The New Testament: An Introduction

Volume II

The Acts of the Apostles

A Study of Paul and the Pauline Letters

The New Testament:
An Introduction

Volume II

The Acts of the Apostles
A Study of Paul and the Pauline Letters

Richard E.A. Rodgers

2018

The New Testament: An Introduction – Volume II: *The Acts of the Apostles, A Study of Paul and the Pauline Letters* — published by the Rev. Dr. Ashish Amos of the Indian Society for Promoting Christian Knowledge (ISPCK), Post Box 1585, 1654, Madarsa Road, Kashmere Gate, Delhi-110006.

ISBN: 978-81-938241-0-8

Cover Credit: Internet Sources

Laser typeset at **ISPCK,** Post Box 1585, 1654, Madarsa Road, Kashmere Gate, Delhi-110006.

Tel: 23866323, Fax: 91-11-23865490

e-mail: ashish@ispck.org.in • ella@ispck.org.in

website: www.ispck.org.in

Contents

Section I
The Acts of the Apostles

CHAPTER - 1

Introduction to the Acts of the Apostles

CHAPTER - 2

Birth and Spread of the Church I (Acts 1-14):

Section II
The Study of Paul and the Pauline Letters

❖ ❖ ❖

The New Testament – An Introduction

Purpose: The empowerment of the λαος (*laos* = laity) – the people of God.

1. To acquaint the reader with a brief geographical, historical and religious background of the New Testament in order to be familiar with the context in which the writings originated.

2. To provide an introduction to the books of the New Testament, and a short commentary, in order to give the reader a background from which to interpret texts while preaching or leading in Bible Study.

3. To provide beginners and laypersons with the basic tools required for an informed understanding and interpretation of the New Testament.

VOLUME I

Background Studies and the Synoptics

Chapter I: Background to the New Testament

Map: Palestine in New Testament Times

1.   Historical Background

   A. Diaspora in Assyria. Diaspora in Babylon. Rise of the Persian Empire. Restoration under Ezra and Nehemiah. Rise of the Greek Empire under Alexander the Great.

   B. Origin and Development of Hellenism. Jewish reactions to Hellenism.

   C. The Maccabean Revolt. Rise of the Hasmonean Dynasty and its decline.

   D. Rise of the Roman Empire. The administration of Palestine under the Romans.

   E. Palestine under the Herods and Roman Governors.

   F. Fall of Jerusalem – A.D. 70, and destruction – A.D. 135.

   G. Persecution of Christians under later Roman Emperors.

2.   Social Background

   A. Cities, Population, Common practices and beliefs

   B. Wealth/Poverty/Slaves

   C. Education

3.   Religious Background

   A. The Temple. Sanhedrin. The Synagogue.

   B. Sectarian Judaism: Sadducees, Pharisees, Scribes, Zealots, Essenes, the Qumran Community and the Dead Sea Scrolls.

CHAPTER II

Formation of the New Testament Canon

CHAPTER III

Study of the Gospels

C. What do the Gospels contain?

D. Gospels as documents of faith used in proclamation, teaching, and preservation.

E. Gospels as faith's interpretation of history.

F. Textual and Literary considerations.

G. Form and Redaction in the Gospels.

H. Modern approaches to the study of the Gospels.

Select Bibliography

CHAPTER IV

The Synoptics

A. Why the first three gospels are known as "the Synoptics" and the Synoptic Problem.

B. Brief introduction to each of the Synoptics:

1. Matthew : authorship, date, place of writing, purpose. Brief analysis of and commentary on the text.

Select Bibliography

2. Mark : authorship, date, place of writing, purpose. Brief analysis of and commentary on the text.

Select Bibliography

3. Luke : authorship, date, place of writing, purpose. Brief analysis of and commentary on the text.

Select Bibliography

CHAPTER V

Selected studies

Theme studies

1. Infancy Narratives – theological motifs

2. Parables – meaning, use and interpretation; value as teaching aids; use in preaching and teaching today

3. Miracles – meaning, use and interpretation. Value in preaching and teaching today

4. Kingdom of God – meaning, use and interpretation

5. Passion, death and Resurrection Narratives

6. Jesus and children

7. Jesus and women

8. Christian discipleship – the Sermon on the Mount.

Mission Perspectives

1. The Nazareth Manifesto – proclamation and participation

2. Confrontation with socio-religio-political powers/structures

3. Developments as Christianity spread from Palestine (Jewish) into the Hellenistic (Greek) world

4. Mission as promotion of peace and justice.

Eschatology and the Hope for the future. The universal reign of God

VOLUME II

The Acts of the Apostles
A Study of Paul and the Pauline Letters

Section I

The Acts of the Apostles

Chapter I

Introduction to the Book of Acts of the Apostles. Authorship. Date. Place of writing. Purpose.

Chapter II

Birth and spread of the Church I (Acts chapters 1 – 14): Brief analysis and commentary on the text. Jerusalem. Persecution of the Church. Ethiopia. Introduction to Saul/Paul. Conversion of Cornelius. Spread beyond Judaism/Palestine. Church in Antioch. Paul's First Missionary Journey.

Chapter III

The Jerusalem Assembly (Acts chapter 15): Brief analysis and commentary on the text. The Jew-Gentile controversy and its resolution in Acts.

Chapter IV

Birth and spread of the Church II (Acts chapters 16 – 28): Brief analysis and commentary on the text. Paul's journeys. Paul's imprisonment and journey to Rome.

Chapter V

History and Theology in the Book of Acts.

Select Bibliography for Section I.

Section II

A Study of Paul and the Pauline Letters

Chapter I

General Introduction to New Testament Letters.

Chapter II

Paul's Life

Primary sources for information on Paul (his letters), secondary sources (Acts). The background of Paul. Conversion. His work. Table of suggested Pauline chronology. Table of suggested chronology for all Pauline letters. Paul as interpreter of Christ to the Jews and Gentiles. Select bibliography.

Chapter III

An introduction to Paul's own letters: A. Romans B. The Corinthian Correspondence – I & II Corinthians C. Galatians D. Philemon

Founding of the community. Authorship/authenticity and integrity.

Date. Occasion and Purpose.

Brief analysis and commentary on the text of each of the letters.

Select Bibliography for each letter.

Chapter IV

An introduction to the deutero-Pauline letters: A. Ephesians B. Philippians C. Colossians D. The Thessalonian Correspondence – I & II Thessalonians

Founding of the community. Authorship/authenticity and integrity.

Date. Occasion and Purpose. Place of writing.

Brief analysis and commentary on the text of each of the letters.

Select Bibliography for each letter.

Chapter V

An introduction to the trito-Pauline letters – The Pastorals:
A. I Timothy   B. II Timothy   C. Titus

The Addressees. Authorship/authenticity and integrity.

Occasion and Purpose. Date.

Brief analysis and commentary on the text of each of the letters.

Select bibliography for the Pastorals.

Chapter VI

Some issues in Pauline thought

A. Sin. Law. Righteousness. Salvation. Justification by faith.

B. Ἐν Χριστω (en Christo): Life in Christ. Individual and corporative perspectives.

C. The Church: Jews and Gentiles in the Church. The Body of Christ. Sacraments. Spiritual gifts. Γλωσσαλαλια (glossalalia) – speaking in tongues.

D. Eschatology and the summing up of all things in Christ.

E. The place and contribution of women in the Church. Women as partners in ministry.

F. Creation and ecological concerns (Rom. 8:18-25; Col. 1:15-20).

Select Bibliography

VOLUME IV

The Epistle to the Hebrews. The Epistles of James, I & II Peter, Jude

Chapter I

The Epistle to the Hebrews

Chapter V

Church Organization and Structure in the New Testament

Acknowledgements

Any writing work requires one to put aside other things and bring to bear time and concentration on the writing. This means that the burden of household chores and social obligations falls on others in the family. In this case my wife, Sunita, has taken over my responsibilities in addition to her own commitment to the home and willingly foregone her own interests so that I could have time to write. In a time of retirement when we both should be finding relaxation and joy in each other's company, I have been sitting with the computer! There are no words that can express my gratitude to her for her love and sacrifice. Nevertheless, thank you, dear wife, for making it possible for me to devote time to writing; I hope these books will be a reward for your patience and love.

Other members of our family – our children Rahul, his wife Neha, and our grandson, Jared, my mother, my sisters Geraldine and Chrystal, my brother Norman and their families, my sisters-in-law, Usha, Asha, Saroj, and their families – have all shared in the intrusion into family life and the priority that these writings have taken. All of them, and many loving friends – colleagues and former students – have been supportive and encouraging and are still cheering along the track waiting for the books to cross the finishing line!

The Board of Directors of Leonard Theological College, and the Delhi Regional Conference of the Methodist Church in India, were gracious in granting me a year's Sabbatical Leave (2015-2016) during which I should have completed this work but was unable to do so. My grateful thanks to the College and Regional Conference authorities.

To the many students, who may find themselves reflected in these pages, my grateful thanks for your interactions and interventions, and for keeping me focused.

The publishers and distributors, ISPCK, Delhi, the General Secretary and all the Staff, have been most gracious in their handling of my text, making suggestions for improvement, and overall technical input in printing, the cover design, and the many times they accommodated me in the corrections to the text. Their enthusiasm that these books will make a contribution has been a great encouragement. My grateful thanks to the General Secretary and the whole team at ISPCK.

This volume is dedicated to three remarkable women who have kept me focussed and challenged: my paternal grandmother, Mrs. Alice Margaret Rodgers, a lady of great and simple faith who implicitly trusted God for everything and in every situation; all she knew was God's redeeming love in Jesus Christ (and even this would have been too much of a theological statement for her!). Her love, gentle and unassuming, along with her strong sense of quiet, yet no nonsense discipline, kept all the grandchildren in line. She has long since passed to her heavenly reward, but her early influence on my life was immeasurable especially her encouragement for me to stay close to the Church in the formative years of growing up, and then for my being sure of God's call to the ministry. I hope that she takes pride in my work. The other two women are my mother, Mrs. Lillian E. Rodgers, and my mother-in-law, Mrs. Primrose RadhaKrishan. Both ladies have faced many challenges in life and both have suffered much for the family, the children, and the truth for which they stood. They have been an inspiration. It may not be possible for my mother to make all the connections to appreciate the work (at 93 her span of attention and memory is not what it used to be when we brothers and sisters were children!), nevertheless, this work is offered in reverence, gratitude and love. My mother-in-law too keeps indifferent health, but her memory and sense of history are still a corrective and a guide. To all three remarkable women: my acknowledgement of their roles in my life and my grateful thanks.

Richard E. A. Rodgers
Jabalpur, M. P., India
Pentecost 2018

Preface

This series of four volumes on introductory material to the New Testament, and a short commentary on each book, has at least three reasons for their origins.

1. When I joined Leonard Theological College, Jabalpur (LTC), for my BD studies, the only model of ministry that was before me was the pastoral ministry. My family and I had been greatly helped by a loving, caring pastor at Centenary Methodist English Church, New Delhi; he and his wife were my role models, and almost 50 years later, I still think of them as my parents in the ministry because it was their example that influenced me in my decision to join full-time church work. During the course of studies, I felt a shift in my understanding of ministry, and slowly, but surely, I came to realize that my calling was to the teaching ministry – theological teaching. Further, under the guidance and influence of excellent teachers, my focus narrowed to the field of New Testament studies. After the required time spent in pastoral ministry at my home Church in New Delhi, and having been ordained, the Bishop was pleased to grant me study leave for my M.Th. in New Testament at the United Theological College, Bangalore (now Bengaluru).On completion of that, an invitation was received from LTC to serve on the faculty; I was excited at the thought of going back to my *alma mater* that I loved. The request was sent from LTC to my Bishop who was again pleased to release my services to LTC (for the next 37 years, consecutive Bishops released my services to LTC). The paradigm shift that I had experienced and dreamt about was becoming a reality. The ease with which all of this happened (no red tape and pulling of strings and playing politics!) convinced me that

God was indeed calling me to the teaching ministry. As I submitted to this understanding of ministry, I felt at ease within myself, and the love affair with the College which began on the day I entered it as a student, opened up new avenues for flowering and flourishing in teaching, research, and in preparing students for responding to the endless possibilities of ministry to which God had called them. This does not mean that the 'pastoral' aspect of ministry totally gave way to the 'academic'. Over the 37 years of teaching/academics/ administration at LTC, I know that dealing with staff and students who are hurting and confused and need a parental touch, has been an exercise of pastoral ministry – reaching out to them in love and caring yet with a sense of discipline. Indeed, I learnt that 'pastoral' and 'academic' are two sides of the same coin. I do earnestly hope that God has blest those efforts of pastoral care as much as God has blest my efforts at being a faithful teacher.

So, my first reason is to acknowledge the love and care that I have received all along the journey; the encouragement, through letters and constant communication from my pastor, church leaders, teachers, colleagues, friends and students. In a very small way, may this be an acknowledgement, from a grateful heart, of all that I have received from them.

2. Over the years of teaching, I have always been intrigued by the unquestioning acceptance with which people, and especially my students, approached the New Testament. In my own experience, throughout the years of religious education (Sunday school, youth groups etc…), I had always been taught to ask questions, to rationalize, and to try to reckon how people understood God as speaking to them, and how we understand God as speaking to us today. The unquestioning acceptance is often described as "blind faith", "simply believe", "God's will" etc…. It has always been my endeavor to inculcate in my students a questioning mind – to approach the text with critical questions, to bring to bear on the text their knowledge from history, sociology, religions, anthropology, language, literature, various other sciences etc…. Or in technical terms, to use the methods of modern historical-critical studies. It has never been my intention

to undermine my students' faith or to question what has been deeply implanted in their psyche, but to get them to understand their faith and beliefs in a more informed way rather than through "blind faith" often bordering on superstition. The first few classes of any course were usually spent in an unlearning process so that the class was open to new approaches and fresh understandings of God's word which would strengthen and undergird the faith. This was never a one-sided exercise; no matter how many times I taught a course, each time I learnt, unlearnt, and re-learnt how God speaks to us through God's word; a hermeneutical exercise that led to a greater appreciation of the New Testament both as literature and as a document of faith. However, I was also aware that such an approach could have ended in a negative way leading to destruction of faith and beliefs. Therefore, a very careful handling of the critical approach had to be nurtured. This resulted in a challenge to me regarding the content and presentation of my lectures, and then to reshape my lectures into books/literature that would lead to a deepening of faith and greater appreciation of God's word through this critical approach. Books/ literature were not always available, even in the best stocked libraries, because most books are too expensive for individuals, and also most books assumed a certain level of critical understanding which was difficult to find in our rather conservative religious ethos.

So, my second reason was to develop literature/books/guidelines as a "primer" before the student/seeker could go on to more complicated theories and hypotheses in advanced commentaries. However, the pressures of work (Church, University, personal interest involvements), and the administration of a college did not permit the time to devote to this task. Now, in retirement, I rely on the many, many files of notes made over the years of teaching and on personal insights gained from the constant interaction with the text. This series is offered as a small contribution to the onward journey of faith and of being an interpreter of God's word in today's world.

3. The third reason arises from a concern to provide the church with literature which could be used by the layperson – literature that would

help the layperson to grapple with issues, but at the same time would avoid the hassles of plunging into academic niceties such as ponderous references, credits in footnotes and bibliography which are absolutely fatal for the beginner! (these should be left to professional courses and research papers); technical language will be largely avoided, or further explained when its use is unavoidable; important Greek words will be found in transliteration. The intention is to lead the person into a critical understanding of scripture even in the absence of a professional such as a theological teacher/theologically trained person. For several years I wanted to give my time, and efforts to this concern which would undergird the theological foundations of Christian doctrine. As the Principal of the College, I had even proposed that Leonard Theological College, Jabalpur – its resources in terms of library, faculty, and the structure of the College's School of Research – could be the locus for this endeavour with an on-going programme for constantly producing literature for the Church but this was not to be. Giving expression to this concern of mine is now my retirement project!

So, my third reason is that I should bring together my concern for developing easily available resources, at least for the New Testament, which could be used by laypersons, and students in external study programmes, in their devotions and study, especially those who are also entrusted with pastoral and preaching responsibilities. It is hoped that these books will fill some of the gap that exists when laypersons seek guidance in the interpretation of the New Testament.

Finally, I hope that this series will make a contribution to theological literature that is available for the layperson, especially in various programmes developed for empowering laypersons through external studies, as a token of my own concern and work in this area of preparing persons for ministry in the Church.

Outline of the series

1. Volume I: General Introduction to the New Testament. Formation of the New Testament Canon. Study of the Gospels. The Synoptic Gospels.

2. **Volume II: The Acts of the Apostles. A Study of Paul and the Pauline Letters.**

3. Volume III: The Gospel of John. The Epistles ofI, II, III John. The Book of Revelation

4. Volume IV: The Epistle to the Hebrews. The Epistles of James, I & II Peter, Jude. Church Organization and Structure.

There are many outlines and introductions to the New Testament, each with their own perspectives and approaches, and while I am aware that the above is not the usual outline for studies in the New Testament, over the years of teaching, I have developed this approach, and I hope to show in the course of the series, and below, that there is some logic in the grouping of books for the purpose of historical and theological continuity. A detailed discussion on the salient points will be given when dealing with each book, but for the sake of perspective and introduction, the following points are to be noted:

1. Vol. I: A General Introduction is always necessary before coming to the text itself. This helps to place the text within a context, to understand the forces that impacted the text, and to understand how and why writers responded to situations, and expressed themselves, in the way in which they did.

   The Synoptic Gospels (Matthew, Mark, Luke) are studied first as they outline the story and presentation of the understanding of Jesus, the central figure of the New Testament, in a way that indicates that they have a common perspective (synoptic: σὐνὀψσις = seeing together). Studies about Jesus therefore forms the base from which other New Testament writings can be understood.

2. **Vol. II: The Acts of the Apostles purports to tell the story (history and theology) of the early movement which became the Church – its formation, mission, the spread of the Gospel, issues faced etc...It takes the message of the good news a step further than the Gospels – from Jesus, Judaism and Palestine into the Gentile Hellenistic/Greco-Roman world. It also sets the stage to understand Paul and his writings which are an**

interpretation of Jesus and the implications of Jesus' message including instructions to regulate community/congregation life, to understand and develop approaches to everyday situations/relationships in the light of the new faith in Jesus, to warn against false teachers, and to provide guidelines for church order – part of the development of Christianity in the Pauline and post-Pauline eras. So, taking the two together (Acts and Paul) brings about a logical step from the beginnings of the community to the development of its theological expressions that emerged from various life situations and later became the scriptures and doctrines of the Church.

3. Vol. III: The Gospel of John, though also a part of the story of Jesus has a different perspective from that of the Synoptics and it has to be approached in a different way in order to appreciate its message. Writings related to the Gospel of John – I, II, III John and the Book of Revelation – are also taken up here so that they can be grouped as having a common perspective and background.

4. Vol. IV: The remaining letters – Hebrews, James, I & II Peter, Jude, – reflect a later date and address situations towards the end of the first century/beginning of the second century. The various communities/congregations seem more settled in their thinking and life-style, and earlier concerns about conversion, Jew-Gentile relationships etc… are not touched upon, instead the concerns are for practical living, an apologetic for suffering and persecution etc….Each of the writings have their own concerns, but this overall generalization helps to keep them together for the purpose of study. The last chapter in this Volume will deal with the development of Church organization and structure in the New Testament.

It is important to note three points in the methodology followed:

1. the sections on analysis and commentary of the texts is to provide the reader with tools for interpretation; the analysis and commentary will not go into homiletics, i.e. the development of the text into a sermon. Each reader is in a different context and should use the

background and tools of interpretation provided here for their own homiletic development and to suit their own contexts.

2. each writing/book is studied in and by itself. No attempt is made to present a unified/comprehensive/compendium of thought as though there is only one picture and one theological expression in the New Testament. This approach used here results in different formats being used to present the studies. It is hoped that these different formats/ numbering/arrangement etc... will only help the reader/student to appreciate the variety of the material in the New Testament and that these writings cannot be squeezed into one mould.

3. in dealing with Paul and the Pauline letters, a different method is used in this study: the letters are grouped into three categories (Paul, deutero-Pauline, trito-Pauline), and the compilations are taken in the order of chronological development (e.g. see the Corinthian Correspondence consisting of seven letters; Philippians; Pastorals).

In this way, it is hoped that the 4 Volume series is not just a compilation but will also make a contribution to New Testament studies and research.

All biblical quotations are from the Revised Standard Version (1952) and are given in italics. Where a quotation is from the section under discussion, only the text is given in italics; other texts have references mentioned. The reader is advised to constantly refer to the biblical text. Several quotations are given in Greek (from The Greek New Testament, edited by K. Aland, M. Black _et al_, Third Edition, United Bible Societies, 1975) for the more advanced student who can appreciate the Greek idioms/phrases/ vocabulary that have come to be associated with a particular writer/ author both in theological understandings and in meaningful expression and usage in the original language.

It is hoped that this overly simple explanation of the rationale for the series will suffice for the moment and that the readers will be in a better position to appreciate the outline at the end of the series.

Readership

The concern for theological writings for laypersons has been mentioned earlier in the Preface and must be stressed again. The series has been written to fill the need for a basic introduction to the books of the New Testament which would not require professional expertise/lectures. The readership kept in mind is the person in the pew who would like to know more about scripture and have guidelines for its interpretation. Therefore, the accepted norms of detailed references and footnotes, and an extensive bibliography have been avoided; also, after years of lecturing on the subject one is not quite sure of what is one's own and what is borrowed! I hope I may be forgiven if sometimes in my 'borrowings', that have been so long appropriated, I have forgotten that they are borrowings! The series is not intended to take the place of a formal study of the New Testament undertaken in a theological college; those preparing for theological degrees need to be familiar with much more advanced material even if they find some of the basics in this series to be helpful and which open up the possibility for further study and research. The advanced student will be able to identify the sources on which this series has relied; my students will find a similarity to my class lectures. I hope that all who engage in Bible Study may find in this series some material which will help to light up the New Testament and that this will serve the purpose of stressing how important it is for the New Testament – a vital part of our scripture and theological formulations – to be constantly studied and interpreted to build up the faith and to help in an informed and relevant proclamation of the Gospel.

Richard E. A. Rodgers
Jabalpur, M. P., India
Pentecost 2018

SECTION I

The Acts of the Apostles

Chapter - 1

Introduction to the Acts of the Apostles

1. General Introduction. 2. Authorship. 3. Date. 4. Place of writing. 5. Purpose.

1. General Introduction

The book of the Acts of the Apostles opens with these words; *In the first book, O Theophilus, I have dealt with all that Jesus began to do and teach, until the day He was taken up, after He had given commandment through the Holy Spirit to the apostles whom He had chosen (1:1-2).* These opening words provide several clues when dealing with the Book of Acts:

A. Acts is a sequel to a first book;

B. The dedication to Theophilus is also found at the beginning of the Third Gospel (Lk. 1:1-4);

C. The First Book deals with what Jesus taught and did, up to the Ascension;

D. The Second Book deals with the work of the Apostles; the Holy Spirit takes the place of the physical presence of Jesus.

Each of these points from the opening words of Acts will be taken up in detail in subsequent sections of the study.

The acceptance of Acts as the sequel to the Third Gospel not only comes from the internal evidence of the two writings (references given above) but also from external evidence from around the end of the second century. Three great theologians of that time – Irenaeus, Tertullian, and Clement of Alexandria – all attest the presence of Acts in the canon of the New Testament along with the four gospels, thirteen Pauline letters, and a few other writings. Further they all hold that Acts is the sequel to the Third Gospel and that both books were written by Luke. One of the earliest canons of the Church – the Muratorian Canon (representing the development of the canon in the Western Church around the end of the second century) – includes Acts and states that Luke was the author of the Third Gospel and Acts. This close association of Luke, Third Gospel and Acts prevailed in scholarship and led to the widespread usage of the phase "Luke-Acts". Further discussion, below, will justify why this two-volume work is studied as one writing coming from the same author.

Although the writing is entitled "Acts of the Apostles", it deals almost exclusively with Peter and Paul; other apostles are mentioned only as incidental to the stories of Peter and Paul. It is only a much later tradition of the Church that entitles the writing as "The Acts of the Apostles". However, the title, "Acts of the Apostles" helps to divide the book into three major sections for the purpose of study and interpretation: **1.** where Peter and Jerusalem are the centres (chapters 1-14); **2.** Where the Jew-Gentile controversy is settled (chapter 15); and **3.** where Paul and churches outside Jerusalem are the centres (chapters 16-28). Luke-Acts could also be divided geographically : the Gospel starting and ending in Jerusalem; the book of Acts starting with the Apostles in Jerusalem as the controlling factor in the new movement and then slowly moving away from Jerusalem (chapters 1-14); the decision to admit the Gentiles and therefore a movement away from Jerusalem (chapter 15); and the spread outward (Acts 1:8) *to the end of the earth (chapters 16-28).* In the brief commentary that follows, the outline for study will be: **1.** Jerusalem as the centre of mission chapters 1-14); **2.** The Jerusalem Council (chapter 15); and **3.** The spread of the mission beyond Palestine (chapters 16-28). The commentary will also use general headings/themes/topics/journeys rather than proceed verse by verse. These groupings seem to be a better way to study Acts and to follow the story that it seeks to tell.

2.   Authorship

The dedication to Theophilus in Lk.1:1-4 and the dedication to the same person in Acts 1:1-2 indicates that the author of these two writings is the same. But nowhere in Luke or in Acts is there a mention of the author's name. The earliest tradition concerning these writings comes from Church Fathers and the Muratorian Canon – a list of books being used by the Western Church towards the end of the 2nd. century. The explanation given there is that the Third Gospel and Acts were authored by Luke, a companion of Paul (Col. 4:14, Phlm. 24, II Tim.4:11). According to the information from Pauline writings, Luke was a physician who became a part of the Pauline group; this is especially reflected in what is known as the "we" passages where the author/ writer is included in the group travelling with Paul (Acts 16:10-17, 20:5-15, 21:1-18, 27:1-28:16). *[Note: Perhaps there was a first edition of the writing which began with the so-called "we passages" – from Ch. 16 to Ch. 28 – and later on chps. 1-15 were added to complete the narrative and to fit into the author/writer's scheme of telling the story especially from the point of view of Paul as the main character.]*

The language and grammar of Luke and Acts suggests an educated person whose native language was Greek. As his name suggests, Luke was probably a Gentile; he was not a first-generation disciple of Jesus (Lk. 1:1-4); he was a convert to the new movement. Thus, the New Testament evidence gives very little direct information about the person Luke; it is only indirectly, from the tradition of the Church that the name appears. **Therefore, the author of the Book of Acts remains anonymous/unknown; the writing found acceptance in the Church only because the 'unknown' author was thought to be Luke and then because of the association of Luke with Paul.**

3.   Date

Although the earliest mention of Acts comes from the end of the 2nd century, nevertheless, four gospels and Acts were known to church leaders by the end of the 1st century. If Acts is the sequel to the Third Gospel, then the earliest possible date for its circulation is about 90 A.D. Accordingly, the accepted date for the circulation of Acts is between 90-100 A.D. though it may have been written much earlier depending on the purpose of writing. *[Note: If there was a first edition of Acts – chps. 16-28 – telling only the story of Paul, then this section could be dated within the lifetime of Paul for the information of the Roman judge who was trying Paul's case, i.e. before A. D. 64. The final edition which would have included chps. 1-15 would come from a later date.]*

4.   Place of writing

Since Luke-Acts has been closely associated with Paul, the discussion concerning the place of writing Acts has usually been around the centres of the Pauline mission – Caesarea, cities in Asia Minor, and most of all Rome. However, the place cannot be determined with any certainty. The only thing that all the traditions point to is that the writing must have originated outside of Palestine.

5.   Purpose

Luke mentions that he intends to write *an orderly account* (Lk.1:3) for *most excellent Theophilus, that you may know the truth concerning the things of which you have been informed* (Lk.1:4). The opening verse of Acts also refers to Theophilus and *all that Jesus began to do and teach…and the work of the Apostles whom He had chosen* (Acts 1:1-2). So primarily Luke's purpose is to tell the story of Jesus and the story of the work of the Apostles, and he does so by bringing out the theological significance of the work, i.e. the story is not just biographical/chronological history, but what Jesus meant to the generations that came after him and how this movement developed into the Church. As one great Lucan scholar, Hans Conzelmann, says that Luke is interested in the *heilsgeschichte* – the history of salvation. In bringing out this interest, Luke writes an apologetic for Christianity by bringing out **1.** that Christianity is politically harmless, that Roman authorities had nothing to fear from this new religion and that followers of Jesus need not be in conflict with the Roman authorities; and **2.** that the spread of the Jesus movement (later the Church) was part of God's plan of salvation for all. Conzelmann also shows that Luke looks at history in three sections: 1. the time of Israel (Lk. 16:16); 2. the time of Jesus (Lk. 16:16ff); and 3. the time of the Church – the time between Jesus and his coming again – the Book of Acts.

The incidences relating to Gentiles in the Gospel and the mission beyond Palestine in Acts brings out another purpose in Luke showing how the Gospel message shifted from a basically Jewish movement to a movement that included Gentiles.

There is also the question of the identity of Theophilus, to whom both Luke and Acts are dedicated, which would be related to the purpose of the writing. 'Theophilus' is a Greek name meaning 'friend of God' (_theos_=θεος=God; _philos_=φιλος=friend). One hypothesis holds that Luke was writing to a particular individual who was a potential convert and who needed more information. The suggestion is also expanded to include anyone who was seeking more information about Jesus and the spread of the movement. However, the most attractive hypothesis is that 'Theophilus' was the Roman judge appointed by Caesar to try Paul's case, hence the story is presented in such a way so as to be politically correct and to show that the new movement was not a threat to the Roman government. This would mean that parts of the writing may have originated by the early 60's, later additions would have been made adding the pre-Pauline material, and then would have become public and received wide circulation only by the end of the first century.

CHAPTER - 2

Birth and Spread of the Church I (Acts 1-14):

Brief analysis and commentary on the text. Jerusalem. Persecution of the Church. Ethiopia. Introduction to Saul/Paul. Conversion of Cornelius. Spread beyond Judaism/Palestine. Church in Antioch. Paul's First Missionary Journey.

A.   Chapters 1 – 2: *Jerusalem*

The Gospel of Luke ends with the instruction to the disciples to stay in Jerusalem (Lk. 24:44-53). The opening scene in Acts is set in Jerusalem (1:4-5). At the end of Luke's Gospel, Jesus seems to have ascended, but in Acts, the resurrection appearances last for forty days (a figure perhaps referring to situations from the Hebrew scriptures and early Christian tradition, e.g. Moses, wilderness wanderings; and to Jesus' period of fasting before the temptations). Four important things take place in the opening chapters:

1. The commission to be witnesses in Jerusalem, all Judea, Samaria and the ends of the earth (1:8). Just prior to this commission is the question of the restoration of the kingdom – the disciples were still looking for a political kingdom (Lk. 22:66ff – the High Priest is concerned about a Kingdom; Lk. 24:13ff – the disciples on the road to Emmaus are concerned about a Kingdom). However, the expectations of a kingdom are pushed into the distant future, instead there is the commission to the disciples that through their witness in the proclamation of the good news, the Kingdom will evolve. This forms the scheme/outline of Acts as the spread of the mission is traced. The mission starts in Jerusalem and spreads out till Rome is reached. Rome as the capital signifies that the whole Empire has been reached (the ends of the earth). Once this commission is given, then Jesus is taken up and the mission of the disciples begins.

2. The completion of the circle of disciples with the choice of Matthias to replace Judas (1:21-26). It seems to have been important to the early community that the circle needed to be completed; this does not happen when another vacancy arises (see 12:2-3). The completion of the vacancy is not an on-going institution in the Church, but necessary for the start of the mission (it could have been that the number 12 was an important symbol of the continuation with the 12 tribes of Israel and therefore a continuation of the _Heilsgeschichte_). Hence the qualification that the person should have been with the group from the beginning and should have been an eye witness to the resurrection (1:21-22). The selection of Matthias indicates the democratic process followed in the early community and also indicates the start of the election process followed today in choosing leaders; the choice is seen both as the selection of the community and the will of God. Interestingly, Matthias appears only here and is not heard of again in the New Testament or in the history of the Church.

3. The coming of the Spirit (chapter 2). Once the commission is given and the apostolic circle is completed, the stage is set for the coming of the Spirit. The event is referred to as the Day of Pentecost. Pentecost was the Jewish festival occurring 50 days after Passover and celebrating the giving of the Law on Sinai. Pentecost was a pilgrim festival so Jews from all over the world were expected to travel to Jerusalem to celebrate. Rabbinic interpretations were that the Law was given in all the languages of the earth, therefore in Acts 2, the languages could be understood and communication was possible (2:11) [see also the section on γλωσσαλαλια or 'speaking in tongues' given below]. In depicting God's appearance at Sinai, the scene is described as one including thunder, lightening, smoke etc.... (Exodus 19:16). Rabbinic interpretations hold that angels took the Law on tongues of flame to the people at the bottom of the mountain and to all the people on earth. Acts evokes the same imagery and presents Pentecost in Jerusalem as the renewal of God's covenant. This covenant covers a broad sweep of the Roman Empire and thus Pentecost symbolizes the vast reach of evangelism that will ultimately bring the Gentiles also into the fold of the people of God. It should also be noted that Peter's speech following the Pentecost event closely links the event with the history of Israel thereby indicating that the mission that will follow is a continuation of God's mission with Israel – the *heilsgeschichte* (Conzelmann's understanding of salvation history) – the history of salvation continued in the Church.

This is the impact of Pentecost: the disciples had become a broken group, leaderless and directionless; it was the end of their world. With the coming of the Spirit at Pentecost, the end becomes a new beginning, a new life; the lack of leadership and direction is transformed into an experience of the empowerment of believers who will become the Church.

B. Chapters 3 – 5: *The beginning of the new community*

At the end of Chapter 2, about 3000 were added to the new group and then it goes on to describe how they lived – a new community had come into existence. Four features of the new community emerge (2:42-47):

1. Κοινωνια or fellowship or communion or community (2:44). It shows that those in the new group felt that they had much in common which was binding them together – the Spirit binding them together into a shared communion and therefore a community. To be noted is that the community shared all their goods (2:44) – perhaps a first experiment in what many centuries later developed into communism.

2. *Worship (2:46):* the community attended the temple (Jewish) worship. This reflects that they were still closely associated with Judaism and Jewish practices. It is also an indication that the first members of the community were from Judaism. Later, non-Jews began to be

part of the community and there was a break with Jewish worship practices when Christian worship/liturgy emerged.

3. *Breaking of bread (2:46):* A distinctive Christian commemoration of Jesus' life, death and resurrection linked with the hope of his coming again. Interestingly, here it was celebrated in private homes whereas after Christian liturgy developed and there was a break with Judaism, the breaking of bread (eucharist) became a central and definitive part of Christian worship.

4. *Apostolic teaching (2:42):* The examples of speeches in chapters 2 & 3 showed that apostolic teaching began with Jewish scriptures and was re-interpreted in terms of the understanding of the life and work of Jesus and how his ministry is a fulfillment of Jewish scriptures. This re-interpretation became the authoritative norm of apostolic preaching and teaching and was later used as the criteria for determining orthodoxy when controversies and heresies arose. The criteria of the apostolic norm was also used when determining the books of the New Testament canon.

    The two examples of speeches in Acts (chps. 2 &3) also indicate the theology of the writer – the continuity of salvation history *(heilsgeschichte)* which began with Israel and continued with Jesus and further continued with the early community (Church).

The above features of the Jerusalem community brings out two points:**1.** continuity with Judaism and fellowship with other Jews whom they met in the temple and synagogue worship; and **2.** growing self-awareness and the potential to break away from Judaism. These two features were opposite in character and would result in tensions and rejection before Christians could become a distinguishable separate group.

Once the *heilsgeschichte* has been established, then from now on in Acts, it is the history of the followers of Jesus and the spread of the mission – the beginning of the history of the Church.

C.   Chapters 6-7: *Persecution*

The first healing takes place when Peter and John go to the Temple (3:1-10). This follows the pattern of Jesus in Luke 4:31-37. The healing is in the name of Jesus (3:6), *I have no silver and gold, but I give you what I have, in the name of Jesus Christ of Nazareth, walk.* The healing is not through any special gifts/power of the apostles (also see 3:16). The healing is followed by a sermon (3:11-26). Just as Jesus' ministry combined healings and words, so too the apostolic ministry. The speech also illustrates how Jewish texts were used to understand and present Jesus, especially to a Jewish audience. Apostolic activity led to the beginning of persecution – Peter and John were arrested (4:1-22) for the night and the next morning, after a warning, were released. The apostolic response was again an understanding of God's salvific work through Israel and Jesus; later their prayer of triumph also reflects the same theology (4:23-31).

The end of Chapter 4 is a summary of the *koinwnia* (κοὶνωνια) community life – with the stress on having everything in common including selling of one's property and pooling the money for the good of the whole community.

As is usually the case, dissension/dissatisfaction begins from within the community. The story of Ananias and Sapphira (5:1-11) illustrates the punishment for danger of pretense and the violation of purely voluntary actions. The community faced its first internal opposition in which it understood the divine initiative in protecting/preserving the community.

A second confrontation with Jewish authorities (5:12-42) parallels the first though it is intensified. The first confrontation was a result of the healing of one man, the second confrontation is the result of many signs and wonders; the first was local – in Jerusalem, the second involves people from the surrounding towns and villages. The reaction of the Jewish authorities is also intensified. The apostles are beaten, warned and released. Interestingly, Gamaliel, a Pharisee voices an opinion which sways the vote of the Sanhedrin, whereas Pharisees were opposed to Jesus in the Gospels and were usually not tolerant of any interpretation outside of their own understandings.

A third confrontation is even more highly intensified and ends in the death of Stephen and greater persecution (6:1-8:1). The confrontation with the community which ends in Stephen's death began as a dissension within the community (6:1-6). The Hellenists who dissented were Greek speaking Jews probably from the diaspora (lands outside Palestine) and whose relationship with traditional Judaism was always a problem (to some extent this will also later be reflected in Paul's story). Interestingly, the way of solving the dissension was to have those from the dissenting party to carry out the work that was under question. This effectively stopped the opposition! However, Stephen is not known for running the communal mess; he is known for his evangelistic work probably among other Jewish Hellenists who disagreed with him (6:8-15). Stephen was arrested and his speech that follows is a classic example of apostolic preaching – tracing the history of Israel and relating it to Jesus of Nazareth whom he was proclaiming. The last part of the speech indicates a movement away from Judaism and the Temple, the centre of Judaism – *the Most High does not dwell in houses made with hands* (7:48-50). Finally, Stephen comes out with his punch lines – *you stiff necked people... you murdered the prophets and you murdered the Righteous One...you did not keep the Law as delivered to you.... I see the Son of Man standing at the right hand of God....* This indictment of Judaism, not surprisingly, enraged his hearers who accused Stephen of blasphemy; he is cast out and stoned to death (7:51-60). Saul, later to become a major character in Acts, is introduced as one who was actively consenting to Stephen's death (7:58 - 8:1a).

Certain interesting theological points are to be noted:**1.** The death of Stephen matches closely the death of Jesus in Luke – both speak of the Son of Man on the right hand of God (Lk. 22:69; Acts 7:56); both have a prayer for forgiveness for those executing the death penalty (Lk. 23:34a; Acts 7:60); both have the dying person commend his spirit to God (Lk. 23:46; Acts 7:59). **2.** In Acts, Peter has shown continuity with the ministry of Jesus through teaching and healing;

Stephen shows continuity with Jesus' death, it is not the end, but the work carries on. **3.** The introduction of Saul who in the scheme of Acts will continue the work of Stephen.

At first the persecution led by Saul was aimed only at the Hellenists (8:1b); the apostles were not touched continuing their relationship with Judaism. However, the Hellenists spread out to surrounding areas of Judea and Samaria (8:1b; 9:31) bringing to reality the outline of Acts as given in 1:8. This spread from Jerusalem was not the result of planning but of persecution. So, in a sense, out of suffering emerges the mission. Up to 12:25, persecution is dominant ending in the death of James, the brother of John (12:1-2), and the arrest of Peter who is miraculously rescued from prison (12-3-17). Each time there is persecution, the community spread wider, at first through the Hellenist Christians, and then later through the Hebrew Christians.

D.   Chapter 8: *Ethiopia*

The story of the movement/spread of the gospel is continued after the death of Stephen in the evangelization of Samaria (8:6-25). The Jews regarded the Samaritans as racially impure and religiously polluted, so Phillip's willingness to work in Samaria marked a significant development in the spread of the gospel. However, Jerusalem was still regarded as the centre of the movement, so it was necessary for the apostles, Peter and John, to visit Samaria and to confirm the work there; the Spirit is given only after the prayers of Peter and John; it is a point to be noted that the Holy Spirit is imparted only through the laying on of hands by the apostles (8:17) (later in the history of the Church this would become part of the reasoning for apostolic succession). At the end of the Samaritan mission, the group returned to Jerusalem, the headquarters. The point is powerfully made: that **at this point of time, Jerusalem is the centre of the mission.**

After the movement to Judea and Samaria, evangelization by the Hellenists is continued in the story of Phillip and the Ethiopian eunuch (8:26-40). This is a continuation of *being witnesses to the end of the earth* (1:8). The first preaching to the Hellenists and conversion, in areas outside of Jerusalem has begun. In the story of the eunuch, it is interesting to note that this is the first conversion of a Gentile (although many see the Cornelius episode as the first Gentile conversion. Since the Cornelius story is repeated – chapter 10 and retold in chapter 15 – it receives more emphasis. Also, the Cornelius story is the first one in which an apostle is involved in the conversion). Further, the eunuch was only baptized, the gift of the Holy Spirit is not mentioned perhaps because no apostle was present. However, it must also be noted that the eunuch may have been part of the _diaspora_ Jews which is why it is not considered as a Gentile conversion although eunuchs would not have been part of the assembly of Israel (Deut. 23:1). It is suggested that the eunuch's conversion is the first Gentile conversion which prepares the reader for the story of Cornelius with Peter as the agent. Also, this episode prepares the ground for the work of Saul (later Paul) who is seen as the great apostle to the Gentiles. Hence the story of the Ethiopian eunuch allows the writer to use the next chapter to introduce Saul/Paul into the scheme of Acts.

(It is interesting to note that the Coptic Church in Ethiopia traces its origin back to this story in Acts and claims a very ancient place in the history of the Church. The Coptic versions of the New Testament play a great role in the textual history of the New Testament. The Church still exists today and has contributed much to liturgy and worship in Christianity.)

E.   Chapter 9: *Introduction of Saul/Paul*

Acts 9:1-19 is the first account of the conversion of Paul in Acts. There will be two more accounts given in Acts (22:3-21; 26:2-23) during Paul's speeches of self-defence. In Acts the conversion experience is very dramatically expressed whereas in his letters, Paul does not refer to this experience in the same way; he only refers to it as a "revelation" but gives no further details (Gal. 1:12ff. See note below). Therefore, it is not important to verify historical details in the conversion accounts in Acts; it is more important to understand the points that Acts is trying to make in the accounts which helps the story that Acts is trying to tell. In other words, the theology of Acts is being brought out in these dramatic presentations. The following three points, at least, come to the fore in this conversion account: **1.** Personalizing Saul's hostility – *"Saul, Saul why do you persecute me?* (9:4).**2.** The reluctance of Ananias to have anything to do with Saul because he is a feared persecutor (9:13-14). These two points bring out very powerfully the complete change from the persecutor to the evangelist (9:20). This seems to be the intention of Acts at this point in the story. In the later two accounts, the mission to the Gentiles is incorporated into the story thereby giving it a slightly different emphasis. **3.** Saul/Paul receives the Holy Spirit (9:17). This brings Paul within the circle of the early community and authenticates his preaching, placing him on level with the other apostles. Clearly the emphasis in ch. 9 is to show that the persecutor had undergone a major change and had become an evangelist proclaiming the very person that he had persecuted – *scales fell from his eyes… he proclaimed Jesus saying, He is the Son of God….and confounded the Jews …. by proving that Jesus was the Christ.*

Saul's/Paul's activities in Damascus are met with hostility by the Jews and they plotted to kill him. So, he was sent to Jerusalem where he was met with suspicion and fear since he was a persecutor. However, he was befriended by Barnabas ("son of encouragement") who introduced him to the leaders of the community. Even though he seems to have been accepted, the plot to kill him catches up and Saul/Paul is hastily sent away to Caesarea and thence to Tarsus. Saul/Paul will reappear when Barnabas brings him from Tarsus to Antioch (11:19-26). What exactly he did during these 'silent years' is not known; however, it is safe to assume that he would have been involved in some form of ministry and perhaps even preparation for future ministry. Saul/Paul's mission activities will be described after further stories of Peter and the conversion of Cornelius.

Note on the post-conversion experience in Acts and Gal. 1:12ff. In Acts 9, after preaching in Damascus Saul/Paul is brought to Jerusalem where he interacts freely with the apostles before being sent off to Tarsus (9:27-30). In Paul's own letter in Gal. 1:12ff, there is a different story: Paul did not go to Jerusalem but went immediately into Arabia; after three years he went to Jerusalem for 15 days where he met privately with Peter and James and then he went to Syria and Cilicia; he was still unknown to the churches in Judea (therefore Saul/Paul could not have been present and recognizable at the time of Stephen's death in 7:58, but it suits the story in Acts to show the persecutor dimension of Saul/Paul). In view of this information from Paul himself, the accounts in Acts must be examined more in the light of the theology of Acts and the role the characters are playing to bring out that theology, rather than accepting the information as verifiable historical data.

F.   Chapters 10:1-11:18: *Conversion of Cornelius*

Peter was the spokesperson of apostolic missionary activity in chps. 2-5; he is now brought back to centre stage again in mission activity. In the earlier chapters it was seen that Peter could preach and heal in the name of Jesus; now further echoes of Jesus' activity are seen: the curing of Aeneas (9:32-35) echoes the curing of the paralyzed man in Lk. 5:24-26, and the raising of Tabitha (9:36-43) echoes Jesus' action in the raising of Jairus' daughter in Lk. 8:49-56. Indeed, the Church is seen as carrying on the ministry of Jesus. However, Jesus' ministry began and ended within the confines of Judaism; chapter 10 will take the movement beyond the confines of Judaism into the Gentile world and ultimately to Rome the capital and representative of *the ends of the earth.*

The story of the conversion of Cornelius (a Gentile who participates in synagogue prayers and accepts the moral demands of Judaism) is reported in the third person in Chapter 10:1-48 and repeated in the first person in chapter 11:1-18. This repetition indicates that the story is of great importance and will have far reaching consequences. It is also important from the point of view of Peter (representing the Church) for the 'conversion/new vision' experience of bringing Gentiles into the new community. The story of Cornelius' conversion can be studied under the following divisions:

a. 10:1-8 – Cornelius in Caesarea has a vision to send for Peter;

b. 10:9-16 – Peter at Joppa has a vision telling him that foods traditionally considered ritually unclean in Judaism are in fact not unclean;

c. 10:17-23a – While pondering on this vision, the messengers from Cornelius arrive and request Peter to accompany them to Cornelius' house in Caesarea;

d. 10:23b-33 – Cornelius and Peter compare visions;

e.   10:34-48 – Peter preaches, and the Holy Spirit descends on the uncircumcised; Peter orders them to be baptized;

f.   11:1-18 – on return to Jerusalem, Peter is questioned about baptizing Gentiles and he gives his explanation by recounting the visions etc…

The visions indicate that the baptism of the Gentiles was uniquely God's will and this is recognized by the Jerusalem community in 11:17-18 although Peter is first questioned by the *circumcision party* about why he associated with the *uncircumcised*. The emphasis on the visions and the recognition that the conversion of the Gentiles was God's will was necessary as this marks a major break from Judaism and a new direction for the mission. The break from Judaism is to recognize that all foods are ritually clean thus breaking down all barriers between Jews, Hellenists, and Gentiles; this is authenticated and authorized by the Jerusalem community and by no less a person than Peter himself, the head of the community (11:12). The new direction in the mission is that the Gentiles can be admitted into the new community as they too have received the Holy Spirit (11:15-18). The story of Cornelius' conversion and the acceptance of the Gentiles into the community also indicate that the ritual of circumcision was not necessary for admission – a point of great debate and division later on. However, by involving Peter in the conversion and admittance of Cornelius, Acts clearly portrays that the procedure has apostolic sanction and there is nothing illegal in accepting and admitting the Gentiles. The Cornelius story therefore is of major significance in Acts and has far reaching consequences.

The section ends with a summary statement on the state of the Church (9:31) which Luke periodically makes (see 2:47; 6:7; 12:24; 16:5; 19:20; 28:30-31) as if to show the triumphant on-ward journey of the community that grows from strength to strength despite many hurdles and opposition.

G. Chapter 11:19-13:3: *Spread beyond Judaism/Palestine; Church in Antioch*

Attention now switches to the movement beyond Judaism especially the mission work of the Church in Antioch where the followers of Jesus were first called Christians (11:19-26) (In the New Testament, when people are called 'Christian' it sometimes means they have caused trouble; so, the name need not necessarily be a complimentary one). The story of the activity of the Hellenists, who were persecuted in Jerusalem and were last mentioned in Chapter 8, is taken up again. In chapter 8 they were active in Samaria, now the mission field is wider – Phoenicia, Cyprus and Antioch in Syria, preaching at first to Jews only but then gradually also to the Gentiles (11:20). The mission to the Gentiles had begun in earnest and was first carried out by the Hellenists. Barnabas was sent from Jerusalem to check on this new development and he approved it (11:2-23). Barnabas also brings Saul to Antioch from Tarsus and a vibrant mission centre is established in Antioch (11:25-26).

The developments in Antioch are important as just at this time two things happen to the Jerusalem community: **1.** Jerusalem is struck by famine (11:27-30) which opens up the possibility of Antioch helping the community there – a part of the κοινωνια, or fellowship characteristic of the early community; and **2.** the outbreak of persecution against Jewish Christians resulting in the martyrdom of James the brother of John under Herod Agrippa I and Peter is also arrested (12:1-3). Persecution allows the community to bear witness through martyrdom. Slowly there is not only separation from Judaism, but also hostility between Judaism and Christianity.

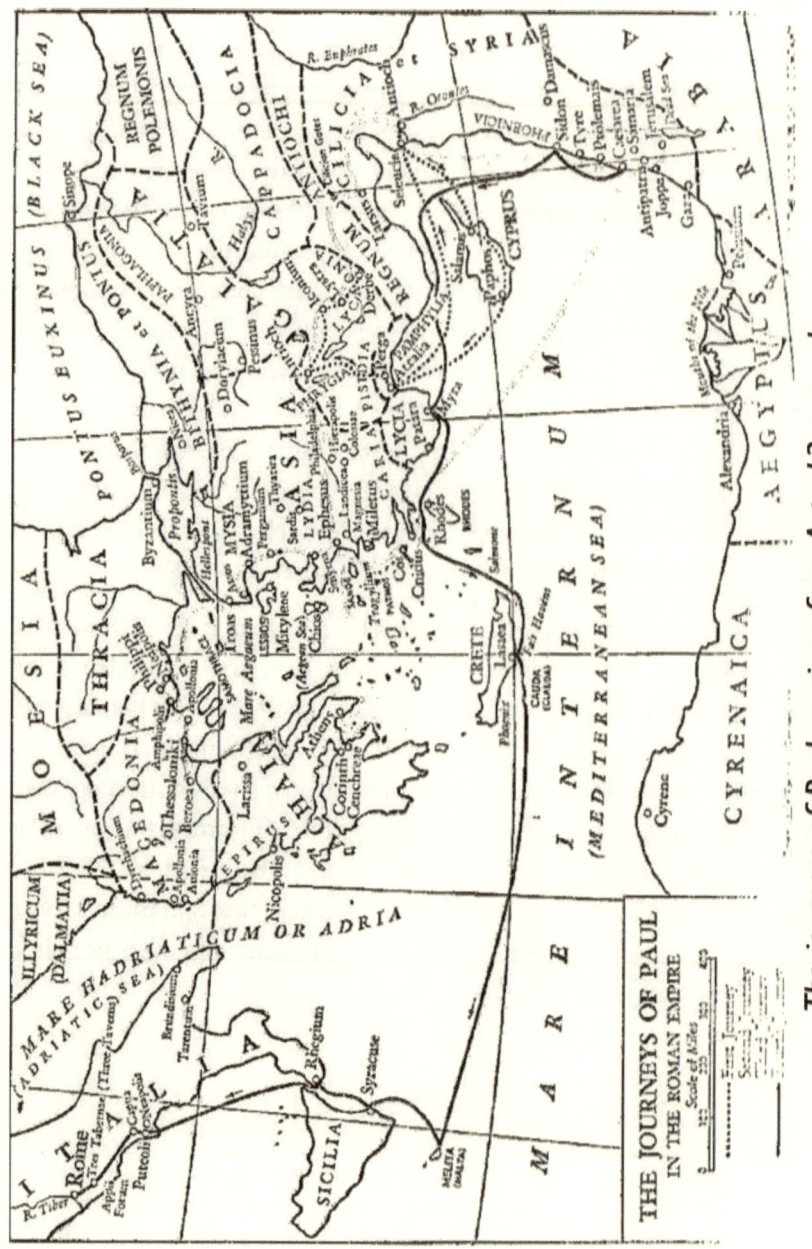

The journeys of Paul as given from Acts 13 onwards

Peter is rescued by angels (12:6-11). Divine intervention shows God's care for God's people, and the punishment of those who dare to raise their hand against God's people – the horrible death of Herod (12:23). The tragedies of chapter 12 end on a joyful note: God's word grows and multiplies, Barnabas and Saul return from Jerusalem bringing John Mark to Antioch (12:24-25). A new phase in mission is about to begin. Again, it should be noted that mission is not the result of a planned programme, but the result of suffering and persecution.

H. Chapters 13:4-14:28: *Paul's First Missionary Journey*

This section begins with a short description of the Church in Antioch (13:1-3). It would seem that in the scheme of Acts, Antioch has now become a major centre of mission; the focus of attention is slowly shifting from Jerusalem; this is part of the movement away from Jerusalem (1:8). The mission centre – Antioch – sets aside Barnabas and Saul for an outreach programme (13:2-3). The journey that follows is often referred to as "Paul's First Missionary Journey" and usually dated around A.D. 46-49. John Mark accompanies them at the beginning of the journey.

The first stop on the journey is Cyprus, the home town of Barnabas (13:4-12) where they preach in the Jewish synagogues maintaining the relationship with Judaism. In Cyprus, they come across Bar-Jesus or Elymas, a false prophet (perhaps a magician) and he is struck blind. This is reminiscent of Peter and Simon Magus (8:14-24).

From Cyprus, the journey continues to Antioch of Pisidia in Asia Minor (13:13-50). *En route,* they pass through Perga where John Mark leaves the group (reason unknown, but which creates a later problem with Paul, 15:37-39). An interesting piece of information is mentioned almost as an aside in 13:13 – the name "Paul" is used, and the order is changed; from henceforth it is "Paul and .....". It is almost as though the writer is saying that it is only in mission work that the great missionary finds his identity and status. Paul's speech to the synagogue (13:16-41) follows the same pattern as the earlier speeches of Peter and Stephen. Thus, apostolic preaching is quite consistent in starting from Jewish scriptures and then moving to an interpretation of Jesus from that perspective.

The group encounters hostility and they move on to Iconium (13:51-14:5). The same pattern of preaching in synagogues was followed with good results, but then ends in persecution and they have to leave the place.

They move on to Lystra (14:6-18) and then to Derbe (14:19-23) where the mission is successful. In Lystra, Paul heals a man crippled from birth just as Peter had done in 3:1-10 – the healing power passed on to Peter has also been passed on to Paul. They retrace their stops on the return journey making sure that there will be someone to oversee the work that was begun (14:23).

They returned to Antioch in Syria from where they had been sent out (14:24-28). The report of their journey and the success they had met with was well received. Antioch was particularly pleased that *a door of faith to the Gentiles had been opened.* It is therefore to be assumed that the mission did not only deal with the Jews, but that there were Gentile converts as well on this first missionary journey.

CHAPTER - 3

The Jerusalem Assembly – (Acts 15)

Brief analysis and commentary on the text. The Jew-Gentile controversy and its resolution in Acts.

Paul's missionary activity in Antioch, Syria, Cilicia, Perga, Pamphylia, Iconium, Lystra, Derbe etc... listed in Acts 12-14 would have included preaching to, and conversion of, the Gentiles; this was indicated in 14:27. Such a mission is now confirmed in 15:1ff when the matter of the admission of the Gentiles into the new community without first becoming Jews is raised and there are objections (15:1): *unless you are circumcised according to the custom of Moses, you cannot be saved,* i.e. Gentiles must first become Jews and then Christians. To become a Jew was not just a matter of circumcision, but it would also involve dietary restrictions (no eating of unclean animals), worship regulations etc.., in short it would involve a complete change in lifestyle which would be burdensome and would ultimately serve no purpose. Further, to insist on becoming a Jew first would also upset the κοινωνια (fellowship) that existed among the members of the new community. The effect of this would be that even if the Gentiles became Christians, they would not be able to eat together with the Jews (such a situation may perhaps be reflected in Gal. 2:11ff where Peter separates himself from the Gentiles to eat with the Jews). This meant that there was a threat to the unity of the Church right at the beginning of its mission. It also meant that the mission of the Church would be limited to Jews only. It was therefore a serious issue which had to be settled as early as possible.

At first it could be thought that the matter was settled when Peter reported the conversion of Cornelius in chapter 11; however, this does not seem to be the case. It may have been that there was an acceptance of the Cornelius conversion as it was a stray incident and an exception especially since Cornelius was reported to have been a close follower of Judaism. Now however, the community is faced with a mass conversion of the Gentiles and whole new Gentile congregations who had had nothing to do with Judaism. It would mean a complete break in relations and the conservative element, or circumcision party – the Jews from Jerusalem – were not willing to take that risk.

The issue was so serious that Paul and Barnabas were deputed by the Church in Antioch to go to Jerusalem and present their case (15:2). Four issues emerge: **1.** the requirement to become a Jew first and submit to all the laws of Judaism; **2.** the limitation of the mission to Jews only; **3.** the threat of a split in the unity of the new community; and **4.** the authority of the group at Jerusalem to make major decisions. This 'consultation' in Jerusalem turned out to be a major decision-making conference. It is often referred to as the Jerusalem Council/Assembly though no formal notice was issued nor was the agenda circulated in advance outlining the issues on which decisions had to be made. Some historians/theologians also refer to it as the First Ecumenical Council. However, by whatever name it might be called, it is a major turning point in the story in Acts; some scholars refer to it as a "watershed" (a turning point) – the whole story of the church's mission takes a new direction after this consultation/conference/council/assembly.

How the Jew-Gentile controversy was resolved

With reference to the four points outlined above, the Jerusalem Assembly resolved the issue in the following way:

1. Since the issue had to deal with the conversion of the Gentiles without submitting to Jewish regulations, the prosecution is first heard – *it is necessary to circumcise them, and to charge them to keep the law of Moses* (15:5). Peter speaks for the defense although he does not directly refer to the Cornelius incident; his speech is more an indirect but practical reference to the admission of the Gentiles

(15:7-11). Paul and Barnabas also speak for the defense from the point of view of their experience in dealing with the Gentiles (15:12). After having heard both sides, James gives his judgement (15:13-21). James refers to the Jewish scriptures to support his judgement. In other words, his judgement is based on very firm grounds and reasoning which would appeal to and be accepted by both sides. James quotes the scriptures (Amos 9:11-12, Jeremiah 12:15, Isaiah 45:21, and Leviticus 17-18) to show how the uncircumcised Gentiles could live among the Jews provided that they abstained from certain pollutants – from eating blood, from eating what has been strangled, from unchastity, and from worshipping idols (Lev. 17-18). James' judgement is accepted by both sides and the issue seems to have been settled.

2.   Once it is agreed upon that the Gentiles can be accepted without first becoming Jews, then the mission field is thrown wide open – no more limitations; mission can be to the Jews and Gentiles and both can be accepted into the new community.

3.   The threat of a split in the Church is also averted. Both factions can live together, worship together, and eat together in fellowship.

4.   The Assembly, however, indicates the authority of the Jerusalem group headed by the apostles. The church in Antioch had to receive orders from Jerusalem in order to ratify the mission among the Gentiles which they had supported; they could not vouch for the validity of the mission by themselves. In bringing this out, Acts paints a picture of the authority of the apostles in Jerusalem – all major decisions had to be made by them. However, once the decision to admit the Gentiles is taken, then Jerusalem has served its purpose and fades out of the picture. The attention now focuses on Paul and his missionary work which is completely in Gentile territory and among the Gentiles.

(Two interesting factors are to be noted: 1. There is no appeal to Jesus – to His words or actions or directions. The Gospel of Luke places emphasis on Jesus interacting with Gentiles (e.g reference to Hebrew scriptures in Lk. 4:25ff; 8:26ff; 8:40ff; 10:25ff; 17:11ff etc....) which could have been

used as a precedence, but none of this is quoted in Acts. **2.** The account
of the Jerusalem Assembly and its decision is at variance with Paul's
version given in Galatians chp. 2. These two factors could perhaps make
for interesting further study.)

Thus, in a three-fold manner, the author of Acts expresses this historical
issue in theological terms:

1.   The mission was willed by God;

2.   It was approved by those who stood in the direct line from Jesus
     – the apostles – who ensured the continuity of redemptive history
     (the *heilsgeschichte*) or the continuity of the mission from Jesus;

3.   There was scriptural proof for the mission.

Interestingly, the issue of circumcision which was the reason for the
Assembly does not figure, or find mention, in the final decision!

Finally, the decision of the Assembly is put down in writing and
sent to the Churches (15:22-31). This is referred to as the *Apostolic
Decree*.   .

The Apostolic Decree

Approving the Gentile mission without/outside the Law is not all
that there is in Acts 15. There is also the so-called 'Apostolic Decree'
(15:22-19) which imposes on the Gentiles four conditions with which
they have to comply: **1.** to abstain from what has been offered to idols;
2. to abstain from blood; **3.** To abstain from what has been strangled;
and **4.** to abstain from unchastity.

Here too, as in the case of the Assembly/Council itself, the ground-work
for the 'decree' has already been laid in the story of the conversion of
Cornelius. Peter's vision (10:11-16) which is indicated as the means by
which God made God's will known with regard to the conversion of
the Gentiles, has, in the strict sense, everything to do with Jewish food
regulations, and nothing to do with the conversion of the Gentiles.
Peter's response that he had never eaten anything unclean bears this
out (10:14). If the vision is taken to refer to food laws and interpreted
accordingly, then the conclusion is that there are no unclean foods.

This stand-point was never recognized by the Jerusalem community. In fact, this is where they call Peter to book (11:3), for eating with the Gentiles. Also, if the Jerusalem community recognized that all foods were clean, then there would have been no need to mention food regulations in the 'Apostolic Decree'. Only if the vision is taken to refer to clean and unclean people, i.e. Jew and Gentile, does it serve the purpose of the theology of Acts, for only then can the vision be interpreted to mean that *"God has given repentance unto life to the Gentiles also"* (11:18). However, this interpretation suggested by Luke himself, still does not solve the problem of the table-fellowship between Jews and Gentiles either socially or sacramentally. In fact, the Assembly/ Council's decision to admit the Gentiles without the Law, has a potential disunifying factor, i.e. the Gentiles may be admitted but they may not eat with the Jews! (see Gal. 2:11ff where Peter separates himself from the Gentiles to eat with the Jews). Yet Luke's concern is to show the continuity of redemptive history to remove the potential disunifying factor(s)..

Here again the hand of Luke, the theologian, is seen resolving this seeming impasse. In the same colours as the author painted the mission to the Gentiles without/outside the Law as standing in the continuity of redemptive history, he now uses those very colours to show that there is no barrier between the Jew and the Gentile. He does so in the three-fold manner met earlier:

1. **By the Divine will:** Acts 15:28 says, *it has seemed good to the Holy Spirit....* In this there is obviously a reference to the highest authority, that it is God Godself, who gives sanction for the observance of the four prohibitions.

2. **By Apostolic authority:** Acts 15:28, *it has seemed good to the Holy Spirit and to us....* Here the apostles/Jerusalem congregation is shown as being in full accord with the divine will as revealed by the Holy Spirit.

3. **By scriptural proof:** The food regulations laid down in the 'Apostolic Decree' are precisely those which are required of Gentiles living in Israel in the law of Moses – Lev. 17 & 18 (see also Amos 9:11-12, Jeremiah 12:15, Isaiah 45:21).

Thus, the observance of the four prohibitions are thought to be "necessary" (15:28) from the point of view of Acts.

It is in this way that Luke portrays that the mission to the Gentiles without/outside the Law stands in the continuity of redemptive history and at the same time preserves the unity of the Church once it has burst the swaddling bands of Judaism. It is in this way that the author solves the problem of how the Church could abandon its links with Judaism and yet remain in unity within the continuity of redemptive history.

Thus, within the theological scheme of the book of Acts, chapter 15 embodies the principle of continuity and therefore stands as the link between the later church and Israel ensuring that the mission to the Gentiles without/outside the Law was fully integrated into redemptive history.

In this way Acts 15 resolves the Jew-Gentile controversy and sets the stage for a full-blown Gentile mission which will extend to the ends of the earth.

CHAPTER - 4

Birth and Spread of the Church II – (Acts 16-28)

Brief analysis and commentary on the text. Paul's journeys. Paul's imprisonment and journey to Rome.

The second half of Acts is almost exclusively the story of Paul. Food laws and circumcision are no longer discussed. There is a wide range of travel and the spread of the Gospel from Palestine to Asia Minor and for the first time, to Europe. Probably these events took place during the years 50–58. Most likely the undisputed letters of Paul were written during this period. It would seem that the decision to freely accept the Gentiles into the new community, and the settling of the dispute in Antioch (ch. 15), allowed Paul to function independently (15:36-40), and served to bring out the most creative years of Paul's life.

A. Chapters 15:36-18:22: *Antioch-Asia Minor-Greece-Antioch – The "Second Missionary Journey"*

1. The sharp dispute between Paul and Barnabas over John Mark (see 12:25 – 13:13) accompanying them on their journeys reached such a level that they had to part ways. Barnabas and John Mark went separately while Paul chose Silas to accompany him. In a way this dispute sets Paul free to concentrate on the mission rather than worrying about personnel accompanying him.

2. Paul and Silas set out from Antioch and the first part of the journey is to revisit earlier places (16:1-5). An interesting feature of this revisit is the mention of the circumcision of Timothy. The historicity of this event is questioned as it goes against the decision which had been reached in chapter 15 and further, it goes against Paul's own conviction that circumcision was not needed in order to be part of the new community. Quite possibly, the circumcision of Timothy could have been a much earlier event while Timothy was still a baby because circumcision would have been necessary to include him in the Jewish community since his father was a Greek (it was not normal for the Jews to accept conversions at a later date). The historicity of the events can be further questioned as Timothy is nowhere seen to have any mission to the Jews nor is he associated with a Jewish community. So, the event does seem to be totally out of character with what is known of Paul's story.

3. The journey continues through Phrygia, Galatia and Troas (16:6-10). Two important points are highlighted in this section: **1.** The strong feeling not to continue the mission in Asia Minor, instead the decision to move to Macedonia in northern Greece which is seen as divine guidance and so put down as a vision. The implication of this which is highlighted here is that for the first time, the Gospel moves into Europe. The history of Christianity will bear out this momentous decision to move into Europe although perhaps the author of Acts would not have been aware of the tremendous consequences of this decision – the spread of the good news through Europe and from the colonial powers of that continent to the ends of the earth. **2.** The divinely inspired moment becomes part of the author's own experience as the "we" passage begins from Troas. This is the first of the "we" passages found in Acts (see Authorship issues above) which form part of the travelogue indicting that the author is part of the group travelling with Paul.

4. The stay in Philippi (16:11-40) brings out the best and the worst in the mission to the Gentiles: the generous support of Lydia (16:11-15) which becomes a model of a Christian household and hospitality. Then the legal and financial problems presented by the girl who had a spirit of divination (16:16-24) indicating the difficulties of ministering in a world of superstition and resulting in a public beating and imprisonment.

Only Paul and Silas are thrown into prison; others in the group are not mentioned, especially the person who writes as though he/she were included in the use of "we".

The miraculous release from prison (16:25-28) parallels the earlier release of Peter from prison (12:1ff) and it also echoes the firm belief that God protects God's workers even in the midst of seemingly impossible situations. The understanding being brought out is that God's mission must continue, and nothing can stop it.

The legal complexity of Paul's trial (16:29-40) provides for an opportunity to proclaim the Gospel resulting in the conversion of the jailer and his household bringing out another model of Christian hospitality. The legalities involved also show how early Christians had to use every means under Roman law to protect themselves and to ensure that they were justly treated. This again serves as a model for Christians to be aware of their rights ensured and protected under the law of the land.

Towards the end of the chapter, the "we" passage seems to have stopped and the pronoun used is "they" indicating that the writer is no longer part of the group. Does it mean that this anonymous companion stayed on in Philippi and rejoined the group when Paul returned (20:5ff)? If so, it would have been a long wait of several years. What was the work of this person during those years which would surely have been acknowledged by Paul?

5. The next stage of the journey brought Paul and Silas to Thessalonica (17:1-9) and Beroea (17:10-15). At Thessalonica, they ran into Jewish opposition. It is interesting to note that the charges against Paul resemble the charges brought by the Jewish authorities against Jesus (Luke 23:2ff) perhaps showing the link between Luke and Acts. Jewish opposition in Thessalonica forced Paul and Silas to move on to Beroea where they were accorded a more cordial welcome, but in the light of the opposition having followed the group from Thessalonica, Paul had to be smuggled out to Athens leaving Silas and Timothy to follow later.

6. There is an appreciation of Greek religious traditions, philosophies, and culture in Athens (17:16-34). Epicurean and Stoic philosophies were very much a part of Hellenistic philosophical thinking and Athens was a major centre where these philosophies were expounded. The philosophers tried to fit Paul's message into their own categories and so took him to the public place – the agora – on the hill of the Areopagus in order to hear him as new thinking was of great interest to them (17:16-21).

The sermon delivered there is in chaste Greek with an awareness of the many temples and statues in the city. There is a cultured and poetic quality in the language and approach quite unlike the other speeches in Acts. Possibly an indication that the author is aware of the highly educated nature of the listeners. The reaction to this eloquence is that some believe (Dionysius and Damaris are named), some mock, some want to hear more. However, there is no persecution, instead a curiosity. The first major speech in Europe ends with an open reaction – open to the message of the Gospel provided it is presented in language and thought patterns that can be grasped. The speech in Athens is an example of Paul's missionary strategy and an example for those in mission in lands of cultural and religious plurality.

7. The mission moves on to Corinth (18:1-17), the capital of the province of Achaia. This first visit to Corinth along with the later two letters probably provides the most information about the place and the social setting of any of the churches founded by Paul. Priscilla and Aqulia (probably a wife-husband team) are met in Corinth and a firm friendship began, especially since they shared a common trade – tent making. They had come to Corinth from Rome as they had to leave under the Edict of Claudius that required all Jews to leave Rome. Romans 16:3 indicates that this couple preceded Paul in Rome and had established a church in their house in Corinth. Silas and Timothy joined Paul in Corinth. The ministry in Corinth lasted a year and a half (18:11). Some of the salient features of this stay and ministry are:

a. The tent making ministry – mission being primarily supported by one's own work rather than being dependent on support from outside. Such a ministry helps in determining one's own priorities rather than have one's agenda written elsewhere because of financial support.

b. Cultivating a circle of colleagues who would continue the work with the same emphasis and thinking: forming a school of thought. In this case, a school of thought that becomes the basis of Christian doctrine and theology.

c. Cutting one's losses and moving on to new areas of mission. When the Jews in the synagogues would not accept the message and caused problems, Paul moved on to a new area of mission – the Gentiles (18:6).

d. The naming of Gallio as proconsul (Governor) is an important reference: Roman records show that Gallio was proconsul of Achaia between AD 51-52. It is from this reference that a chronology of Paul's life and missionary activity can be calculated.

e. The unwillingness of the Roman authorities to get involved in religious matters (18:12-17) especially in the pre-Nero period thereby opening the field for greater missionary activity.

f. Paul's missionary activity at Corinth is often viewed as the ideal missionary strategy to be followed when engaged in mission.

Cenchreae-Ephesus-Caesarea-Antioch (18:18-22). At the end of the so-called "second missionary journey" there is a very brief mention of various cities before the return to Antioch. At Ephesus, Paul leaves the group behind with the indication that he will visit again; perhaps setting the stage for the "third missionary journey". The journey comes to an end with the return to the mother church and mission centre, Antioch.

The accomplishment of the mission has been the establishment of many churches, developing leadership among the group around Paul, learning to deal with opposition even to the extent of using Roman law to one's advantage, interpreting the Gospel according to the context in which it is being preached, and financially supporting one's activity by working at one's trade.

The "second missionary journey" also serves to show that the mission has moved far away from the borders of Palestine and the confines of Judaism in which it all began. The Gospel, its interpretation and message, no longer uses the vocabulary and setting of Palestinian Judaism, or of Hellenistic Judaism, but has now moved beyond those boundaries into the thought patterns of the Gentile (Hellenistic-Roman) world. The mission "to the ends of the earth" is slowly unfolding.

B.   18:23 – 21:14: *Antioch-Ephesus-Greece-Caesarea– the "Third Missionary Journey"*

1. After staying in Antioch for a while, Paul set out from Antioch again to re-visit places and to establish new contacts. He first went through Galatia and Phrygia (18:23).

2. The author introduces Apollos (18:24ff), an educated and eloquent person. His origin in Alexandria would presuppose that he was highly educated as Alexandria was a University city and scholars from there were held in high regard. It is rather peculiar that Apollos knew only the baptism of John and knew nothing of the Holy Spirit; Acts does not offer an explanation other than an indication that Priscilla and Aquila were instrumental in updating Apollos thereby making them Paul's co-workers in the ministry.

3. In Ephesus Paul stays for about three years (3 months in 19:8, 2 years in 19:10 and "stayed in Asia for a while" in 19:21-22). He had earlier promised the Ephesians to return (18:21) and this long stay eliciting the comment that "all the residents of Asia heard the word of the Lord" indicates that Ephesus was now to be considered as a major centre for mission alongside Jerusalem and Antioch. The mission in and from Ephesus is seen to be a successful one (19:11-20), where Paul's name becomes a powerful instrument for exorcisms, giving rise to the summary that "the word of the Lord grew and prevailed mightily". In 19:21 there is the first indication of Paul's plan to ultimately go to Rome – perhaps an indication of the direction in which the book of Acts will move.

During Paul's stay in Ephesus, there is a detailed account of the riot caused by the silversmiths and the concern for their business of making silver statues of Artemis, patron goddess of the Ephesians (Ephesus was known for its fine crafts in silver). The story is an example of how easily the crowds can be aroused and also of how the appeal to law and order was heeded indicating a very sophisticated social order (19:23-41). This brings to an end Paul's stay in Ephesus, but by the time he moved on, Ephesus had been established as a centre for Christianity in Asia Minor.

4. The next leg of the journey took Paul through Macedonia and Greece – Corinth (20:1-4) where he spent three months, then retraced his path through Macedonia instead of going on to Syria in order to escape from plots made against him. There was also quite a cosmopolitan group around Paul who accompanied him.

5. Time is now spent between Troas and Philippi where a "we" passage begins again (20:5-15). The writer seems to have rejoined the group again after chapter 16. At Troas, Paul raises Eutychus to life after he had fallen out of a third storey window of the room where Paul was talking till the early hours of the morning. The incident parallels Peter raising Tabitha to life in Joppa (9:36-42). There is an interesting reference to the group having "broken bread" (20:11): a Eucharistic reference or simply a reference to a shared breakfast?

6. Acts 20:13-16 recounts some of the ports at which they stopped on their way to Jerusalem where Paul wanted to observe the day of Pentecost. At Miletus, Paul gave an eloquent farewell address to the elders of the Church at Ephesus (20:17-38). The address touches upon the success of the mission in Asia, of the persecution that must follow, but the assurance of the presence of the Holy Spirit in all circumstances, and Paul's commitment to the preaching of the Gospel. The warning against false teachers (20:30) – something that was very prevalent after about AD 70 (strongly mentioned in later New Testament writings such as the Catholic Epistles and the Pastoral Epistles). There is also mention of the uncertainty of what awaits Paul in Jerusalem – possibly setting the stage for the further direction of the writing. The speech also serves to indicate that the elders receive the care of the Church from Paul –

the first mention of passing on authority to the next in line – Paul's final directives to those whom he will never see again (20:25, 38).

7. After the farewell at Miletus, the journey to Jerusalem continues with another dramatic farewell at Tyre (21:1-6) and thence to Caesarea (21:7-14). In Caesarea they stayed at the house of Phillip, the evangelist (last heard of as speaking to the Ethopian eunuch in 8:26-40). Paul is symbolically warned of impending disaster in Jerusalem but is insistent that he should go forward. Thus, Paul's road to Jerusalem echoes Jesus' journey to Jerusalem (Luke 9:51, 13:33).

At the end of the "Third Missionary Journey", Acts shows that the Gospel is well entrenched in Asia and Europe – churches/congregations had come up in all major cities and Ephesus was a new mission centre. There is also the concern for the on-going work indicated in Paul handing over charge to the elders of the Church in Ephesus in his farewell address at Miletus. There also seems to be the urgency to move toward Jerusalem perhaps setting the stage for the end of the mission work in Asia Minor and moving on westwards to Rome. The mission "to the ends of the earth" comes to an end in one area with a movement as to its continuation in another direction.

C. 21:15 – 26:32: *Arrest in Jerusalem, imprisonment and trials*

1. In Jerusalem, Paul reports to James (Jesus' brother who is head of the community in Jerusalem) and others in the Jerusalem community (21:17-26). The Jew-Gentile feelings seem to surface again though in a rather subdued form. Paul is asked to show his loyalty to Judaism by purifying himself, but this advice, good as it may be, fails when a riot is started claiming that Paul had defiled the Temple (21:27-36) by bringing Gentiles into it. Paul is saved from being lynched by the intervention of the Roman tribune with soldiers. After being arrested, Paul uses his Roman citizenship and proficiency in Greek and he is allowed to speak to the people.

2. Paul's speech of defence (22:1-21) was delivered in Aramaic to catch the attention of the people and reassure them that he was one of them. The speech recounts his conversion with some variants from 9:1-30.

The question is again raised as to whether Paul was in Jerusalem at the time of Stephen's death as later he says that he was not known by sight to the church in Jerusalem. When Paul explains his mission to the Gentiles, the crowd reacts violently, but Paul's Roman citizenship wins him protection (22:24-29). The next day Paul is brought before the Sanhedrin to explain himself (22:30).

3.   Paul before the Sanhedrin (23:1-35)

Paul claims his Pharisaic origins – belief in the resurrection – to divide the Sanhedrin which consisted of Sadducees and Pharisees (23:6-9). As a result of the divided opinion, the Tribune took charge of Paul since no decision of the Sanhedrin was possible. The indication that the movement is towards Rome is seen in 23:11. Since the Sanhedrin could not resolve the issue and since there was little hope that a decision could be reached, a plot was hatched to assassinate Paul before he could get to the Sanhedrin chambers (23:12-15). The involvement of the Sadducees to do away with what does not suit them at this highest level of decision making is reminiscent of the trial of Jesus recorded in the Gospels where the Sadducees roused the people to do away with Jesus and release Barabbas (Luke 23:1-25).

The plot to assassinate Paul came to be known by his nephew and then brought to the notice of the Tribune (23:16-22). Realizing that Paul was not going to get a fair trial before the Sanhedrin, and probably also keeping in mind that Paul was a Roman citizen, the Tribune sent Paul, under escort, to Felix the Governor in Caesarea. In his letter to Felix, the Tribune, Claudius Lysias, plays it safe and washes his hands off the whole matter (23:26-30). So, Paul is brought to Felix in Caesarea, and as per Roman law, the trial proceeded only when both parties were there to present their case; until such time the prisoner is kept safe (23:31-35).

4. Trial before Felix (24:1-27). Felix was Procurator in Palestine between AD 52 and 60. Possibly Paul's appearance before him was towards the end of his term as Paul appears before Felix's successor as well. The charges against Paul were mentioned to Felix (24:1-9). Then Felix gave Paul a chance to defend himself (24:10-21). Paul's defense is a

dependence on his Jewish background and especially his Pharisaic background. Both parties acknowledge that Felix is well versed in the history and practices of Judaism (24:2-3; 10). Verse 22 also shows that Felix is quite up-to-date on Jewish sects/movements. As procurator, he probably kept tabs on potential areas of trouble, especially concerning the Jewish religion which was always a contentious issue. The outcome is that Felix is really unable to make a judgement and so postpones the matter with a liberal sort of "house-arrest" having been ordered for Paul (24:22-23). However, Felix's interest in the case continues whether from a genuine desire for understanding the issues involved or from the hope of getting a bribe from either of the parties (24:24-26). Finally, Felix's term ends (after two years of Paul's imprisonment) and he is succeeded by Porcius Festus but does the Jews a favour by keeping Paul in jail (24:27).

5. Paul before Festus (25:1-27). Festus was procurator from AD 60 to AD 62. The Jews asked him to conclude the case against Paul requesting that the trial be conducted in Jerusalem (25:1-3) but Festus decided that the trial would be at Caesarea and asked the accusers to appear there (25:4-5). However, Festus wanted to play the popularity card and offered Paul the choice to go to Jerusalem for trial (25:6-11a). Paul, knowing that he would not get a fair trial in Jerusalem, made the ultimate appeal available to a Roman citizen – the appeal to Caesar for justice (25:11b). Once this appeal is made, the procurator has to make all arrangements so that the person is sent safely to appear before Caesar in Rome (25:12).

6. Paul before Agrippa II (25:13 – 26:32). The parallelism to Jesus' trial in Luke's Gospel (Lk. 23:7) is continued in Paul's appearance before the Herodian, Agrippa II. In Jesus' case, it was Herod Agrippa I, one of the sons of Herod the Great. The person mentioned in Acts 25 & 26 was King Agrippa II, a distant relative of Herod the Great who lived in an incestuous relationship with his sister Bernice, and thus was not acceptable to the Jews in addition to being from the hated family of Herod. Agrippa II was given the title of king by the Romans probably as a measure to keep a still powerful family loyal to Rome.

However, Agrippa II had no powers; he had a title which possibly gave him some measure of social standing and respect, but that was about all. Nevertheless, having come from a family that had some connection with Judaism, Agrippa II was quite knowledgeable about Jewish rites, traditions and laws (26:2) which was why Paul's case was presented to him, more for information (entertainment?) than for any legal purpose/opinion (25:13-27).

Paul's defence was his Jewish background, and a re-interpretation of the law in terms of his new found means of salvation (26:2ff) and a repetition of his conversion experience for the third time in Acts (26:9-20). This account also has differences from the earlier two accounts. Agrippa II is sympathetic, but nothing more and has no choice but to go along with the procurator's decision that since Paul had appealed to Caesar, he should be sent to Caesar (26:30-32).

Some interesting points are to be noted in these trial accounts:

A. The author is definitely on Paul's side and presents the story from that point of view; the other side is always wrong / unethical, and guilty of trying to circumvent justice.

B. The insistence that the Jewish law is now to be reinterpreted in terms of what God has done in Jesus Christ.

C. The continuing antagonism between the authorities of Judaism and the new group that has formed around Jesus which seems to pose a threat to Judaism.

D. The careful narration that presents Roman law as being just and fair and that its enforcers (governors/procurators/administrators) were well-versed in the law and eager to uphold it. In this sense, Acts shows that in no situation was Roman law called into question, but rather, its provisions were upheld in the most honourable way. In other words, the new group on trial (Christians) were law abiding and peaceable citizens of the Empire.

D.   27:1 – 28:16: *Journey to Rome*. 28:17-31: *In Rome*

1. Since Paul had appealed to Caesar, it was mandatory for Festus to ensure that Paul was safely brought to Rome to face trial before Caesar. So, begins a long journey, employing the "we" formula, up the Syrian coast (Caesarea to Sidon, 27:1-3), past Cyprus (27:4), past the southern coast of Asia Minor and docked at Myra (27:5). A change of ships at Myra, then sailing along the southern coast of Crete, they docked at Fair Havens (27:6-8). But due to winter storms, it was necessary for them to reach a safe harbor and although Paul warned against moving on, the centurion was anxious to reach Rome as soon as possible (27:9-12) and so moved on. But a winter storm blew them off course and with difficulty they reached the island of Cauda (27:13-16), but they kept moving with loss of cargo and fear of being ship wrecked (27:17-20).

However, the author of Acts sees the hand of God leading Paul to Rome, so no loss of life occurred (27:21-26).Finally, they were driven ashore on a strange island (later identified as Malta in 28:1) and the ship was destroyed in the shallow sea, but all lives were saved (27:27-44). An interesting note here is verse 35 where Paul took bread, gave thanks, broke it and began to eat. Is this a reflection of the Eucharist? The language used, and the imagery employed are the same as the Eucharistic accounts. Perhaps the author is trying to bring out that the whole situation in which they found themselves was part of a divine plan and the Eucharistic vocabulary used is a reassurance of God's presence and guidance.

Survival of storms, ship wreck, and snakebite (28:1-6) illustrate God's care for Paul whose missionary zeal and concern for companions on the journey are again and again mentioned (28:7-10).

Finally, they sailed from Malta up the west coast of Italy to a landing at Puteoli near Naples (28:11-16). The journey probably began towards the end of AD 60 and Paul would have arrived in Rome towards the end of AD 61. Paul was welcomed by the community in Rome, several of whom came to Puteoli to meet and escort him to Rome (28:14-16). With Paul's arrival in Rome, the scheme outlined in Acts 1:8 – *to the ends of the earth*– is now coming to fulfillment. Rome, as the capital city, was connected to all parts of the empire, and so, in a sense, the Gospel has moved to the ends of the earth.

2. 28:17-31: **Paul in Rome**

In Rome, Paul seems to be under some kind of semi house arrest – he can stay by himself with a soldier to guard him (28:16).

There is already an established Jewish community in Rome as is evidenced by 28:17. By the early 60s, the Roman Jewish community which must have been established at least 25 to 30 years before, came to be highlighted only when the great Christian missionary himself arrived there. Interestingly, the "we" passage ends with Paul's arrival in Rome. Does the author not continue with Paul's group? Paul appealed to the Jewish community in Rome and he explained his situation to them (28:17-20), while they indicated that they had not received any reports against Paul (verse 21), but that the sect that he was proclaiming was spoken against (verse 22); this follows his missionary strategy of always going first to the Jews with his message of the Gospel.

Paul's preaching about Jesus seems to have had no success among the Jews (28:23-28) and the last words attributed to Paul in Acts were that the Gospel had been sent to the Gentiles and that they would believe (28:28).

In summary, Paul seems to be quite free to continue meeting people and preaching – a semi house arrest situation continues for two years (28:30-31). It must be noted that the author of Acts is always careful to present the Roman authorities and the Roman legal system in good light so no threats are made on Paul and he remains in protective custody of the Roman authorities.

In a sense it is an anticlimax at the end of Acts' story and many questions are left unanswered especially as to what happened after the two-year period. However, from the literary and internal point of view, the narrative cannot proceed as Acts comes to an end since it has reached the climax of its outline – in Rome from where the Gospel will move to the ends of the earth.

It is ironic that Paul arrived in Rome because of his appeal to Caesar, and so under Roman law, he is a protected person until Caesar disposes of his case – in other words, Roman law assisted in the Gospel reaching Rome and thus to the ends of the earth.

[Some traditions claim that after his trial and on being set free, Paul went on to Spain as he at one time had planned (Romans 15:23-24); this is supported by a tradition in Spain (see below in life of Paul). There is also the speculation of a "second career" for Paul after his release from Roman imprisonment, based on II Timothy and Titus: that Paul went East to Crete and then to Asia; he was again arrested and taken as prisoner to Rome where he died. However, the general belief, and strong tradition of the Church, is that Paul died in Rome in the persecution under Nero between A.D. 64-66 during the imprisonment recorded in Acts.]

CHAPTER - 5

History and Theology
in the Acts of the Apostles

Acts is not a literary work that can stand on its own; as the dedication to Theophilus shows (1:1), Acts carries forward the story started in Luke's Gospel, and therefore the two constitute one large writing and must be taken together; hence the writing is usually referred to as "Luke-Acts". The earliest scholarship of the book indicates that Acts was thought to be the history of the early church and thus the approach to Acts was that it was recording history. However, in the nineteenth century (about 1838) the thesis put forward was that Acts originated in the late period of primitive Christianity (i.e. between AD 80 – 100) with the intention to show the settlement of the dispute between Jewish Christianity and Gentile Christianity (which is very prominent in the letters of Paul), and to show that both parties were accommodated by the decisions of the early church. This hypothesis raised the question as to whether Acts should be approached as a strict recording of history or whether Acts was also theologically motivated. As scholarship moved on, the contents of Acts came under scrutiny and the way in which the story is told – the first part mostly Peter and centered in Jerusalem (chapter 1-14), the second part exclusively centered around Paul (chapters 16-28) and missionary activity outside of Jerusalem in Gentile areas, while the Apostolic Decree in chapter 15 stands as the turning point in the book moving from Jewish Christianity (with Peter as the main figure) to Gentile Christianity (with Paul as the main figure). In this way, Acts smoothens the very strong dispute between the two parties. It led scholars to exclaim that in Acts, "Peter is not Paulinized, nor is Paul Peterized, but both Peter and Paul are Lucanized"! It was felt that Acts was an apology for Christianity against Jewish accusations, addressed to Gentile society with the aim of showing that the world mission of Christianity had superceded Judaism – the history of salvation (*heilsgeschichte*), begun with God's dealings with the Jews, was now continued in Christianity.

In the twentieth century, Hans Conzelmann dominated the scene with his scholarship in Luke's Gospel followed by his scholarship in Acts where he convincingly showed that in Luke-Acts there is a theological interpretation of history always controlled by the *heilsgeschichte* – the history of salvation. The story in Acts probably covers a period of about 30-35 years after Jesus but only a few incidents are narrated which help in moving the story forward in terms of the *heilsgeschichte;* the two main centres of Christianity are mentioned, but in the movement from Jerusalem to Antioch, nothing is mentioned about the spread of the mission to Eastern parts of the Empire (including India where Thomas is traditionally believed to have evangelized about AD 52), North Africa, or even how, and by whom, Christianity was first taken to Rome. Therefore, the material in Acts is highly selective, both chronologically and geographically. Whether all the historical references to Jerusalem and the situation there can be proved is very doubtful (e.g. tongues of fire and speaking in various languages on the day of Pentecost, the harassment of Peter and John by Jewish authorities, the killing of James, son of Zebedee by Herod Agrippa I, the martyrdom of Stephen), though these are all quite plausible even if the author romanticizes the early Christian picture of the Jerusalem Church in terms of rapidly increasing numbers, the quality of life (including the generous giving up of possessions and having all things in common). Although he does modify his picture somewhat by including the story of the deceptiveness of Ananias and Sapphira (ch. 5) and the division between the Hebrews and Hellenists (ch. 6), giving it a very human touch, nevertheless the stories are used as entry points/stepping stones to the larger picture of the on-going *heilsgeschichte*.

The speeches in Acts also reflect this interest in moving the story forward – showing how the new sect proclaiming Jesus had taken the place of, and gone beyond, Judaism. Thus, for the most part they are the creation of the author although they may have a genuine base in what was believed and proclaimed.

Paul's missionary travels are also questioned. The author of Acts seems to be included in the "we" passages, but these are only a few. Where did the author get information regarding the majority of the travels and activity involved? How much co-relates with Paul's own letters? There is no mention of Paul's writings in Acts which is Paul's major legacy.

So how is Acts to be approached – history or theology? Perhaps the choice should not be "either/or" but "both/and". As modern scholars point out, Luke-Acts is the theological interpretation of history and perhaps the clue to this lies in the author's own description – the author of Luke-Acts thought of his/her work as διηγησις *(diegesis)* – narrative. The narrative is to undergird historical events with theological insight. Therefore, whatever history is recorded in Acts, it is put to the service of theology – to strengthen and proclaim the faith. By writing with the objective of proclaiming God's redemptive act in Jesus, coming to a climax of preaching in Rome, the author has created a literary form of combining history and theology in such a way that there was no precedent for such a literary endeavour and no successor. The author has used a literary method to represent his/her view of history along with his/her theological intentions. The author's choice of material and narrative presentation is therefore shaped not only by what happened (history) but also by what it means (theology). So, Acts is a combination of history and theology telling us about events and interpreting those events in terms of God's act of redemption in Jesus for the whole world – *"you shall be my witnesses…to the ends of the earth."*

Select Bibliography for Section I

Brown, R. E., *An Introduction to the New Testament*. Bangalore: Theological Publications in India, 2000.

_____, et. al., *New Jerome Biblical Commentary*. Englewood Cliffs, NJ: Prentice Hall, 1990.

Bruce, F. F., *Commentary on the Book of Acts*. Grand Rapids: Eerdmans, 1980.

Conzelmann, H. *Acts of the Apostles* (Translated by James Limburg et. al.). Philadelphia: Fortress, 1987.

_____, The *Theology of Saint Luke* (Translated by Geoffrey Buswell). New York: Harper, 1961.

Fitzmyer, Joseph A. *The Acts of the Apostles,* The Anchor Bible, Vol. 31. New York: Dooubleday, 1998.

Foakes Jackson, J., and K. Lake (eds), The *Beginnings of Christianity. The Acts of the Apostles* (5 vols.). London: Macmillan, 1920-1933.

Haenchen, E. *The Acts of the Apostles: A Commentary* (Translated by Bernard Noble et. al.). Philadelphia: Westminster, 1971.

Hengel, M., Acts *and the History of Earliest Christianity.* Philadelphia: Fortress, 1979.

Kee, H. C., and F. W. Young, The *Living World of the New Testament*. London: Darton, Longman & Todd, 1966.

Kummel, W. G. *Introduction to the New Testament* (Rev. Ed.). London: SCM Press, 1975.

Venkataraman, Babu Immanuel. "Acts" in Brian C. Wintle (General Editor), *South Asia Biblical Commentary* (Udaipur, Rajasthan: Open Door Publications, 2015) pages 1451-1509.

Winter, B. W., et. al. (eds.), The *Book of Acts in its First Century Setting* (6 vols.). Grand Raids: Eerdmans, 1993-1997.

SECTION II

A Study of Paul and the Pauline Letters

CHAPTER - 1

General Introduction to New Testament Letters

Letter/Epistle

There are 21 writings that come under the category of **"letter"** or ἐπιστολη out of the 27 writings that comprise the New Testament. It is therefore necessary to have some understanding of the format of these writings and how they are used in communication. It is generally accepted that a 'letter' is written on a particular occasion, directed to a specific person or group of people, written with the purpose of direct communication and with no thought of wider distribution. It is also generally accepted that 'letter' and 'epistle' are interchangeable terms referring to the same writing. A few remarks on these 'generalizations' would be in order before proceeding further.

The accepted definition of a letter today may not quite fit the New Testament writings that come under this category. In the early 20th century, a German scholar, A. Deissmann (*Light From The Ancient East*, London, 1927) made a distinction between 'letter' and 'epistle'. Deissmann held that an epistle was an artistic literary device dealing with a moral/theological/philosophical issue presented to an audience/readership in a written form; whereas a letter was a non-literary (non-grammatical/colloquial) means of communicating between two persons separated at a distance from each other. Deissmann's definitions were not fully accepted by New Testament scholars but it did make a contribution in that it helped to have greater clarity and critical thinking on these 21 writings in the New Testament. It was recognized that not all the 21 writings met all of Deissmann's criteria for classifying them strictly as either 'letter' or 'epistle': several are long writings and could better be classified as essays (Hebrews); several do not have an epistolary/letter structure (e.g. James; Ephesians); only a few are addressed to individuals (e.g. II & III John; Philemon; Timothy; Titus); most are addressed to cities/communities (e.g. Romans, I & II Corinthians, Colossians) to address particular circumstances and contexts; they are therefore meant to be read aloud and shared e.g. I Thess. 5:27; Col. 4:16). The letters/epistles bring together several stylistic forms: missionary address, especially in proclamation and worship, preaching, exhortation, instruction, exegesis of scripture and hermeneutics, hymns, recording of already shaped traditions, warning against heresy, ecclesiastical order, etc…It must also be remembered that these letters were not originally divided into chapters and verses (these were introduced much later – 10th century); the letters were intended to be read as a whole rather than just picking and choosing passages. The New Testament 'letters' or 'epistles' can therefore be seen as a contribution to Greek literature and to literary classifications by combining the personal letter form and the essay form in one writing. Hence the strict differentiation between 'letter' and 'epistle' may not be possible to maintain and so the interchangeability of the terms to describe/refer to these New Testament writings would be appropriate.

Format of ancient letters

Many ancient Greek and Latin letters and fragments of papyrus manuscripts from Egypt have come to light in archaeological discoveries, dealing with all kinds of subjects – legal matters, friendship, business correspondence, family matters and love-letters. From examination of these evidences, the usual format of a letter can be discerned:

A. The Opening Formula: The opening formula of a letter consisted of three basic elements: the sender, the addressee, greetings. **The sender** involves the personal name of the author (the author may have dictated the letter rather than have written it him/herself, e.g. Romans 16:22; I Peter 5:12), and/or may contain the signature of the author (e.g. I Cor. 16:21; Gal. 6:11; Col. 4:18; II Thess. 3:17). There could also be co-senders of a letter: e.g. Timothy (II Cor. 1:1; Col. 1:1), Silvanus and Timothy (I Thess.

1:1; II Thess. 1:1). This distinguishes between 'author' (the authority behind the writing) and 'writer' (the one responsible for the script). The author could also add further identifications for the purpose of stressing his/her authority: e.g. *Paul, a servant of Jesus Christ* (Rom. 1:1); *Paul, called by the will of God to be an apostle* (I Cor. 1:1); James, *a servant of God* (Jam. 1:1); *Peter, an apostle of Jesus Christ* (I Peter 1:1).

The addressee could be a personal name, e.g. *to the beloved Gaius* (III John); *to Philemon our beloved fellow worker* (Philemon); or the addressee could be a group, e.g. *to the saints and faithful brethren in Christ at Colossae* (Col. 1:1); *to the church of the Thessalonians* (I Thess. 1:1, II Thess. 1:1).

Greetings were usually expressed at the beginning (II Cor. 1:2; I Tim. 1:2) and also at the end of the writing (see the Concluding Formula below).

B. Thanksgiving: It was customary that after the opening formula, the sender would give thanks for specified reasons, e.g. deliverance from a calamity, recovery after illness etc.... Many of Paul's letters state, *I/we give thanks because....* Usually it is thankfulness for the life and faithfulness of the congregation (Philip. 1:3; Col. 1:3). In II and III John there is no expression of thanks, but an expression of joy which served the same purpose. These expressions help to compliment the one being addressed and allow for a benevolent mood to receive the message of the writing.

C. Body of the writing: Normally this is the portion between the opening formula and the concluding formula; not much thought has been given to its set form probably because it is more difficult to analyze and put into a pattern since a variety of topics may be covered. The body of the writing would contain exhortation, admonition, teachings, arguments on points of controversy, warnings, directions for the future. It is here that the letter takes on an essay form of addressing issues in worship, preaching, ethical behaviour, instructions, interpretation of scripture, formulation of doctrine, and biographical details etc...

D. Concluding Formula: A letter would usually end with a word of greeting and farewell. Paul usually concludes with his own greetings and greetings from those who were with him at that time (e.g. Philip.

4:21-22; Titus 3:15). In Romans 16:22 it is mentioned that Tertius was the writer of the letter or the amanuensis, i.e. one who wrote while the author dictated or the author's literary assistant. II & III John have greetings sent to the addressees from the community where the letter was written. Paul sometimes concludes with a doxology – an ascription of glory (Rom. 16:25-27; Philip. 4:20) and/or a benediction (II Cor. 13:14; Philip. 4:23; Col. 4:18). Other letters also have doxologies and benedictions – I & II Peter, Jude, Hebrews. In some letters, the greeting was to be done *with a Holy kiss* (e.g. Rom. 16:16; I Cor. 16:10; I Peter 5:14). Greeting one another with a kiss would seem to be an accepted practice (Genesis 33:4, 45:15; II Sam. 20:9; Lk. 15:20), so it did not draw attention when Judas identified Jesus with a kiss (Matt. 26:47-50 and parallels). The 'Kiss' had become a sign of fellowship; it was 'Holy' because it was exchanged among the saints in the community. At the end of the letter, there may be mention of signing in one's own hand thereby suggesting that the letter was written by another, but that the author had agreed to its contents so that it could justifiably be sent in his name (I Cor. 16:21; Gal.6:11; Col. 4:18; II Thess. 3:17).

Keeping the above criteria in mind, 21 of the New Testament's 27 books have been classified as letters/epistles. It was the easiest way of maintaining communication with distant places and providing further instruction in one's absence; the letter substituted for the physical presence of the apostle/writer. All the authors wrote with some awareness that their letters would be accepted because of their apostolic authority and that what they had written would be read within the community and shared with other communities. It is important therefore to have a knowledge of the historical, cultural, social, religious background of the communities/individuals addressed in the letters in order to fully appreciate their message. The requirement of the mission, edification and instruction, warnings against heresy and guarantee of ecclesiastical order comprise the potent force of the letter/epistle not only as a means of internal communication for Christianity but also made a contribution to Greek literature. By inclusion in the canon of scripture, these letters became far more than just writings to a particular situation in a particular historical context; they became God's word still speaking to the church today.

Pseudonymity and Anonymity in New Testament writings

When dealing with the New Testament letters, an issue faced is that of *pseudoepigraphy* (ψευδο = false + γραφη = writing; literally 'false writing') or *pseudonymity* (ψευδο = false + νομος = name; literally 'false name'). These writings were purported to have been written by an authoritative figure, but which may have been written by his/her disciples/followers many years after his/her death. Today, pseudoepigraphy and pseudonymity are not well accepted and there is a need to have several legal clearances in order to use it. But this was not the case till about the 4th century A. D.; pseudoepigraphy and pseudonymity were commonly used and an accepted method of writing. Similarly, the issue of anonymity (ἀνομος = no name): anonymous writings were commonplace, especially in situations where the writing could get the writer into trouble with the authorities, or even get the whole community into trouble. Christian writings of the first century faced this issue as communities were under pressure and threat of persecution from the Roman government or from local bodies. So, writers kept themselves anonymous to keep themselves and their communities from running into trouble with the authorities. Thus, it can be seen that pseudoepigraphy, pseudonymity, and anonymity were accepted methods of writing in the ancient world and flourished from about 200 B. C. till about A.D. 400.

These are difficult methods of writing to understand in the modern day and age, and to more fully understand these methods, a distinction must be made between 'writer' and 'author'. Normally, today 'author' means both the one responsible for the ideas contained in a writing and also the 'writer' who drafted the wording; today these are synonymous terms. But in the ancient world, 'author' was only the authority behind the writing; the 'writer' could be anyone else. If the author/writer was an easily identifiable figure, then there would be no need for pseudonymity; the writing would simply be kept anonymous. All four Gospels, the book of Acts, and Hebrews have no author/

writer mentioned and fall in this category of anonymous writings (see sections on authorship of each writing in Vols. I, II, III, IV).

This method was especially followed by 'schools of thought' where a disciple/follower wrote in the name of the authoritative figure (perhaps even after the person's death) as the writer wanted the work to be received authoritatively and also because he/she considered himself/herself as an authoritative interpreter of the person whose thought was being endorsed and/or expanded to suit new situations. This was especially the case where the authoritative figure was dead, and the situation necessitated his/her authority to be stressed to meet new contexts. So, the writing was attributed to the authoritative figure, or left anonymous, and was accepted as though it had come from the person himself/herself; the authoritative figure was regarded as the authority behind the writing while the writing itself was done by someone else, usually someone who stood in the line and carried on the work of the authority. Such an attribution would serve to continue the authority of the person concerned and to take the place of the person's physical presence. Thus, those who considered themselves in the school of Paul, or James, or Peter, or Jude, or John, or Matthew, or Luke, may have either written in their authority's name or left the writing anonymous because the authority was a well-known and easily identifiable person.

This is also found in the Hebrew scriptures, the Old Testament: The Books of the Law were written about 700 – 800 years after Moses, but were written in his name since he was considered to be the great Law-giver; the Book of Psalms was collected in the name of David even when some other name is specifically mentioned because David was considered a great composer of psalms and lyrics; many wisdom writings are attributed to Solomon, even those written 800 years after his death, because Solomon was considered the wise man *par excellence*; parts of the prophetic book of Isaiah, written 200 years after the prophet's death, were included in the prophetic book of Isaiah, because of the similarity of thought pattern. Thus pseudoepigraphy, pseudonymity, and anonymity were accepted contributions to the literature of the time and were treated with the same authority as if the main figure was actually present.

Keeping this background in mind, **it is important to note that many New Testament works can be put down to being pseudoepigraphy, pseudonymous and anonymous writings but which in no way lose their relevance and authority as the word of God.**

Select Bibliography

Aland, K. "The Problem of Anonymity and Pseudonymity in Christian Literature of the First Two Centuries" in *Journal of Theological Studies, No. 12, 1961, pages 39-49.*

Doty, W. G. *Letters in Primitive Christianity,* Philadelphia: Fortress Press, 1973.

Kummel, W. G. *Introduction to the New Testament.* London: SCM Press, 1975.

Murphy-O'Connor, J. *Paul, the Letter Writer.* Collegeville: Liturgical, 1995.

CHAPTER - 2

Paul's Life

Primary sources for information on Paul (his letters). Secondary sources (Acts). The background of Paul. Conversion. His work. Table of suggested Pauline chronology. Table of suggested chronology of all Pauline letters. Paul as interpreter of Christ to the Jews and Gentiles. Select Bibliography.

The New Testament canon (27 books) contains 21 writings which can be classified as letters/epistles and of these 13 letters are associated with the name of Paul. It has meant that Paul has probably been the most influential of the New Testament writers when it comes to interpreting Jesus and the implications for particular individuals and communities. After the story of the earthly Jesus in the Gospels (Vol. I in this series), the Acts of the Apostles and the Pauline Letters take the story to the next level of development: the on-going life of the community that came into existence as a result of the work of Jesus' disciples and workers like Paul. By inclusion in the canon, these writings affect every Christian in terms of beliefs, doctrines, church order, and ethical norms and it is therefore necessary to include a study of the letters and their contribution in any introduction to the New Testament.

Paul's letters

The 13 letters which bear the name of Paul do not all necessarily originate from Paul. In the mid-18th century, F. C. Baur, and his students from the University of Tubingen (Germany) who formed the Tubingen School, first questioned Paul's authorship of I & II Timothy and Titus and then later I & II Thessalonians, Ephesians, Philippians, and Colossians. Their argument was that only four major writings – Romans, I & II Corinthians and Galatians – could be considered as genuinely coming from Paul as they reflect the time and age of the concerns of Paul which they understood to be the struggle against "judaizing" elements (i.e. those who wanted converts to first become Jews, submit to all the laws of Judaism, and then become Christians) and in that process, gave rise to the major doctrinal contribution of Paul in his theology of justification by faith (whereas in Judaism the emphasis was on justification by works). The short writing of the letter to Philemon was included in the genuine letters since it was a very personal letter and as it illustrated, in a way, the theological implications of justification by faith when applied to daily life situations (see commentary below for further details). The objection to the Tubingen School was that it places Paul in too narrow a framework to do justice to the vast contribution of his thought to Christian theology. However, the position taken here, which is also widely accepted in New Testament scholarship, is that even where Paul's own authorship cannot be proven/accepted, nevertheless the thought pattern and theological development, if reconcilable with the four major writings, can be accepted as 'Pauline' i.e. the writing may not be from Paul himself, but from the school of thought that arose around Paul's writings (see Pseudonymity in letter writing, above) and which developed Paul's thought to meet the needs of the mission as it moved further on from Paul both in time and context. Based on the above criteria, this volume will classify the writings as follows:

- **from Paul himself:** Romans, I & II Corinthians, Galatians, Philemon. These deal with arguments against the Judaizers and the development and implications of justification by faith, and the practical dimension of putting faith into action in the new relationships in Christ (Philemon).

- **deutero-Pauline:** Ephesians, Philippians, Colossians, I & II Thessalonians. These deal with a concern for Christology, ecclesiology, and eschatology – a logical development from Paul's basic theology of justification by faith. These could also be combinations/compilations of parts of several letters (see commentary on each writing for details).

- **trito-Pauline:** the Pastorals – I & II Timothy and Titus. These deal with a further development of addressing the on-going concern for church organization, administration, and leadership (pastoral concerns, especially the concern for 'sound teaching') as the mission expanded and communities were established in far-flung regions.

In addition to the above 13 letters which have been preserved in the canon, three other letters are mentioned which may be "lost" – *I wrote to you in my letter...* (I Cor. 5:9); *I wrote to you out of much affliction....* (II Cor. 2:4); *.... see that you read also the letter from Laodicea* (Col. 4:16). It may be possible that these letters are not "lost" but have been preserved in part or wholly in a larger writing within the New Testament (see commentary below for detailed study).

The above classification will serve as the basis for understanding the life and thought of Paul, of his contribution to the New Testament and to the formulation/development of Christian doctrine.

Sources for information on Paul

After Jesus, Paul is probably the most influential figure in the history of Christianity, and just as in the case of Jesus, little or nothing is known about their person. What is known has to be gleaned from scant references here and there, so the authenticity of these sources of information must always be validated. On any figure of historical interest, there are two sources of information: the primary source – what the person says about himself/herself i.e. autobiographical information; and secondary sources: what someone else (third party) has to say about the person. This is the case with Jesus where the sources of information are biographical and theological not primarily historical and certainly not autobiographical. The situation is similar and yet different with Paul. There is both autobiographical information (from his letters) and biographical/historical information (from Acts) though this may be put in the context of the third party's perspective/

interpretation. These two important sources for the life of Paul can be summed up as follows:

Primary source

Paul's own letters and the Pauline letters (letters in which he may not be directly involved but which come from the Pauline School and therefore reflect Paul himself).

Secondary source

Information about Paul from a third party; in this case the Acts of the Apostles which begins to trace Paul's activities from Acts 7:58.

There are several occasions when the information given by these two sources is at variance. Therefore, it becomes necessary to develop a methodology and to state how these two sources are to be used. There are three approaches: **1.** complete trust in Acts as a source in drawing up a life of Paul, adapting the information from elsewhere into the outline given in Acts. This is the traditional view which is still a popular method of outlining the life of Paul. **2.** distrust in Acts as a source and use of only the information found in the Pauline letters. This stems from a basic questioning of the historical value of the material found in Acts. **3.** a mediatory position which uses Paul's letters as the primary source and cautiously supplements information found in Acts, the secondary source. In this way, both Paul's letters and Acts become sources for information, and the question of 'either/or' is avoided especially since both Paul and Acts have to be held within the canon. This third option will be the approach in this work, presuming that the author of Acts was Luke a companion of Paul in his missionary activity and especially on his journeys (see chapter on Acts above).

A critical view must also take into account that Acts offers a theological interpretation of Paul, bringing his role into the overall view of the spread of Christianity *to the end of the earth* (Acts 1:8). Moreover, the author of Acts may have had only some details of Paul's life and work usually related to accompanying Paul on his travels (the "we" passages in Acts). Acts does not mention many events in Paul's life especially the writing of letters to churches/communities/individuals which is

Paul's major legacy; Acts tends also to compact many complex issues so that the actual struggles of the apostle, as reflected in his letters, is missing. Nevertheless, the information in Acts is useful for providing supplementary knowledge of Paul. Therefore, both sources, primary and secondary, help in putting together an understanding of the life and work of this great missionary, evangelist, and servant of God.

The background of Paul

At present there is no certain fixed point for arranging the events in Paul's life or a chronology of the life of Paul. The only event for which a possible date is proposed is the inscription in the letter of the Emperor Claudius to the city of Delphi written for the twenty-sixth time he was acclaimed as Emperor. The inscription mentions that Gallio was proconsul of the province of Achaia; this corresponds to the mention of Gallio in Acts 18:12-17 before whom Paul was brought by the Jews in Corinth. The proconsuls normally held office for a year beginning from April-May (i.e. after the Senate session in March in which they were appointed) to the following April-May when the next proconsul would have been appointed. The twenty-sixth acclamation of Claudius as Caesar would have occurred in A.D. 52, so the appearance of Paul before Gallio would have been in May-June of A. D. 52. It is from this date that a chronology of Paul can be worked backwards and forwards using the sources mentioned above.

Most assumptions are that Paul was either contemporary with, or a little older than, Jesus, i.e. born in the closing years of the last century B.C. when Caesar Augustus was ruling. In Acts 7:58 he is described as a *young man* at the stoning of Stephen; in Philemon 9, in a textual variant, he is described as *an old man* (see section on Philemon (below) for dating – sometime after A. D. 55 during one of Paul's imprisonments). Jews in the diaspora during this period often had two names: a Roman/Greek name and a Jewish name. "Paul" was a well-known Roman family name; since he describes himself as being from the tribe of Benjamin (Rom. 11:1; Philip. 3:5) there is no reason to doubt Acts that Paul's Jewish name was "Saul" – probably named after Israel's first king who was from the tribe of Benjamin. Paul never mentions his place of birth, but Acts mentions that he was a citizen of Tarsus, the capital of Cilicia (Acts; 21:39; 22:3). Paul was a Roman citizen (Acts 16:17-18; 22:25-29) though how he became a citizen – whether by birth (as suggested by Acts 22:29), or by acquiring it through payment, or as an honour bestowed on the family for services rendered to Caesar – is not disclosed. However, he seems to have made full use of the privileges of his citizenship – to get out of prison, to demand proper treatment, and finally in his appeal to Caesar.

Hellenistic (Greek) background

Paul was probably reared and had an education in Tarsus. This can be seen from his writings which are in good Greek and use of rhetorical skills and dialectic; he quoted from the Greek translation of the Hebrew scriptures (LXX). Perhaps he also learned the trade of tentmaking (Acts 18:3) – a trade that helped him to support himself rather than depend on others for financial support during his missionary activity (I Cor. 9:14-15; II Cor. 11:8-9). As a tradesperson, he would have been part of the lower social order or working class. His education in a Hellenistic environment would have opened him up to the varied possibilities of acculturation (being exposed to many cultures), and perhaps even assimilation of cultural ideas. He would certainly have known about the various religions and mystery religions of the Hellenistic world in which he lived. His education would have provided him with the knowledge of Greek philosophy, especially the moral and ethical values espoused by the Stoics, the Cynics, and the Epicureans. Above all, he would have known how ordinary people lived and their needs, hopes and fears especially since he often used the imagery and vocabulary of a household when he wrote on theological issues. His Hellenistic (Greek) background would certainly have prepared him to be an apostle to the Gentiles (Gal. 1:15-16).

Jewish background

There was another side to Paul's upbringing: his thorough knowledge of Hebrew scriptures, language, and customs could only have come from an intimate association with Judaism. Acts 22:3 claims that Paul was educated in Jerusalem at the feet of Gamaliel *according to the strict manner of the law of our fathers.* The dates for Gamaliel are usually accepted as A.D. 20-50, yet nowhere is it suggested that Paul saw Jesus or came across any of the teachings/miracles that made Jesus popular. So, Paul's continuous presence in Jerusalem is questionable. Paul describes himself as a Hebrew and a Pharisee (II Cor. 11:22; Philip. 3:5), which goes along with the description in Acts 23:6 and 26:4-5 and Acts 22:2 shows that he is well conversant with Hebrew and Aramaic. His strict Pharisaic background would have made Paul a persecutor of the new group forming around Jesus and his disciples as what they were preaching raised questions against the very basic tenets of Judaism and was certainly contrary to the Pharisaic interpretation of the Law (I Cor. 15:9; Gal. 1:13; Philip. 3:6); thus, his zeal for the Law turned him into a persecutor – one who was violent and brutal (Acts 8:3, 9:1) so that his reputation went before him (Acts 9:13, 26) even if they had not personally seen or encountered Paul.

These two backgrounds show Paul as being very familiar with two worlds which in many ways were quite different from each other. From this background emerged a man who reached out from the boundaries of his upbringing to bring the two worlds together, to touch the lives of others with his own experience of making a life-changing decision when confronted with the message of the Gospel to become a servant/ slave of Jesus Christ, and his conviction of having been sent with a message (ἀποστολειν/ἀποστολος) to the Gentiles: the message of God's love in Jesus Christ for Jews and Gentiles.

Conversion

Acts 9:21 is a good summary of the Jewish reactions to Paul's preaching after conversion; therefore, it is appropriate to understand his conversion experience. Paul's letters state that he was a persecutor of the Church of God (I Cor. 15:9; Gal. 1:13; Philip. 3:6) which is also mentioned in Acts 8:3; 9:1-2; 22:3-5,19; 26:9-11. His zeal for the Law, as a Pharisee, made him immediately recognize how basically the law was called into question by the Hellenistic mission, and therefore the first phase of persecution was against the Hellenistic Christians (e.g. Stephen) who were proposing that God had acted outside of Judaism on several occasions to bring salvation to the Gentiles (see speeches in Acts of Peter, Stephen etc....). This meant that the salvation being proclaimed was really God's judgement on the Jewish understanding of striving after righteousness by fulfilling the works of the Law. As a zealous Pharisee, Paul had to reject such an idea and such a proclamation had to be violently put down. It is this Pharisaic perspective which is involved in his conversion experience.

Paul himself has little to say on the details of his conversion experience; he mentions that it was by *revelation* (Gal. 1:11-16); in I Cor. 9:1 and 15:8-9 Paul claims to have *seen* Jesus, but this is not supported by Acts, nor does Paul make it the basis of his conversion. More likely, this "seeing" Jesus is a myth (the language used to express a deep spiritual and life-changing experience) by which Paul was convinced of the truth of the Gospel and that indeed it was God's judgement on Jewish striving after righteousness by doing the works of the Law. In Philip. 3:4ff while recounting his rich Jewish heritage Paul states, *whatever gain I had* (his Jewish heritage), *I counted as loss for the sake of Christ. Indeed, I count everything as loss because of the surpassing worth of knowing Jesus Christ my Lord...suffered loss of all things, and count them as refuse...not having a righteousness of my own, based on law, but that which is through faith in Christ....* For Paul his conversion experience was a complete submission/ surrender of his Jewish heritage. Paul's conversion, therefore, "was not the result of an inner moral collapse (he was blameless with regard to the Law – Philip. 3:6), nor was it a conversion of repentance or of some emancipating enlightenment, rather it was obedient submission to the judgement of God, made known in the cross of Christ, upon all human accomplishment and boasting" (R. Bultmann, *Theology of the New Testament, Volume I,* London: SCM Press, 1971, pages 187-189)This conversion experience is later reflected in his theology of justification by faith as a free gift and not by works of the Law (Romans chapters 2, 3, 4, 5).

On the other hand, Acts presents Paul's conversion in very dramatic form: once as a third person narrative (Acts 9:1-9), and twice as part of Paul's speeches (Acts 22:6-11; 26:9-18). In the narrative of Acts, the conversion has to be dramatized in order to powerfully bring out the complete change from persecutor to missionary and therefore

many dramatic images are presented – lights, voices, blindness etc....
Nevertheless, when the accounts in Acts are demythologized (i.e.
stripped of the language and expression of a deep spiritual and life-
changing experience), then it is seen that Acts does not ignore the
point that Paul's conversion was indeed a basic calling into question
of his Pharisaic zealousness for the Law in the light of God's grace
freely available in Jesus.

Therefore, Paul's conversion experience, both from his own letters
and as described by Acts, prepares him for his mission among the
Gentiles (Gal. 1:16) and by implication, prepares him to bring to bear
a new understanding/interpretation of salvation which includes both
Jews and Gentiles in the *heilsgeschichte*.

His work

A detailed description of his relationship with each of the churches to
which he writes will be discussed in the commentary section. In this
section, only a brief overview of his work will be outlined (see below)
which would help in drawing up a chronological table.

Paul does not mention where his conversion took place only that
it was during the time when he was persecuting the Church; further
Paul refers to this experience as a "revelation", i.e. a personal inner
conviction rather than an overt external situation. Acts 9:1-9, 22:5,
26:12 mentions that the experience took place while Paul was on the
way to Damascus to persecute Christians there. After the experience,
Gal. 1:17-18 records that Paul went into Arabia and Damascus for
three years before going to Jerusalem. The work in which Paul was
involved in Arabia is not known, but he surely would have preached,
perhaps with no success. It seems that he fell foul of the authorities for
II Cor. 11:32-33 narrates an escape from Damascus when King Aretas
of the Nabatean Kingdom (Arabia) tried to seize him. Since Aretas
was given control of Damascus by the Emperor sometime between
A.D. 37-41, Paul's conversion could be placed around A.D. 31/32 and
his visit to Jerusalem, three years later, around A.D. 35 (the crucifixion
of Jesus based on the dates for Pontius Pilate as Governor, and Passover falling
on the day before Sabbath, could be placed at A.D. 27. see Vol. 1 for Jesus' dates).

Gal. 1:18-19 tells of Paul going to Jerusalem for the first time after conversion (i.e. corresponding to three years after conversion) and conferring with Peter and James, the brother of the Lord, but no one else is mentioned. In I Cor.11:23 and 15:3 Paul talks of the "tradition" about Jesus which he had received. This meeting may have been a time when those 'traditions' (Eucharist and resurrection appearances) were passed on. The stay was a brief one and then Paul went to Tarsus in Cilicia (Gal. 1:18; Acts 9:30, 22:18) – back to his home-town. His next visit to Jerusalem was fourteen years later (Gal. 2:1), however, in the meantime he was introduced to the Church in Antioch by Barnabas (Acts 11:25-26) to be part of the mission to the Gentiles being organized by the Church in Antioch. Paul spent a year in Antioch before being sent to Jerusalem with famine relief (Acts 11:26-30). In a subtle way, Luke prepares the way in Acts for the centre of the Gentile missionary enterprise to shift from Jerusalem to Antioch and from the original twelve to Hellenists (e.g. Stephen and Philip) and then to Paul.

According to Acts, the next major event in Paul's work is the so-called First Missionary Journey. It is referred to as 'so-called' because such a clear compartmentalization of Paul's work/journeys is not found in any of his letters. In fact, even Acts does not clearly specify the three journeys; the three journeys are only a convenient classification developed by biblical scholars for studying the life of Paul and understanding the theology of Acts. This convenience also helps to place the "we" passages (see Section on authorship of Acts), which occur on journeys, from ch.16, into the story of Acts.

Acts 13:3 – 14:28 narrates the 'First Missionary Journey' from Antioch in Syria to several places in Asia Minor. The group consisted of Paul, Barnabas and Barnabas' nephew, John Mark. The journey took them through Cyprus, then to the Asia Minor cities of Perga (where John Mark left the group to return home to Jerusalem), Antioch in Pisidia, Iconium, Lystra and Derbe before coming back to Antioch in Syria. The mission strategy was to first preach in synagogues and then move out to others, especially the Gentiles among whom the Gospel was well received. Paul does not specially mention this journey in any of his letters but in Gal. 2:1-3, Paul recalls having preached to the

Gentiles before the Jerusalem Council (*ca.* A.D. 49), so the journey could be dated A.D. 47/48-49; further in II Cor. 11:25 he mentions being stoned (see Acts 14:19 where he was stoned in Lystra). According to Acts 10:44-48 and 11:20-21 there were others before Paul who were instrumental in the conversion of the Gentiles. Perhaps these converts were easily absorbed into Jewish Christian communities, whereas Paul's mission activity resulted in the formation of Gentile Christian communities on their own with little or no attachment to Judaism. In Acts, this raised questions regarding the validity of such a mission, and so Paul and Barnabas were sent by the Antioch church to Jerusalem to seek clarification.

The Council at Jerusalem is a major event in the book of Acts although Acts 15 and Gal. 2:1-10 differ. However, there is agreement on the major players at the Conference/Council – Peter, James, the Lord's brother, and Paul. The final decision was declared by James, the Lord's brother, who seems to have been regarded as the spokesperson/ head of the Jerusalem community. In Gal. 2:9, Paul reports that the Jerusalem community recognized Paul's apostolate to the Gentiles and extended to him the right hand of fellowship, i.e. in Paul's understanding his apostolate was on par with that of the original disciples/apostles and that there was no hindrance to accepting the conversion of the Gentiles nor was any requirement placed on them to first become Jews (see the commentary, above, for the position in Acts), only to remember the poor which was Paul's intention in any case (Gal. 2:10). However, the Jerusalem Council and its decisions did not seem to have settled the issue because the issue is still reflected in the letters of Paul to the Romans, in the Corinthian correspondence, and in the letter to the Galatians. For Paul, placing any restriction on the Gentiles would amount to being a contradiction of the Gospel (Gal. 2:11ff). This festering issue is what places these four letters in a category by themselves; by the early 60s the issue seems to have been settled/accepted as more Gentile Christian communities came into existence and concerns moved on to other areas/theological issues.

On their return to Antioch the dispute on observing Jewish purity laws, especially food regulations, seems to have led to difficulties with

Paul continuing his association with that centre (Gal. 2:11ff), and on planning further missionary activity, Paul and Barnabas parted ways (Acts 15:36-40 glosses over this serious issue assuming that it had been settled by the Council's decision, and refers to the split as being over the issue of allowing John Mark to accompany them). There are hints in Acts 15:36-40 that there was a sharp difference of opinion between Paul and Barnabas over the issue of taking John Mark with them on their next missionary journey. However, Luke seems to gloss over a much more serious issue – the relationship of the Jews and Gentiles in a mixed community. Paul brings the matter out very clearly in Gal. 2:11ff.: Paul and Barnabas were at Antioch, the mother church and sponsor of missionary activity to the Gentiles (the so-called First Missionary Journey); Peter (Cephas) came to Antioch for whatever reason, but saw no need to interfere with the freedom enjoyed by the mixed community in Antioch as compared with the more rigid standards observed in the Jerusalem community, i.e. in Antioch, Gentiles were accepted without circumcision and both Jews and Gentiles shared common meals. Peter entered into the life of the church at Antioch and even shared common meals with the Gentiles. However, when members of the Jerusalem community visited Antioch, they must have expressed surprise at Peter's acceptance of such a liberal attitude with the result that Peter began to distance himself from the Gentile group. The group from Jerusalem insisted on circumcision and on Jews eating separately from the Gentiles; they were so persuasive that even Barnabas began to distance himself from the Gentiles and to side with Peter. Unfortunately, the common meal which was meant to express the unity of the community had become the major cause of division (Acts 15:1,2; Gal. 2:13). Paul reacted very strongly to this changed scene and *opposed Peter to his face*. It resulted in personal conflict among the leaders of the community. The matter also spread to Galatia (see Galatians, below), so a very strong action was called for. The conflict was so great that Paul and Barnabas parted company and don't seem to have worked together again; Barnabas took John Mark as his assistant, while Paul took Silas on his next journey which brought the Gospel into Europe. Thus, Jerusalem and then Antioch lost their importance as mission centres; the centres now shifted to cities where new communities were formed, and which supported the mission which included Gentiles – Ephesus, Corinth, Philippi, and finally Rome.

From now on, as reflected in Paul's letters, Antioch does not play a central role in the Pauline mission; he is much more on his own, and is not obligated to anyone, in his further missionary activity.

The so-called 'Second (Acts 15:40-18:22) and Third (Acts 18:23-21:14) Missionary Journeys' can be seen as Luke's illustration of Paul's wide-ranging mission enterprise of taking the Gospel to the Gentiles without having to adhere to Jewish conversion laws.

The first part of the enterprise or the 'Second Missionary Journey' (Acts 15:40-18:22), can be dated *ca.* A.D. 49/50-52/53,and which reports that Paul revisited cities in Asia Minor that he had evangelized earlier. Then there is the important move to enter Macedonia (Acts 16:9-10) so taking the Gospel for the first time into Europe. There his travels took him to Philippi, Thessalonica, Beroea, Athens, and Corinth. Three of these five cities would later have letters addressed to them. One of the earliest writings of Paul, a part of I Thessalonians, may have been written while Paul was in Corinth (Acts 18:11 – he stayed in Corinth for a year and a half) expressing concern for a church he had recently founded. A year and a half was the longest time that Paul had stayed in any church that he had founded; it was later to be plagued by many issues which he had to write about and misunderstandings with the apostle (see chapter on the Corinthians Correspondence). Aquila and Priscilla, became co-workers with Paul in Corinth, later Ephesus and then in Rome. Paul appearing before Gallio, the proconsul, in Corinth is a key figure and date in Pauline chronology (see above on Life of Paul). Thus, Paul's year and a half stay at Corinth can be dated *ca.* A.D. 50-52/53. Paul moved on from Cenchreae (one of the port cities of Corinth) to Ephesus and Caesarea, finally ending in Antioch to greet the Church there.

The second part of the enterprise or the 'Third Missionary Journey' (Acts 18:23-21:14), which can be dated *ca.* A.D. 53/54-58, began after spending some time in Antioch, revisiting Galatia and Phrygia and arriving in Ephesus, the most important city in the Roman province of Asia. He stayed in Ephesus for three years, *ca.* A.D. 54-57. Paul never explicitly refers to the events that took place at Ephesus – struggle with the seven sons of the Jewish high priest who were exorcists and the riot by the silversmiths who were devotees of Artemis – although he may implicitly include them in the list of hardships mentioned in II Cor. 11:23-26 and *the affliction we experienced in Asia* (II Cor. 1:8), or *I fought with beasts at Ephesus …..there are many adversaries* (I Cor. 15:32 and 16:8-9). There is no record either in Paul's letters or in Acts of Paul having been in prison in Ephesus; an important point since some of the so-called 'prison' letters/epistles (Philippians, Colossians and Philemon in particular) are thought to have originated in Ephesus. Most would accept that the letter to the Galatians may have originated in Ephesus during Paul's stay there along with I Corinthians (I Cor. 16:8) and some other parts of the Corinthian correspondence – the letter of tears (II Cor. 2:3-4:6) and the "painful" visit (II Cor. 2:1); Acts is completely silent about the difficult dealings with the Corinthian church. After the spring of A.D. 57, Paul left Ephesus for Troas and then crossed over to Macedonia. He met Titus there with the good news that the Corinthian problems had been resolved (II Cor. 2:12-13), so a letter of thanksgiving was written, which may now comprise most of II Corinthians. This was followed by a three month visit to Achaia and Corinth in the winter of A.D. 57/early 58. The letter to the Romans may have originated during this stay at Corinth with Paul explaining that he will deliver the collection for the Jerusalem church and then visit Rome on his way to Spain (Romans 15:24-26). From Corinth Paul spent Passover at Philippi (spring of A.D. 58), then worked his way down to Miletus where he gave a farewell address to the elders of Ephesus who had come to meet him (Acts 20:17-38). Even though there is a foreboding of disaster awaiting him in Jerusalem, Paul is determined to go there (Acts 21:13-14).

In Jerusalem (by summer of A.D. 58), Paul is received gladly. The last few years of Paul are covered by Acts 21:15-28:31; they were marked by suffering – constant harassments and four imprisonments. There is nothing in Paul's letters that confirms the events of this period. In

Jerusalem Paul is received by James, the brother of the Lord, and told to behave as a pious Jew while in Jerusalem (Acts 21:17-26). However, his presence in the Temple creates a problem resulting in the intervention of the Roman Tribunal in order to maintain the peace. When he was brought before the Sanhedrin, he managed to divide the house between the Sadducee and Pharisee members so that no decision was possible, hence he was taken to the Roman Governor, Felix, at Caesarea. But Felix, expecting a bribe, kept the case pending for two years (Acts 24:22-27) probably from A.D. 58-60. Even after that, Felix did not complete the case and left it for his successor, Festus. In the trial that followed, Festus did not find anything that would warrant drastic action, but Paul knowing that he would not get a fair trial either at Caesarea or in Jerusalem appealed to Caesar as was his Roman right (Acts 25:9-12). However, in an attempt to let tempers cool down further, Festus asked Paul to appear before Herod Agrippa II. Agrippa was also of the view that Paul had done no wrong, but the appeal to Caesar was final and could not be undone (Acts 26:31-32). Arrangements were therefore made to send Paul as a protected prisoner to Rome to appear before Caesar (Acts 27:1).

The final months of imprisonment at Caesarea, the sea voyage and the land journey which finally brought Paul to Rome are described in Acts 27:1-28:31 and probably took place *ca.* A.D. 60-62. The sea journey is vividly described in Acts with storms, shipwreck, and stranded on an island for a whole winter. Paul is warmly welcomed in Rome and according to Acts 28:30-31 he *lived there for two whole years at his own expenses* (*ca.* between A.D. 62-64) under a sort of house arrest that allowed him to meet people and preach but did not permit him to go out. The story of Paul ends at this point.

There are however, the references in Romans that indicate that Paul's intention was to go on to Spain from Rome and there is an early tradition reflected by I Clement 5:7 towards the end of the first century, that Paul indeed went on to Spain. When dealing with the Pastorals, especially II Timothy and Titus, another hypothesis is presented: that Paul had a 'second career' i.e. after release from Roman imprisonment, he came East to Crete and other cities in Asia, that he was again taken as a prisoner to Rome where shortly before his death he wrote II Timothy. However, the most accepted tradition is that there was only one imprisonment in Rome as reflected in Acts and that Paul was martyred in Rome in the persecution under Nero, sometime between A.D. 64-66.

This summary of Paul's work, using both primary and secondary sources, brings out a picture of a zealous Jew who, when confronted with the Gospel became an ardent missionary and whose work laid the foundation not only for the spread of Christianity but also for its doctrinal basis and formulations.

Suggested chronology for the life of Paul

The following chart summarizes his life and work and suggests a chronology for the life of Paul:

Date	Event
ca. 31/32	Conversion
32-35	Three years in Arabia
35	Visit to Jerusalem (after 3 years in Arabia)
35-46	In Syria and Cilicia and Damascus
46/47-49	'First Missionary Journey' and visit to Jerusalem 14 years after conversion
49	Council at Jerusalem
49/50-52/53	'Second Missionary Journey' including 18 months at Corinth and appearance before Gallio, Proconsul of Achaia
53/54-58	'Third Missionary Journey'
58	Arrival in Jerusalem and arrest
58-60	Prisoner in Caesarea. Appearances before Felix, Festus and Herod Agrippa II. Appeal to Caesar.
61-62	Journey to Rome (long sea voyage, shipwreck etc...)

62-64	Prisoner in Rome awaiting trial, but free to meet people
64-66	Martyrdom under Nero in Rome. Some traditions have mission to Spain and 'second career' in Asia.

Paul as interpreter of Christ to the Jews and Gentiles

Probably one of Paul's first tasks was to find ways to present an essentially Jewish messiah to a non-Jewish audience/readership but this also involved having to first present his message to a Jewish audience. In Acts, Paul is introduced when consenting to the death of Stephen – a case that questioned the very basic tenet of Judaism that God was at work only within the confines of the Law. In Stephen's case, he had proclaimed that God was at work even outside the Law – i.e. God was at work among the Gentiles. This was an interpretation to which a strict Pharisee like Saul/Paul had to take objection. The very basis of Judaism that the Jews had a special relationship to God as God's chosen people was called into question. Further, the promises made by God with regard to a Messiah pertained only to the Jews, so to include the Gentiles within the ambit of those promises was anathema to a Pharisee. Still further, the promise was believed to be fulfilled in the restoration of the kingdom of David, so a political messiah, or at least a warrior messiah to overthrow foreign powers, was expected. But the understandings of Jesus that were being proclaimed – a suffering messiah – based on an interpretation of Jewish scriptures, was, in Pharisaic terms, totally unacceptable and blasphemous. If the Pharisees disagreed with other Jewish leaders on matters of interpretation, they were at least agreed on this: Jesus was not the expected messiah and the attempt to find justification for such a belief on the basis of scripture, had to be quashed.

Therefore, for Paul, Jesus had to be presented as a fulfillment/ continuation, and yet expansion, of the promises made to Israel. According to Acts 24:14, Luke says that Paul stated: *according to the Way, which they call a sect, I worship the God of our Fathers, believing everything laid down by the Law or written in the prophets.* Such an unequivocal statement calls for understanding Paul as an interpreter of Christ to the Jews. Paul goes back to Abraham to present a strong argument from Jewish scriptures. His understanding/interpretation of *Abraham, our forefather* (Romans 4), is that Abraham was justified by his faith rather than by his works and that too before circumcision (the sign of the covenant between God and Israel), as the historical position of Abraham was much before the Law was given through Moses, *because the purpose was to make Abraham the father of all those who believe without being circumcised and who thus have righteousness reckoned to them, and likewise the father of the circumcised who are not merely circumcised but also follow the example of the faith which our father Abraham had before he was circumcised.* The result of this interpretation was that Abraham became the father of not only Jews but also of the Gentiles as well, with the rider that the Jews had also to show the faith of Abraham. This is how Paul presented the universality of Abraham, *the father of all the families of the earth* (Genesis 12:1-3) to the Jews. So, for Paul, circumcision was of value only if one had the faith of Abraham, otherwise it had no value (see notes on Romans 3:1-2 and Gal. 5:2). This would not only take into consideration the Jewish understanding of God's dealings with them but would also expand that understanding to include the Gentiles.

Paul uses the typology of Adam (Romans 5) to say that all humanity shares in the sin of Adam, i.e. both Jews and Gentiles, and therefore all share in the salvific/redemptive work of Christ: *sin came into the world through one man.....and therefore all have sinned.....One man's trespass led to condemnation for all, so one man's act of righteousness leads to acquittal and life.* So, like the example of Abraham, Paul takes a Jewish concept and gives it a universal application thus equalizing both Jew and Gentile with the result that he can state, *there is neither Jew nor Greek.... you are all one in Christ Jesus* (Gal. 3:28).

Having been convinced of this universality of sin and salvation and of the heritage from Abraham, and understanding these in the light of the person and work of Christ, Paul can declare of his Jewish heritage of which he was so proud and of his right to God's salvation: *whatever gain I had, I counted as loss for the sake of Christ.....for the surpassing worth of knowing Christ Jesus my Lord* (Philip. 3:4-8). Paul's conversion, then, was when he realized that salvation was by faith in what God had done, rather than in trying to attain one's own righteousness by doing the works of the Law.

In this way, Paul interprets Jewish Law and theology in such a way so as to uphold Judaism and yet go beyond its narrow thinking/confines. This would result in Paul espousing his theology of justification by faith which served to equalize both Jew and Gentile.

As an interpreter/missionary to the Gentiles, Paul's background and conversion experience shows that he stood within the framework of Hellenistic Judaism which prepared him for his work among the Gentiles. As such, he made a major contribution to Hellenistic Christianity, raising the concerns of the Hellenistic churches to the level of theological clarity and formulations – justification by faith (Romans and Galatians), the equality of the Jew and Gentile in that all have sinned and all stand in the need of salvation (Rom. 3:21-26; Gal. 3:28), issues regarding marriage, food restrictions, spiritual gifts, speaking in tongues etc... (Romans and I Corinthians) – and since his writings were the earliest Christian documents, hence in a sense Paul became the founder of Christian theology (R. Bultmann, *Theology of the New Testament, Volume I,* page 187).

Notwithstanding his early visit to Jerusalem, from the time that Paul became active in the mission enterprise, he was associated with the Hellenistic Church and made no hesitation to proclaim his independence from the authority of Jerusalem (Gal. 1 & 2) unlike Acts where Paul had to take the permission of Jerusalem to legitimize his mission to the Gentiles (Acts 15). Paul's letters show no influence of the Palestinian tradition, reflected in the Gospels (except I Cor. 11:23 and 15:3) concerning the life and work of Jesus; indeed, the central message of Jesus on the Kingdom of God hardly finds a place in the message of Paul, and neither is the central message of Paul on justification by faith reflected in the message of Jesus. When Paul refers to Jesus, he is thinking not of the historical Palestinian Jew, but of the pre-existent

Jesus (Philip. 2:5ff) whose salvific work is to be appropriated through faith by the believer; and of the returning Christ who will transform the perishable into the imperishable and the mortal into immortality (I Cor. 15:51-57). This places Paul and his work very definitely within the realm of Hellenistic Christianity and it is there that Paul's work and message and lasting contribution must be placed and understood.

In this way, Paul became an interpreter of Jesus to both Jew and Gentile and in finding expression for his interpretation, Paul laid the basis of Christian theology. It is therefore understandable that the Church returns again and again to affirm Paul in every movement of reformation (Zwingli, Luther, Calvin, Knox, Wesley, Abraham Malpan), and that the 13 Pauline letters play a vital role in understanding Christianity.

Suggested chronology of Paul's and Pauline letters

(see also table for suggested
chronology for life of Paul, pages 71 and 72, above)

Letter	Place of writing	Date of writing	Details given on
I. Paul's letters			
Romans	Corinth	56-57	pages 79-105
Corinthian Correspondence			pages 105-155
1. "Lost Letter" : II Cor. 6:14 – 7:1	Ephesus?	53-54	
2. I Corinthians	Ephesus	54-55	
3. "Letter of Tears" II Cor. 10 – 13	Ephesus?	55-56	
4. "Letter of Thanksgiving" II Cor. 2:14 –6:13 & 7:;2-16	Macedonia	mid 56	

5. "Epistolary Formula"   Macedonia   end 56

    II Cor. 1:1 – 2:13

6. "Restart Collection"   Macedonia   early 57

    II Cor. 8

7. "Urgency to complete   Macedonia   mid 57
the Collection" : II Cor. 9

Galatians	Ephesus? / Macedonia?	55-57	pages 156-168
Philemon	Ephesus?	53-57	pages 169-177
	Caesarea?	58-60	
	Rome?	62-64	
II. Deutero-Paul			
Ephesians	Asia Minor?	80-100?	pages 178-190
Philippians	Compiled in Philippi?	70-90?	pages 191-205
Colossians	Asia Minor?	80-100?	pages 206-217
Thessalonian Correspondence	Compiled in Thessalonica?	80-100?	pages 218-231
III. Trito-Paul			pages 232-256
I Timothy }			
II Timothy }	Asia Minor?	120-140?	
Titus }			

Select Bibliography

Bornkamm, G.*Paul*, New York: Harper & Row, 1971.

Brown, R. E., *An Introduction to the New Testament*. Bangalore: Theological Publications in India 2000.

Bultmann, R. *Theology of the New Testament, Volume I*, London: SCM Press, 1971.

Kasemann, E.*Perspectives on Paul*, Philadelphia: Fortress Press, 1971.

Knox, J.*Chapters in the Life of Paul*, Nashville: Abingdon Press, rev. ed. 1987.

Kummel, W. G. *Introduction to the New Testament*, London: SCM Press, 1975.

Murphy-O'Connor. Jerome *Paul, A Critical Life*, Oxford: OUP, 1996 (1997).

Sanders, E. P. *Paul and Palestinian Judaism*. Philadelphia: Fortress Press, 1977.

_____, .*Paul*, Oxford: Past Masters, 1991.

Stendhal, K. *Paul Among Jews and Gentiles*. London: SCM Press, 1977.

CHAPTER - 3

An Introduction to
Paul's Own Letters

*A. Romans B. The Corinthian Correspondence — I & II Corinthians
C. Galatians D. Philemon. Founding of the community, authorship/
authenticity and integrity, date, occasion and purpose. Brief analysis
and commentary on the text of each of the letters. Select bibliography
for each letter.*

The following chapters will introduce each of the 13 letters attributed
to Paul and provide a brief commentary on the text of each of the
letters. As mentioned above in the section on Paul's letters, five letters
– Romans, I & II Corinthians, Galatians, Philemon – will be taken as
genuinely having come from the Apostle himself (see below); five letters
will be placed in the deutero-Pauline category – Ephesians, Colossians,
Philippians, I & II Thessalonians (see chapter IV, below); and three letters
will be placed in the trito-Pauline category – I & II Timothy and Titus
which are also called the Pastorals (see chapter V, below). In the study of
the writings, the canonical order will be followed. Within the canonical
order, a chronological order of each part/section of the writing, if
discernable, will be followed.

Paul's own letters:

A. Romans

The founding of the community. Authorship / authenticity and integrity. Date and place of writing. Occasion and purpose of the letter. Brief analysis and commentary on the text. Select bibliography for Romans.

The community at Rome

The earliest knowledge of a Christian community in Rome is the letter to the Romans itself. The community existed before Paul arrived in Rome as attested by the report that Christians from there came to meet Paul and brought him to Rome (Acts 28:15). Paul also wrote that *I have longed for many years to come to you* (Rom. 1:13, 15:23) which implies that there must have been Christians in the capital city. Further, the Roman historian, Suetonius, wrote that *Claudius expelled the Jews from Rome since they had been continually causing disturbances at the instigation of a certain Chrestos* . Since *Chrestos* was another form for *Christ*, the information pertains not to Jewish insurrectionists against the Roman empire, but to Jesus Christ whose Gospel brought great unrest among the Jewish community in Rome thus providing occasion for the Emperor Claudius to expel the Jews or at least a section of them. The edict of Claudius is dated A.D. 49, so the Jewish and Christian community must have been present in Rome for quite some time before then. The mention of Aquila and Priscila who had arrived in Corinth from Rome because of the Edict of Claudius (Acts 18:2-3) and who became part of the Pauline mission enterprise, also confirms that Christianity was well established in Rome. Aquila and Priscila are Roman names but are of Jewish origin thus showing the integration of Jewish and Roman backgrounds in the Roman community.

Judaism had established itself in Rome through the trading community, through immigrants looking for better job opportunities, through captives taken to Rome by Pompey (between B.C. 50-40); so, there was at least a century of Jewish presence in Rome by the mid-first century. Much later the Jewish community was added to by captives taken to Rome by Titus after his invasion of Palestine and the fall of Jerusalem, around A.D. 70. The early part of the first century saw a close relationship of Rome with Palestine, especially after Rome became the dominant power and began to directly rule Palestine. Herod the Great's successors had to go to Rome for approval of their status as Kings; Herodian princes were sent to Rome for their education where they met the leaders of the Empire and were friends with the Emperors; after A.D. 70, Titus brought Herod Agrippa II (mentioned in Acts 25:23-26:32) and his sister, Bernice, became Titus' mistress. Given this long Jewish presence in Rome, it would not have taken long for the Christian mission to find its way to Rome. The Edict of Claudius in A.D. 49 shows that Jewish Christians were already established in Rome long enough for trouble to arise in the community. Paul's letter dated around A.D. 56-57 showed that the Christian community also consisted of Gentile Christians who continued to live in Rome as the Edict of Claudius did not affect them. Hence it would be possible to say that Christianity must have reached Rome by the late 30's/early 40's of the first century.

Nowhere is the founder of the Christian community in Rome mentioned in the New Testament nor is there any mention of a mission to Rome from any of the mission centres, Jerusalem, Antioch, Ephesus, Philippi etc... although Acts 28:21 indicates that there were links between Jerusalem and Rome. It is often thought that Peter was the founder of the Church in Rome, but there is no New Testament evidence for this, even more so in the light of Paul's statements that he would not intrude on someone else's mission territory (Rom. 15:20; II Cor. 10:15ff). Therefore, Christianity probably entered Rome through the world of commerce, politics, and through movements in the diaspora and it is safe to conclude that Christianity in Rome already had a stretch of history behind it by the time Paul wrote to the community there.

Composition of the community

Much of the letter is a debate between the gospel as Paul interprets it (see his references to "my gospel", e.g. Rom. 16:25 and elsewhere in Romans where he espoused that the promise of God for salvation was open to the Gentiles as well without first having to become Jews thus opening the way for justification by faith) and Judaism (chapters 1-3), so that in the first instance it can be presupposed that the recipients were Jewish Christians. However, there are also specific statements that indicate that the letter was addressed to Gentile Christians (1:5, 1:13, 15:15ff.); in chapters 9-11, Paul speaks to the non-Jews concerning his own people. Therefore, the letter to the Romans was addressed to a community that consisted of both those of Jewish and Gentile backgrounds.

Authorship and Integrity

The authorship of Romans has never been in any serious doubt. From the earliest traditions of the Church, Romans has been attributed to Paul. The epistle very clearly mentions that Tertius was the writer (Rom.16:22) – amanuensis/literary assistant – the one who wrote while Paul either dictated or directed him. There have, however, been questions about the ending of Romans.

There are final greetings at the end of Chapter 16 (verse 23); and many ancient textual witnesses add verse 24, *the grace of our Lord Jesus Christ be with you all. Amen.* Verses 25-27 appear as the ending of the Marcionite text which closes Romans at 14:23. So Marcion (end of 2nd century/mid-3rd century), who had edited many of the other New Testament writings (see Vol. I on the Canon of the New Testament), completely deleted chapters 15 and 16 of Romans and composed a doxological ending for chapter 14 (the language, style, and theology are completely different from what is found in the rest of the letter or in any other Pauline letter). However, it is widely held that the text of Romans, as found in the canon today, is a corrected copy of Marcion's text made by Origen and other church leaders in the mid-3rd century; they restored chapters 15 and 16 and shifted the ending of chapter 14 to the end of chapter 16 after the original had ended at 16:24: *the grace of our Lord Jesus Christ be with you all. Amen.*

There has also been the question of whether chapter 16 could have been part of the letter to the Romans as it is most unusual for a whole chapter to be devoted to a long list of names with greetings. The usual arguments for these questions is that it is difficult to imagine that Paul knew so many people in a congregation that he had not visited before and whether it would have been more appropriate for Paul to greet the leader of the congregations rather than his old friends. Further, it is difficult to understand how all these people are in Rome when they are last heard of in Ephesus (e.g. Phoebe – 16:1; Prisca and Aquila – 16:3; Epaenetus, the first convert in Asia – 16:5; Apollos – 16:10). Some scholars have concluded that Rom. 16 was originally part of a letter addressed to Ephesus, but how it came to be attached to Romans is not adequately explained even if the benediction at the end of chapter 15 (15:33) was the original ending of Romans.

Therefore, none of the questions about the authenticity/integrity of the ending of Romans can be answered with any finality. The most convincing hypothesis is to say that the original probably ended with 16:23/24, with the Marcionite ending (16:25-27) being added at a later date to conclude the letter.

Date and place of writing

The information in Romans is that Paul had been travelling in Macedonia and Achaia and had collected money to take to the Jerusalem community to help with the famine relief there (15:25-29). **He was enjoying the hospitality of Gaius in Corinth (16:23).** He also mentions that after delivering the famine relief, he would proceed to Spain via Rome as he felt that his mission in the East was over (15:24-25). This information combined with the information from Acts 18:1ff (Paul's appearance before Gallio in A.D. 52 and a year and half stay at Corinth) and 20:31 (three years in Ephesus) and a few months' further stay in Corinth (Acts 20:3), along with the fact that when he reached Jerusalem with the famine relief, Paul was arrested (Acts 21:27ff) would place **the date for writing the letter to the Romans around A.D. 56-57.**

Occasion and purpose

The occasion of the epistle is derived from the plans of the apostle. Paul does not know the Christian community at Rome personally and had never visited there, but he hoped to visit and from there to move on to Spain (1:15; 15:15, 23-24). So, it is probable that Paul intends to use Rome as a missionary base for his mission westwards since he felt that his mission in the east had been completed (15:23). This announcement accounts for the external occasion and immediate aim of the letter, but the debate with Judaism on several theological issues that are found in the letter presuppose that the letter must have had deeper reasons and purpose.

It is often suggested that Romans is Paul's doctrinal presentation of the Christian faith (Melanchthon, a church reformer in the middle ages, called Romans *a compendium of Christian doctrine*). But this view cannot be fully substantiated since Romans does not contain much on major doctrines such as ecclesiology and Christology; Eucharist and church order are not touched on at all. Since Paul was seeking to make contact with the Roman community, it was appropriate that he told them of what he thinks is the essence and content of the Gospel which he preached to the Gentiles. Firstly then, the letter serves as an introduction to Paul's understanding and presentation of the Gospel. Secondly, it is a letter that originated in the context and on-going plans of Paul's missionary work, and it also gives Paul an opportunity to express his theological concerns. Thus, Romans is often referred to as Paul's testament (Bornkamm, a leading Pauline scholar, calls it *Paul's last will and testament*, i.e. Paul's legacy to the development of Christian doctrine). So, the letter serves to introduce Paul himself and his perception of his apostolic ministry, and also an introduction to the gospel he preached.

Yet this "testament" does not simply contain abstract theological formulations, but grapples with concrete local situations being faced by the Roman community, he may have especially hoped to heal the animosities in the relationship between Jewish and Gentiles Christians (cf. chapters 1-3 and 9-11; and further, directions to "the weak" and "the strong" in chapters 14 & 15), and in the process of dealing with that situation, Paul develops one of the clearest expressions of the Gospel having universal significance – justification by faith. In doing so, he develops his arguments utilizing rhetorical styles (diatribe) employed by Stoic and other Greco-Roman philosophers, resulting in a major writing that goes beyond the limitations of the strict letter format, and so also contributing a new literary form.

The purpose of Romans therefore, is multi-faceted: a document of personal introduction, a document of missionary strategy, a document of doctrinal/theological importance, a document of pastoral concern for the mixed community in Rome, and a document that contributes to the ancient letter writing format. In this sense it is a testament, not only for the Roman community to whom it was immediately addressed, but also an emphatic statement and doctrinal formulation for the whole of Christianity in the first century and through the ages.

Brief analysis and commentary on the text

1:1-7 – The Opening Formula

The Opening Formula expresses a whole host of theological statements which must be understood, especially since Paul is writing to a church he had not founded and to a church he had not visited. In many ways, it is a sort of self-introduction which would not only catch the attention of the readers but would also give them a glimpse of the person's theological stance.

Paul, a servant of Jesus Christ.... the Greek word used is δουλος, more accurately translated as "slave" – a person who is totally under the control of the master, even to die at the master's wish. Paul understands himself as such a person.

*...called to be an apostle, set apart for the gospel of God....*An apostle – ἀποστολος – is one who has a particular mission, therefore the apostle is *set apart for the gospel* - εὐαγγελιον– the good news that has its source and origin in God.

.... promised beforehand through his prophets....God's Son descended from David... Paul presents the gospel as a fulfillment of earlier promises; a continuation of the *heilsgeschichte* or God's salvific dealings with Israel. The descent from David – Son of David used in the Gospels (Matt. 15:22; Mk. 10:47, 12:35-37) – is also part of Jewish messianic understanding, strengthening the link with Judaism.

... designated Son of God in power... Jesus given the messianic title of Son of God, a title given to those who were specially called to fulfill a particular purpose, e.g. prophets and kings of Israel.

.... Jesus Christ our Lord... The Christological title of Lord – κυριος – is particularly one that was developed in the Hellenistic world and used consistently by Paul. The title of Son of Man, a particularly Jewish title, is not used outside of the Gospels.

It is a long self-introduction in one sentence (verses 1-6). It is recognized that Paul is here using a Jewish Christian formulation of the gospel which would have been acceptable to the mixed Roman community. Since he has no personal contact with this community, Paul uses a formula which would show that his preaching was not at variance with the preaching of those who had evangelized the Roman community.

To all God's beloved in Rome, who are called to be saints... The inclusiveness of the greeting brings both Christians of Jewish and Gentile backgrounds on par.

*Grace to you and peace ....*The greeting of *grace* - χαρις — commonly used in the Hellenistic world, and the greeting of *peace – shalom*/ειρηνη – commonly used in Judaism – again suggests an inclusiveness while addressing the Roman community. Both words imply an unearned consideration/kindness, good health, well-being and prosperity.

1:8-15 – After the opening greetings, Paul talks of the common bonds between him and the Romans, his desire to have had visited them, and now his intention to visit them in his future expansion plans.

1:16-17 – The righteousness of God. These two verses form the central message of the letter:

I am not ashamed of the Gospel: the origin of the Gospel from a nondescript village in Palestine, by an uneducated man who made great claims, and eventually died a criminal's death may have been cause for many to feel ashamed of professing faith in him and/or of proclaiming him even if they were convinced of his messiahship. This unequivocal statement would reassure the Roman community of Paul's credentials.

...everyone who has faith, to the Jew first and also to the Greek. The inclusiveness of the Gospel message. The phrase, *the Jew first and also to the*

Greek, occurs several times in Romans, expressing Paul's understanding that the Jews were the original recipients of God's promises but now that has been extended to include the Greeks/Gentiles, therefore both stand within the ambit of God's salvific act in Jesus.

...in it the righteousness of God (δικαιοσυνη Θεου) *is revealed....* In Greek, the possessive genitive case used for God indicates that the quality of righteousness belongs to God; it is God's righteousness. This quality of God is revealed – made known – in and through the Gospel. 'The righteousness of God' is also the trustworthiness of God, a quality that cannot be emulated by anyone else. This is a very strong Jewish theological position with regard to the nature of God; thus, Paul is basing himself firmly in Judaism, but then goes a step further –

.... The person who through faith is righteous shall live (ὁ δε δικαιος ἐκ πιστεως ζησεται). God exercises the quality of righteousness and imparts it to human beings, so that the person can appropriate this quality by faith and can be said to be righteous – by accepting God's gift. 'Righteousness' is not a quality that a person can claim as a right, nor can a person call themselves righteous; it is a quality that has to be recognized by others and in recognition thereof, the person is called righteous. It is a Greek legal term whereby a judge pronounces the person as 'not guilty', so the person can be said to be righteous or 'right-wised' or in favourable standing, or the relationship is restored and treated as if nothing had happened. This quality of righteousness, which belongs only to God, is imparted, through Jesus Christ, on humanity. In this sense, it is not only the Jew, but all humanity which can avail of this benefit. The original quotation is from Habakuk 2:4 which is in the context of the prophet encouraging the people to trust God when they were under attack by the Babylonians; in good rabbinic style, Paul takes this quotation and interprets it far beyond its original context.

After these opening statements and till the end of chapter 15, Paul deals with various theological issues which must have been part of the unsettled thinking in the mixed Roman community; it was also a reasoned expression of his own stand on these issues. The statements and guidance that Paul provided for the Romans became the norm for the Church and the basis for doctrinal developments. It would be methodologically more appropriate to deal with these chapters in large sections that cover a particular thought pattern rather than a verse by verse exegesis.

1:18-32 – The wrath of God

Paul's affirmation of God's righteousness is balanced by his thinking on God's wrath (ἡ ὀργη του Θεου). Paul holds that the truth about God is known from the beginning of creation and so the Gentiles cannot plead ignorance just because they had not received the revelation of God like the Jews. Instead *they exchanged the truth about God for a lie and worshipped and served the creature rather than the Creator.* Their ignorance was not an excuse, so God gave them up to God's wrath– separation from God – resulting in social disintegration and sexual confusion. God's wrath, then, is not a display of anger, but the allowing of a separation, *God gave them up to dishonourable passions* which led to disarray and crisis where natural heterosexual relations were exchanged for unnatural homosexual relations. Also, a result of *God gave them up to dishonourable passions,* was *a base mind and improper conduct;* a list of actions that would be considered improper conduct is mentioned. It is a list that describes the total depravity of the human condition which can only lead to death, and *people not only do them but approve those who practice them.*

The human condition described by Paul is a graphic image that shows the human being having sunk to the depths of depravity. In much of this portrait of the Gentiles, Paul may be drawing on a standard Jewish understanding, especially a Hellenistic Jewish understanding, that formed part of his Jewish background. As such, Paul stands, at the moment, within the bounds of Judaism and the Jewish understanding of the fate of the Gentiles.

2:1-29 – God shows no partiality

Paul used the Stoic diatribe method of presenting his argument, i.e. asking a question and answering it himself. Here the imagined person – *you* – being addressed could be either a Jew who might be passing judgment on the Gentiles as doing the things listed in chapter 1, or, *you* could be a Gentile being judgmental about others But in a remarkable twist, Paul says, *in passing judgment upon others, you condemn yourself, because you, the judge, are doing the very same things.* Then there follows a series of questions that in Greek syntax areso phrased that the answer is "no": *do you think you will escape the judgment of God?. do you presume upon the riches of God's kindness and forbearance and patience?.* Then expecting the answer "yes": *do you not know that this is meant to lead you to repentance?* Paul sums up his argument that there will be tribulation and distress *for the Jew first and also the Greek, but glory and honour and peace for everyone who does good, the Jew first and also the Greek. For God shows no partiality.*

In making such a statement, Paul equalizes the Jew and the Greek (Gentile); all are judged by the same standard. Paul goes on to explain how the standard applies to both Jews and Gentiles.

Those without the Law (Gentiles): It is not the hearers of the Law (the Jews), but the doers of the Law (Jew and Gentile alike) who will be justified. The Gentiles are justified when they unknowingly do what the Law requires, *they show that what the Law requires is written on their hearts, while their conscience also bears witness.* This according to Paul is *my gospel* i.e. Paul's particular/peculiar interpretation that places Jew and Gentile on an even footing.

Those who have the Law (Jews): Greater responsibility is placed on the Jews because they have the Law and the promises and are to be the example for others, but because they do not follow any of the precepts that they teach and preach, the Law is of no avail to them, instead, *the name of God is blasphemed among the Gentiles because of you.*

Both: The observance of the rite of circumcision was the main issue that set the Jews apart from the Gentiles, but Paul held that *circumcision is of value only if you obey the Law, otherwise your circumcision becomes uncircumcision.*

So, the Jew cannot claim any special relationship with God simply on the basis of circumcision; the Gentile can claim a special relationship with God by doing the works of the Law. This does not support a theory of salvation by works but is a way of expressing the equality of both Jew and Gentile before God and of the criteria for God's impartial judgment. Paul ends with a much deeper interpretation of the meaning of circumcision: *he is not a real Jew who is one outwardly, nor is true circumcision something external and physical. He is a Jew who is one inwardly, and real circumcision is a matter of the heart, spiritual and not literal.* Such an interpretation widens the whole understanding of how circumcision is an instrument for relationship with God – an understanding that would include **all** people. Paul has actually recovered/re-iterated this interpretation which was already known in Judaism (Deut. 10:16; 30:6; Jer. 4:4; 9:24-26), but probably deliberately overlooked as it would mean that Israel had no 'special' status before God. In effect Paul is showing how Christians continue to stand in the line of promises and in the continuity of the history of God's salvific acts.

3:1-20 – all are under the power of sin

If God shows no partiality and treats Jews and Gentiles alike, *then what advantage has to Jew?* Is there any benefit of being God's chosen people? or *what is the value of circumcision?* As a good Jew and brought up in the strictest school of Jewish thought – Pharisees – Paul cannot totally discard Judaism but has to re-interpret/understand it in a new way that would include those who were not Jews as well. Therefore, the Jew has an advantage – *they were entrusted with the oracles of God.* However, in their observance and implementation of these oracles (Law), the Jews had been unfaithful, but their unfaithfulness did not negate the faithfulness of God who makes a way of salvation open to all. Paul quotes several passages from Hebrew scripture (Ps. 5, 10, 14, 36, 53, 140, Is. 59:7-8) to make his point that like all others, the Jews too stand under the power of sin (see Chapter IV below for further discussion on sin, righteousness etc....). The oracles/Law of God could have been used for salvation, instead through misuse/misinterpretation, the oracles/Law brought the knowledge of sin.

3:21-31 – God's gift of salvation

The Apostle describes what was promised in the Law and the Prophets, i.e. in Hebrew scriptures, that *the righteousness of God* (ἡ δικαιοσυνη του Θεου πεφανερωται) *has been manifested apart from law...through faith in Jesus Christ for all who believe.* In other words, God's righteousness (God's essential being in relation to humans) justifies in Christ, without distinction, Jew and Gentile alike. Paul verbalized one of the basic tenets of the Christian faith that *since all have sinned and fall short of the glory of God, they are justified freely* (δικαιουμενοι δωρεὰν τη αὐτου χαριτι) *by God's grace as a gift... to be received by faith.* Since God took the initiative in this act of salvation, neither Jew nor Greek has any ground for boasting because a person does not do work for salvation (i.e. doing the works of the Law) but is *justified by faith apart from the works of Law.... God will justify the circumcised on the ground of their faith and the uncircumcised through their faith.* So, all are equalized. This does not overthrow the Law as if it had no value; instead it upholds the Law as the Law should lead a person into the proper understanding of the relationship with God. Paul will resort to the story of Abraham to illustrate the basis of his argument in the next chapter.

4:1-25 – the example of Abraham

In chapter 3 Paul cited the Law and Prophets to bring out his understanding of God's faithfulness and salvation; he now turns to the story of Abraham (Gen.12) who was considered to be the ancestor of the Jews. He claimed that Abraham was not justified by his works but by his faith which was *reckoned to him as righteousness* (see also Gen. 15:6). Paul's argument is that Abraham was justified and considered righteous before he was circumcised (Abraham's circumcision takes place in Gen. 17, whereas he was considered righteous in Gen. 15). Thus, Paul goes a step further back than Abraham being only the father of the Jews; since he was considered as righteous before circumcision, Abraham became the father of all those who believe. The promise to Abraham that he and his descendants would inherit the earth was fulfilled, not through the Law (which was given many centuries later through Moses), *but through the righteousness of faith.... he received* circumcision *as a sign or seal of his righteousness.* So, while the Jews would have looked on Abraham as their ancestor and thus made Judaism a very exclusive faith determined on biological descent, Paul opens up the understanding of Abraham so that he can be seen as *the father of us all.* Abraham's hope and faith defied all human expectations as both he and Sarah, his wife, were old and past the age of child-bearing; it was this hope and faith that was counted as his righteousness. The story of the righteousness of Abraham ends with Paul's main point, *it was written not for his sake alone but for ours also. It will be reckoned to us who believe...in Jesus our Lord, who was put to death for our trespasses and raised for our justification.* This envisages a much greater inclusion than just biological descent; it goes beyond individual believers to describe a collective relationship to one another – a community of believers or a church, just as Israel was once considered a covenanted people.

5:1-21 – Results of Justification: Reconciliation with God: Free from wrath

Paul starts this section with "therefore" (οὖν) indicating that it includes all the discussion that has gone before – justified through Christ and now reconciled to God. This reconciliation brings the benefits of *rejoicing in suffering knowing that suffering produces endurance, and endurance produces character, and character produces hope,* and also the benefits of peace with God, hope of sharing God's glory, and an outpouring of God's love through the Holy Spirit. The description of how Christ's death accomplished justification (5:6-11) is one of Paul's great explanations of what is involved in God's love: a willingness to die for sinners who do not deserve such graciousness. Paul now compares what has been accomplished through Christ with the state of all human beings stemming from Adam: grace and life as compared to sin and death (here 'death' is not simply the cessation of life, but the negation of life – an existence apart from God). *If many died through one man's (Adam's) trespass, much more have the grace of God and the free gift in the grace of that one man Jesus Christ abounded for many....if because of one man's trespass, death reigned... much more will those who receive the free gift of righteousness reign in life.....* Since all share in Adam's humanity, so Paul's argument is that all share in Adam's sin; an argument that later led Augustine, in the 4th century, to develop the theology/doctrine of 'original sin', but *where sin increased, grace abounded all the more, so that, as sin reigned in death, grace also might reign through righteousness to eternal life through Jesus Christ our Lord* (refer also to Paul's view on 'sin' below). Paul contrasts the two Adams:

Humanity through Adam	Humanity through Christ
Condemnation (5:16)	Justification
Many made sinners (5:19)	Many made righteous
Sin increased (5:20)	Grace much more abounded
Sin reigned to death (5:17)	Grace reigned through righteousness

This reconciled state of peace with God sets the believer free from the wrath of God (ἡ ὀργη του Θεου) i.e. God and the believer are no longer separated but live in reconciled relationship.

6:1-23: Results of Justification: Reconciliation with God: Free from sin

Chapter 5 ended with Paul affirming that where sin increased, grace did much more abound. So, the logical question is asked at the beginning of chapter 6: *are we to continue in sin that grace may abound?* The answer is a strong phrase in Greek – μη γενοιτο– definitely not. This chapter deals with freedom from sin (refer also to the Pauline understanding of 'sin' below) – a result of justification brought about through baptism. This is the longest treatment of the topic in all the letters of Paul but even here, Paul only uses baptism as a metaphor/symbol of understanding the initiation into a new relationship with Christ: *do you not know that all of us who have been baptized into Christ Jesus were baptized into his death? We were buried therefore with him by baptism into death, so that as Christ was raised from the dead by the glory of the Father, we too might walk in newness of life.* The power of Sin is broken by the death and resurrection of Christ and the efficaciousness of this is passed on to the believer through being united with Christ – *the old self was crucified with him...we might no longer be enslaved to sin. But if we have died with Christ, we believe that we shall also live with him.* In the final analysis, *you also must consider yourselves dead to sin and alive to God in Christ Jesus.*

Paul further uses the metaphor of being under a government/rule. In baptism, members have changed the ruling power – *sin will have no dominion over you, since you are not under law but under grace.* In chapter 5 Paul held that all share in the sin of Adam, i.e. Sin seen as a power that keeps humanity enslaved; but in chapter 6, Paul affirms that this power of Sin is broken by the death and resurrection of Christ and therefore humanity has the choice not to be enslaved by sin. By using the words 'sin' and 'law' interchangeably, Paul will spell out his position in chapter 7. However, for the moment, the same question arises: *are we to sin because we are not under law but under grace?* The answer is again the same strong refutation – μη γενοιτο– certainly not! A person becomes a slave to the power to which they yield themselves – to sin which leads to death, or to obedience which leads to righteousness – *thanks be to God…. having been set free from sin, you have become slaves of righteousness. Just as you once yielded your members to impurity…now yield your members to righteousness.* Paul is using the imagery and vocabulary of the slave market where a slave receives no wages but is totally at the disposal of the master. The result of such an enslavement would be that being a slave to sin leads to death and becoming a slave to righteousness leads to life. In conclusion Paul shifts his vocabulary and imagery to that of a servant who gets paid for his/her services/ loyalty, to describe the freedom from sin and the new relationship with God through Christ: *the wages of sin is death, but the free gift of God is eternal life in Christ Jesus our Lord.*

7:1-25: Results of Justification: Reconciliation with God: Free from law

In chapter 7 Paul returns to the theme of the Mosaic law; the chapter is addressed very much to *those who know the law.* He illustrates that the law is binding only as long as a person is alive; if the person is dead, the law has no jurisdiction. So, Paul says, *you have died to the law through the body of Christ, so that you may belong to another…*Paul builds on the previous chapter that the believer is dead to sin and so set free from the power of Sin therefore all that is part of the old dispensation has no more hold over the believer. Is the law 'sin' because it belongs to the old dispensation? The answer is again an emphatic μη γενοιτο— certainly not. The law is not sin, in fact the law is *spiritual,* but the law arouses sinful passions: *our sinful passions aroused by the law…. if it had not been for the law, I should not have known sin.*

Throughout chapter 7, Paul uses the first person pronouns 'I', 'me', 'my'; it relates the matter being discussed to himself in a dramatic fashion and makes it vivid for the readers especially the impassioned helpless cry that shows a person torn between their helplessness, and what they really want to do: *I do not do what I want, but I do the very thing I hate…. Nothing good dwells in me…. I can will what is right, but I cannot do it. For I do not do the good I want, but the evil I do not want is what I do.*

So, Paul sees the person under the law to be bound by the requirements of the law to the extent that the person loses the freedom to make a choice. As long as there was no law, sin was not defined, but with the coming of the law, sin was defined and became active, leading to death (separation from God). This utter frustration is expressed vividly: *wretched man that I am! Who will deliver me from this body of death?* However, because he is now free from the law, Paul can exclaim in affirmation, *thanks be to God through Jesus Christ our Lord!*

It is interesting that Paul's basic Jewish background is put on the block here – the place of the law. The law was intended to give life, but with the coming of sin, the law became powerless to give life and therefore became a burden in the human attempt to observe every requirement *(the very commandment that promised life proved to be death to me).* The chapter brings out that for Paul freedom from the law meant that a person no longer had to do the works of the law in order to attain salvation; salvation now comes from a gracious God through faith in Jesus Christ. However, Paul does not reject the demands of the law – the practical, ethical element – that determines one's relationship to God and to the rest of humanity. The ethical aspects of having only one God, honour parents, do not steal, do not kill, do not commit adultery, do not bear false witness, are still to be practiced. Paul is therefore able to preserve his Jewish background as well as show that the believer is free from trying to fulfill the demands of the law as a means of salvation.

8:1-39: Results of Justification: Reconciliation with God: Free from death

There is therefore now no condemnation for those who are in Christ Jesus. For the law of the Spirit of life in Christ Jesus has set me free from the law of sin and death. For God has done what the law, weakened by the flesh could not do.... The opening verses of chapter 8 are a summary of Paul's argument of the last few chapters. If the believer is free from wrath, free from sin, free from the law, then the believer is also free from death, i.e. free from all that separates humans from God. This freedom comes from God's initiative, not human works/striving to keep the law. Therefore the believers *are not in the flesh but in the Spirit....for all who are led by the Spirit of God are children of God.* This status of children of God permits the believer to address God in the same way as Jesus did: *Abba, Father.* Further, this ensures that the believers as children are *heirs of God and fellow heirs with Christ...provided we suffer with him in order that we may also be glorified with him.*

In the story of creation in the Hebrew scriptures the earth was cursed because of Adam's sin (Gen. 3:17-19; 5:29), and so in Jewish apocalyptic thought there will be *a new heaven and a new earth*(Is. 65:17; 66:22), therefore, Christ's healing effect – salvation – is on all creation; creation will be freed from the bondage of decay: *creation waits with eager longing.....creation was subjected to futility ....creation will be set free from its bondage to decay and obtain the glorious liberty of the children of God. Creation has been groaning in travail* (the Greek words used are συνστεναζει και συνωδινει from the images and vocabulary of a woman at the time of childbirth; intense pain followed by joyous reward). Creation too will be transformed and renewed in accordance with God's plan of salvation. Paul's understanding of salvation is therefore inclusive of all creation; an insight into the inclusiveness of salvation which it has taken Christendom 2000 years to recognize and articulate in the concerns

for creation/ecology/ecotheology/green theology/environment etc...;
Paul was far ahead of his time!

The believer does not as yet see all this happening, yet *we groan
inwardly as we wait for adoption...for in this hope we were saved.* The believer
hopes and waits with patient endurance *and the Spirit helps us in our
weakness...the Spirit intercedes for us with sighs too deep for words....* None
of this is left to chance; both justification and glorification are part
of the plan of salvation that God has predestined (προεγνω και
προωρισεν– foreknew and predestined) from the beginning. This is not
predestination in the sense of a predetermined, prospective plan
being put into action, but predestination in a retrospective sense that
on looking back one can say that God has done everything well: *in
everything God works for good with those who love God.*

The chapter ends with one of the great affirmations of the Christian
faith – God's limitless love: *If God is for us, who shall be against us? who
shall separate us from the love of God in Christ? Shall tribulation, or distress,
or persecution, or famine, or nakedness, or peril or sword?...No, in all these things
we are more than conquerors through God who loved us....neither death, nor life,
nor angels, nor principalities, nor things present, nor things to come, nor powers,
nor height, nor depth, nor anything in all creation, will be able to separate us
from the love of God in Christ Jesus our Lord.*

In many ways, chapter 8 concludes Paul's introduction of himself
and his theological position – *my gospel.* Having established his credentials,
Paul can go on with dealing with some of the issues that concerned
the Roman community.

9:1-11-36: The place of Israel

In chapters 9-11, Paul deals with the place of Israel in the salvific
plan of God. How is justification reconcilable with God's promises
to Israel? How is it that the Israelites, who had received the promises
through the Law and the Prophets, rejected Christ? These are the
questions that Paul sets out to answer in chapters 9-11; the chapters
are best taken as a unit rather than piecemeal.

The first issue to recognize is that Paul is defending himself against the charge that he was more concerned about the salvation of the Gentiles than the salvation of his own people – the Jews. In fact, he goes so far as to say that *I have great sorrow and unceasing anguish in my heart for I could wish that I myself were accursed and cut off from Christ for the sake of my brethren, my kinsmen by race.* His anguish is all the more since he lists, in 9:4-5 that the people of Israel had received all the blessings from God: adoption, glory, covenant, law, worship, promises; the patriarchs belonged to them and Christ descended in the flesh as a Jew. However, Paul insists that *it was not as though the word of God had failed*, but it is an emphasis on the freedom of the human being to make a choice whether to be obedient or not and on the freedom of God to make God's own choices. So, *not all who are descended from Israel belong to Israel, and not all are children of Abraham because they are his descendants:* God chose Isaac as the son of promise over Ishmael and similarly God chose Jacob to continue the line rather than Esau – the understanding of 'election' of the Jews as the favoured nation. God exercised God's freedom of choice and humans exercised their freedom by choosing obedience to God. Therefore, there is no injustice on God's part – the strong Greek negative, μη γεvoιτo– refuted any thought of injustice on God's part. The exercise of God's choice and power is also brought out in the quotation from Ex. 13:19 – *I will have mercy on whom I have mercy, and I will have compassion on whom I will have compassion.....so that my name may be proclaimed in all the earth.* In this sense, humans are left with no choice just as the clay cannot object to the shape that is given to it by the potter. Again, there are quotations to show that God's choice includes the Gentiles as well as the Jews.

The strong emphasis that God's choices preclude any human choice is dealt with in 9:30ff, that righteousness has to be pursued by faith and not by works of the law. This means that humans have to make a choice and their choice leads either to death (trying to follow every demand of the law) or to life (accepting God's provision through faith). This choice to be made cannot be taken away therefore human decision is very much involved in responding to God's act of salvation. Paul interprets the Isaianic prophecy that only a remnant of Israel would be saved (Is. 20:22-23) which again emphasizes that it is only those who exercise their freedom of choice and respond to God's salvific activity who can be saved. This freedom of choice is open to both Jews and Gentiles. So, while the chapter begins on a note of sorrow for the Jews, it ends on a note of consolation that there will be a remnant from among the Jews who would be saved along with the Gentiles who respond positively to God.

In chapter 10 Paul continues to plead for the Israelites, *my heart's desire and prayer to God for them is that they may be saved.* Their zeal was misplaced, *for, being ignorant of the righteousness that comes from God, and seeking to establish their own, they did not submit to God's righteousness.* Then Paul also summarizes the position of the law – *Christ is the end of the law,* because a person no longer has to work for righteousness; or the futility of seeking to be righteous before God on the basis of works, but a person is justified by faith – *if you confess with your lips that Jesus is Lord and believe in your heart that God raised him from the dead, you will be saved.* Hence *there is no distinction between Jew and Greek; the same Lord is Lord of all...everyone who calls on the name of the Lord will be saved.* Paul offers Israel little excuse – the gospel was preached to them by the prophets, but Israel did not believe, they were disobedient and defiant, but the Gentiles have responded positively. For Paul, therefore, God's plan of salvation includes both Jew and Greek.

Again, the rhetorical question: *has God rejected God's people?* and the emphatic answer μη γενοιτο – certainly not. He cites his own example – *an Israelite, a descendant of Abraham, a member of the tribe of Benjamin.* He cites examples from Israel's history where the majority failed, but a remnant was preserved; in fact he feels that everything will work out well; Israel's stumbling was providential in allowing salvation to come to the Gentiles; this will make Israel jealous and more will be saved: *if their failure means riches for the Gentiles, how much more will their full inclusion mean!*

In 11:13, it is very clear that the community in Rome consists of Gentiles as well and Paul can talk to them with authority as he claims to be the Apostle to the Gentiles. He encourages them to adjust and accept the Jews for that would be for the enrichment of the whole community.:*if their rejection means the reconciliation of the world, what will their acceptance mean but life from the dead?* Gentile believers should not boast; they are a branch of a wild olive tree grafted on to a cultivated olive tree in place of some of the branches that have been cut off. The grafting is for the purpose of the conversion of Israel. Paul is using an agricultural metaphor to make the same point – that the conversion of the Gentiles would make Israel jealous and therefore lead to them being saved. All have been disobedient, but their disobedience is so that God may have mercy on all. The section ends with a hymn praising the depths, and riches and wisdom of God: *O the depth of the riches and wisdom and knowledge of God! How unsearchable are God's judgements and how inscrutable God's ways!..for from God and through God and to God are all things. To God be glory forever. Amen.*

Thus, in this section, Paul brings out that Israel had a special role to play in God's salvific plan, and their election is irrevocable. However, only a few – remnant –remained true to God and are truly Israelites. Along with this honour, also goes the responsibility to brings others in, but because they failed in their responsibility, they too have to rely on Jesus and the acceptance of salvation as a gift. So, while Paul defends Judaism and Israel as God's 'elect', Paul also goes beyond the borders of Judaism to include the Gentiles. In this way, Paul is true to the Gospel he preaches that Jew and Gentile are included in God's salvation. He cannot then be accused of neglecting/rejecting the Jews but interprets the place of the Jews in a wider perspective of being instruments of God's salvific plan.

12:1-13:14: Hortatory section I

Till chapter 11 Paul has been dealing with theoretical issues; he now turns to the practical implications of living under God's grace and the sort of conduct that must govern God's people. The sections are known as 'hortatory' or exhortations for daily living – hortatory because this is advice not just for others (readers) but also for the author (hortatory includes the speaker/writer).

The section starts with the vocabulary of the temple sacrificial system – *offer your bodies to be a living sacrifice.* A living sacrifice is almost a contradiction in words; a sacrifice is the presentation of a gift to God and if it is in the form of an animal, it is killed in the ritual of offering. Here the sacrifice is to be living – i.e. the offering must live a life *that is holy and acceptable to God.* In order to do this, Paul describes the process in two almost untranslatable Greek words: *do not be conformed (*συσχηματιζεσθε*) but be transformed (*μεταμορφουσθε*);* the word translated 'conformed' comes from the Greek word *schema* – the outward/exterior form/shape of a person. This outward form changes from age to age; a person at 20 does not have the same form as at 50; a person's outward appearance can be altered to suit fashion; so, to be 'conformed' is to follow current trends which may lead to popularity/ recognition etc… The word translated 'transformed' comes from the Greek word *morphe* – the essential being of the person which does not change. The usual example given is that of the transformation of a caterpillar into a butterfly – the process is known as metamorphosis – an irreversible change of the essential being. The living sacrifice that Paul calls for is this irreversible inner change by the *renewal of your minds* which must also find its expression in the outward/exterior changes of behavior and relationships. The renewed mind must move towards perfection (John Wesley), for this is the will of God.

To bring about this movement towards perfection, Paul talks of humility – *not to think of oneself more highly than they ought to, but to think with sober judgment.* Then he goes on to express that this is necessary because the community is like a body having members with different functions – *for as in one body we have many members, and all the members do not have the same function, so we, though many, are one body in Christ, and individually members one of another.* Each member has a different gift – prophecy, serving, teaching, exhorting, giving in liberality, and doing acts of mercy with cheerfulness. All these gifts need to be exercised in unison in order to make the body – the community – functional. And overall, there is an emphasis on love that has to be exercised by all members of the community – *let love be genuine.*….(12:9-21). All this is part of not being conformed to the world but renewed in the new age inaugurated by Christ.

The directive to be subject to governing authorities (13:1-7) is particularly appropriate in a letter to the capital city of the Empire. By the time Romans was written, the Emperor Claudius who had expelled the Jews from Rome was dead, and the new Emperor, Nero, had not yet shown hostility to Christians. So, Paul can say, *there is no authority except from God, and those that exist have been instituted by God.* The instructions to pay taxes and to respect authorities would make ideal citizens of the Christians. Did these instructions come from Paul's own favourable dealings with Roman authorities as in Acts 18:12-17, and other places where his Roman citizenship was honoured? (e.g. Acts 16:25-40; 23:12ff; 24:1ff; 25:1-12). Or were his instructions a defence strategy against the charge that his theology of freedom fostered dangerous civil irresponsibility? Or was Paul pastorally concerned that the recent expulsion of the Jews from Rome (A.D. 49) by annoyed authorities should not be repeated in the case of Christians? (In later writings of the New Testament, there will be a different attitude towards the Emperor and Roman authorities due to imperial persecution and harassment). Perhaps Paul is aware of all these reasons, but unable to quite spell it out as he was writing to the capital. And so, as a hortatory advice he writes, …. *love one another…the commandments are summed up in this, "you shall love your neighbour as yourself" …. love is the fulfilling of the Law.*

Paul ends this section with a reference to eschatology – *you know what hour it is, how it is full time now for you to wake from sleep…. The night is far gone, the day is at hand.* However, he does not elaborate on eschatological beliefs and events; his warning is to bring to the notice of the Romans that it is the opportune time, the καιρος (*kairos*) time – the imagery of night versus day, works of darkness versus armour of light – which must be taken advantage of or lost forever. So, his warning ends with the exhortation to *put on the Lord Jesus Christ.*

14:1-15:13: Hortatory section II

The use of terminology such as "weak" and "strong" suggests that the Jew-Gentile controversy had not yet settled down – there were still problems in the relationship especially in the area of eating habits and dietary restrictions stemming from the Mosaic law. Whether the "weak" are to be identified as Jewish converts and the "strong" as the majority Gentile converts is not certain; in fact, it may be possible that both groups observed certain rituals and dietary restrictions on certain days – *one esteems one day as better than another, while another esteems all days alike....the one who eats, eats in honour of the Lord....while the one who abstains, abstains in honour of the Lord.* The point that Paul is concerned about is that the two groups should not act as judges of one another and therefore cause divisions in the community. The factor holding the community together is Christ and not food regulations: *none of us lives to themselves, and none of us dies to themselves.... whether we live or whether we die, we are the Lord's.... so why do you pass judgment on another or why do you despise another?* So, Paul advises *do not for the sake of food destroy the work of God...it is right not to eat meat or drink wine or do anything that makes another stumble.*

(Some ancient manuscripts end the letter with 14:23 – see section on *Authorship and Integrity* above)

Paul ends this section with an appeal for the "weak" and the "strong" to make an adjustment with one another: *let each of us please our neighbour for good, to edify them.* He gives the example of Christ who did not please himself but through his work he confirmed the promises made to the patriarchs (Jews) and also opened the way for salvation for the Gentiles, so therefore, they ought to *welcome one another, as Christ has welcomed you, for the glory of God.* Quotations are given from the three divisions of Hebrew scriptures that concern and confirm God's plan for the Gentiles: Deut. 32:43 (Law); Is. 11:10 (Prophets); Ps. 18:49; 117:1 (Writings). The source of all blessings is *the God of hope* – a familiar theme from Isaiah whom Paul has just quoted (Is. 40:31, 42:4, 49:23, 51:5) – so that *by the power of the Holy Spirit you may abound in hope.*

15:14-33: Concluding Section I

Paul concludes his letter by summarizing his dealings with the Romans: *you yourselves are full of goodness, filled with all knowledge, and able to instruct one another...I have written boldly.... because of the grace given to me by God to be a minister* (λειτουργὸν) *of Christ Jesus to the Gentiles.* The word for minister is used in the liturgical function of a Jewish priest; therefore, Paul sees himself and his preaching as a liturgical service so that the Gentiles might become acceptable offerings to God. For this service, he has every reason to be proud of his ministry which has taken him from Jerusalem to Illyricum in Western Greece and he now hopes to push further West but not duplicating the work started by someone else. But now he reckons that his work is over in the Eastern, and North Eastern, parts of the Empire, so he wants to go westwards to Spain (the New Testament does not talk of any work as far west as Spain, so this would be new mission territory); perhaps the intention is to make Rome as a mission centre as was Jerusalem, Antioch, Ephesus etc… However, he had first to deliver the collection made in Macedonia and Achaia for the needy in Jerusalem. The collection is not just an expression of concern for those in need, but Paul gives it a theological flavor: *indeed they (Gentiles) are in debt to them (Jews), for if the Gentiles have come to share in their spiritual blessings, they ought also to be of service to them in material blessings.* However, Paul is uncertain about the reception he will receive in Jerusalem – whether he will escape the hostility of *the unbelievers in Judea*(presumably Pharisees and members of the Sanhedrin who felt that Paul had betrayed them by going over to the group that he had persecuted), and whether the collection will be accepted by the saints in Jerusalem since he had said/written some hard words against them (Gal. 2:6,9 – facetiously referring to them as *reputed to be pillars;* II Cor. 11:13 *false apostles;* II Cor. 12:11 – *I am not at all inferior to those superlative apostles*). So, Paul wants the Romans to pray for him and perhaps hints that the Romans should put in a good word for him to Jerusalem.

The chapter ends with a concluding benediction (see section on *Authorship and Integrity* above).

16:1-23: Concluding Section II

Since Paul is intending to visit Rome, he also needs to make personal contact with people there. Chapter 16 is a long list of greetings to people whom Paul knows and who are now in Rome; a few of these people are mentioned in Acts and in other Pauline letters; however, none of the other Pauline letters has a list this long (26 people) who are greeted in the same city (see section on *Authorship and Integrity* above). Possibly this is Paul's attempt to make contact with a community that he had never visited before and with which he was not so familiar having only" heard" of their faith (Rom. 1:8ff). It is noteworthy that there are many women mentioned in the chapter either as holding an office (Phoebe, a deaconess) or are listed as Paul's fellow workers (Prisca, Mary, Junia, Tryphaena, Tryphosa, Persis) There is the warning to deal severely with those who cause dissensions in the community (16:17-20a), indicating both a pastoral and administrative oversight. In conclusion, those who were with Paul at the time of writing, and the writer Tertius, sent their greetings. 16:20b again seems to be an ending of the letter which was moved to the end thus giving rise to the creation of verse 24 (see section on *Authorship and Integrity* above).

The doxology – 16:25-27 – is missing from many ancient manuscripts, but has a history attached to it stemming from the work of Marcion (see section on *Authorship and Integrity* above). However, most New Testament studies today would accept that Romans 1-16 is an integrated writing and that while it directly addressed the issues at Rome, nevertheless its contents are also applicable to other churches of other places and times.

Select Bibliography for Romans

Barrett, C. K. *A Commentary on Romans.* London: SPCK, 1932.

_____. Paul: *An Introduction to his Thought.* London: Chapman, 1994.

Bornkamm, G. *Paul.* New York: Harper & Row, 1971.

Bowen, Roger. *A Guide to Romans.* Delhi: ISPCK, 1983.

Brown, R. E., An *Introduction to the New Testament.* Bangalore: Theological Publications in India, 2000.

Bultmann, R. *Theology of the New Testament, Volume I.* London: SCM Press, 1971.

Dodd, C. H. *The Epistle of Paul to the Romans.* London: Hodder & Stoughton, 1960.

Kasemann, E., *Perspectives on Paul.* Philadelphia: Fortress Press, 1971.

_____, Commentary *on Romans*, Grand Rapids: Eerdmanns, 1980.

Knox, J. *Chapters in the Life of Paul.* Nashville: Abingdon Press, rev. ed. 1987.

Khatry, Ramesh "Romans" in Brian C. Wintle (General Editor), *South Asia Biblical Commentary*, Udaipur, Rajasthan: Open Door Publication, 2015, pages 1511 – 1554.

Kummel, W. G. *Introduction to the New Testament.* London: SCM Press, 1975.

Morris, Leon. *The Epistle to the Romans.* Leicester: Inter Varsity Press, 1988.

Murphy-O'Connor. Jerome *Paul, A Critical Life.* Oxford: OUP, 1996 (1997).

Paul's own letters

B. The Corinthian Correspondence – I & II Corinthians

The founding of the community. Authorship / authenticity and integrity, occasion, purpose, dates and places of writing of the Corinthian correspondence. Brief analysis and commentary on the text. Select bibliography for the Corinthian Correspondence.

Founding of the community

Corinth was a rich trading centre standing between two ports: Cenchreae on the East and Lechaum on the West; and situated astride the important north-south land route. Roman records show that from about 30 B.C., Corinth was the seat of a proconsul and the capital of the senatorial province of Achaia (see Life of Paul, above). The city had a mixed population in which religious syncretism flourished; the population's addiction to vice and immorality was a by-word. On his so-called 'second missionary journey' (see Life of Paul, above), Paul passed through Macedonia and Athens and reached Corinth, later to be joined there by his helpers Silvanus and Timothy (II Cor. 1:19; Acts 18:5). At first Paul stayed with Aquila and Prisca since they seemed to have known each other and were of the same trade (I Cor. 16:19; Acts 18:1-2). Paul first taught in the synagogues, then following a conflict with the Jews, he moved to the house of Titius Justus, a Gentile (Acts 18:4ff) symbolizing a shift of the mission strategy to the Gentiles. Paul supported himself and his mission by working at his trade, tentmaking (Acts 18:2ff; I Cor. 4:12; 9:1ff; II Cor. 11:7ff). After a year and a half of Paul's ministry (Acts 18:11), there was a large community consisting of Gentile Christians (I Cor. 12:2) mostly from the lower classes (I Cor. 1:26ff), and of Jewish Christians (Acts 18:4; I Cor. 7:18); there were also those from the upper social and economic strata as well (I Cor. 1:26ff; 11:21ff; Acts 18:8; Rom. 16:23).The names mentioned in I Cor. 16:15-18 and Romans 16:21-23 indicate the presence of both Jews and Gentiles among the community at Corinth. After Paul, Apollos, a rhetorically gifted Jew from Alexandria, carried on the work in Corinth (Acts 18:24ff; I Cor. 3:5ff).

Thus, it was in this flourishing Greek town that Paul left behind a 'vibrant' Christian community in the seven/eight years during which he had personal contacts, and contacts through friends and letters. The word "vibrant" is used to describe the community, not in the sense that it had no problems and was a constantly developing and expanding community, but "vibrant" in the sense that the range of problems (rival theologians, factions, civil court cases, problematic sexual practices, marital obligations, dietary restrictions, liturgy and eucharist, speaking in tongues, resurrection, eschatology etc...) encountered in the Corinthian correspondence is an indication that the community was struggling to find direction and faithfulness with regard to concerns/ issues that it met in daily life and that on many occasions they had to be corrected leading to strained relations with Paul, but just as many times finding again a bonding and lasting friendship with the founding Apostle. It was also "vibrant" in the sense that the community brought together people of widely differing educational backgrounds, differing financial resources, differing religious backgrounds, differing social backgrounds etc.... The community had the potential for great unity and equally potential for great dissension. Hence it is understandable that there is more Pauline correspondence with the Corinthians than with any other community in the Pauline circle and from the issues dealt with in the correspondence, more is known about the Corinthian community than any other Pauline community, and in that process, much can also be known about Paul.

The authenticity, integrity, occasion, purpose, dates and places of writing of the Corinthian correspondence

There has never been any serious doubt regarding the authenticity of I & II Corinthians. The earliest traditions mention Paul as the author of these letters. Indeed, as the founding missionary, Paul exercises his prerogative in continuing to guide the community and suggest ways/ means of regulating their lives in such a way that they are found to be faithful witnesses to the Gospel. However, also from early times there have been questions about the integrity of the correspondence: are I & II Corinthians, as found in the canon today, internally unified writings or are each compilations of several letters? Since the two writings are closely related, it would be best to study them together in the sequence that is suggested below. This is not the normal approach to the Corinthian correspondence as scholars prefer to take each book separately, but if there are several letters included in the correspondence, then it would be better to identify and study each as a separate unit which addresses different situations in the congregation.

The New Testament contains two letters of Paul to the Corinthians, but in those two letters there is mention of two other letters – the 'previous' letter not to associate with immoral persons (I Cor. 5:9), and the 'letter of tears' (II Cor. 2:4) – so four in all. From the end of the 18th century, New Testament scholars have posited a variety of hypotheses even suggesting a compilation of as many as nine letters within the canonical I & II Corinthians. A reconstruction of all the details, and sequence of events, would lead into complicated theories and presuppositions;[1] moreover, complete objectivity is not possible

---

1 One sequence of letters which form II Corinthians that is proposed by some scholars is: II Cor. 8 (regarding the collection for Jerusalem) was written first and sent with Titus. Titus brought back news of trouble at Corinth, so Paul wrote II Cor. 2:14-7:4 – a letter that failed. So, Paul visited Corinth, but that visit was a disaster. The result was that Paul left Corinth and wrote II Cor. 10-13 – the letter of tears – and sent it with Titus. This time Titus brought back good news, so Paul wrote II Cor. 1:1-2:13 and 7:5-16. Finally, to express the urgency of completing the collection for Jerusalem, Paul wrote II Cor. 9. An attractive sequence but involving too many assumptions and presuppositions which cannot be substantiated. Another scholar suggests that in the collection of Pauline letters, there were three letters

when dealing with ancient texts as every literary judgment embodies a subjective element, more especially when dealing with texts that are now accepted scripture. Hence only the position accepted here will be outlined.

I Corinthians can be studied with greater ease than II Corinthians with regard to a theory of compilations/partitions. Any theory with regard to I Corinthians must take into account the sources of information that Paul had available to him. The first source would be firsthand knowledge of the community as the founder missionary; obviously Paul would make use of that knowledge in addressing the community. The second source of information was *Chloe's people* (I Cor. 1:11) who reported *that there is quarreling among you*. A third source of information was *concerning the matters about which you wrote* (I Cor. 7:1). A fourth source of information was the visit of *Stephanas and Fortunatus and Achaicus* (I Cor. 16:17) who were perhaps the bearers of the letter mentioned in 7:1 and who carried Paul's reply back to Corinth. The complexity of issues from these four sources (see the composition of the community above; and the detailed historical and literary contexts below) indicate that the community was quite a mixed group and that their behavior would therefore pose problems for any pastoral oversight. However, based on this information from the text, it is possible to view I Corinthians as a combined response to oral and written reports that the factionalism and dissentions within the community are not to their advantage and therefore the letter can be viewed as internally consistent and a writing that exhibits a basic unity.

II Corinthians poses a different picture: not only does one have to look for sources of information, but also to construct contexts in order to understand the text. This is clearly seen in the difference in tone and subject between chapters 1-7 (opening epistolary formula + rejoicing at reconciliation after misunderstandings between Paul and the Corinthians and which mentions a *letter written out of much affliction and anguish of heart and with many tears* – II Cor. 2:4) and chapters 10-13 (reproaches and sarcasm, and a defense of his

---

to the Corinthians – I Cor., II Cor. 1-9, and II Cor. 10-13 brought together in decreasing order of length. However, the person who made the combination did not notice that he/she had joined two separate letters in II Cor.!

apostleship); added to this are chapters 8 and 9 which deal differently with the same subject (to re-start the collection for Jerusalem and to urgently complete the work) with no reference to each other.

The result of this all too brief summary can be stated as follows:

1. The "Lost/previous" letter mentioned in I Cor. 5:9 (possibly found in II Cor. 6:14-7:1);

2. I Corinthians: responses to reports from Chloe's people and responses to written questions;

3. II Corinthians 10-13 – the letter of tears mentioned in II Cor. 2:4;

4. II Cor. 2:14-6:13 and 7:2-16 – letter of thanksgiving;

5. II Cor. 1:1-2:13– opening epistolary formulae and exhortation;

6. II Cor. 8 – letter to re-start the collection for Jerusalem (cf. I Cor. 16:1-4);

7. II Cor. 9 – letter expressing urgency regarding the collection for Jerusalem.

Thus, it is suggested that the canonical I and II Corinthians are a compilation of at least 7 letters. The historical events (**A – I** below) and the literary contexts of this suggestion can be tabulated as follows:

A. Founding visit

B. I Cor. 5:9 – the 'lost/previous letter' found in II Cor. 6:14-7:1

C. I Cor. – responses to oral reports and written questions

D. 2nd visit – unsuccessful and resulting in conflict

E. II Cor. 10-13 – 'letter of tears' and Apostolic defense

F. II Cor. 2:14-6:13 and 7:2-16 – 'letter of thanksgiving'

G. II Cor. 1:1-2:13 – opening epistolary formulae and exhortation which could have been attached to F, H, or I

H. II Cor. 8 – letter to re-start the collection for Jerusalem

I. II Cor. 9 – letter expressing the urgency of completing the collection for Jerusalem.

The literary contexts must now be examined in a little more detail.

1.   I Cor. 5:9 – the 'lost/previous letter':

In this reference, Paul writes, *I wrote to you in my letter not to associate with immoral persons*....Prior to I Corinthians, Paul had already written to the Corinthian community advising them against having dealings with immoral persons. Corinth was well known for its permissive life style where all kinds of 'immorality' – sexual, greed, idolater, reviler, drunkard, robber (I Cor. 5:11) – were prevalent. Paul was probably trying to set some ethical standards based on Jewish and Greek philosophical schools and it was necessary to write to the community about the matter after his founding visit. The advice was interpreted to mean immoral persons outside the community (unbelievers), but here Paul clarifies that what he meant was persons within the community (I Cor. 5:9-13). According to the summary of the contents of this 'lost' letter given in I Corinthians 5:9-13, it seems possible that the letter is preserved either in whole or in part in II Cor. 6:14-7:1 which deals with the subject of being *mismated with unbelievers...let us cleanse ourselves from every defilement of body and spirit...* Further, 6:14-7:1 breaks the continuity and thematic link between 6:23 and 7:2 so it seems that 6:14-7:1 is an insertion. It is therefore held that the first letter written to the Corinthians can be found in the text of II Cor. 6:14-7:1. If I Corinthians can be dated between A.D. 54-55 (see below), then this **'Lost letter' must predate I Corinthians, so it could be A. D. 53-54 after Paul had left Corinth after the founding visit. The place of the writing cannot be determined, but it could be Ephesus where Paul spent three years from 54-57.**

2.   I Corinthians

There has never been any serious doubt about the integrity of I Corinthians. Once the sources of Paul's information are established, then it can be seen that I Corinthians is a unity first responding to oral reports from Chloe's people (I Cor. 1:11ff) and then answering written questions (I Cor. 7:1) perhaps brought by Stephanus, Fortunatus and Achaicus (I Cor. 16:17ff). The concerns expressed over the oral reports, and Paul's guidance in the matters can be found in chapter 1-6: divisions within the community based on personality cults and appeals to Greek intellectual, abstract philosophies for rhetoric (chapters 1-4), unacceptable sexual relations (chapters 5 and 6) even in the context of a permissive Corinthian society; going to courts of law to solve internal issues (chapter 6). The written questions for clarification include thinking regarding asceticism (chapter 7), social issues such as food offered to idols (chapter 8), participation in the Lord's Supper, drunkenness at the eucharist and the differences that it brought out between the rich and the poor (chapters 10-11), an understanding of 'spiritual gifts' and the unity of the 'body' (chapter 12), 'love' as the force for overcoming differences and determining relationships (chapter 13), the issue of 'speaking in tongues' and behavior in worship (chapter 14), questions about the resurrection (chapter 15), personal notes and closing greetings (chapter 16). Many of the issues may have arisen from the intellectual style of preaching of Apollos which may have resulted in dissatisfaction in the congregation and therefore gave room for "spirited' elements to enter into the community advocating a more spirited/charismatic type of preaching and worship coupled with the permissiveness of the Corinthian society. Most of I Corinthians is given over to countering such a movement within the community. Therefore, I Corinthians shows that it is a basic unity in the consistent deliberative argument to dissuade the Corinthians from factionalism. As it stands inthe New Testament canon, I Corinthians can be regarded as a unified writing and Paul's second letter to the Corinthian community.

The occasion seems to have been that on hearing unfavourable reports about the situation in Corinth, Paul had sent Timothy through Macedonia to Corinth, while Paul himself stayed in Ephesus (4:17; 16:8,10; Acts 19:22). While awaiting Timothy's return, a delegation from Corinth of Stephanas, Fortunatus and Achaicus (16:17) reached Paul with written questions that he answered as found in I Cor. 7:1 to the end of the writing. Paul's stay in Ephesus could be dated between 54-

57 and his plans are to stay there *till Pentecost* (16:8) with the hope that he can spend a longer time at Corinth during winter (16:5-6) especially since he had not visited Corinth for some time (4:18-19). Accordingly, **I Corinthians can be dated during Paul's stay in Ephesus in the spring of A. D. 54-55.**

3.   II Cor. 10-13 – the 'letter of tears'

During Paul's second visit to Corinth (the first visit being the founding visit) some tension seems to have arisen between Paul and the community (II Cor. 13:2) and he threatens that he will not spare them on his next visit. This second visit must have occurred after the writing of I Corinthians, for in that writing there is no indication of strained relations but an expectation that the Corinthians would obey him. Some of the issues raised against Paul are sarcastically mentioned in various parts of II Corinthians: he is unstable (II Cor. 1:15ff), his letters are unclear (II Cor. 1:13ff), his preaching is not clear (II Cor. 4:3), his behavior is offensive (II Cor. 5:11ff; 10:2), he harms the community and enriches himself (II Cor. 7:2; 12:16), he is courageous at a distance (II Cor. 10:1,10), he is an inferior apostle (II Cor. 11:5; 12:11), he is not an apostle (II Cor. 12:12) and Christ does not speak through him (II Cor. 13:3) etc..... Paul is polemicizing against specific people who have attacked him from within the community (probably coming from a Gnostic-Jewish Christian, anti-Pauline background), disparaging his person and who question his apostolic office. These people, described by Paul as *false prophets* (II Cor. 11:12-15), had gained entrance into the community and had raised several objections (e.g. II Cor. 3:1; 10:12, 18; 11:4, 22; 12:1,7,11, 21; 13:2). It is clear that this is a new situation not found in I Corinthians. The result is that Paul's second visit ended in disaster (see II Cor. 2:5-11; 7:12);he had to leave Corinth in great distress and write a severe letter – *I wrote to you out of much affliction and anguish of heart and with many tears not to cause you pain but to let you know the abundant love that I have for you* (II Cor. 2:4). It is suggested that this 'Letter of Tears', either in whole or in part, is found in II Cor. 10-13. The letter was sent with Titus (II Cor. 12:18; II Cor. 7:6-7 mentions Titus' return with the good news that the Corinthians had received him well). It is a complete refutation of all the allegations made against him and a spirited defense of his apostolic office in a strong and forceful presentation completely different in tone from other parts of the Corinthian correspondence, indeed completely different in tone and expression from any other Pauline writing. It is suggested that this is the third piece of Paul's correspondence with the Corinthian community.

Paul left Corinth after his second visit, which resulted in difficulties and tensions between him and the Corinthians, perhaps **returned to Ephesus and wrote the 'letter of tears' which was sent through Titus. The 'letter of tears' can therefore be dated between A.D. 55-56.**

4.   II Cor. 2:14-6:13 and 7:2-16 – letter of thanksgiving

There were anxious moments for Paul as to whether the Corinthians would receive Titus well and whether there could be a reconciliation between Paul and the Corinthians especially in the light of the severe letter. Hence in II Cor. 7:6-7, 15, Paul expressed the relief he felt at Titus' return with good news that Titus had effected a reconciliation and that all was well between Paul and the Corinthians. His immediate response was to write the letter of thanksgiving and to plan a third visit to Corinth (II Cor. 1:15-16?). It is suggested that this is the fourth piece of correspondence with the Corinthians.

The 'letter of thanksgiving' was probably written from Macedonia (it would be difficult to pinpoint the exact location in Macedonia) **towards mid/end of A.D. 56.**

5.   II Cor. 1:1-2:13– opening epistolary formula and exhortation

This section of the letter could be seen as the epistolary opening section of the letter of thanksgiving (see 4 above), but the absence of the mention of Titus as the key figure in the reconciliation process is missing which seems to separate this section from the rest of the letter of thanksgiving. The section could also have stood as either the opening formulae for the letter at chapter 8 or for the letter at chapter 9. Further, since the contents seem to sum up the whole troublesome period of the relations with the Corinthians and to present Paul's apologetic/explanation for the letter of tears – *not to cause you pain but to let you know the abundant love that I have for you* (II Cor. 2:4), then attaching the section to any letter would unnecessarily rake up issues that were best laid aside since they had already been settled. Since there are difficulties in attaching this section to any of the three sections mentioned, therefore this section of paranesis/exhortation is treated as independent and can be considered as the fifth piece of correspondence with the Corinthians.

This paranesis/exhortation section is either simultaneous or shortly after the 'letter of thanksgiving' written from Macedonia and can be dated towards the end of A.D. 56.

6.   II Cor. 8 – letter to re-start the collection for Jerusalem

In I Cor. 16:1-4, Paul had given instructions to collect money for the church in Jerusalem. However, in the intervening period, and with strained relations between Paul and the Corinthians, the collection for Jerusalem seemed to have suffered. Moreover, one of the allegations against Paul was that he had enriched himself through the collection (II Cor. 7:2; 12:16), so until the matter was cleared, the collection had to be placed on hold. In chapter 8, the Corinthians are urged to continue with the collection working with Titus and others to raise funds for Jerusalem (II Cor. 8:6, 10, 16-24) which had begun over a year ago. The collection for Jerusalem was not simply a matter of raising funds; for Paul it had theological implications: sharing with the needy (II Cor. 8:14) as an expression of God's concern for those in need; as a unifying factor that Jews and Gentiles mutually support one another (cf. Gal. 2:9-10); the Gentiles had shared in the Jews' spiritual blessings, so they should share their material blessings with the Jews(Rom. 15:27), so that supporting one another becomes a unifying factor. It is suggested that this letter to re-start the collection under the guidance of Titus and two others is Paul's sixth communication with the Corinthians.

The letter was probably written in Macedonia following the 'letter of thanksgiving' and the opening formula section and sent with Titus to Corinth in early A.D. 57.

7.   II Cor. 9 – letter expressing urgency regarding the collection for Jerusalem

The collection seems to have resumed, but the work is slow-going. The matter had now become urgent as Paul was on his way to Corinth, along with others, to collect the offering (II Cor. 9:1-5); he urges the Corinthians to donate generously since he had boasted to the Macedonians that Corinth (Achaia) had collected a good amount. Yet Paul addresses this issue not as a command or order, but to contribute as a generous gift: *God loves a cheerful giver* (II Cor. 9:7). Paul outlines a whole theological basis for sharing the abundance of God's blessings (II Cor. 9:10-15). Whether the Corinthians matched the Macedonians in their gift is not known, but the collection was taken by Paul to Jerusalem (Acts 20-21); probably making this Paul's last visit to Corinth. It is suggested that II Cor. 9 expressing the urgent need for completing the collection is the seventh letter to the Corinthians.

Paul and company were on their way to Corinth (Achaia) from Macedonia, so the letter must have been written from Macedonia to express the urgency of completing the collection so as not to embarrass Paul on his arrival (II Cor. 9:5). The letter could be dated mid-57.

The above analysis indicates that there was much correspondence and interaction between Paul and the Corinthians and that what we have preserved in the New Testament is a compilation of numerous letters from Paul to the Corinthians. However, the links between the letters (historical and literary links as mentioned above) indicates that the compilation took place within the lifetime of Paul and so the compilation of the seven letters into two major collections may be treated as genuine writings from Paul.

Earlier (see above), the Corinthian community was referred to as "vibrant" and the analysis shows that "vibrant" described the community's struggles with day to day issues, struggles with human tendencies of jealousies, mistrust, disbelief, struggles to understand theological issues and find theological expressions etc.... and that out of the interactions, Paul developed his theology not based on abstractions and speculations, but on a vibrancy of how human beings are to find an expression of their faith in and through the everyday issues of life. The Corinthian correspondence, therefore, while being complex as a literary work, is nevertheless one of Paul's great contributions to the development of theology as representative of the people's concerns, or a theology of, and for, and by, the people of God.

Brief analysis and commentary

The brief analysis and commentary will follow the chronological order of the writings in the Corinthians correspondence as outlined above.

1.   I Cor. 5:9-11 – the 'lost/previous letter' – II Cor. 6:14 – 7:1

The reference is to *I wrote to you in my letter*....It is normally referred to as the 'lost letter' but the description given in 5:9-11 corresponds to the contents of II Cor. 6:14-7:1; moreover, this block of material breaks the connection between 6:13 and 7:2 indicating that it is an insertion. Therefore II Cor. 6:14-7:1 is normally accepted as the letter that Paul wrote prior to I Corinthians (see above) and so stands as the first piece of correspondence with the Corinthians. Corinth was famous for its permissive, multi ethnic and cross cultural society; converts from among the Jews would have brought with them the strict laws of Judaism regarding irresponsible and unacceptable behavior; however, the Gentiles would not have had the same background and presuppositions. So, a problem would have occurred within the community of association with *immoral persons*. Immoral behavior also included *the greedy and robbers, idolators, revilers, drunkards*. The instruction was *not even to eat with such a one*.

Possibly after the founding visit, and before the writing of I Corinthians, Paul had heard of immoral relations among the Corinthians and wrote a quick note to give them directions. It would seem that this 'note' was misunderstood/misinterpreted to mean those outside of the community – *not all at meaning the immoral of this world* – and so Paul had to write to correct the community: *rather I wrote to you not to associate with anyone who bears the name of brother* (i.e. someone from within the community). They are not to judge those outside the church; but the church must exercise discipline over its own members – *is it not those inside the church whom you are to judge? God judges those outside.* The final instruction is that the wicked person must be expelled, invoking the strict law of Deut. 22:22: *drive out the wicked person from among you.*

II Cor. 6:14-7:1 – The theme of associating with immoral persons is referred to in this section, linking it with I Cor. 5:9-11. The basic message is that believers cannot form mismatched relationships with unbelievers because this would compromise their faith which he expresses in a series of sharply worded questions showing the mismatch: *righteousness and iniquity ... light with darkness...Christ with Belial...believer with unbeliever...temple of God with idols?* These questions bring out very emphatically that the Christian faith stands in direct opposition to the immorality and permissiveness of society that was accepted in Corinth, and so he warns the Corinthians to stay away from contacts that would lead them away from the strict morality of their new faith, reminding them that *we are the temple of the living God.* In other words, if God dwells in a person, then that person cannot indulge in immoral behavior. This is supported with quotations from Lev. 26:11-12, Jer. 32:38, and Eze. 37:27 where the promise is that *I will be a father to you, and you shall be my sons and daughters.* Paul sees this promise as being fulfilled now in the Christian community. Paul is affirming that believers are called to be a counter-culture to the world (*transform* the world, and *not be conformed* to the world as in Rom. 12:1-2).So he ends with the exhortation which includes himself (1ˢᵗ person plural) that in a city such as Corinth known for its permissiveness, Paul is stressing the necessity of a strict morality that must characterize the community, anything less would be unacceptable: *let us cleanse ourselves* (καθαρισωμέν ἑαυτους) *from every defilement of body and spirit, and make holiness perfect* (ἐπιτελουντες ἁγιωσυνην)*in the fear of God.*

2.   I Corinthians: responses to reports from Chloe's people and responses to written questions

The Corinthian community had been founded by Paul and the report that there were factions and other problems by Chloe and her people

(1:11) was deeply disturbing. On hearing these unfavourable reports about the situation in Corinth, Paul had sent Timothy through Macedonia to Corinth, while Paul himself stayed in Ephesus (4:17; 16:8,10; Acts 19:22). While awaiting Timothy's return, a delegation from Corinth of Stephanas, Fortunatus and Achaicus (16:17) reached Paul with written questions that he answered from chapter 7 onwards. The presence of the Corinthian delegation also meant that Paul could verify the information received from Chloe's people and all the information that Timothy was to bring back was now readily available. Paul was therefore in a position to write to the Corinthians addressing issues which he considered problematic and issues which the Corinthians had specifically asked him and to send his reply back with the delegation of Stephanas, Fortunatus and Achaicus (see Occasion, date, place of writing etc…above).

1:1-9 Opening greetings

Paul refers to himself as *called by the will of God to be an apostle* (κλητος ἀποστολος δια θελημϰτος Θεου); it stresses his apostolic authority and sets the tone for giving directions. The co-sender of the letter is *Sosthenes,* perhaps the same person who was the ruler of the Corinthian synagogue and was beaten when Gallio refused to judge Paul (Acts 18:17); if he is the same person, it would mean placing him in Ephesus from where Paul was writing the letter and it would also mean that he had been absent from Corinth for quite a while since he could not collaborate the news that Paul received about Corinth. Sosthenes could also have been the scribe writing the letter as Paul dictated it. The Corinthians who are addressed are also *called and sanctified in Christ Jesus;* they make up the church in Corinth. Such greetings which were also addressed to the Gentile converts would have been a boost to them and placed them on the same level as the Jewish converts. The opening greetings includes references to subjects that will be taken in detail later in the letter:

1. Many references to *Jesus Christ* which would serve as the introduction to Paul's correction to the factionalism that was part of the Corinthian problem;

2. Paul also mentions that the Corinthians have been given *grace* (χαρις) – a subject he would deal with later when talking about their charisms and the problems that it was causing;

3. As the opening thanksgiving comes to an end, the topic of *the day of our Lord Jesus Christ* is introduced which Paul would take up in detail at the end of the letter.

1:10-31 Divisions at Corinth

The next few chapters are addressed to the issues that *Chloe's people* reported. The first of these are the divisions or factions that have arisen in the community – there were conflicting personal loyalties among the Corinthian community each having a declared preference of their own: *"I belong to Paul"* or *"I belong to Apollos"* or *"I belong to Cephas"* or *"I belong to Christ"*. No information is given about the groups, but it can be reckoned that the "Paul" group stood for an openness of Jews and Gentiles in the community without background restrictions; "Apollos" may represent the intellectual/philosophical/wisdom sort of presentation of Christ which would appeal to only a few; "Cephas" may represent those from a Jewish background who insisted on the law being followed, i.e. Judaisers; the "Christ" party may be an open group accepting all. Paul's reaction is not to support the group that has declared loyalty to him, but to ask, *Is Christ divided? Was Paul crucified for you? Or were you baptized in the name of Paul?* Later Paul stresses that *whether Paul or Apollos or Cephas...all are yours; and you are Christ's; and Christ is God's* (3:22-23). The division that affirms loyalty to Apollos the philosophical/intellectual/wisdom group is dealt with in the next few chapters. Paul states that he was sent to preach *not with eloquent wisdom, lest the cross of Christ be emptied of its power*. For Paul, the preaching of Christ should not be cloaked in a presentation which would effectually hide, and perhaps even dilute, the message. Thus, the *word of the cross is folly to those who are perishing, but to us who are being saved it is the power of God* (δυναμις Θεου ἐστιν). Possibly it was difficult to explain the suffering and death of Jesus as part of the salvific activity of God, but for Paul this was the essence of the gospel message and he uses Is. 29:14 to bring this out – that which seems foolish is actually the power of God at work for salvation. This is again emphasized: *for Jews demand signs and Greeks seek wisdom, but we preach Christ crucified, a stumbling block to the Jews and folly to Gentiles, but to those who are called, both Jews and Greeks, Christ the power of God and the wisdom of God.*

Paul then substantiates his argument by the example of the composition of the Corinthian community: *consider your call…not many of you were wise…not many were powerful, not many were of noble birth.* The community would seem to basically consist of ordinary, middle class men and women, though as in all communities, there would have been exceptions. But predominantly the community consisted of God's choice of those who were *foolish in the world…weak in the world…low and despised in the world.* These were the people to refute worldly standards so that there is no cause for boasting about one's achievements, for *it is Christ Jesus whom God made our wisdom, our sanctification and redemption* (σοφιά δικαιοσυνή ἅγιασμος και ἀπολυτρωσις).Therefore, the only possible cause for boasting is to *boast of the Lord.* In other words, Paul would not tolerate any divisions in the community.

2:1-5 Paul's style of preaching

The Corinthian community seems to have been influenced by the intellectual/wisdom style of preaching/presentation whereas Paul was a much more down-to-earth evangelist: *I did not come proclaiming to you the testimony of God in lofty words of wisdom.* In a philosophical/intellectual oriented society, Paul's message would have been very different, perhaps even unappealing to some. His preaching strategy was to proclaim *nothing among you except Jesus Christ and Him crucified.* In fact, Paul affirms: *I was with you in weakness and in much fear and trembling; and my speech and my message were not in plausible words of wisdom.* Paul affirms that it was not his persuasive speech or any efforts on his part, but that his message allowed the *demonstration of the Spirit and power, that your faith might not rest in human wisdom but in the power of God.*

2:6-16 The Wisdom that Paul preached

Paul proclaimed the mysterious wisdom of God hidden from those who crucified Jesus but proclaimed in the power of the Spirit: *we impart a secret and hidden wisdom of God...none of the rulers of this age understood this, for if they had, they would not have crucified the Lord of glory...God has revealed this to us in the Spirit.* Those who are able to comprehend this are those who appreciate *wisdom among the mature.* They especially appreciate that this wisdom comes from the Spirit who *searches everything, even the depths of God.* So, what is this "mysterious wisdom"? For Paul it would be Christ crucified which can be understood only by the power of the Spirit that comes from God *in words not taught by human wisdom but taught by the Spirit;* to all others it is folly, i.e. it is unexplainable how a crucified Christ becomes the messiah. Thus the wisdom that Paul preached is the wisdom that comes from the new relationship with Christ which he describes as *having the mind of Christ* (ἡμεις δε νουν Χριστου ἐχομεν).

3:1-23 The foundation that Paul laid

Paul has laid the foundation by preaching Christ. It is this foundation that must be relied on to heal factions/divisions in the light of some of the claims *"I belong to Paul", "I belong to Apollos".* Both Paul and Apollos are *servants through whom you believed* – i.e. they are instruments and not an end. He uses an agricultural illustration to make his point – *I planted, Apollos watered, but God gave the growth. So, neither the one who plants nor the one who watersis anything, but only God who gives the growth.* So, it is foolish to pay allegiance to human leaders, for human leaders are *fellow workers for God.*

He has *laid the foundation like a skilled master builder* (σοφος ἀρχιτεκτων θεμελιον ἐθηκα); *another can build on the foundation, but with care, for there can be no other foundation than that which has been laid.* The foundation that has been laid should lead to the understanding that *you are God's temple* (ναος Θεου) and that *God's spirit dwells in you.* In the closing verses of the chapter, Paul again condemns anyone who thinks that they are wise – *the thoughts of the wise are futile.* So any divisions based on wisdom are to be rejected *for all things are yours... and you are Christ's and Christ is God's* (ὑμεις δε Χριστού Χριστος δε Θεου).

4:1-21 A fatherly appeal

In this chapter, Paul confronts those whose attitude towards him has changed because of the appeal to wisdom. He was being judged as an inferior speaker since he did not indulge in or resort to the wisdom/intellectual style of preaching. Paul is concerned that this would affect the Corinthians' attitude towards the gospel and cause divisions in the community.

He insists on calling himself (and Apollos?) as *servants of Christ* (ὑπηρετας Χριστου) *and stewards of the mysteries of God*. The Greek word used for "servant" refers to the very lowest level of servant who has to do all the dirty work that not even another servant would do. At the same time, he is a "steward" – one entrusted with the running of the household. Both 'servant' and 'steward' need to be *found trustworthy*, and if God has found them trustworthy, then no one should judge them – *it is the Lord who judges me*. Paul closes his arguments regarding divisions based on the 'wisdom' style by giving the Corinthians another model – *I have applied all this to myself and Apollos for your benefit that you may learn by us to live according to scripture*. He posits three harsh rhetorical questions, i.e. he answers the questions himself: 1. *Who sees anything different in you?* 2. *What have you that you did not receive?* and 3. *If you received it, why do you boast as if it were not a gift?* He reminds them that they are no different from others and have received God's blessings as a gift, so they have nothing to boast of. The new model that he presents to them is that of the apostles who *are fools for Christ's sake, but you are wise in Christ. We are weak, but you are strong. You are held in honour, but we in disrepute*. He then goes on to list the sufferings which they have had to endure becoming *the refuse of the world, the off scouring of all things*.

Finally, like a father after harshly correcting the child, Paul speaks kindly and in love: *I do not write this to make you ashamed, but to admonish you as my beloved children…I became your father in Christ Jesus through the Gospel. I urge you then, be imitators of me*. He then talks of an impending visit and the sending of Timothy as an advance party to remind them of Paul's ways and his teaching about Christ in all the churches. He promises to deal the arrogant sternly, but at the same time, like a father, he hopes that they will change: *shall I come to you with a rod, or with love in a spirit of gentleness?*

5:1-6:20 Dealing with local problems

The first problem that he deals with is a case of immorality – **5:1-13** – of such a nature that *is not found even among pagans; for a man is living with his father's wife.* Even for a permissive society such as found in Corinth, such immorality/incest is shocking and unacceptable. Paul betrays his Jewish roots in the outrage that he feels – sexual relationships among those of such close relations are not to be tolerated (Lev. 18:8; 20:11). The man has to be removed from the community as a disciplinary measure. The Corinthians have nothing to boast about when such behavior is found among them; they are to *cleanse out the old leaven so that they may be a new lump.* He is using leaven as an alternate word for 'sin'. The symbol of leaven carried the message that like leaven permeates all the dough, so one person's immorality could permeate and spoil the whole community one bad apple spoils the basket). The imagery is from the Passover rituals and celebrations when households would clean out the vessels so that none of the old leaven is carried over into the festival(Ex. 13:7; Deut. 16:4); they could then celebrate the feast of Passover and Unleavened bread without the contamination of the old (the Jews had to eat unleavened bread on the night of Passover as there was no time for the leaven – yeast – to work in the dough. Christians emulate this on 'Shrove Tuesday', when households, and especially kitchens, are cleansed of any yeast left overs on the day before the Lenten period (repentance and penitence) starts on Ash Wednesday). His appeal is, *let us, therefore, celebrate the festival, not with the old leaven, the leaven of malice and evil, but with the unleavened bread of sincerity and truth.*

Paul then goes on to outline his earlier letter that dealt with associating with immoral persons – see Section 1 in the brief analysis and commentary above.

The second issue that he picks up is the matter of community members going to the civil courts against one another – **6:1-11**. Paul insists that disputes are to be settled within the community rather than go before Gentile judges: *when one of you has a grievance against another, do* *they dare to go to law before the unrighteous instead of the saints?* The Roman system permitted one to go to court against someone of equal or lower social ranking; those in higher social circles could not be taken to court by those of lower status. So, going to court meant that they were taking equals or lower status persons to court while the real culprit, the higher class, were not affected at all. It was an unfair system that ensured that the lower classes would not get justice, so it would have been better to settle disputes within the community, ensuring justice for all. He then invokes an apocalyptic picture of saints judging the world, even angels, and if this is what they are going to do, then *are you incompetent to try trivial cases? can it be that there is no one among you wise enough to decide between members?* He then goes on to give a list of vices that the Corinthians were guilty of – a list that leaves nothing to be proud about! But these have to be left behind for they have no place in the *kingdom of God* (a rare occurrence of the phrase 'kingdom of God' which is found often on the lips of Jesus in the Gospels).Paul was not advocating sweeping matters under the carpet or not washing dirty linen in public, but he was making the point that the Corinthians should grasp the opportunity to demonstrate the power of grace and justice to those outside the community by resolving disputes within the community. This would be a mission strategy to demonstrate grace at work and so settling disputes within the community would be seen as a witness to the gospel and a form of evangelism.

The third issue is that of freedom – *all things are lawful for me* (παντα μοι ἐξεστιν) – **6:12-20**. This seems to have been a popular slogan in Corinth justifying their behavior which Paul counters with *but not all things are helpful* (ἀλλ οὐ παντα συμφερει). The license for freedom that the Corinthians thought they had is immediately stopped by Paul: *the body is not meant for immorality, but for the Lord, and the Lord for the body….your bodies are members of Christ…you cannot therefore make it a member of a prostitute….* Sexual immorality of various degrees from visiting prostitutes, homosexuality, and other practices was high on the list of vices in Corinthian society, only they did not think that these practices were vices; this was part of their background with which they were comfortable and which they were bringing into the new community.

But they were being taught that in the new community to which they now belonged, these practices were unacceptable because *do you not know that your body is a temple of the Holy Spirit... so glorify God in your body.* So, it is not a matter of doing what one pleases as *all things are lawful for me,* but it is a matter of what builds up the body as an instrument demonstrating the presence of God in every word and action.

7:1-40 Answers to written questions – Marriage, Divorce and Mixed Marriage

In the next few chapters, Paul sets out his answers to the written questions (περι δε ὧν ἐγραψατε) brought to him from the Corinthians by Stephanas, Fortunatus and Achaicus (16:15-17; see I Corinthians above). The first of the topics deals with marriage and sexual relationships both within and outside of marriage (it is interesting how much of I Corinthians is given over to topics relating to sexual relationships; in a permissive and promiscuous society, this was certainly a problem – administratively, theologically, and pastorally – and ethical norms had to be laid down).

7:1-7 deals with marriage in general. Paul states that both partners in the marriage have equal conjugal rights over each other: *the husband should give to his wife her conjugal rights, and likewise the wife to her husband.... the wife does not rule over her own body, but the husband does; likewise the husband does not rule over his own body, but the wife does.* Sexual relationships in marriage are mutual, even abstinence for a season, but this not lead to loss of self-control. Paul wishes that all were like him: *I wish that all were as I myself am* (θελω δε παντας ἀνθρωπους εἶναι ὡς και ἐμαυτον). This statement has given rise to much speculation – was Paul married, or divorced, or living apart, or a bachelor, or one who has taken vows of celibacy? Paul does not answer the question in any of his writings nor is there any information from Acts. An important point is that Paul sees both partners in a marriage as having equal status – bound to each other in submission and commitment.

7:8-9 is advice to the unmarried and widows – *it is well for them to remain single as I do* (he still does not answer the question regarding his marital status). But if they are unable to control their passions, it is better for them to marry.

7:10-11 is advice to the married – husband and wife should not divorce/separate, but if they do, they should remain single.

7:12-16 deals with mixed marriages. Mixed marriage (believer and non-believer) is not a ground for divorce. The unbelieving husband or wife can be an instrument for communicating the gospel to their partner; *wife, how do you know whether you will save your husband? Husband, how do you know whether you will save your wife?* However, in the event that the unbelieving partner wants to separate, it may be done in the interests of maintaining peace in the community and in personal relationships.

7:17-24 – the advice to remain in whatever state one is: *was anyone at the time of his call already circumcised? Let him not seek to remove the marks of circumcision...was any uncircumcised, let him not seek circumcision...were you a slave? Never mind. Were you a free person? You are now a slave of Christ.... so in whatever state each was called, there let them remain with God.*

7:25-40 – Paul's own advice which is somewhat apocalyptic – expecting the early return of Christ at the end of history – therefore to change one's state would be a waste of time and an exercise in futility: *I think that in view of the impending distress it is well for a person to remain as they are....the appointed time has grown very short...the form of this world is passing away.* The unmarried are anxious about the affairs of the Lord while the married are anxious about worldly affairs; whereas *good order is to be maintained and to secure your undivided devotion to the Lord.* Therefore, people should remain in whatever state they are in unless there are passions and circumstances beyond one's control, then order and ethical behavior is to be maintained. He ends by stating, *I think that I have the Spirit of God.*

The chapter shows that Paul views behavior in marriage, and outside of marriage, as an important part of one's witness to the gospel and a lifestyle that reflect Christian discipleship. Even if this is only for a short interim period, nevertheless ethical norms must be consistently followed.

8:1-13 Answers to written questions – Food offered to idols

Paul starts by putting aside 'knowledge' which tended to induce a superior attitude; instead he advocates an attitude of 'love' which builds up: *all of us possess knowledge; knowledge puffs up, but love builds up.* So, having set this as the perspective by which to approach the subject, Paul talks about an everyday matter which has become an issue of separation/division among the Corinthians – *the eating of food offered to idols.*

His first response is theological – *an idol has no real existence…for us there is one God, the Father, from whom are all things* (ἐξ οὗ τα πάντα) *and for whom we exist, and one Lord, Jesus Christ, through whom are all things* (δι οὗ τα πάντα) *and through whom we exist.* It is a theocentric (God centered) and diachristic (through Christ) statement. This response supports his statement that there are no idols nor is there any challenge to the omniscience and omnipotence of God.

Paul's second response is at a more everyday level – some are accustomed to eating meat slaughtered in the name of an idol (probably the only meat available in the market), but *we are no worse off if we do not eat, and no better off if we do.* The factor to be considered is what he began with – love – *take care lest your liberty become a stumbling block to the weak… food should not become a cause of my fellow believer's falling.* Paul realizes that the only meat available in the markets would have been slaughtered in the name of a god or goddess (somewhat like *halal* (where the animal is slaughtered slowly and the blood is allowed to flow out, as per Jewish and Muslim regulations) *and jatka* (where the slaughter is in one stroke) meats sold in Indian markets) so the confusion was whether it was proper to eat such meat. This does not just pertain to meat, but to all foods that have been offered in worship. In India this would include the response to eating sweets or other special preparations especially at festival times – *Prasad* – receiving and eating food as a sign of God's blessings and favour. Paul advises that the attitude and perspective should be to build one another up rather than cause another to stumble because of one's choices. Therefore, the choice to eat meat/food or not should be determined on how such a choice would affect the other person; love is to be the central criteria.

9:1-27 Answers to written questions – Apostolic Defence

Paul defends his rights as an Apostle possibly in response to questions raised as to whether he is an apostle or not. He has seen the risen Lord and his work is proof of his apostleship: *if to others I am not an apostle, at least I am to you, for you are the seal of my apostleship in the Lord.* Paul could have asserted his status as an apostle by demanding to be fed, and supported, and accompanied by a wife: *those who proclaim the gospel should get their living by the gospel,* i.e. a missionary/preacher should be supported by the local community just as other employees like farmers, soldiers, herdsmen are supported by their trades. Instead, *we have not made use of this right, but we endure anything rather than put an obstacle in the way of the gospel of Christ.* So, he supported himself (a tent making ministry) in order that he *may make the gospel free of charge, not making full use of my right in the gospel.*

This mission strategy allows him to be free from any unwritten agendas that people may have had and permitted him for the sake of the gospel, to be a *slave to all. To the Jew I became as a Jew, in order to win Jews; to those under the law I became as one under the law that I might win those under the law. To those outside the law I became as one outside the law.... that I might win those outside the law...I have become all things to all people, that I might by all means save some.* Paul's strategy is that he was first and foremost a missionary and that he has struggled to remain faithful to his calling: *woe to me if I do not preach the gospel.* He uses the imagery of athletic competitions which would have been very familiar to the Corinthians due to the Isthmian games held there from time to time (somewhat like the Olympic games). He subjected himself to this grueling discipline *to pommel my body and subdue it, lest after preaching to others I myself should be disqualified.*

10:1-33 Answers to written questions – Lessons from Israel's history and warning against idolatry

Paul cites the exodus story of being led under *the cloud* passing through the Sea (Ex. 14:19-22) as a form of baptism and then refers to eating *the same supernatural food and all drank the same supernatural drink* – obvious references to manna which was supplied daily and the drinking water from the Rock(Ex. 16:1-17:7). These events from Israel's history are re-interpreted in terms of baptism and eucharist: *the Rock was Christ.* But in spite of these acts of God, the people did evil and were punished. This should serve as a warning *not to indulge in immorality as some of them did and were destroyed...we must not put the Lord to the test as some of them did and were destroyed...these things happened to them as a warning...they were written down for our instruction, upon whom the end of the ages has come...So, take heed.* But Paul is confident that *God is faithful and will not let you be tempted beyond your strength, but with the temptation will also provide a way of escape, that you may be able to endure it.*

Paul then goes on to supply some important insights into sacramental theology – baptism and eucharist – in which God meets the believer and sustains the believer, yet still holds the believer accountable for their sin and liable for punishment. Participation in baptism and eucharist is irreconcilable with participation in idol worship: *therefore, my beloved, shun the worship of idols...the cup of blessing* (eucharist) *which we bless is it not a participation in the blood of Christ? The bread which we break, is it not a participation in the body of Christ?* (images from the Passover liturgy explained in the relevant gospel sections in Vol. I) *...You cannot drink the cup of the Lord and the cup of demons. You cannot partake at the table of the Lord and the table of demons.* Again, Paul appeals to the community to build one another up: *let no one seek their own good, but the good of their neighbour.* This approach permits community members to share meals among themselves and with outsiders without having any problem about meat/food having been offered to idols: *so, whether you eat or drink, or whatever you do, do all to the glory of God* (παντα εἰς δοξαν Θεου ποιειτε). *Give no offence to Jews or to Gentiles or to the church of God...* The guiding principle/criteria should always be whether social relationships and behaviour bring glory to God.

11:1-16 Answers to written questions – Women in worship

This section raises some difficult questions in the light of modern-day women's movements with regard to women in worship. Two backgrounds should be understood before exegeting the passage: first – the place of Jewish women in society and worship. The rabbinic interpretation of Gen. 2:18-22 was used in Jewish circles to show that women were inferior to men and were therefore subordinate to men, both socially and in matters related to worship. Secondly – women in the Greco-Roman world where they were treated as equals; however, women who were temple prostitutes (those who indulged in sexual acts with men as symbolic of uniting with the god/s) often displayed unusual behavior when possessed by the spirit. In a state of ecstasy, they would untie their hair, or let it come loose; uncovered heads, disheveled hair and swaying movements of the head were typical signs of ecstasy in the spirit. So loose hair and/or uncovered heads would indicate that the woman was either a prostitute or engaged in the ecstatic worship of the mystery cults. Such an interpretation, or traditional understanding accepted by society, would have defeated the purpose and meaning of Christian worship; hence the problem and Paul's response.

Paul starts with praising the Corinthians for maintaining the *traditions* (παραδοσεις) *as I have delivered* (παρεδωκα) *them to you*. 'Tradition' is an important concept here; Paul will also talk about another tradition later in the chapter. Paul first gives the traditional theological response that *the head of every man is Christ, the head of a woman is her husband, and the head of Christ is God… man was not made from woman, but woman from man…*This is the traditional Jewish understanding, with the Christological addition, that covering the head in worship for women, or uncovered heads for men, brings honour to the head of the person, not the person themselves. It is the traditional understanding of the Gen. 2:18-22 story which shows God as having created man and woman in different ways and which is used to justify the social and religious position that women are subordinate to men. In other words, gender difference was part of God's plan for humanity, and so must be preserved. Hence a man should look like a man – short hair and head uncovered – and a woman should look like a woman – long hair and head covered. However, Paul is aware of the changed scenario in Christ where all are equal before God, so he gives a very clear statement, the only explicit statement in the New Testament, that men and women are equal and should live in mutual interdependence: *nevertheless, in the Lord woman is not independent of man nor man of woman; for as woman* *was made from man, so man is now born of woman. And all things are from God.* Paul overturned the traditional argument of the chronological priority of man (that man was created first) by pointing out that the chronological priority of woman in the birth of a male is as much a part of God's plan for the order of God's creation. Gender equality of male and female was the issue that was established.

Thus, Paul's advice on the issue of women's behaviour in worship is not to resort just to the traditional Jewish or Greco-Roman understanding only, but to go beyond that – to develop the criteria for attitudes in worship by evaluating one's behaviour in the light of Christ and equality before God: *we recognize no other practice, nor do the churches of God.*

11:17-34 Answers to written questions – The Lord's Supper

In chapter 10 Paul had taken up the issue of sacramental theology – baptism and eucharist;in the second half of Chapter 11, he returns to the theme of eucharist and the meal in which it was set. The divisions that had come up amongst the Corinthians were carried over into their observance of the Lord's Supper: *when you assemble as a church, I hear that there are divisions among you...when you meet together it is not the Lord's Supper that you eat. For in eating each one goes ahead with their own meal, and one is hungry and another is drunk...Shall I commend you in this? No, I will not!* Presumably, a common meal preceded the liturgical re-enacting/ remembrance of what Jesus said and did on the night he was betrayed; at this common meal (pot-luck, i.e. each brings something to share), *those who have nothing are excluded and humiliated,* and so go hungry; this lack of concern for others who do not have excludes the meal from being the Lord's Supper. This practice may reflect that the house in which the community assembled was small, so that only a few could be accommodated in the eating area, but then it would have been the duty of the host to see that all participated in the meal, not just a few who were of equal or higher status than the host. This show of inequality and lack of sharing at a meal that affirmed that Christ died for all could not be accepted by Paul.

Paul affirms that he has *delivered* (παρεδωκα) what he had *received* (παρελαβον) – the same words that he had used earlier in chapter 10. Paul is stating that the liturgical observance/remembrance of the events on the night that Jesus was betrayed had already become a tradition (written in the mid-50's, this was at least 15 years before the first gospel was written and already being referred to as 'tradition', so the liturgical remembrance was a very early Christian tradition). It was to be observed in all solemnity and without social distinctions for at the Lord's table all were one. The observance seems to have a fixed formula – tradition – for the institution of the elements of the meal: *on the night that he was betrayed…my body which was given for you…. the new covenant in my blood…* The observance of this ritual is to be done again and again, *for as often as you eat this bread and drink the cup, you proclaim the Lord's death until He comes.* So, for Paul, the Lord's Supper was not just a liturgical observance/ritual, but also a proclamation – a preaching, a witness, to the Gospel. In this sense therefore, Paul calls for a self-examination before participation in the Lord's Supper: *whoever eats the bread or drinks the cup of the Lord in an unworthy manner will be guilty of profaning the body and blood of the Lord.* The whole purpose of the sacred breaking of the bread is koinwnia– fellowship/commonness – not to highlight social or theological divisions of the community, *whoever , therefore, eats the bread and drinks the cup of the Lord in an unworthy manner will be guilty of profaning the body and blood of the Lord…. Anyone who eats and drinks without discernment, brings judgment upon themselves.* So, his final advice, as in all other situations, is that they should be considerate of one another – *when you come together, wait for one another.*

12:1-31 Answers to written questions – The gifts of the Spirit and the body of Christ

Chapters 12 and 14 deal with the gifts bestowed on the community by the Spirit, gifts which seem to have caused problems because the possessor of a particular gift feels that he or she is better off than one who does not possess it. So, the place of these gifts in the life of the community had to be put into perspective. (See also note on *glossalalia* – γλωσσαλαλια – below).

The first thing to be noted is that no one can say *"Jesus be cursed!"* *And no one can say "Jesus is Lord"* except by the Holy Spirit – the Spirit controls all speech.

The second point to be noted is that *there are varieties of gifts* (χαρισματων εἰσιν). The Greek word *charisma* that is used means 'grace', so these are 'grace gifts'; they are not something that one acquires on one's own merit; they are undeservedly – grace – given by God.

The third point to be noted is that all these gifts come from *the same Spirit; and there are varieties of service, but the same Lord; and there are varieties of working, but it is the same God who inspires them all in everyone.*

The fourth point is that since the source is the same, there is also a unity in the gifts – *to each is given the manifestation of the Spirit for the common good.* The gifts – *charismas* – may be given to individuals, but the *charisma* is to be exercised within the community for building up the community.

A list of the various gifts – *charismas* – is given, but some who have one gift want another and so the metaphor of the human body has to be given to emphasize unity – *just as the body is one and has many members, and all the members of the body, though many, are one body, so it is with Christ.* There is a basic unity in the diversity of many members as by one Spirit all were baptized into one body – *Jews or Greeks, slaves or free, all were made to drink of one Spirit.* For Paul, the sacraments, and their understanding in sacramental theology, were the unifying factors in the community. So a particular member of the body cannot opt out of the total body structure – *if the foot should say, "because I am not a hand, I do not belong to the body", that would not make it any less a part of the body....there are many parts but one body...God has so adjusted the body... that there may be no discord in the body, but that the members may have the same care for one another.*

This metaphor of the unity of the body (a metaphor from Stoicism used to explain the unity of the political system as against factionalism) is applied to the community – *you are the body of Christ and individually members of it.* In the light of this unity of *charismas* there are also offices to which people are appointed: *apostles, prophets, teachers* etc… All cannot have the same office; it is necessary to have this diversity of *charismas* and offices in the unity of the body in order that the body may function properly. The community as the body of Christ where each part has to function according to its role in order for the body to hold together is a very powerful image to express the unity of the community (from Greek philosophical systems). It can be inferred from chapter 12 that *charismas* and offices in the community had become a troublesome feature as one was thought to be more superior than the other; the 'charismatic', 'led-by-the-spirit' sort of behavior and worship which had infiltrated the Corinthian community would only result in chaos, indiscipline and finally disintegration; Paul saw that this danger had to be avoided. The *charismas* were not being belittled or discriminated against but were being seen from the perspective of the whole community with emphasis on interdependence and recognition of the fact that not all members possess gifts and offices: the basic message is that all the *charismas* and offices are needed for the common good and to build up the community.

13:1-13 The Hymn to Love as an answer to factionalism:

As all commentators state, this chapter contains some of the most beautiful lines penned by Paul and has a poetic ring to it, hence the title "hymn". Paul uses the word *agape* – ἀγαπη – throughout the chapter to refer to divine love, the sacrificial love of God in Christ, the love that confers goodness on the object loved without thought of reward or reciprocation. In this chapter, Paul personifies love and makes it the subject of many verbs, almost making love and Christ interchangeable. The believer becomes a channel of passing that love on to others, not evaluating their goodness and without motivation.

Paul brings out this concept of love to emphasize *a still more excellent way* to use the *charismas* in the community – all gifts find their proper place in serving others in love; it is the essential quality of Christ and therefore of the Christian life. All speech, even the language of angels, has no value without love: *if I speak in human tongues and of angels, but have not love, I am a noisy gong or a clanging cymbal.* Even the gifts of prophecy and knowledge have no value without love; self-denial and sacrifice of one's body is nothing without love. The qualities that love exhibits are:

- Patience and kindness

- Not jealous, boastful, arrogant, rude

- Does not insist on its own way

- Is not irritable or resentful

- Does not rejoice at wrong, but rejoices in the right

- Bears all things, believes all things

- Hopes all things, endures all things

- Love never ends even when other things pass away

- Love is perfect and when love comes the imperfect will pass away

- Now there is only a dim reflection, but when love comes, then things will become clear

- Now there is only partial knowledge, but when love comes knowledge will be complete.

In the end, *faith, hope and love abide, these three...* faith and hope will be absorbed/will come to fruition in the coming of the kingdom; only love will remain as the basis for all relationships – *the greatest of these is love.* What Paul had always advised in practice – to love one another as the binding force in the community – he now articulated as a principle – faith in Jesus alone did not make a person a Christian; a believer had to live in love – *without love I am nothing* and a believing community had to exhibit the qualities of love in their relationships; love is the sole binding imperative of the new community in Christ, the salient feature of Christ's humanity, and therefore the only true quality that remains because it is the very essence of the Christian life – *faith, hope and love abide....but the greatest of these is love.*

14:1-40 Answers to written questions – Speaking in tongues and order in worship

Paul picks up the issues that he left off at the end of chapter 12and continues to talk about speaking in tongues which seemed to have been a very divisive issue. Perhaps this was so because it was the most visible of the *charismas*. Paul critiques the situation in several ways:

1. *One who speaks in a tongue speaks not to people but to God….*

2. *Those who speak in tongues edify themselves….*

3. *The one who prophesies is greater than the one who speaks in tongues….*

4. *Speaking in tongues requires an interpreter otherwise it is not beneficial….*

Paul's critique was a direct answer to the spirit-people who had infiltrated the community and who insisted that speaking in tongues was the ultimate demonstration of a person having received salvation. He contrasts speaking in tongues with the gift of prophecy:

1. Tongues benefits the individual, prophecy benefits the whole community;

2. Tongues edifies the individual, prophecy edifies the whole church;

3. Prophecy is a higher gift than tongues as tongues are not beneficial unless there is someone to interpret.

4. Tongues does not help unbelievers – *if they hear, will they not say you are mad?* but prophecy is for both, believers and unbelievers; believers will be built up, and unbelievers will be convicted and corrected and will worship God declaring that *God is really among you.*

He asks the rhetorical question: *if I come to you speaking in tongues, how shall I benefit you…. unless I bring you some prophecy?* His answer is: *if you in a tongue utter speech that is not intelligible, how will anyone know what is said? For you will be speaking into the air…. if I do not know the meaning of the language, I shall be a foreigner to the speaker and the speaker a foreigner to me…* He advises that *since you are eager for manifestations of the Spirit, strive to excel in building up the church.* The criterion for the exercise of a gift is always for the good, the building up, of the community: and the answer to his rhetorical question is: *in church I would rather speak five words with my mind, in order to instruct others, than ten thousand words in a tongue.*

Modern charismatic movements from the 19th century onwards exhibit a variety of *charisms*, but the greatest attention is paid to speaking in tongues. Paul's corrective to the Corinthian situation is as valid today, as it was in Paul's time, and should be paid attention to when there is a challenge, and when the only criteria for being a Christian is to speak in tongues.

The sort of disorder that speaking in tongues caused when they came together for worship had also to be corrected: *when you come together, each one has a hymn, a lesson, a revelation, a tongue, or an interpretation. Let all things be done in order for edification.* There follow instructions for proper order to be maintained in worship so that all are edified rather than allow confusion to prevail *for God is not a God of confusion but of peace.*

There are strong restrictions mentioned about women participating in worship: *women should keep silence in the churches...they are not permitted to speak...let them ask their husbands at home...shameful for a woman to speak in church.* This is in direct contrast to Paul's earlier stand on women in worship (see section on 11:1-16 above, and Women in Ministry below). It can only be assumed that the ecstatic experiences of the Greek religions which focused around women's behavior in worship, were being incorporated into Christian worship and were a cause of problems, so a word of correction was in order. But the corrections here cannot be taken as the Pauline normative teaching as it contradicts other passages in which women are equal partners with Paul in the task of the gospel.

Finally, Paul asserts that what he is writing is a *command of the Lord.* This is a rare use of his apostolic authority because on other occasions he exhorts/appeals to them to follow his teachings. Perhaps this "command" is indicative of the fact that he felt strongly about the issues of speaking in tongues and order in worship which he could see were divisive forces and a threat to the unity and witness of the

Church: *so earnestly desire to prophesy, and do not forbid speaking in tongues, but all things should be done decently and in order.*

15:1-58 Answers to written questions – the Resurrection of the dead

This chapter is one of the few occasions when Paul comes close to but does not actually narrate the story of the historical Jesus. His narration is still an interpretation: *in what terms I preached to you the Gospel, which you received, in which you stand, by which you are saved.* These "terms" are that Paul *delivered* (παρεδωκα) *to you as of first importance what I also received* (παρελαβον)…both words were used earlier (chapters 10 and 11) to describe the passing on of tradition (the development of the oral tradition – see Vol. I for detailed discussion). The contents of what was being passed on was the purpose of the death of Christ in accordance with the scriptures (i.e. Hebrew scriptures), burial, resurrection and resurrection appearances. Along with the tradition in 11:23ff concerning the Lord's Supper on the night that he was betrayed, it shows that a tradition regarding Jesus' earthly career, especially the Passion Narrative (see relevant passages from the Gospels in Vol. I) was developing alongside Paul's preaching even though this preaching did not depend on the historical veracity of the events. This chapter was an explanation about those who have died in Christ, but it has become the main focus of the Pauline theology of the reality of the resurrection of Jesus and therefore the resurrection of believers. The tradition passed on was that the risen Jesus *appeared to Cephas, then to the Twelve* (the tradition forgets that Judas was supposedly dead and that his successor had not yet been elected/appointed; nevertheless "Twelve" was the normal way of referring to the disciples/apostles). *Then he appeared to more than five hundred people at one time* (incident not found in the Gospels) …*then he appeared to James* not found in the Gospels). This indicates that the developing tradition went beyond the historical facts as known from the Gospels. However, after quoting the tradition, Paul includes himself: *last of all, as to one untimely born, he appeared also to me* – the only New Testament writer to claim to have personally witnessed an appearance of the risen Lord (however, it is to be noted that Paul does not attach this appearance to his conversion as done by the author of Acts). This appearance is connected with his mission – he considers himself *the least of the apostles, unfit to be called an apostle, because I persecuted the church of God. But by the grace of God I am what I am....* He then goes on to list his missionary endeavours and that he worked harder than anyone else. For Paul, the appearances of the risen Lord to him forms the background of his later arguments in the chapter on the resurrection of the body even if the body is transformed.

The reason for the detailed arguments on the resurrection was that *how can some of you say that there is no resurrection from the dead?* Paul's answer is that *if there is no resurrection from the dead, then Christ has not been raised; if Christ has not been raised, then our preaching is in vain and your faith is in vain ...Then those who have fallen asleep in Christ have perished.* He is quick to affirm that *in fact Christ has been raised from the dead.* He then makes a contrast between Adam and Christ: *in Adam all die; in Christ shall all be made alive. The first man Adam became a living being; the last man Adam became a life-giving spirit.* Paul outlines the eschatological picture of the end when *the last enemy to be destroyed is death,* then the Son will hand over the kingdom to God *that God may be everything to everyone.* To be noted is that no eschatological time-table is proposed, just the surety of an eschaton and an order of events: first Christ, then those who belong to Christ, then Christ hands over the kingdom to God and the Son will also be subject to God.

Paul contends that all the dead are to be raised, that the resurrection is future, and bodily; those who have fallen asleep in Christ are not lost because Christ is the first fruits of those who have fallen asleep. Resurrection was not an abstract issue for Paul rather resurrection was an expression of hope which sustains the person in the face of persecution: *what do I gain if, humanly speaking, I fought with beasts at Ephesus if the dead are not raised?* (the letter was written from Ephesus where Paul faced persecution).

The next question he deals with is *how are the dead raised? With what kind of body do they come?* His answer is one the greatest classical statements on the resurrection of the body: *what is sownis perishable* (φθορη), *what is raised is imperishable* (ἀφθαρσια). *It is sown in dishonor, it is raised in glory; it is sown in weakness, it is raised in power. It is sown a*

physical body (ψυχικον), *it is raised a spiritual body* (πνευματικον)....
Resurrection will involve a transformed body, both for the living
and the dead – imperishable, powerful, spiritual, in the image of the
heavenly, for *flesh and blood cannot inherit the kingdom of God, nor does the*
perishable inherit the imperishable.

In the final verses of the chapter (part of the liturgy of the resurrection
used in every funeral service), Paul talks of the resurrection as a mystery
– something that cannot be fully explained this side of the grave but
which can only be thought of in eschatological language/terms: *we*
shall all *be changed...twinkling of an eye...last trumpet.* But he ends with
the absolute assurance and shout of triumph that *when the perishable*
puts on the imperishable, and the mortal puts on immortality, then shall come to
pass the saying "death is swallowed up in victory. O death where is thy victory?
O death where is thy sting?" The sting of death is sin... but thanks be to God
who gives us the victory through our Lord Jesus Christ.

In the light of all his arguments and the assurance of the
resurrection, he exhorts the Corinthians to *be steadfast, immovable, always*
abounding in the work of the Lord, knowing that in the Lord your labour is
not in vain.

16:1-24 Closing instructions and greetings

The closing section of 16:1-4 is an appeal to the Corinthians to take
up the collection for Jerusalem and gives instructions how to go about
it in the same way as he had instructed the churches in Galatia: *As I*
directed the churches in Galatia, so you also are to do. On the first day of every
week, each of you is to put something aside.... Weekly savings were certain
to produce a greater sum than a onetime donation at short notice.
An important aspect of the collection is the example of Paul's role:
he is not responsible to collect the funds and not responsible for
safeguarding and delivering the funds: *when I arrive, I will send those whom*
you accredit by letter to carry your gift to Jerusalem. If it seems advisable that I
should go also, they will accompany me. Paul was involved only to the extent
of providing the motivation for the collection and to provide a letter
of reference if he did not accompany the representatives (despite these
precautions, he would later be accused of pilfering the funds – see section on II

Cor. 10-13); it was the responsibility of the representatives for seeing to it that the funds were delivered to those for whom it was meant.

Paul outlines his plans to visit Corinth and to spend the winter there, but for the moment he will stay in Ephesus: *perhaps I will stay with you and even spend the winter...for I do not want to see you in passing, I hope to spend more time with you...I will stay in Ephesus until Pentecost.* His stay at Ephesus was between 54-57, so possibly he is writing in the spring of 54-55. The visit that he was planning would have been the second visit to Corinth after the first founding visit, however, it was conditional: *if the Lord permits.* Paul mentions that further opportunities for evangelization have opened up: *a wide door for effective work has opened to me...*The Corinthians seemed to have missed the conditionality and would later accuse Paul of inconsistency in his planning.

Timothy, one of Paul's co-workers and known to the Corinthians, is to be treated well when he arrives: *see that you put him at ease among you....let no one despise him...speed him on his way in peace...* Apollos, another co-worker, had somehow found an objection to visiting Corinth (perhaps the factions/divisions caused by his 'intellectual/wisdom' approach was still fresh in his mind). The concluding greetings were warmly sent and included the exhortations to be *watchful, stand firm in your faith, be courageous, be strong. Let all that you do be done in love...I rejoice at the coming of Stephanas, Fortunatus, Achaicus...the churches of Asia send greetings, Aquila and Prisca together with the church in their house...greet one another with a holy kiss.... my love be with you all.* Paul adds the final greetings with his own hand and closes with an ancient formula of hope in the original Aramaic – *Marana tha* (μαρανα Θα) – *Our Lord Come.*

3.   II Corinthians 10-13 – the Letter of Tears mentioned in II Cor. 2:4

(read introduction to the Corinthian correspondence along with the literary and historical analysis above)

During Paul's second visit to Corinth (the first visit being the founding visit) some tension seems to have arisen between Paul and the community (II Cor. 13:2). The result is that Paul's second visit ended in disaster (see II Cor. 2:5-11; 7:12); he had to leave Corinth in great distress and write a severe letter – *I wrote to you out of much affliction and anguish of heart and with many tears* (ἐκ γαρ πολλης θλιψεως και συνοχης καρδιας ἐγραψα ὑμιν δια πολλων δακρυων) *not to cause you pain but to let you know the abundant love that I have for you* (II Cor. 2:4). It is suggested that this 'Letter of Tears', either in whole or in part, is found in II Cor. 10-13. The letter was sent with Titus (II Cor. 12:18; II Cor. 7:6-7 mentions Titus' return with the good news that the Corinthians had received him well).

This second visit must have occurred after the writing of I Corinthians, for in that writing there is no indication of strained relations. The earlier chapters of II Corinthians shows a reconciliation between Paul and the Corinthian community, so it is hardly possible that a completely different writing like that of II Cor. 10-13 could have been the conclusion of the celebratory chapters of II Cor. 1-9. This leaves the following conclusions: Paul left Corinth after his second visit, which resulted in difficulties and tensions between him and the Corinthians, perhaps he returned to Ephesus and wrote the 'letter of tears' which was sent through Titus. The 'letter of tears' can be dated A.D. 55-56. Though these four chapters are emotionally intense, they provide a great deal of autobiographical information that contributes towards the understanding of Paul, the person, his life, his mission.

II Cor. 10:1 – 13:10: Since the whole section holds together under a single theme of Paul's defence of his apostolic authority in answer to criticisms being leveled against him, it would be methodologically proper to look at the whole section as a single unit, rather than piecemeal. In chapters 10-13, Paul makes a defence of the authority *which the Lord gave for building you up and not for destroying you* (10:8; 13:10) and therefore he threatens to be severe when he visits Corinth for the third time (10:2,6,11; 12:14; 13:2).

There is a sudden change in tone from 10:1ff.; the previous chapters were affectionate and suggested a warm relationship between Paul and the Corinthians; but now suddenly there are reproaches and sarcastic self-vindication and a strong defence of the challenges to his apostolic authority. There have been *superlative apostles* (11:5; 1211) undermining Paul at Corinth portraying him as weak and unimpressive and a poor speaker, but uses strong language when writing from a distance; there is also the matter of financial assistance: the *superlative apostles* did not like the idea of Paul supporting himself as the tradition was that a true apostle should be supported by the community; further they cast aspersions on his character that he was helping himself from the funds being raised for Jerusalem. But as far as Paul was concerned they were *false apostles and servants of Satan* (11:13-15) who will be punished. What these false apostles were successful in achieving was that they drew out of Paul the longest and most impassioned description of his own apostolic service. Paul counts his apostolic authority not in terms of his great achievements or numbers converted or churches established, but on the promise he received when he asked the Lord to remove the *thorn in his flesh* that "*my grace is sufficient for you* (ἀρκεῖ σοι ἡ χαρις μου), *for my power is made perfect in weakness". I will all the more gladly boast of my weaknesses, that the power of Christ may rest upon me. For the sake of Christ, then, I am content with weaknesses, insults, hardships, persecutions, and calamities; for when I am weak, then I am strong* (12:7-10). Paul sets a new standard for assessing service to the Lord – although *the signs of a true apostle were performed among you in all patience, with signs and wonders and mighty works* (12:12), he lays much more stress on the following as signs of a true apostle and of which he could boast: *far more imprisonments, with countless beatings, and often near death. Five times I have received at the hands of the Jews the forty lashes less one. Three times I have been beaten with rods, once I was stoned. Three times I have been shipwrecked, a night and a day I have been adrift at sea; on frequent journeys, in danger from rivers, danger from robbers, danger from my own people, danger from Gentiles, danger in the city, danger in the wilderness, danger at sea, danger from false brethren, in toil and hardship, through many a sleepless night, in hunger and thirst, often without food, in cold and exposure* (11:21b-28)......*if I must boast, I will boast of the things that show my weakness* (11:30). These are more important to Paul as an expression of true apostleship and concern for the churches (11:28-29). This enumeration of his apostolic sufferings was not simply a matter of arousing pity for him, but for Paul it was to serve as an example to ensure that divisions and corruption and vilification of him would cease before he visited so that *when I come I may not have to be severe in my use of the authority which the Lord has given me for building up and not for tearing down* (12:20-13:10). So even though he had promised severe disciplinary action in dealing with those causing trouble, Paul's pastoral concern is seen in his hope that there will be repentance.

13:11-14: Therefore, in the concluding formula, Paul can say, *mend your ways, heed my appeal, agree with one another, live in peace, and the God of love and peace will be with you.* The Trinitarian benediction is given at the end (13:14) – a full expression of God, Jesus and Holy Spirit, used in most Christian liturgies even today.

4.   II Cor. 2:14-6:13 and 7:2-16 – Letter of Thanksgiving

(read introduction to the Corinthian correspondence along with the literary and historical analysis above)

There were anxious moments for Paul as to whether the Corinthians would receive Titus well and whether there would be a reconciliation between Paul and the Corinthiansespecially in the light of thesevere letter (see II Cor. 10-13). In II Cor. 2:12-13, Paul indicates that his departure from Ephesus was motivated by his affection for the Corinthians and his desire to have news of them. He went to Troas where he did not stay even though there was the possibility of mission work, then from Troas to Macedonia. Later in II Cor. 7:6-7, 15, Paul expressed the relief he felt at Titus' return with good news that Titus had effected a reconciliation and that all was well between Paul and the Corinthians. His immediate response was to write the letter of thanksgiving and to plan a third visit to Corinth (II Cor. 1:15-16?).The 'letter of thanksgiving' was probably written from Macedonia (it would be difficult to pinpoint the exact location in Macedonia)in mid/end of A.D. 56.

2:14-17: Paul's expression of thanksgiving

The 'letter of thanksgiving' must be read and understood in the light of the Corinthian crisis that prompted the 'letter of tears'. Paul's response and relief at the good news of the restored relationship brings out some remarkable passages and phrases from Paul(these are in italics as quotations from the text), the privilege of apostolic service as a servant of Christ: *the fragrance of the knowledge of him everywhere....we are the aroma of Christ...we are not pedlars of God's word but people of sincerity, as commissioned by God...*

3:1-18: Being continually changed into God's likeness

Are we beginning to commend ourselves again? This is an oblique reference to one of the allegations made against Paul by those who had infiltrated the Corinthian community and caused trouble. He assures them that he thinks of them as *you yourselves are our letter of recommendation, written on your hearts, to be known and read by all...* He goes on to express his confidence in God through Christ of which he is minister *of a new covenant, not written in a code but in the Spirit; for the written code kills, but the Spirit gives life.* Paul compares the life-giving power of the Spirit to that of the written code that kills. He goes back to Israel's history recalling that when Moses came down the mountain with the written tablets of the law, his face shone so much that he had to wear a veil, until the glow faded, so that people could look at him; if this was the case with the written code, then much more *would not the dispensation of the Spirit be attended with greater splendor?* He makes several contrasts with the law and the Spirit finally saying that *if what faded away came with splendor, what is permanent must have much more splendor.* He uses an allegory (the physical veiling of Moses to illustrate the spiritual veiling of Israel) to indicate that Israel still reads the law with a veil over its face, i.e. Israel does not understand the purposes of the law: *their minds are hardened; for to this day, when they read the old covenant, that same veil remains unlifted, because only through Christ is it taken away.* The Lord who is the Spirit lifts the veil and brings a sense of freedom from the law so that *we, with unveiled face, beholding the glory of the Lord, are being changed into his likeness from one degree of glory into another....*

4:1-18: Treasure in earthen vessels

In an indirect reference again to allegations cast on him, Paul talks of the ministry given to him by the mercy of God: *we have renounced disgraceful, underhanded ways; we refuse to practice cunning or to tamper with God's word, but by open statement of the truth we would commend ourselves to everyone's conscience in the sight of God....for what we preach is not ourselves but Jesus Christ as Lord, with ourselves as your servants for Jesus' sake.* Paul refers to human beings as *earthen vessels* (ἔχομεν δε τον θησαυρον τουτον ἐν ὀστρακινοις σκευεσιν), i.e. vulnerable vessels that can break, but he affirms that these earthen vessels contain a treasure – it shows that *the transcendent power belongs to God and not to us.* The 'earthen vessel' is subjected to many onslaughts – despair, persecution, forsaken, etc... but it still does not break; in a series of contrasts (seen/not seen, outer/inner, naked/clothed) Paul explains why he does not lose heart and this is *all for your sake, so that as grace extends to more and more people it may increase thanksgiving to the glory of God. So, we do not lose heart...* His troubles are momentary as compared to the glory to come which will be eternal: *this slight momentary affliction is preparing us for an eternal weight of glory.... the things that are seen are transient, but the things that are unseen are eternal.* Paul lives in the tension of the 'already' (the present) and the 'not yet' (the future); tension because most people are generally on one side or the other, but Paul brings about a balance – the present leads to the future.

5:1-10: A house not made with hands

The tension between the present and future helps him to affirm that when the present passes away, there is still a house with God: *we know that if the earthly tent* (ἡ ἐπιγειος ἡμιν οἰκια) *we live in is destroyed, we have a building from God, a house not made with hands* (οἰκιαν ἀχειροποιητον), *eternal in the heavens....So we are of good courage...* The section ends with the apocalyptic image of the final judgment *so that each one may receive good or evil according to what they have done in the body.*

5:11-15: The love of Christ

The love of Christ is demonstrated in his death and resurrection. It is this love that is the controlling factor, *for the love of Christ controls us... he died for all, that those who live might live no longer for themselves but for him who for their sake died and was raised.* 'The love of Christ controls us' (ἡ γαρ ἀγαπη του Χριστου συνεχει ἡμας) – a summary of Paul's devotion and motivation for ministry.

5:16-19: A new creation

The section is one of the most outstanding statements of Paul: *if anyone is in Christ, they are a new creation* (εἰ τις ἐν Χριστῳ, καινη κτισις)*; the old has passed away, behold the new has come.* There could not have been a better understanding of Paul's own life and an expression of what it means to have received salvation. Added to this is the distinct theological understanding of what God has achieved in Christ's death and resurrection: *God, through Christ, reconciled* (καταλλαξαντος) *us to Godself.* Because of this, the human responsibility is: *(God) has given us the ministry of reconciliation...God was in Christ reconciling the world to Godself* (Θεος ἦ ἐν Χριστῳ κοσμον καταλλασσων ἑαυτῳ) *not counting their trespasses against them, and entrusting to us the message of reconciliation.*

5:20-21: Ambassadors for Christ

The ministry of reconciliation makes the believer *an ambassador* (πρεσβευομεν) *for Christ.* To be an ambassador for Christ is first of all to be reconciled to God through Christ whose death is described as *made him to be sin, who knew no sin, so that in him we might become the righteousness of God* (δικαιοσυνη Θεου). This is a theologically 'loaded' passage outlining the understanding of Christ's work, death, and implications/efficaciousness of that death.

6:1-13: Appeal to the Corinthians

Having outlined his response in a reconciliatory manner, Paul appeals to the Corinthians *not to accept the grace of God in vain...now is the acceptable time; behold now is the day of salvation* (ἰδουνυν ἡμεραν σωτηριας). Paul assures them that he would not put a block in anyone's way to carry out their ministry. He then goes on to emotionally list all the problems that he and his colleagues had faced in the course of carrying out their ministry: *afflictions, hardships, calamities, beatings, imprisonments, tumults, labours, watching, hunger...* He understands all of this as contributing to the richness of their lives and faith: *we are treated as imposters, and yet are true; as unknown, as yet well known; as dying, and behold we live; as punished, and yet not killed; as sorrowful, yet always rejoicing; as poor, yet making many rich; as having nothing, and yet possessing everything.* Paul enumerates all this so that the Corinthians, whom he considers his children, may be encouraged to return the affection he and his team have for them: widen *your hearts also.*

(6:14-7:1: see 'lost letter' above)

7:2-4: Open your hearts

It is clear that 7:2-4 is in continuation of 6:13. In 7:2-4 Paul would like the Corinthians to be open and frank with him just as he has been with them assuring them that, *I have great confidence in you; I have great pride in you; I am filled with comfort. With all our afflictions, I am overjoyed.* Paul comes back to the theme of rejoicing over the good news brought by Titus that there is reconciliation in the relationship between him and the Corinthians.

7:5-16: Relationship with the Corinthians and mission of Titus

Paul returns to outlining his relationship with the Corinthians and how the return of Titus has gladdened his heart; he was restless since there was no news from Titus and had even set out from Ephesus to meet Titus on the way. They met up at Macedonia, but not before there was further anxiety over Titus' delayed arrival: *even when we came into Macedonia, our bodies had no rest but we were afflicted at every turn – fighting without and fear within.* When Titus arrived, Paul breathed a sigh of relief and thanksgiving: *God comforted us by the coming of Titus, and not only by his coming but also by the comfort with which he was comforted in you, as he told us of your longing, your mourning, your zeal for me, so that I rejoiced still more.* Paul makes reference to the 'letter of tears' that grieved the Corinthians, but also understands the letter as a means of rejoicing: *I see that the letter grieved you...I rejoice not because you were grieved, but because you were grieved into repenting... therefore we are comforted.* The 'letter of tears' had had its effect; the individual causing the problems had been dealt with and the relationship between Paul and the Corinthians had been restored. The key person who represented Paul in bringing about the reconciliation was Titus; his role is commended and he has been refreshed by the Corinthians, *we rejoiced still more at the joy of Titus, because his mind has been set at rest by you all,* with the result that *his heart goes out all the more to you, as he remembers the obedience of you all....* Paul ends by expressing, *I rejoice, because I have perfect confidence in you.*

This is a warm letter of thanksgiving putting aside all the issues that caused a problem and much heartache. It shows Paul as an administrator who can be a stern disciplinarian, but also a pastoral person who advises repentance and who can be loving, kind, and supportive of those who repent.

5.   II Cor. 1:1-2:13 – opening epistolary formula and exhortation:

(read introduction to the Corinthian correspondence along with the literary and historical analysis above)

This section of the letter could be seen as the epistolary opening section of the letter of thanksgiving (see 4 above), but the absence of the mention of Titus as the key figure in the reconciliation process is missing which seems to separate this section from the rest of the letter of thanksgiving, unless 2:14-6:13 and 7:2-16 – the 'letter of thanksgiving' (where Titus is a central figure) are added to this epistolary opening. The section could also have stood as either the opening formulae for the letter at chapter 8 (see above) or for the letter at chapter 9 (see above). However, since the contents seem to sum up the whole troublesome period of the relations with the Corinthians and to present Paul's apologetic/explanation for the letter of tears – *not to cause you pain but to let you know the abundant love that I have for you* (II Cor. 2:4), then attaching the section to any letter would unnecessarily rake up issues that were best laid aside since they had already been settled. Therefore, since there are difficulties in attaching this section to any of the three sections mentioned, it would be best to treat this section of paranesis/exhortation as an independent writing.

This paranesis/exhortation section is either simultaneous or shortly after the 'letter of thanksgiving' written from Macedonia and can be dated towards the end of A.D. 56.

1:1-11: Opening formula

The letter is from Paul, *an apostle of Christ Jesus by the will of God, and Timothy, our brother.* Timothy was a known co-worker of Paul and was associated with the community in Corinth (I Cor. 4:17). During Timothy's work in Corinth, the situation there got vitiated against Paul with the arrival of those who spoke against him, and many Corinthians were inclined to side with the outsiders. Timothy went to Ephesus to report the situation to Paul who then visited Corinth, but which resulted in relationships getting even more strained, so Paul had to leave along with Timothy. But now it seems that the problems have been settled and Timothy's role of carrying tales to Paul has been forgiven; hence he is also included in the opening greetings. The letter is addressed not only to Corinth but also to *all the saints who are in the whole of Achaia.* Perhaps this reflects that the issues that caused a break in the relationship were not just local but had spread beyond Corinth. Paul then speaks of the trials he suffered at Ephesus – *the affliction we experienced in Asia* – a situation that highlighted his weaknesses and the comfort of Christ that he had experienced. The opening serves as a background for his recent dealings with Corinth.

1:12-2:13: Dealings with Corinth

Paul outlines his relationship with the community in Corinth *we behaved toward you in holiness and godly sincerity, not by earthly wisdom but by the grace of God.* He writes about the plans that he had to visit Corinth, but plans that he could not carry out due to the situation there and for which an allegation was that he was undependable, *was I vacillating? Do I make my plans like a worldly person ready to say Yes and No at once?* He justifies his change of plans theologically that *in Jesus Christ whom we preached among you, it was not Yes and No; but in Him it is always Yes* ἀλλα ναιεν αὐτῳ γεγονεν). *For all the promises of God find their Yes in Him. That is why we utter the Amen through him, to the glory of God. God establishes us with you in Christ... and put God's seal upon us and given us God's Spirit in our hearts as a guarantee.* So he goes on to say that *it was to spare you that I refrained from coming to Corinth...I made up my mind not to make you another painful visit...* Paul is obviously referring to the second visit to Corinth when he was confronted with opposition and the Corinthians' seeming to side with the opponents which was a very painful situation for him (see historical and literary contexts, above). So instead paying another painful visit to those who should have made him rejoice (a proposed third visit to Corinth), Paul wrote to them instead, *I wrote to you out of much affliction and anguish of heart and with many tears (see 'letter of tears' chs. 10-13, above).* But the purpose of the letter was *not to cause you pain but to let you know the abundant love that I have for you.*

From verses 5 to 13, Paul talks about the pain that was caused. Apparently, it was by a person who seemed to have had enough influence, or rhetoric, or backing of influential persons who cast doubts on Paul's apostolicity, preaching, life style and authority. The person was persuasive enough to sway the Corinthians away from Paul and thus cause divisions within the community. It had created a very disturbing situation especially to Paul, the founder of the community. However, since the person seems to have repented after the 'letter of tears' and Titus' intervention, Paul is willing to forgive the person and asks that the Corinthians also forgive the person: *you should rather turn to forgive and comfort him, or he may be overwhelmed by excessive sorrow. So, I beg you to reaffirm your love for him.... Anyone whom you forgive, I also forgive.* His concern for healing the relations with the Corinthians was so great that he was willing to interrupt his ministry in Troas in order to cross over to Macedonia to await the arrival of Titus from Corinth and the news of the effect of his 'painful letter written with tears': *when I came to Troas to preach the gospel of Christ, a door was opened for me in the lord, but my mind could not rest because I did not find my brother Titus there. So, I took leave of them and went on to Macedonia.* Once again, the administrative/disciplinarian side of Paul tempered with his pastoral concern can be seen in his dealings with the Corinthians; he was a disciplinarian not in a vindictive sense, but with a redemptive intention.

6.   II Cor. 8 – letter to re-start the collection for Jerusalem

(read introduction to the Corinthian correspondence along with the literary and historical analysis above)

In I Cor. 16:1-4, Paul, in response to a request from the Corinthians, had given practical directions to collect money for the church in Jerusalem. However, in the intervening period, and with strained relations between Paul and the Corinthians, the enthusiasm of the Corinthians for the collection for Jerusalem seemed to have suffered especially in the light of factional disputes within the community. Moreover, one of the allegations against Paul was that he had enriched himself through the collection (II Cor. 7:2; 12:16), so until the matter was cleared, the collection had to be placed on hold. In chapter 8, after reconciliation had taken place between Paul and the Corinthians, they are urged to resume work on the collection which had begun over a year ago. Titus is sent with the letter and the recommendation to continue the work of the collection (probably early A.D. 57)

The letter starts with a commendation, and the example of the churches in Macedonia who have made a good contribution: *for in a severe test of affliction, their abundance of joy and their extreme poverty have overflowed in a wealth of liberality on their part. They gave according to their means…and beyond their means, of their own free will ….* This was probably a gentle push to get the Corinthians to do better! Added to this is the example of Jesus himself, *who though he was rich, yet for your sakes he became poor, so that by his poverty you might become rich.* Paul's main concern was that the gift to Jerusalem should reflect equality: *as a matter of equality your abundance at the present time should supply their want, so that their abundance may supply your want, that there may be equality.* Paul then cites, in Rabbinic style (because it does not directly relate to the equality of sharing finances), the experience of the Israelites in the wilderness who always had enough manna to meet their need whether they gathered more or less.

Titus and another *brother who is famous among all the churches for his preaching of the gospe* (II Cor. 8:6, 10, 16-19) were entrusted with the work of raising the collection at Corinth. The 'other brother' is probably to ensure that the allegation leveled against Paul of dipping into the collection for his own purposes is avoided and that there is transparency in the handling of money, *we intend that no one should blame us about this liberal gift which we are administering for we aim at what is honourable not only in the Lord's sight but also in the sight of people.* It is surprising that the 'other brother' is well known for his preaching, but his name is never mentioned. Along with these two is yet another person, *our brother,* who is not named but who seems to have been a well-known figure. This would ensure that accountability and transparency are visible in handling money.

The letter concludes with the appeal *so give proof, before the churches, of your love and of our boasting about you to these persons.*

7.II Cor. 9 – letter expressing urgency regarding the collection for Jerusalem

The collection seems to have resumed, but the work is slow-going. The matter had now become urgent as Paul was on his way to Corinth, along with others, to collect the offering (II Cor. 9:1-5); he urges the Corinthians to donate generously since he had boasted to the Macedonians that Corinth (Achaia) had collected a good amount: *Now it is superfluous to write to you about the offering for the saints, for I know your readiness of which I boast about you to the people of Macedonia saying that Achaia has been ready since last year,..* So, in order not to be embarrassed, Paul sent an advance party: *so I thought it necessary to urge the brethren to go to you before me, and arrange in advance for this gift* (letter probably written in mid A.D. 57).

Paul addresses this issue not as a command or order, but as a *willing* and generous gift: *God loves a cheerful giver* (II Cor. 9:7). Paul outlines a whole theological basis for sharing the abundance of God's blessings (II Cor. 9:10-15) ending with *thanks be to God for God's inexpressible gift.* Whether the Corinthians matched the Macedonians in their gift is not known, but the collection was taken by Paul to Jerusalem (Acts 20-21); probably making this Paul's last visit to Corinth towards the end of A.D. 57.

The collection for Jerusalem was not simply a matter of raising funds; for Paul it had theological implications: sharing with the needy (II Cor. 8:14) as an expression of God's grace and concern for those in need; as a unifying factor that Jews and Gentiles mutually support one another (cf. Gal. 2:9-10); the Gentiles had shared in the Jews' spiritual blessings, so they should share their material blessings with the Jews (Rom. 15:27), so that supporting one another becomes a unifying factor. Above all, it is an expression of God's grace that supplies all material needs and God's grace that prompts a person to share with those who are in need. In this way, a person becomes an instrument of God in providing for the needs of others.

Chapters 8 and 9 along with I Cor. 16:1-4, though each was written separately, show Paul at his best as a fund raiser. He avoids any hint of tension and criticism; instead he sets up an administrative structure for the collection, commends the group, exhorts them, tells them of how he expects the best from them and boasts of them to others, and finally does not order them, but appeals to them to give generously. He sees to it that others – neutral, well known and respected persons – are involved to ensure accountability and transparency in the handling of funds; all lessons that fund raisers, and those who are appointed to exercise financial responsibilities, can learn for today.

Select Bibliography for the Corinthian correspondence

Barrett, C. K. "Paul's Opponents in II Corinthians", *New Testament Studies*, Vol. 17, 1970-71, pages 233-254.

Beasley-Murray, G. R. *2 Corinthians*, Nashville: Broadman, 1971.

Bornkamm, G. "The History of the Origin of the So-called Second Letter to the Corinthians," *New Testament Studies*, Vol. 8, 1961-62, pages 258-264.

_____., Paul, New York: Harper & Row, 1971.

Brown, R. E., An *Introduction to the New Testament*. Bangalore: Theological Publications in India 2000.

Bultmann, R., The *Second Letter to the Corinthians, Minneapolis*: Augusburg, 1985.

Cherian, Jacob. "2 Corinthians", in Brian C. Wintle (General Editor).*South Asia Biblical Commentary*, Udaipur, Rajasthan: Open Door Publication, 2015, pages 1585 – 1614.

Conzelmann, H. *I Corinthians: A Commentary on the First Epistle to the Corinthians.* Hermeneia, Philadelphia: Fortress, 1975.

Furnish, Victor P., *II Corinthians*, Anchor Bible Commentary. Garden City: Doubleday, 1984.

Hanson, R. P. C., *II Corinthians.* London: SCM Press, 1954.

Hering, J. *The Second Epistle of Saint Paul to the Corinthians.* London: Epworth, 1967.

Kummel, W. G. *Introduction to the New Testament.* London: SCM Press, 1975.

Murphy-O'Connor. Jerome *Paul, A Critical Life.* Oxford: OUP, 1996 (1997).

Philip, Finny "1 Corinthians", in Brian C. Wintle (General Editor), *South Asia Biblical Commentary*, Udaipur, Rajasthan: Open Door Publication, 2015, pages 1555 – 1584.

Paul's own letters: C. Galatians

The founding of the community. Authorship / authenticity and integrity. Date and place of writing. Occasion and purpose. Brief analysis and commentary on the text. Select Bibliography for Galatians.

The founding of the community

The *Galatai* had a long and proud history and were related to invaders who had come from Western Europe and who had settled in the area. They were taken over by the Romans after their last king died in 25 B.C. The area became the Province of Galatia with major cities in the South. However, there were ethnic Galatians who were not descendants of the West European invaders and who lived mostly in the northern areas of Galatia – the Territory of Galatia. Since the cities in the South were easily accessible by sea and land routes and used for commerce, they were cosmopolitan cities with people from many areas settling there; also, the Roman headquarters for the Province was situated in the South. Acts 16:6-7 reports that Paul, Timothy, and Silas went through the regions of Phrygia and Galatia (on the so-called Second Missionary Journey), probably referring to places in the North. However, there is no report of missionary activity, but it would seem that there were converts made as Acts 18:23 reports that Paul *went from place to place through the region of Galatia and Phrygia, strengthening all the disciples.*

So, the first question that is raised when dealing with the Epistle to the Galatians is who exactly are the Galatians? The above shows that many complicated theories as to the identity of the Galatians are possible, but simply put there are two dominant theories: 1. the South Galatian or the Province Hypothesis which identifies the populated cosmopolitan cities in the South which lay along the major West-East trade route: Antioch in Pisidia, Lystra, Derbe, Iconium. 2. The North Galatian or the Territory Hypothesis tries to identify cities in the North or District of Galatia which were sparsely inhabited and mostly by ethnic Galatians.

In Acts 13:3 – 14:28, the so-called 'First Missionary Journey' narrates Paul's travels from Antioch in Syria to several places in Asia Minor. The group consisted of Paul, Barnabas and Barnabas' nephew, John Mark. The journey took them through Cyprus, then to the Asia Minor cities of Perga (where John Mark left the group to return home to Jerusalem), Antioch in Pisidia, Iconium, Lystra and Derbe before coming back to Antioch in Syria. The mission strategy was to first preach in synagogues and then move out to others, especially the Gentiles among whom the Gospel was well received. In the cosmopolitan cities of the South, there would have been many Jews and so the presence of synagogues. Paul does not specially mention this journey in any of his letters but in Gal. 2:1-3, Paul recalls having preached to the Gentiles before the Jerusalem Council (*ca.* A.D. 49), so the journey could be dated A.D. 47/48-49. This information from Acts would identify the cities in the South and would lean toward the South Galatian/Province Hypothesis. These communities founded by Paul were re-visited on the so-called Second Missionary Journey (Acts 16:1ff) showing that Paul was closely associated with cities in the South as their founder. Further, in Gal. 2:1, Paul mentions Barnabas who was part of the group on the 'First Missionary Journey' but who, according to Acts 15:36-40 was not part of the group on the 'Second and Third Missionary Journeys', so the inclusion of the name of Barnabas, who would have been known in the South, strengthens the South Galatian or Province Hypothesis. However, in Gal. 3:1 the people addressed are called "Galatians" – a name used only for the ethnic people of the region, and not for the people of the Hellenized cities of the South. Further, in the remote cities in the North which were sparsely populated, there would have been a lesser possibility of the presence of those from Jewish ancestry; but Paul was writing mainly to Gentiles who were being pressurized to first become Jews.

Therefore, there are strong arguments for both hypotheses, but in the final analysis, the message of Galatians is not affected by either hypothesis. Sufficient at this point to say that Paul was the founder of the communities and that as the founder, he wrote to 'Galatia' – South and North – to exercise his prerogative to advise, deal with problems, correct and encourage them.

Authorship and integrity

There have never been any doubts about the authorship and integrity of the Epistle to the Galatians; any doubts have been quickly laid to rest because of the very nature of the writing which is in response to issues faced by Pauline communities of the mid 50s of the first century. **From the earliest traditions, Paul has been acknowledged as the author; Galatians has always been accepted as a genuine letter of Paul.**

Date and place of writing

The relationship of Galatians and the problems outlined in II Cor. 10-13 have usually served to place these two writings close together – problems of people with Jewish backgrounds (Judaisers, perhaps from the Jerusalem and Syrian Antioch centres) who insisted that converts become Jews first, follow all Jewish requirements, and then become Christians, and also questioning Paul's apostolic authority. **Since place of writing and date are closely related, the Epistle to the Galatians could have been written either in Ephesus or Macedonia between A.D. 55-57.**

Occasion and Purpose

In his letter to the Galatians, Paul addresses his converts as 'you' (e.g. 3:1-5), and others as 'some people', 'anyone', 'they' (e.g. 1:7; 1:9; 4:17; 6:13) clearly differentiating between groups and identifying the adversaries as intruders. There is no evidence of what exactly these 'adversaries' were propagating except by mirror-reading, i.e. looking at what Paul had written and trying to frame the issues to which he was responding; in other words, what was the question with regard to the answers that Paul supplied or framing the opposite of what Paul was saying. From this perspective of mirror-reading, the adversaries can be identified as Christians of Jewish origin – they belonged to the 'circumcision' (6:13), preaching another gospel (1:7), i.e. their understanding of what God had done in Christ was different from Paul's; they appealed to Israel's history to substantiate their message (3:6-9); they had their own interpretation of the Law as a means of salvation (3:10-29); they considered their message to the Galatians as 'a gospel' (1:6-9). All these issues point to the adversaries being 'Judaisers' who may have originated in Jerusalem or in Syrian Antioch as these were the great centres of Jewish Christianity. When Paul founded the churches in South Galatia he had been acting as an emissary of Antioch. However, the Antiochian community, under pressure from Jerusalem (2:11-21) had opted for a Judaized version of Christianity which Paul could not accept as he felt that this was being unjust to the Gentile converts and also restricted freedom from the Jewish law. This difference of opinion ultimately led to a complete break between Paul and Antioch, resulting in Barnabas going separately with John Mark and Paul taking Silas for further missionary work (see also section on Paul's life and work, above). This break in the relationship probably led the Antiochian group to thinking that areas that had been evangelized by Paul, while he was their representative, now no longer came under the authority of Paul and so their attempt to take over. Thus, when the Judaisers made their appearance in areas which had been evangelized by Paul (e.g. Corinth and Galatia), Paul had to write strongly to defend the gospel that he had preached and continued to uphold. As far as Paul was concerned, the Judaisers were intruders and had no business interfering in his areas of work especially when he did not interfere with others' areas of work (1:16-17; 2:9; Rom.15:20-21). The methodology of the Judaisers was two-fold and was directed to both those of Jewish origin and those of Gentile origin:

1. They had to undermine the authority of Paul; they had to discredit him (a good example is the mirror-reading of II Cor. 10-13, above). These intruders held that the Jerusalem leaders, and by extension the Antiochian leaders (all from Jewish backgrounds), were the only persons with authority to define and preach the true gospel (1:6-9, 11-12), and that they too had the best interests of the Gentiles at heart. They felt that Paul was assuming too much authority and was mistaken in his claim that he alone possessed the truth; the law-free gospel that he was preaching had no basis as it was his own interpretation and that he did not receive it from the apostles in Jerusalem(1:13-2:10; 5:1-12; 6:11-15); in fact they publicly disapproved of Paul's behavior and encouragement of the

Gentiles as shown in the confrontation between Peter and Paul over Jewish dietary laws (Gal. 2:5-11).

2. They had to put across their version of Christianity: they could not simply say that Paul was wrong; they had to provide a viable alternative. They began with the history of Israel and the story of Abraham being called to be a blessing to all nations (Gen. 12:3). Abraham was a convert, so he was given the sign/commandment of circumcision (Gen. 17:10) and Rabbinic interpretation holds that though Abraham did not have the law, nevertheless he observed all the precepts of the law and all Jewish rituals. Later the law was given through Moses (Gal. 3:1-29) and the coming of the Messiah confirmed God's law revealed to, and observed by Abraham, and spoken through Moses. They claimed that Jews were the descendents of Abraham through Isaac, and that the Gentiles were descendants of Abraham through Ishmael, thus both are actually siblings. The descendants of Ishmael are to cast off their enslavement to the evil one and turn in repentance to God and follow God's commandments just as Abraham did – i.e. observe circumcision and all the laws and festivals, including dietary laws (Gal. 2:11-14; 4:10; 6:13). The differences that appeared among the community members was put down to the fact that Paul did not give them the proper gospel nor a guide map of how to tackle issues, thus unless they are fully incorporated into Abraham (Gal.3:29) as Abraham's descendants, and observe all the Jewish requirements, they cannot truly benefit from the Messiah's coming. Such was the alternate presentation of the gospel through Jewish Christianity – a presentation and understanding that went completely contrary to Paul's presentation and understanding. In a sense, Paul's message of freedom from the law left the Galatians, and other Pauline communities, at a loss as to how to tackle issues of right and wrong, what rituals were needed to correct transgressions etc... This freedom was in fact frightening because it left the converts rudderless, and in such a situation, going back to the law would have provided a steadying influence. Paul had to write against such presentations and outline his own rabbinic interpretation of the Abraham/Sarah/Isaac/Hagar/Ishmael stories.

Therefore the occasion and purpose of the letter to the Galatians, whether in the North or in the South, to counter the work of the Judaisers was two-fold: 1. To preserve the unity of the church which was threatened by the disruptive work of the intruders; and 2. To restore the credibility of Paul as an apostle of the message of freedom from the law.

Brief analysis and commentary

1:1-5 Opening formula

Paul designates himself as *an apostle* (Παυλος ἀποστολος) – *not from humans nor through humans, but through Jesus Christ and God the Father.* It is as though Paul is immediately establishing his credentials as an apostle and emphasizing that he was not appointed by any human authority; the true source of his apostleship is Jesus Christ and God. As indicated in the introduction to the letter, Paul's apostolicity and message were under attack and therefore offense was the best form of defence. He does not mention the names of co-workers who were with him, only a general reference to *all the workers who are with me.*

To the churches of Galatia (ταις ἐκκλησιαις της Γαλατιας): As suggested above, the best understanding of this phrase would be to understand it to refer to both the cosmopolitan communities/churches in the South as well as the more predominantly ethnic Galatian communities/churches in the North.

Verses 3-5 is a passage which is the gospel that Paul preached in a nutshell. He was under attack, and so his opening formula was not a thanksgiving (as customary in other letters), but a statement of belief and a Christology that finds its roots in theology: *our Lord Jesus Christ, who gave himself for our sins* (του δοντος ἑαυτον ὑπερ των ἁμαρτιων ἡμων) *to deliver us from the present evil age, according to the will of our God and Father* (κατα το θελημα του Θεου και πατρος ἡμων)...

1:6-10: Introduction to the occasion for the writing

The letter starts with an expression of astonishment: *I am astonished that you are so quickly deserting him who called you...and turning to a different* gospel (ἕτερον εὐαγγελιον)... Paul gets right to the point and outlines the issue and seriousness of the case: *not that there is another gospel but there are some who trouble you and want to pervert the gospel of Christ. If anyone should preach a gospel contrary to that which we preached to you, let them be accursed.* Paul felt very strongly about those creating a problem in the churches in Galatia; the gospel that they were preaching was contrary to what Paul had preached and which had been accepted by the Galatians.

1:11-2:21: Details, arguments, explanations

Using the rhetorical pattern, Paul asks a series of questions which he answers himself and offers as an apologetic (explanation). It is almost as though Paul is using the rhetorical pattern that was common in the Roman courts – the preachers who have come into Galatia with a 'different' gospel are the accusers, Paul is the defendant, and the Galatians are the judge. To appreciate this courtroom style presentation, the occasion and purpose of the writing (as given above) should be kept in mind.

The first point that Paul makes is that *the gospel which was preached by me is not from human beings* (οὐκ ἐστιν κατα ἀνθρωπον)*; I did not receive it from humans, nor was I taught it, but it came through a revelation* (ἀποκαλυψεως) *of Jesus Christ.* To illustrate this claim, he narrates the story of his conversion experience – before and after – from a persecutor of the church *extremely zealous for the traditions of my fathers* (referring to both the written and oral laws of Judaism) to an equally zealous missionary, *when God who had set me apart before I was born, and called me through God's grace, was pleased to reveal God's son to me, in order that I might preach him among the Gentiles, I did not confer with flesh and blood, nor did I go up to Jerusalem to those who were apostles before me...* Paul does not give details of the "revelation" he received but probably this came through an understanding of God's act of salvation in Jesus rather than in a dramatic form as presented in Acts (Acts 9:1-19; 22:6-16; 26:12-18) – an understanding that widened the sphere of God's salvific act to include the Gentiles. The point being made was to show that Paul was independent of the church leaders in Jerusalem.

An interesting point that is made here is that Paul was *still not known by sight to the churches of Christ in Judea; they only heard it said, "he who persecuted us is now preaching the faith he once tried to destroy"* …. Interesting because Acts 7:58 narrates that Paul was present at the stoning of Stephen and that the people recognized him: *and the witnesses laid down their garments at the feet of a young man named Saul.* This is an issue in methodology that the autobiographical statements given in Paul's own writings are to be preferred over information given in secondary sources as these sources have their own narratives and points to make.

Paul goes on to present his defence referring to his post-conversion experience that Jerusalem had approved of (not in the sense of giving permission but in the sense of agreement) his presentation of the gospel which he preached to the Gentiles and that they did not insist on circumcision, *even Titus who was with me was not compelled to be circumcised though he was a Greek* (compare this with Acts 21:17-26 which has Paul bowing to Jewish pressure to observe the requirements of the law)....*because of false preachers secretly brought in that they might bring us into bondage – to them we did not yield submission even for a moment, that the truth of the gospel might be preserved for you.* Further, recognizing that Paul had been entrusted with the gospel to the uncircumcised just as Peter had been entrusted with the gospel to the circumcised, *James and Cephas and John, who were reputed to be pillars, gave to me and Barnabas the right hand of fellowship...* So, Paul's defence is that though he did not receive his commission and message from humans, nevertheless, he had been recognized by the highest possible human authorities, the closest disciples of Jesus; this verifies his claim that his apostleship came directly from God, so *they glorified God because of me.*

Paul then links those who had come from Jerusalem to Antioch claiming to represent James (tradition holds that he was the brother of Jesus and head of the Jerusalem church; James the disciple had been beheaded by Herod Antipas – Acts 12:1-2) with those who had come to Galatia and were causing the same problem. Paul is particularly severe in his reference to Peter (using his Jewish name of Cephas indicating that he was talking particularly about those with a Jewish background who reneged on the agreement made earlier when the group from Jerusalem arrived, *before the group came from James, he (Peter) ate with the Gentiles, but when they came he drew back and separated himself, fearing the circumcision party. With him the rest of the Jews acted insincerely, and even Barnabas...* This caused a major split: Paul parted ways with Barnabas and dissociated himself from the Antioch centre to set out on his missionary work alone and without the support of a mission body. He goes on to justify his stand on the issue, *we are Jews by birth...yet we know that a person is not justified* (δικαιουται) *by works of the law but through faith in Jesus Christ...by works of the law shall no one be justified...I died to the law that I might live to God... if justification were through the law, then Christ died to no purpose.* This was a very strong defence of Paul's gospel and the agreements reached with the group from Jerusalem; Paul is in no mood to compromise on his basic theological understanding of freedom from the Jewish law.

3:1-4:31: Further rhetoric and refutation of the Judaisers

Paul presents six arguments to convince the foolish Galatians who have been bewitched! (see above where these arguments were mirror read to understand the Occasion and Purpose of the writing):

1. 3:1-5: when Paul proclaimed Christ crucified, the Galatians accepted the message and received the Spirit without observing the works of the law. *Are you foolish* to think that the works of the law can now be made necessary? He had earlier said that he cannot return to the law because he had died to the law.

2. 3:6-14: The Judaisers kept referring to the circumcision of Abraham (Gen. 127:10, 14), so Paul pointed out that the promise to Abraham that all the nations would be blessed (Gen 12:3) was given independently and before Abraham was circumcised and that he received the promise in faith which was counted as his righteousness. So, in giving the Spirit to the uncircumcised Gentiles, God is fulfilling the promise to Abraham: *that in Christ Jesus the blessing of Abraham might come upon the Gentiles, that we might receive the promise of the Spirit through faith.*

3. 3:15-25: He gives the example of a human will, which once ratified, cannot be annulled by later additions. The law was

given 430 years after Abraham, therefore how can the promises given to Abraham depend on observing the law? *The law which came four hundred and thirty years afterward, does not annul a covenant previously ratified by God, so as to make the promise void. For if the inheritance is by the law, it is no longer by promise; but God gave it to Abraham by a promise.* The law was only temporary because of transgressions until the coming of Christ: *the law was our custodian until Christ came, that we might be justified by faith.... now that faith has come, we are no longer under a custodian.*

4. 3:26-4:11: Since the Galatians who were once *slaves to the elemental spirits of the universe (that which by their very nature were not gods, and observing days, and months, and seasons, and years)* have experienced redemption by God's Son, *who was born of a woman, born under the law, to redeem those who were under the law, so that we might receive adoption as God's children,* why do they again want to become slaves to the demands of the law? Since they are free from the law, *there is neither Jew nor Greek, there is neither slave nor free, there is neither male nor female; for you are all one in Christ Jesus* (οὐκ ἔνι Ἰουδαιος οὐδε Ἕλλην οὐκ ἔνι δουλος οὐδε ἐλευθερος οὐκ ἔνι ἀρσεν και θηλῦ παντες γαρ ὕμεις εἰς ἐστε ἐν Χριστῳ Ἰησου).

5. 4:12-20: The Galatians had treated Paul very well, like an angel, so how could he have now become their enemy as the outsiders were making him out to be? *It was because of a bodily ailment that I preached the gospel to you at first; and though my condition was a trial to you, you did not scorn or despise me, but received me as an angel of God...Have I then become your enemy by telling you the truth?...I am perplexed about you.*

6. 4:21-31: The Judaisers appealed to Abraham, Hagar, Sarah, Ishmael and Isaac, but came to the wrong conclusions. Ishmael, the son of Hagar the slave woman, *was born according to the flesh.* Isaac, the son of Sarah a free woman, *was born through promise.* Paul uses the methods of rabbinic exegesis (assuming much more than what is in the text) and interprets the stories of these women as

an allegory: they represent two covenants – Hagar the covenant at Sinai (the law given through Moses); she represents the earthly Jerusalem (Judaism) which was still in slavery to the law. Sarah on the other hand, represents the heavenly Jerusalem of those who have inherited the promise and are free from the law, i.e. all those in Christ, *we, like Isaac, are children of promise.... we are not children of the slave, but of the free woman.*

Paul raises these six rhetorical questions, in the diatribe question-answer method to show that the Galatians should not be "bewitched" and should not be "foolish". The arguments are strongly worded and indicate Paul's anger and frustration at the Galatians and at the Judaisers who caused the trouble.

5:1-6:10: A passionate exhortation

After the arguments Paul finishes the letter with a passionate exhortation: *for freedom Christ has set us free; stand fast therefore, and do not submit again to a yoke of slavery.* He again emphasizes that circumcision is not necessary, i.e. it is not necessary to become Jews first and then Christians; there is also the warning that becoming a Jew first entails keeping the whole law and also implies that the person is cut off from Christ: *the person is bound to keep the whole law. You are severed from Christ, you who would be justified by the law; you have fallen away from grace.* He again re-iterates that *in Christ Jesus neither circumcision nor uncircumcision is of any avail, but faith working through love,* making it clear that circumcision is not evil but rather something that has no power to bring salvation whether to Jews or to the Gentiles. He expresses his anger against those who are leading the Galatians astray in the strongest possible terms: *those who are troubling you will bear their judgment, whoever they are...I wish who unsettle you would mutilate themselves!* (ὄφελον καὶ ἀποκόψονται οἱ ἀναστατοῦτες ὑμας).

Paul views adherence to the law for salvation as a form of slavery and insists that Christ has set the believer free from the law its slavery: *you were called to freedom, do not use your freedom as an opportunity for the flesh.* As in his other epistles, Paul talks of love as the quality that binds people together and love that should be the controlling factor in all relationships: *through love be servants of one another. For the whole law is fulfilled in one word,* "you shall love your neighbour as yourself". He gives a list of the *works of the flesh* – immorality, impurity, licentiousness, anger etc.... – probably taken over from Stoic lists which emphasized morality and ethical behavior. In a rare use of the phrase, he warns that *those who do such things shall not inherit the kingdom of God.* He then goes on to give a list of qualities that believers are expected to exercise: *the fruit of the Spirit is love, joy, peace, patience, kindness, goodness, faithfulness, gentleness, self-control; against such there is no law.* These are the qualities that should determine how one relates to God and to other human beings – expressions of love. *Let us not grow weary in well-doing, for in due season we shall reap, if we do not lose heart.... let us do good to all....*

6:11-18: Conclusion

Even in the conclusion of the letter, written in his own hand, Paul emphasizes and re-iterates his position against circumcision indicating that he felt very strongly about those who were insisting on the law as it was against his very basic understanding of the salvation that God had made possible in Christ: *far be it from me to glory except in the cross of our Lord Jesus Christ...neither circumcision counts for anything, nor uncircumcision, but a new creation – the Israel of God* ('Ισραηλ του Θεου). The last phrase– *Israel of God– is* a unique way of describing those who now constitute God's family and does not occur in any other letter of Paul. He ends again with a personal reference, *let no one trouble me; for I bear on my body the marks of Jesus* – what Paul has suffered as an apostle is more important for him than the marks of his circumcision! This short epistle, but fervent appeal expressing his views on freedom from the law ends with his benediction of *the grace of our Lord Jesus Christ.*

In the letter to the Galatians, Paul was forced to deal with the problem of the Judaisers and the implications that it would have for the Church – a problem that he had not encountered till then and which forced him to clearly articulate his stand on justification by faith and freedom from the law as a means of salvation. The Epistle to the Galatians therefore exhibits the issues that the churches were facing in the 50's of the first century, including the Epistles to the Romans and I & II Corinthians, issues that seemed to have been settled by the end of the 50's/mid-60's as later epistles do not raise this problem. The troublesome issue of the Judaisers and Paul's response to it is what distinguishes letters that come from Paul's own time from the later deutero and trito Pauline writings.

Select Bibliography for Galatians

Barrett, C. K. *Freedom and Obligation: A Study of the Epistle to the Galatians.* London: SPCK, 1985.

_____. Paul: *An Introduction to his Thought.* London: Chapman, 1994.

Betz, H. D. *Galatian: A Commentary on Paul's Letter to the Churches in Galatia.*, Hermeneia, Philadelphia: Fortress, 1979.

Brown, R. E. *An Introduction to the New Testament.* Bangalore: Theological Publications in India, 2000.

Bruce, F. F. The *Epistle of Paul to the Galatians: A Commentary on the Greek Text.* Exeter: Paternoster, 1982.

Finny, Philip "Galatians" in Brian C. Wintle (General Editor), *South Asia Biblical Commentary.*Udaipur, Rajasthan: Open Door Publication, 2015, pages 1615 – 1630

Murphy-O'Connor, Jerome Paul, *A Critical Life.* Oxford: Oxford University Press, 1996.

Paul's own letters:
D. Philemon

Occasion and purpose. Authorship and integrity. Date and place. Brief analysis and commentary on the text. Onesimus in the tradition of the Church. Select bibliography for Philemon.

The letter to Philemon stands closest in form to ancient Hellenistic private letters and is also the shortest of the Pauline letters (335 words). However, it is not to be evaluated simply as a letter from one person to another asking for a favour. Paul is writing as one who has sacrificed his freedom for Christ – *a prisoner for Christ Jesus* – to ask for another's freedom; he is writing to the head of a house-church and by implication to all the members of the congregation meeting in that house-church. Therefore, the underlying tenor of the letter is the challenge to the normal master-slave relationship because of the changed relationship brought about by the gospel. Thus, while the background of the master-slave relationship must be understood to appreciate the letter, it is also important to note that the thrust of the letter is its theological dimension. It is probably this thrust/focus that brought this private letter into the canon of the New Testament.

It would be appropriate to understand slavery in the time of the mid-first century to appreciate the context of the letter. Slaves were an accepted part of society in the Roman Empire; they were owned by the wealthy class and business houses. The ownerhad complete control over the slave; the slave (male and female) was either brought to the city as a prisoner of war, or kidnapped by slave hunters as there was a flourishing slave market in most cities, or were enslaved due to debt (bonded labourers), and children born to slaves also became slaves; slaves were bought and sold at the slave market, sometimes bought in distant cities and transported. They were entrusted with household chores, business dealings (those who were literate) and any other work which the owner assigned to them or required them to do (including the demand for satisfying sexual desires of family members and at orgies); mostly they were assigned the heavy manual labour of construction work, mining, road building, and farming. Those engaged within the household or in business administration were the favoured ones and from among them many bought their freedom or were set free by the families as a reward of honest and loyal work. A slave was severely punished for any misdemeanor, refusal to work, or attempts to escape, either by having to serve a prison sentence if reported to the law enforcement, or enduring some form of, usually brutal, meted out personally by the owner. However, a slave could appeal to a friend of the owner who could intercede on behalf of the slave so that punishment was waived, and the slave could be restored to his/her previous position.

Occasion and Purpose

The letter to Philemon presupposes that Philemon, Apphia and Archippus (Philemon's wife and son? or daughter and son? or son and daughter-in-law? or daughter and son-in-law?) were a wealthy family who owned at least one slave, Onesimus, and whose house was large enough to have congregational meetings and also the provision of a guest room (*prepare the guest room for me* – verse 22). Paul seems to have met Onesimus in prison (presumably a prison in a city other than where Philemon lived); to be presumed is that Onesimus was in prison for an offence other than running away (he would have been sent back if he had been caught for that offence). Under the influence of Paul, Onesimus became a Christian. Also, to be presumed is that Onesimus was already familiar with Paul through the family connections and the house-church, so finding himself in the same prison emboldened him to seek Paul's help in returning to his master. Onesimus had *wronged you* and so had probably run away to escape punishment. Paul would *have been glad to keep him (Onesimus) with him (Paul),* but Paul observed the legal right which Philemon had over his slave and so sent Onesimus back. Paul's volunteering that if Onesimus owed Philemon anything then, *charge that to my account* may indicate that there was some financial matter involved. Thiswas the immediate factual situation, but Paul's theology was always developed from ground realities, so the new life in the gospel shared by Paul, Philemon and Onesimus became the basis for a theological response to a social issue. Thus, the letter to Philemon was the appeal to welcome Onesimus back *no longer as a slave but more than a slave, as a beloved brother.... receive him as you would receive me.*

The letter to Philemon is a test case for the views on slavery: the author does not say that slavery should be abolished and thereby he would have started a political and social revolution, but the author calls for a new human relationship which transcends the social acceptance of slavery. There are other passages such as I Cor. 7:20-24, Col. 3:22ff, and of course, the passage in Gal. 3:28 where *there is neither Jew nor Greek, there is neither slave nor free, there is neither male nor female; for you are all one in Christ Jesus.* There is no direct call for the liberation of Onesimus, but the author is confident that the Christian faith transcends social barriers of status in the community, so *I am confident of your obedience, I write to you, knowing that you will do even more than I say* is a clear command that the author is directing Philemon to release Onesimus.

Since much of the letter has the same setting and the same people mentioned, as the letter to Colossians (Paul, a prisoner – Col. 4:10-18, Phlm. 1, 9, 23; Timothy accompanies Paul – Col. 1:1; Phlm. 1; Epaphras and Aristarchus – Col. 4:10-12; Phlm. 24; Mark – Col. 4:10; Phlm. 24; Luke – Col. 4:14; Phlm. 24; Onesimus – Col. 4:9; Phlm. 10-12 etc…in both Archippus is among the recipients – Col. 4:17; Phlm.2), it is often suggested that the letter to Philemon is the "lost" letter to the Laodiceans mentioned in Col. 4:16. Epaphras seems to have been the founder of the church at Colossae and also the churches at Laodicea and Hierapolis (Col. 4:12-13); all these towns came within the province of the Lycus Valley of which Ephesus was the capital city. The instruction in Col. 4:16, a*nd when this letter has been read among you,* have *it read also in the church of the Laodiceans, and see that you read also the letter from Laodicea,* is understandable if the two churches are close by and share the same context. It is also suggested here that since there was a commonality between the two churches, then in instructing the Colossians to read Laodiceans (letter to Philemon), is the attempt to muster up support for the issue of the release of a slave which would have affected individuals, community, and society at large, and therefore a supportive group would have been essential to defend the questions that would have been raised.

Philemon is a small letter, but its message had far reaching consequences, socially, legally, and in its theological expression when dealing with the issue of slavery. It is a challenge to a Christian slave owner to defy social norms: to forgive and receive back a runaway slave, to refuse financial reparation when offered mindful of what one owes to Christ, and to go further in generosity by freeing the slave, making the most important theological point of a new relationship as a *beloved brother*. It is no wonder then that this small letter has been preserved and referred to again and again in political, social, and religious history.

Authorship and Integrity

No serious question has been raised with regard to the authenticity of Philemon. The letter is well attested from the end of the first century and included in all Pauline canons; even Marcion who edited much of the New Testament to suit his purposes includes the writing. and since many do not hold to Paul's authorship of Colossians but attribute it to the Pauline school of thought, it is often felt that Philemon too should be placed in the category of deutero-Pauline and pseudonymous writings. But the question of why to include such a small writing with a very limited, though important, perspective is not adequately answered. Therefore, regardless of the position taken *viz a viz* Colossians, **Philemon is, and has been, considered as a genuine letter of Paul, because in it, he actually puts into practice what he has theorized about with regard to relationships and justification by faith.**

Place and Date

For all of its importance, the letter to Philemon does not specifically mention the place of writing which would help in determining the date of writing. Paul writes as *a prisoner for Christ Jesus.... I, Paul, an ambassador and now a prisoner also for Christ Jesus....* Paul himself does not mention the places of imprisonment, but three possibilities arise from Acts – Ephesus, Caesarea, Rome.

Ephesus was close to Colossae where Philemon was located (Epaphras of Colossae knows the recipients of the letter well enough to send greetings – Phlm. 23; Onesimus was from Colossae – Col. 4:9; Archippus of Colossae is among the recipients of both letters - Col. 4:17; Phlm.2); the large number of mission workers mentioned in both Colossians and Philemon show that the two letters were probably written around the same time and context; the letter to Philemon was sent through Tychicus and Onesimus along with the letter to the Colossians (Col. 4:7-9). Hence information from one letter can be used to supplement that of the other. Further, Ephesus being close by would have been the ideal place for Onesimus to find refuge; the instruction to prepare a guest room for him (Paul) would also suggest that he was not far from Colossae.So, this is an attractive suggestion for the place of writing – Paul's nearby physical presence would have enhanced his position as that of an apostolic authority whose directions were to be unquestionably followed. However, the following issues are raised with regard to an Ephesian origin:

1. There is no attestation of Paul having been in prison for an extended period in Ephesus;

2. The presence of Luke is contested as he is nowhere listed as being with Paul in Ephesus;

3. The presence of John Mark is contested as Acts 15:17-39 shows that Mark had not accompanied Paul since the so-called second missionary journey and may only have rejoined the Pauline group in Rome (II Tim. 4:11).

So, Ephesus is a good possibility, but it cannot be uncontested.

Paul was imprisoned in Caesarea for two years, 58-60, while he awaited trial before the Roman authorities (Acts 24:27). The argument regarding John Mark is also valid for Caesarea. Further, Caesarea was a long distance away from Colossae, so Onesimus' running away to Caesarea becomes doubtful.

The final imprisonment of Paul was in Rome, A.D. 62 onwards. The amount of freedom granted to Paul to receive guests etc... (Acts 28:30-31) would have been an occasion to meet Onesimus and others from Colossae and to send letters with them. However, the distance to Rome for Onesimus to travel would make Rome an even more unlikely place of writing.

In conclusion then, it is not possible to pin-point the place of writing as each suggestion has several valid objections. If it is Ephesus (as in the traditional point of view) then the dates would have to be between A.D. 53-57; if Caesarea, then between A.D. 58-60; or if Rome then between A.D. 62-64.

Brief analysis and commentary

1-3: Greetings

It is only in this letter that Paul introduces himself as *a prisoner for Christ Jesus* (δεσμιος Χριστου Ἰησους); his usual introduction is "apostle" or "servant". The recipients of the letter are *Philemon, Apphia, and Archippus....and the church* (ἐκκλησια) *in your house.* The reference to the house-church has given rise to much speculation as to the relationship of the three individuals one to another (see above), but this is hardly a major point. The reference to *the church in your house* would suggest that the letter is to be read to the congregation as well. Paul may well have been aware that the case of Onesimus would not only have consequences for Philemon but would also affect the social structure of the congregation as the slave had now become a Christian.

4-7: Thanksgiving and Prayer

Paul gives thanks because he *has heard of the love and faith which you have toward the Lord Jesus and all the saints.* In these opening verses, Paul has tactfully prepared the ground for the request that he is about to make!

8-20: Request on behalf of Onesimus

Paul avoids using his apostolic authority to make a demand, or *bold enough in Christ to command you to do what is required* but makes his request, *for love's sake I prefer to appeal to you.* Paul stresses his imprisonment as a further testimony of his sufferings in order to gain Philemon's sympathy. Onesimus had become a Christian through Paul's ministry though details are not given; Paul refers to him as *my child* (ἐμου τεκνου) *whose father I have become in my imprisonment.* Onesimus had *indeed become useful to you and to me.* So, Paul is sending Onesimus back to Philemon even though he would have been glad to keep him. Paul says, *I preferred to do nothing without your consent in order that your goodness might not be by compulsion but of your own free will.* Paul is quite confident that Philemon will receive Onesimus with open arms rather than punish him for what he had done.

In this confidence, Paul delivers the *coup d'état*, the main request which may have had disturbing consequences: *you may have him back no longer as a slave, but more than a slave, a beloved brother* (οὐκετι ὡς δουλον ἀλλα ὑπερ δουλον ἀδελφον ἀγαπητου) ...*receive him as you would receive me.* Paul even volunteers to repay whatever it is that Onesimus had stolen or from some behavior for which he had run away. There is no sense of condoning Onesimus' behavior, but there is a sense of seeing that there was a dramatic change in Onesimus; as one who had undergone a dramatic change in his own life, Paul could sympathetically recognize this change in others. The position of a slave in a household was being overturned by the idea of receiving Onesimus as a "beloved brother"; socially, Onesimus can now be on equal terms with his former owners. This is where the community – "the church in your house" – would have to play a role. Would Philemon take the risk of alienating his friends and the larger society by breaking accepted social norms, of sitting with, eating, and conversing with a slave? But Paul is *confident of your obedience.* Indeed, Paul goes a step further: *I write to you knowing that you will do even more than I say* (εἰδως ὅτι και ὑπερ ἅ λεγω ποιησεις). So, while Paul does not advocate the abolishing of slavery or even to request that Onesimus be freed (which is a criticism that Paul faces in the letter to Philemon), he has more than clearly suggested that in Christ there is a new relationship which supersedes societal norms. Thus, he proposes a theology of the Christian response to slavery that arises out of a concrete situation (see above); in Pauline thought, personal justification by faith must also empower others to be justified by faith – the whole of creation has to be brought into a salvific relationship (Rom. 8:22-23).

21-25: Final remarks and closing greetings

Paul closes with a sign of friendship, *prepare a guest room for me.* Such an expression of a close relationship shows that there is an incredible confidence that Philemon will do as requested. There is a final list of greetings from those who were with Paul, many of whom are also mentioned in the letter to the Colossians.

This brief letter is a vivid expression and example of applying the teachings of the Gospel where love is the factor that forgives, restores and reconciles relationships.

Onesimus in the tradition of the Church

Paul may have written many personal letters to individuals, but why was this one preserved? A strong tradition in Ephesus and Colossae was that Onesimus was released by Philemon and returned to work with Paul in Ephesus remaining there even long after Paul was dead. Ignatius of Antioch (late first century/early second century), addressing the Ephesian church states that *in the person of Onesimus, a man of love beyond recounting and your bishop*. It is this witness that gave rise to the tradition that Onesimus was the bishop of Ephesus at the end of the first century/beginning of the second century. However, Ignatius' reference would have been about 40-50 years after Paul, and Onesimus would have been an old man by then (retired) with more of a revered states person presence (*a man of love beyond recounting*) rather than actual hands-on administration (active/in office) expected of a bishop. One attractive hypothesis is that in his retired years, Onesimus made a collection of the Pauline writings with Ephesians as the preface, and out of esteemed memory of the person who had made his career possible, Onesimus lovingly included the letter to Philemon which he had treasured all these years, and which had made his career possible. This is an attractive and sentimental hypothesis, but it is totally without any proof. In fact, it is more possible that the Onesimus being referred to by Ignatius was another person who had taken the name of his revered predecessor.

Apart from the personalities involved and the hopeless task of proving anything, probably the best reason for including Philemon in the canon is that it has an ecclesial significance rather than a purely personal one. Paul's theology was always based on the issues being faced by a congregation, and Philemon is no different. Hence in the address, Paul greets *Philemon, Apphia, Archippus, and the church in your house*. The letter to Philemon raises an important pastoral and theological issue of receiving a run-away slave on terms that would place him as an equal – as *a beloved brother*. Such an issue, and its social implications, would have involved community support not only among the small group that met in the home of Philemon, but in wider society in Colossae (see comments above on Col. 4:16).

It is this that makes the characters in Philemon so endearing; and it is this that provides the enduring character of the letter. However, if the tradition that comes from Ignatius has any substance, then in Onesimus, the Church had one of its first leaders who had risen from the lower ranks   of society yet provided a pastoral leadership which is still an example today when dealing with the issues of slavery, bonded labourers, and dalits.

Select Bibliography for Philemon

(see also Select Bibliography for Ephesians and Colossians)

Knox, J. *Philemon Among the Letters of Paul.* Nashville: Abingdon Press, 1959.

Kummel, W. G. *Introduction to the New Testament.* London: SCM Press, 1975.

Peterson, N. R. *Rediscovering Paul: Philemon and the Sociology of Paul's Narrative World.* Philadelphia: Fortress Press, 1985.

Sanyu Iralu "Philemon" in Brian C. Wintle, (General Editor), *South Asia Biblical Commentary,* Udaipur, Rajasthan: Open Door Publications, 2015, pages 1705-1707.

Wintle, Brian C. and Bruce J. Nicholls.*Colossians and Philemon,* Asia Bible Commentary, Singapore: Asia Theological Association, 2005.

CHAPTER - 4

An Introduction to the Deutero-Pauline Letters

A. Ephesians B. Philippians C. Colossians D. The Thessalonian Correspondence — I & II Thessalonians. Authorship / authenticity and integrity, date, purpose. Brief analysis and commentary on the text of each of the letters. Select bibliography for each letter.

Deutero-Pauline:
A. Ephesians

The founding of the community. Authorship / authenticity and integrity. Occasion and purpose of the letter. Date and place of writing.

Brief analysis and commentary on the text. Select bibliography for Ephesians.

Founding of the community

After the altercation with Peter and the split with Antioch – a split that had clearly demarcated Jewish Christianity and Gentile Christianity (see earlier chapters for details) – and probably in the spring of A.D. 52, Paul took Silas and departed on the so-called Second Missionary Journey (Acts 15:40). It was on this journey through the southern cities of Galatia, Philippi, Athens, Troas and Corinth that Paul came to Ephesus, the leading city in the administrative area of Asia (Asia Minor). The city was located on the western coast of Asia Minor and the seat of the Roman proconsul; it was the site of the Temple of Artemis one of the seven wonders of the ancient world (Acts 19:23ff gives the narrative of Paul in Ephesus and the protest led by the followers of *Artemis of the Ephesians*); there was also a huge theatre built by the Romans which could seat more than 24,000 people; hence Ephesus was a major city for religious pilgrimage as well as for conducting official business at the seat of the proconsul, and a tourist spot. The city was strategically located and a good choice for a mission centre; the surrounding cities of Asia Minor and Achaia – Galatia, Thessalonica, Corinth, Philippi, Antioch in Psidia – which had been evangelized by Paul were easily accessible. Acts 19:8-10 says that Paul's first stay there was two years and three months and Acts 20:31 says that his second stay was for three years. When Paul headed for Ephesus n A.D. 52, it was not his first visit; he had briefly stopped there after founding the church in Corinth (Acts 18:18-19) and he had left Prisca and Aquila there to carry on the work (Acts 18:23-28). When Paul arrived in Ephesus in A.D. 52, Prisca and Aquila had already been at work there for more than a year, and so the credit for the founding of the community must go to Prisca and Aquila, a part of the Pauline circle in a general sense. It is from the missionary centre of Ephesus under the guidance of Paul that there was considerable outreach including the seven churches of Asia mentioned in the book of Revelation which were probably part of the Ephesian outreach with a Pauline foundation (although the absence of letters to most of those churches does not take away from their basic Pauline foundation/origin): Ephesus, Laodicea, Smyrna, Pergamum, Thyatira, Sardis, Philadelphia. Other churches in the area are known from writings of Ignatius and other church leaders in Asia. All these churches/cities are within an easy radius of Ephesus; Ephesus was the new centre from which missionary activity was to expand (I Cor. 16:19 – *the churches in Asia greet you* – indicates that the mission was successful and several churches in Asia had been established). As founder of the missionary outreach, Paul now sees his work in Asia as having been complete – the establishment of Ephesus as a mission centre and successful missionary outreach to surrounding areas; he then turned his attention westwards (Rom. 15:21) to Rome and plans for Spain (Rom. 15:22-24).

Authorship/authenticity and integrity

The letter to the Ephesians was well attested in the early church; several church leaders knew the epistle and quoted from it; since the mid-second century, Ephesians was an uncontested part of the Pauline letters, and its Pauline authorship was accepted without challenge based on Eph. 1:1 which claims Paul as the author. In the 16th century, Erasmus raised doubts about the authorship of Ephesians on the basis that the style of writing differed sharply from other letters of Paul thus it should be seen as having been written by someone else. The next two centuries saw much debate on the authorship question especially since it was shown that Ephesians reflects the period of "early Catholicism" – i.e. the period just after the apostolic age while the doctrines of the church, especially ecclesiology, sacramentalism, hierarchy, ordination etc... were still being debated and formulated and while there was yet no accepted canon; in other words, this was the beginning period of *Catholic Christianity* (Early Catholicism). Today, Paul's authorship of Ephesians is not accepted on the following basis:

A. Language and Style: Ephesians uses other words for important concepts which are not found in other writings of Paul, long and complex sentences (e.g. 1:15-23 is one sentence in Greek which can scarcely be parsed!). Scholars have recognized the presence of *hapax legomena* – rare words not found elsewhere in the New Testament but found in the writings of church leaders of the second century (in the analysis below, the non-Pauline phrases are underlined).

B. Most of Colossians is also found in Ephesians raising questions about the relationship of these two writings. The relationship between these two writings based on language and style is far greater than the relationship between these writings and any other letter of Paul. There are only brief portions of Ephesians that have no verbal parallels in Colossians. Therefore, the question of authorship of these two writings must be taken together.

C. The theology of Ephesians is quite different from the theology of Paul's other letters, though the Ephesian theology, more of a developed Christology, can be seen as a development of more basic ideas found in earlier writings (e.g. Eph. 2:16 presents Christ as the agent of reconciliation, whereas in II Cor. 5:18 it is God who reconciles the world to God self). Similarly, the concept of the church is that of the 'universal church' and not so much of the local community. All these point to a development of theology, Christology and ecclesiology beyond the time of Paul and into the period of early Catholicism.

In view of the above three points, **Paul's authorship of Ephesians is seriously doubted, and Ephesians is placed in the deutero-Pauline epistles as a pseudonymous writing** (see above on Pseudonymous writings)**, i.e. written by someone, possibly a disciple, after the lifetime of Paul showing how Paul's thinking and theological expression was further developed as it moved out into wider areas and met with different contexts.** It is likely that the author was a Jewish Christian as indicated by 2:3, 11, 17 who had strong Hellenistic influences and that he was writing to a post-Pauline situation which had been infiltrated by Gnosticism (see Occasion and Purpose, below).

The literary problem of Ephesians also supports the assumption that it is a pseudonymous writing. The inscription προς᾿Εφεσιους or in some manuscripts, ἐν᾿Εφεσῳ (both meaning *to the Ephesians*) in 1:1 is missing in the earliest manuscripts and found only in manuscripts after the second century. Further, there is a complete lack of details and concrete problems in the letter or spelling out of a relationship between the author and readers; all personal greetings are missing. Paul had spent a total of more than 5 years in Ephesus, so it is inconceivable that he would write to them without mentioning some of their names or reminding them of the time spent together as he does in other writings. In many manuscripts, Ephesians stands at the beginning of the Pauline corpus as though it is a covering note explaining the collection, hence there is no specific issue being discussed and the writing serves as an introduction to all the letters.

The letter to the Ephesians can therefore be placed in the deutero-Pauline writings as a pseudonymous writing.

Occasion and Purpose

The links between Ephesians and Paul are made known in 1:1, 3:1, 4:1, 6:19-22, but as is evident from the discussion on authorship, above, the historical situation reflects a period after the life time of Paul. What can be gleaned from the epistle is that it was addressed to Gentile Christians (2:1ff, 11ff,; 3:1, 13; 4:17) and that the dividing wall between Gentiles and Jews has been broken down: ....*for He is our peace, who has made us both one, and has broken down the dividing wall of hostility*... The letter depicts the comprehensive significance of God's work in Christ and thereby emphasizes the eternal relationship between Christ, the head, and his body, the Church (1:4ff, 22ff; 2:15ff, 21ff; 4:13, 15ff, 5:23ff, 29,32). But what the concrete occasion was for reworking and rewording Paul's own ecclesiology (as outlined in Paul's own writings) is not known. As some scholars put it, Ephesians is the comprehensive and developed presentation of Paul's Christology and ecclesiology of a later generation. Ephesians emphasizes, and reminds its readers that the Christianity of its time includes also a past Jewish component and therefore it is moving towards the universal church – *until we all attain to the unity of the faith and of the knowledge of the Son of God, to mature personhood, to the measure of the stature of the fullness of Christ*. It is clear that there is a two-fold situation being addressed:

1. His religious terminology suggests a background of hellenized Jewish Christianity especially the household admonitions in 5:21-6:9 or the *haustafelen* (German word for household relationships).

2. The development of Christology and ecclesiology suggests a background of hellenized Gentile Christianity influenced by Gnostic ideas.

This two-fold situation builds on Paul's ideas and formulations reflecting the development of Paul's theology as Christianity moves beyond the Pauline era and meets new situations. Since the letter is a comprehensive document, i.e. inclusive of all Paul's writings with a closeness to Colossians, and with no specific historical situation being addressed, it is not surprising that scholars have understood Ephesians to be a "covering" letter for, or an introduction to, the Pauline corpus (collection of Pauline writings).

Therefore, the occasion and purpose for the writing is to address a post-Pauline situation which could have been prevalent anywhere in the Hellenistic outreach of the church and not necessarily only in Ephesus.

Date and place of writing

Since Ephesians is a post-Pauline writing its earliest possible date has to be after A.D.70, and since Ignatius knows the letter, the latest possible date cannot be after A.D. 110. Therefore,**the best dating would be between A.D 80 – 100**. In the light of accepting Ephesians as a post-Pauline writing, the references to Paul as a prisoner(3:1; 4:1; 6:20) can only serve to substantiate the pseudonymous nature of the writing since it was well known that Paul had been a prisoner on several occasions; such references are meant to strengthen the link and add to the authority of the writing. **The affinity with Colossians might suggest Asia Minor as a place of writing, but that can be no more than a possibility.**

Brief analysis and commentary

1:1-2: Opening formula

The letter is introduced as having been written by *Paul, an apostle of Christ Jesus by the will of God.* This is the same opening introduction used in other letters – an introduction that would not have raised any questions of authorship, authenticity, and authority. It is addressed to *the saints who are also faithful...*The Greek words, ἐν᾽ Ἐφεσῳ - in Ephesus – are missing from ancient manuscripts (see details in the introductory issues, above). The opening greeting of *grace* and *peace* are also found in other letters. There is no mention of any past dealings with the readers or any details about them. Therefore, *the saints* could be any Christians, anywhere. However, the mention of Tychicus (6:21, and Col. 4:7-8) may indicate that the readers/recipients of the letter are known to the author and probably can be found in Asia Minor as both Eph. 6:21 and Col. 4:7-8 use the same words. No details are described regarding Paul's situation in either of the texts.

1:3-14: Thanksgiving, Part I

The writer uses the quasi liturgical language of Jewish blessings: *blessed be the God and Father.... who has blessed us...every spiritual blessing* (ἐν παση εὐλογια πνευματκη) *...to the praise of his glory...* The sentences are long and grammatically complicated in terms of subject, excessive adjectives, and theological concepts: *we should be holy and blameless* (εἰναι ἡμας ἁγιους και ἀμωμους) *God destined us in love.... According to the purpose of God's will...in him we have redemption* (ἀπολυτπωσιν) *through his blood, forgiveness of our trespasses, according to the riches of God's grace ....* It is a celebration of Christ and the Christians' role (destined even before creation, προ καταβολης κοσμου) in God's plan *to unite in Christ all things in heaven and on earth.*

1:15-23: Thanksgiving, Part II

The writer acknowledges and gives thanks for the faith and love of the recipients and prays that they may grow in knowledge of the exalted Christ: I have heard of your faith in the Lord Jesus and your love toward all the saints. I do not cease to give thanks for you...may give you a spirit of wisdom and of revelation in the knowledge of him. All this to show the riches of his glorious inheritance in the saints...the immeasurable greatness of God's power...which God accomplished in Christ when he raised him from the dead...and seated him far above all rule and authority and power and dominion, and above every name that is named...and has put all things under his feet and has made him head over all things for the church (και αὐτον ἐδωκεν κεφαλην ὑπερ παντα τη ἐκκλησια), which is his body, the fullness of him who fills all in all. Verses 15-23 is one long and complicated sentence both in Greek and in the English translation! Basically, the writer sees all of God's plan summed up in the church which involves all of creation – a cosmic idea of salvation.

2:1-22: The Household of God

The chapter begins by explaining how God's plan of salvation is manifested in the richness of God's mercy and love. It has converted sinners into saints, the spiritually dead into the spiritually alive: *God has made you alive, you who were dead through the trespasses and sins in which you walked....but God who is rich in mercy, out of God's great love with which God loved us, even when we were dead, God has made us alive, together with Christ...for we are God's handiwork, created in Christ Jesus for good works...* The chapter goes on to show how God's grace has reached out to the Gentiles: *you were once separated from Christ, alienated* (ἀπηλλοτριωμενοι) *from the commonwealth of Israel* (της πολιτειας του Ισραηλ), *and strangers to the covenants of promise, having no hope and without God in the world. But now in Christ Jesus, you who once were far off have been brought near....* The non-Pauline phrases such as 'alienated from the commonwealth of Israel' 'strangers to the covenant of promise' add to the hypothesis of pseudonymity and the deutero-Pauline (post Paul) nature of the writing. In the further description of the oneness of Jews and Gentiles, there are further non-Pauline phrases (underlined; also to be noted are the long sentences and heavy descriptive language quite uncharacteristic of Paul as compared to earlier writings): *for Christ is our peace, who has made us both one, and has broken down the dividing wall of hostility* (το μεσοτοιχον του φραγμου λυσας την ἐχθρων), *by abolishing in his flesh the law of commandments and ordinances, that he might create in himself one new person in place of the two, so making peace...and might* reconcile us both to God, *in one body through the cross, thereby bringing the hostility to an end. He preached peace to those who were far off and peace to those who were near; for through him we both have access in one Spirit to the Father.* Since the community of Israel and the Gentiles are one, they are fellow citizens of the household of God: *you are no longer strangers and sojourners, but you are fellow citizens with the saints and members of the household of God* (οἰκειοι του Θεου). The household is built upon *the foundation of the apostles and prophets, Christ Jesus himself being the cornerstone* (ἀκρογωνιαιου)... *grows into a holy temple in the Lord...you are built into it for a dwelling place of*

God in the Spirit. The people constitute the household of God and the place of God's dwelling; God's dwelling cannot be limited by physical structures in a particular locality; it is universal and present wherever God's people meet.

3:1-21: Apostle to the Gentiles

The writer emphasizes Paul's understanding of having been called to a ministry among the Gentiles. The Gentiles who are now *fellow citizens in the household of God* need to know/be reminded that *the mystery was made known to me by revelation...it has been revealed to his holy apostles and prophets by the Spirit, that is how the Gentiles are fellow heirs, members of the same body and partakers of the promise in Christ Jesus through the gospel* (συμμετοχα της ἐπαγγελιας ἐν Χριστῳ Ἰησου δια του εὐαγγελιου). The writer claims that he/she is a minister of such a gospel and a *prisoner* (δεσμιος) *of Christ Jesus on behalf of you Gentiles.* The writer feels that *though he was the very least of all the saints, this grace was given, to preach to the Gentiles the unsearchable riches* (ἀνεξιχνιαστον πλουτος) *of Christ and to make all see what is the plan of the mystery hidden for ages in God... that through the church he manifold wisdom of God might now be made known to the principalities and powers in the heavenly places.* Long complicated sentence structure and vocabulary characterize the passage as in all of Ephesians. The writer, in the name of Paul, offers his imprisonment and prayers so that the readers will comprehend the love of Christ, *in whom we have boldness and confidence of access.* The writer ends the section with a benediction on the readers: *that you, being rooted and grounded in love* (ἐν ἀγαπη ἐρριζωμενοι και τεθεμελιωμενοι), *may have power to comprehend with all the saints what is the breadth and length and height and depth* (το πλατος και μηκος και ὁψος και βαθος), *and to know the love of Christ which surpasses knowledge, that you may be filled with all the fullness of God.* And a doxology: *to Him who by the power at work within us is able to do far more abundantly than all that we ask or think, to Him be glory in the Church and in Christ Jesus to all generations, for ever and ever. Amen.*

Chapters 2 and 3 form, as it were, the indicative section of the epistle, i.e. making a statement/stating a position without resorting to argument/polemic. It can be seen that in all the statements, there is the influence of a basic idea from Paul, but the form of expression and vocabulary used is not from Paul (can be seen from a comparison with Romans, I & II Corinthians, Galatians) but indicates a development of Paul's thought from a period later than Paul.

4:1-5:20: The plea for unity

Following the 'indicative' or statement section, the writer goes on to challenge the readers with the 'imperative' section, i.e. the indicative must find expression in the imperative – from statement to action. There are 36 verbs in this section which are imperative verbs in Greek, e.g.: ὀργιζεσθε και μη ἅμαρτανετε (be angry but do not sin), μητι κλεπτετω....κοπιατω (let him not steal...let him labour), λογος σαπρος ἐκ του στοματος ὑμων μη ἐκπορευεσθω (let not corrupt words proceed out of your mouth). There is the insistence on unity and oneness: *one body and one spirit just as you were called to the one hope that belongs to your call, one Lord, one faith, one baptism, one God and Father of us all* (ἕν σωμα και ἕν πνευμα....ἐν μια ἐλπιδι....εἰς κυριος, μια πιστις ἕν βαπτισμα, εἱς Θεος και πατηρ παντων), *who is above all and through all and in all.* The writer spells out gifts which are the manifestations of unity/oneness in the Christian life: a diversity of gifts for building up the body of Christ: *His gifts were that some should be apostles, some prophets, some evangelists, some pastors and teachers, for the equipment of the saints, for the work of ministry, for building up the body of Christ.* These gifts were seen to have been divisive in I Cor. 12 but now they are seen as helping *to attain to the unity of the faith, and of the knowledge of the Son of God, to mature personhood, to the measure of the stature of the fullness* (πληρωμα) *of Christ...grow up in every way into Him who is the head, into Christ...*

Since Christ has created a new human being of Jew and Gentile, the new human being cannot live according to the old pattern of life: *put off your old nature which belongs to your former manner of life...and be renewed in the spirit of your minds, and put on the new nature created after the likeness of God in true righteousness and holiness...be kind to one another, tenderhearted, forgiving one another, as god in Christ forgave you. Therefore, be imitators of God, as beloved children.* The rules for the new life reflect the Ten Commandments about relationships with others. When this relationship is actually fulfilled then it results in being *filled with the Spirit, addressing one another in psalms and hymns and spiritual songs, singing and making melody to the Lord with all your heart, always and for everything giving thanks in the name of our Lord Jesus Christ to God the Father.*

5:21-6:9: Household relationships

This section specifies the way Christian life transforms relationships in terms of a household (*haustafel*)– *wives*-husbands, *children*-fathers, *slaves*-masters; these relationships are also treated in Col. 3:18-4:6(see below), but Ephesians is more detailed in its description and approach. The overall pattern is that the *first mentioned* individuals/groups are to be subject and obedient; the second party is to exemplify the characteristics of Christ. However, the passage starts: *be subject to one another* (ὑποτασσομενοι ἀλληλους) *out of reverence for Christ;* thus the overarching theme is that all must relate equally to one another under a Christological umbrella: if the wife is to be subject to the husband, then the husband is also to be subject to the wife; similarly children and parents, slaves and masters. In effect, these instructions as described here are a new way of expressing relationships within the household and by extension, in society. Bringing Christ into the equation of relationships makes the passage a uniquely Christian contribution to society and gives relationships a Christological base. The instruction for the husband to *love* his wife (which is treated more extensively than the wife having to obey her husband), and therefore their whole relationship to be controlled by love, is unique in a social setting where this was not the expected norm; it thus off-sets the instruction that the wife should be *subject* to her husband, and it is given a Christological base: *husbands, love your wives, as Christ loved the Church and gave Himself up for her... husbands should love their wives as their own bodies...* The children-parents instructions are based on the Hebrew scriptures of "honour your father and your mother that it may go well with you and that you may live long on the earth (Ex. 20:12; Deut. 5:16); further, parents *do not provoke your children to anger, but bring them up in the discipline and instructions of the Lord.* In the master-slave instructions, a Christological interpretation is given that the slave *must be obedient as to Christ, as servants of Christ, doing the will* *of God from the heart…*The master must be impartial and must refrain from threatening: *forbear threatening, knowing that He who is both their Master and yours is in heaven, and that there is no partiality with Him.* The writer makes no comment on the practice of slavery, but by describing the basis of the relationship in Christological terms, the practice of slavery is redefined – all are free in Christ irrespective of their social status; all are slaves of Christ, and all are accountable to Christ. The Christological colouring and thrust of these household relationships is part of the gospel that places responsibility and accountability on those who are in positions of power and authority.

6:10-20: The armour of God

Using the figurative language of armour and weapons, there is an exhortation to encourage the reader in the on-going battle, *put on the whole armour of God…for you are not contending against flesh and blood, but against the principalities, against the powers, against the world rulers of this present darkness, against the spiritual hosts of wickedness in the heavenly places…and having done all to stand..having girded your loins with truth, and having put on the breastplate of righteousness* (ἐνδυσαμενοι τον θωρακα της δικαιοσυνης)…*the helmet of salvation* (περικεφαλαιαν του σωτηριου)…*the sword of the Spirit* (την μαχαιραν του πνευματος)… There is an inherent idea of a future eschatology, i.e. the end time taking place at a future point so that the battle continues in the present. The writer requests prayers that he may be faithful in his calling and the task of proclaiming the gospel for which he/she calls himself/herself *an ambassador in chains* (πρεσβευω ἐν ἅλυσει), emphasizing his/her own commitment to the gospel.

6:21-24: Concluding formula

There are minimal greetings and the commendation of Tychicus who is being sent to the addressees as also in Col. 4:7-8 underlining the close relationship and similarity between the two writings. The blessings of *peace …love with faith…grace…* are a benediction on *all who love our Lord Jesus Christ with love undying.*

Select bibliography for Ephesians

(see also Select Bibliography for Philemon and Colossians)

Beare, F. W. *Interpreter's Bible, Vol. 10*.Nashville: Abingdon Press, 1953.

Brown, R. E., An *Introduction to the New Testament*.Bangalore: Theological Publications in India, 2000.

Murphy-O'Connor.Jerome Paul, *A Critical Life. Oxford*: Oxford University Press, 1996.

Ninan, Idicheria "Ephesians" in Brian C. Wintle (General Editor), *South Asia Biblical Commentary*.Udaipur, Rajasthan: Open Door Publication, 2015, pages 1631 – 1647

Kummel. W. G. *Introduction to the New Testament*.London: SCM Press, 1975.

Schnackenburg, R., The *Epistle to the Ephesians*.Edinburgh: T. & T. Clark, 1991.

Wintle, Brian C. and Ken Gnanakan, *Ephesians,* Bangalore/Singapore: Asia Bible Commentary, 2004/2006.

Deutero-Pauline:
B. Philippians

The founding of the community. Authorship/authenticity and integrity. Occasion and purpose. Place of writing and Date. Brief analysis and commentary on the text. Select bibliography for Philippians.

The Founding of the community

The founding of the community at Philippi was Paul's first act on the continent of Europe when he arrived in Macedonia from Asia on the so-called 'second missionary journey' about A.D. 49/50. The city had been built by Phillip of Macedon, father of Alexander the Great, and named for him. The city had been used as a Roman military colony from about 40 B.C. and was the leading city of the district of Macedonia. The story of Paul's first introduction to Philippi is found in Acts 16:11-40. The first convert there was Lydia (originally from Thyatira) who was a dealer in purple goods. After her conversion, she hosted Paul and his group in her home. There was trouble when Paul cast out a "spirit of divination" from a slave girl and her owners complained to the authorities; Paul and Silas were beaten on orders of the city magistrates and cast into prison. The jailor made sure that the prisoners were securely locked in the jail. An earthquake destroyed the jail that night, but none of the prisoners escaped; the jailor saw this as an act of God and was converted and baptized with his whole house. When the magistrates released Paul and Silas, Paul claimed the privileges of a Roman citizen who could not be thrown into prison without proper legal proceedings. This made the magistrates fear drastic consequences, so they apologized and escorted the group out of the city after they had visited Lydia and others. The first visit does not seem to have made many converts – Acts mentions only Lydia and her household, and the jail-keeper and his household; however other names appear in the letter: Epaphroditus (2:25ff; 4:18), Euodias, Syntyche, Clement and an un-named co-worker (4:2ff). The names suggest that the community at Philippi was essentially Gentile Christians. A close relationship had bonded Paul and the Philippians so that they supported him with gifts of money (4:15ff; II Cor. 11:8ff). There is no record of frequent visits to Philippi, but on his frequent journeys between Europe and Asia Minor, Paul must have renewed the ties with Philippi which is why they supported him. He visited the community for the last time in A.D. 56/57 as he journeyed from Corinth through Macedonia to Jerusalem for the purpose of delivering the collection there and probably celebrated Passover in Philippi (Acts 20:3ff). This supplies the picture of a small community but it would seem to be a tightly knit one and also a community that was willing to financially support Paul in his work.

Authorship/authenticity and Integrity

The authorship of the letter to the Philippians has never been seriously questioned. It has always been acknowledged that the letter(s) originate with Paul. However, serious doubts about the integrity of the writing – one letter or a compilation of several letters – has given rise to much debate from the second century onwards (Polycarp mentions Paul's "letters" to the Philippians which implies that several letters must have been combined at a later date) and must be studied before proceeding with the text. Some of the issues on which integrity is questioned are:

1. In 2:23-30 Paul alludes to his travel plans, which he usually does toward the end of his letters;

2. "Finally" in 3:1a sounds as if he is about to close the letter, yet two chapters follow;

3. Would it be logical to mention the sending back of Epaphroditus (2:25-30) before mentioning his arrival with the gifts for Paul (4:18)?

4. The above issues raise the question of whether chapter 3 is a separate, or part of a separate letter.

The following information is found in the letter to the Philippians:

- Paul was in prison (1:7, 13, 17);

- At the place of imprisonment there were members of the "Praetorian Guard" (1:13); there is also mention of "saints" in "Caesar's household" (4:22);

- Paul mentions the possibility that he might die (1:19-21; 2:17) – martyrdom?

- He hopes, however, to be delivered (1:24-25; 2:24);

- Timothy was with Paul (1:1, 2:19-23);

- Christians with different motives are emboldened to speak in Philippi (1:14-18);

- Paul refers to these persons as "dogs", "evil-workers" (3:2);

- These persons seem to be Judaisers insisting on the observance of the Jewish law (3:2ff);

- There were frequent contacts between Paul and the Philippians:

  - ✓ News reached the Philippians of Paul's imprisonment (4:10-13);

  - ✓ They sent Epaphroditus with a gift (4:15), but while staying with Paul he became seriously ill (2:26, 30);

  - ✓ News reached the Philippians of Epaphroditus' illness (2:26-27);

  - ✓ Epaphroditus was distressed that the Philippians had heard of his illness (2:26);

  - ✓ Paul sent Epaphroditus back to Philippi on his recovery (2:25-30);

  - ✓ Paul hopes to send Timothy to Philippi (2:19-23) and also hopes to pay a personal visit to Philippi (2:24).

The point now is to fit these details into a historical situation in the life of Paul.

The book of Acts records two lengthy imprisonments of Paul: Acts 23:33 – 26:32, imprisonment in Caesarea for two years; and

Acts 28:14-31, imprisonment in Rome for two years. Does the letter originate during either of these imprisonments?

The earliest view was that Philippians originated in Rome because of the mention of the "Praetorian Guard" and "saints in the household of Caesar". However, the frequent contacts between Paul and the Philippians while he was a prisoner would have taken more than two years: Rome was too far away for news and responses to travel so quickly. Further, Paul had not visited Philippi after the founding of the community according to 1:26, 30; 4:14ff. But Paul had visited Philippi on his way to deliver the collection for Jerusalem and had spent Passover at Philippi (Acts 20:1ff).So, the statement that he had not visited Philippi would not have been correct if the letter originated in Rome.

The journeys presupposed in Philippians could be better understood if the place of imprisonment was closer – perhaps Caesarea. But the movement from Caesarea to Rome that followed Paul's appeal to Caesar rules out the possibility of Paul's intended visit to Philippi. So,it would seem that a place of imprisonment closer to Philippi and before A.D. 58-60 (the date for the imprisonment in Caesarea) would be more appropriate.

This analysis also raises the question of the integrity of the letter – is it one letter or a compilation of several letters? It has long been recognized that thanks for the gift from the Philippians to Paul at the end of the letter (4:10-20) is not in its proper place particularly because the interval since the gift was brought to Paul must have been long (2:25ff). Therefore, this section is separated out as an earlier letter of thanks. Further, 3:2-4:3 does not presuppose an imprisonment but is a polemic against Christian opponents; 3:3ff warns against Jewish and pagan antagonists. Thus, three letters can be identified in the following sequence:

1. 1st letter: **4:10-20**: the letter of thanks for the gift sent through Epaphroditus.

2. 2nd letter: **1:1-3:1a and 4:21-23**: thanks, after Epaphroditus' recovery and his return to Philippi, and future plans.

3. 3rd letter: **3:1b-4:9**: polemic against Jewish and pagan antagonists which was new information received by Paul.

Hence it can be concluded that **there are three letters by Paul to the Philippians addressed to different situations and that Philippians as it now stands is a later compilation of these three originally independent letters or fragments of letters.** As can be seen from the historical and literary analysis (given below) which does not show a close link between the letters/fragments, it may be concluded that though these letters/fragments may have originated with Paul, they were compiled in the period after Paul and so they are treated as being among the deutero-Pauline letters.

This study accepts/follows the position that there are three letters of Paul compiled in the letter to the Philippians and written in the sequence outlined above. Thus, the analysis of the text will also follow the sequence of the identified letters/fragments.

Occasion and Purpose

1. 4:10-20: The letter of thanks for the gift sent through Epaphroditus

Paul's gratitude for the financial assistance sent by thePhilippians is acknowledged only in this section which stands at the end of the letter – most unusual as the gift would have been acknowledged at the beginning. It therefore raises the possibility that that section was a separate letter and was placed at the end during the compilation; as such, it is the first of the letters written by Paul to the Philippians. There is no need to assume that Paul was in prison as it is not mentioned in the letter, unless the reference to *it was kind of you to share my trouble* can be assumed to refer to an imprisonment. The gift had been sent with Epaphroditus; this was not the first gift received from the Philippians, *for even in Thessalonica you sent me help* and II Cor.11:9 mentions yet another time when the Philippians helped Paul in time of need. The gift represented a community effort and Paul's thanks is directed to the whole church: *I am filled, having received from Epaphroditus the gifts you sent, a fragrant offering, a sacrifice acceptable and pleasing to God.* **Thus, the** occasion and purpose of 4:10-20 is to express Paul's thankfulness for the gift of love that he had received. The place and date of writing cannot be exactly determined although Ephesus, between A.D. 53-55, is a better possibility than other suggestions.

2.   1:1-3:1a and 4:21-23:Thanks, after Epaphroditus' recovery and his return to Philippi, and future plans

After Epaphroditus had reached Paul with the gift from the Philippians, he fell seriously ill and news of his illness reached Philippi: *he (Epaphroditus) has been longing for you all, and has been distressed because you heard that he was ill. Indeed, he was ill, near to death.*So the news of his illness had reached Philippi and the concern that they had expressed had come back to Paul and Epaphroditus. He is now being sent back to Philippi, having recovered (2:25-30). The letter is also to communicate to the Philippians how things are going with Paul (1:12ff), although as a result of his imprisonment (1:7, 13, 17) he cannot come to them at present but hopes to visit them soon; in the meantime, he plans to send Timothy to them(2:19-24). The letter tells more about Paul's situation than it does about the Philippians; this is a reflection that there were noserious problems to be addressed.

Paul indicates that he is being held as a prisoner in the Praetorium (1:13) – the official residence of the Governor. The mention of the *praetorian guard* and *those of Caesar's household* (4:22), does not automatically imply that the place of writing is Rome as these facilities are found in all the provinces where there are official residences of Roman Governors.

The epistolary opening formula is seen in 1:1 and the closing formula begins in 3:1a – *finally, my brethren, rejoice in the Lord* – and is concluded in 4:21-23 – *greet every saint in Christ Jesus....* indicating that this section could stand as a separate letter. The letter would have been written after the letter of thanksgiving and was sent to the Philippians through Epaphroditus on his return after recovering from his illness. **The place and date of writing cannot be exactly determined although Ephesus, between A.D. 53-55, is a better possibility than other suggestions.**

3.   3:1b-4:9: polemic against Jewish and pagan antagonists

The section that begins, *to write the same things to you is not irksome to me and is safe for you....* refers to what follows which indicates a complete change in topic, context, language, vocabulary, and tone. There is no mention of an imprisonment in this section although Paul's sufferings could have been mentioned appropriately anywhere in the section. This might suggest that this letter was written after Paul's release from prison. The concern in this section is that Paul fears Judaizing infiltration in Philippi which seems to have happened in the communities at Corinth and in Galatia: *look out for the dogs, look out for the evil-workers, look out for those who mutilate the flesh...I have often told you about them, and tell you again with tears, they live as enemies of the cross of Christ. Their end is destruction....* The reference to *their god is the belly* may refer to Jewish dietary laws which the Judaisers were emphasizing. Two women – Euodia and Syntyche – seem not to be able to agree with each other and their disagreement was having its effect on the community.

The epistolary ending is present in verses 8 & 9: *finally, brethren.... the God of peace be with you.*

The place and date of writing cannot be exactly determined although Ephesus, between A.D. 53-55, is a better possibility than other suggestions and after the release of Paul from prison.

Therefore, each section of the compiled document has its own occasion and purpose so that its origin is readily understandable. However, the exact immediate historical situation for the composition of each section remains unclear.

Place of writing and Date

It is not certain as to where Paul was when the letters were written and hence the date of their composition is also uncertain. On the basis of the above discussion on the integrity of the letter and the acceptance of the position that there are at least three letters which have been compiled in the period after Paul, the place of writing and the date become more complicated issues. In the hypothesis that the three letters were compiled during Paul's time when he was in prison, then three possibilities arise from the known imprisonments of Paul, two mentioned in the book of Acts (see above), and one assumed from other writings:

1. Caesarea – A.D. 58 – 60. Objections to this place of writing are listed above, especially the fact that during this imprisonment Paul had appealed to Caesar, and he was sent under guard to Rome, so there would have been no possibility of the intended visit to Philippi.

2. Rome – A.D. 62 – 64. The objection to Rome as the place of writing is that it was too far from Philippi in order to fit the frequent contacts, mentioned in the writings, between Philippi and Paul's place of imprisonment.

3. Ephesus – before A.D. 58 and more likely between A.D. 53-55. This is a good possibility given its proximity to Philippi which could accommodate the several journeys back and forth, but there is no clear attestation of Paul having been in prison for an extended period in Ephesus.

Therefore, it is not possible to determine the place of writing and date during the time of Paul. An attempt is made (above section on Occasion and Purpose) to suggest a place of writing and date for each of the component letters/fragments, but the place of compilation and date of Philippians, as it presently stands in the New Testament, cannot be specifically determined. **It can only be assumed that the letters/ fragments may have been compiled in Philippi – where the letters were addressed and collected – after Paul's time. Therefore, Philippians is to be considered in the deutero-Pauline category and perhaps compiled after A.D. 70 and before A.D. 90 since it is known by Church leaders in the last decade of the first century.**

Brief analysis and commentary

Since three letters/fragments have been identified (see discussion above), the brief analysis and commentary will follow the sequence of the letters/ fragments as identified above in the following chronological order:

1. 4:10-20: the letter of thanks for the gift sent through Epaphroditus.

2. 1:1-3:1a and 4:21-23: thanks, after Epaphroditus' recovery and his return to Philippi, and future plans.

3. 3:1b-4:9: polemic against Jewish and pagan antagonists which was new information received by Paul.

1.   4:10-20: the letter of thanks for the gift sent through Epaphroditus.

The Philippians had sent Paul a gift of money with Epaphroditus, *I rejoice in the Lord greatly that now at length you have revived your concern for me....it was kind of you to share my trouble...I am filled, having received from Epaphroditus the gifts you sent, a fragrant offering....* The letter expresses thanks for the gift. It was not the first time that the Philippians had sent Paul a gift: *even in Thessalonica you sent me help once and again,* but perhaps they had not sent a gift/support for some time. II Cor.11:9 mentions yet another time when the Philippians helped Paul in time of need. It reflects the warm and loving relationship between Paul and the community he founded and the effort of the whole community in contributing towards supporting the ministry of Paul.

However, lest he is misunderstood to be complaining and even without the support of the Philippians, Paul had learnt to be content with whatever he had and in whatever circumstances he found himself: *I have learned in whatever state I am, to be content* (ἐγω γαρ ἐμαθον ἐν οἷς εἰμι αὐταρκης εἶναι). *I know how to be abased, and I know how to abound.... I can do all things in Him who strengthens me* (παντα ἰσχυω ἐν τῳ ἐνδυναμουντι με).

The partnership of the Philippians in Paul's ministry is gratefully acknowledged: *you Philippians yourselves know that in the beginning of the gospel, when I left Macedonia, no church entered into partnership with me in giving and receiving except you only...* Paul assures them of his prayers and his conviction that *my God will supply every need of yours according to God's riches in glory in Christ Jesus.* He ends with an ascription of glory to God.

This is a very short intimate letter of thanks to a community with whom the apostle shares a warm and supportive relationship.

It should be noted that nowhere in the letter is there mention of an imprisonment or a mention of Epaphroditus' illness, both issues which are central to other parts of the letter to the Philippians.

2.   1:1-3:1a and 4:21-23: thanks, after Epaphroditus' recovery and his return to Philippi, and future plans.

In the opening address, the warmth of the relationship between Paul and the Philippians is clearly expressed: *I thank my God in all my remembrance of you...thankful for your partnership in the gospel...I hold you in my heart...I yearn for you with the affection of Christ Jesus...* The *partnership in the gospel* (κοινωνια ὑμων εἰς το εὐαγγελιον) refers to the gifts in support of Paul and his work which was time and again extended by the Philippians (see Occasion and Purpose and 4:10-20 above). The strong ties/bonds of love and affection are the main motives of this letter along with information regarding Paul and Paul's plans regarding Philippi.

The information regarding Paul is that he is allegedly writing from prison (1:7, 13, 17), but he is not despondent despite his circumstances and even though he thinks that he will may die: *what has happened to me has really served to advance the gospel...others have been made confident in the Lord because of my imprisonment, and are much more bold to speak the word of God without fear...through your prayers, this will turn out for my deliverance... but with full courage now as always Christ will be honoured in my body, whether by life or by death. For me to live is Christ, and to die is gain* (ἐμοι γαρ το ζην Χριστοςκαι το ἀποθανειν κερδος). Paul ends the letter with his plans to send Timothy to Philippi, *I hope to send Timothy to you soon,* and his commendation of Timothy as a good and faithful worker. There is also the mention that Paul is sending Epaphroditus back to Philippi. Epaphroditus had brought the gift from the Philippians to Paul and was to serve Paul in whatever way possible; he had fallen seriously ill after reaching Paul. News of his illness had reached the Philippians who were very anxious for him; an anxiety that caused distress to Epaphroditus: *I have thought it necessary to send to you Epaphroditus...he has been longing for you all and has been distressed because you heard that he was ill. Indeed, he was ill, near to death.* No news of Epaphroditus' illness was mentioned in the letter of thanksgiving (4:10-20 above).

The information regarding the situation at Philippi is that Paul wants the Philippians to be blameless and to stand firm in the gospel and to be prepared to suffer for Christ: *let your manner of life be worthy of the gospel of Christ...stand firm in one spirit, with one mind striving side by side for the faith of the gospel, and not frightened in anything by your opponents... it has been granted to you...not only believe in Him but also suffer for His sake, engaged in the same conflict which you saw and now hear to be mine...be blameless and innocent ...in the midst of a crooked and perverse generation* There is no mention of who the opponents are or the specific situation, so it seems that this is a general exhortation to the community.

The exhortation is followed by one of the most beautiful passages in the New Testament, the Christological hymn on the humility of Christ (κενωσις– *kenosis* or self-emptying) which should serve as an inspiration and challenge to maintain unity: *if there is any encouragement in Christ, any incentive of love, any participation in the Spirit, any affection and sympathy, complete my joy by being of the same mind, having the same love... Let each of you look not only to their own interests, but also to the interests of others. Have this mind among yourselves, which you have in Christ Jesus, who, though He was in the form of God* (μορφη Θεου) *did not count equality with God a thing to be grasped, but emptied himself, taking the form of a servant* (δουλου or slave) *...humbled Himself and became obedient unto death even death on a cross. Therefore God has highly exalted Him* (ὁ Θεος αυτον ὑπερυψωσεν)...

It has long been recognized that 2:5-11 is Christological hymn – it rhythmical style, parallel patterns etc... set it apart from prose. Incorporating or quoting verses of a hymn into the writing is not unusual in the New Testament; there are other places where the writers incorporate hymns, e.g. Luke 2:14, 29-35; John 1:1-18; Rom. 3:24-26, I Cor. 13; Col. 1:15-20; I Tim. 3:16; I Peter 3:18-22, although there are no introductory formulas to identify the quotation; it is only a literary analysis that brings out the hymnic quality of the quotation and identifies it as a hymn. A close analysis of the hymns suggest that the theology of the community was put down in this rhythmic pattern as a mnemonic aid and also as an expression of faith, much like the function of hymns in the church in the present time.

The description of Christ as a servant (δουλος= slave) who is to be imitated is not only one of the most beautiful passages in the New Testament, but its Christological expression brings together a whole new understanding of Christ. It is probably a pre-Pauline hymn expressing the humility and self-emptying of Christ (κενωσις) bringing into juxtaposition (opposites being brought together) Christ's position at the beginning, his self-emptying humility and acceptance of a most ignomious type of death, and finally his exaltation in glory above every name. The purpose of the hymn in the context of the writing is soteriological – it encourages the readers to follow the example of the humility of Christ for their own salvation. The Philippians are to have the mind of Christ who showed that the way to God was not by grasping at higher positions but by becoming humbly obedient to God, even if it means death on a cross. This understanding of Christ as a humble, obedient servant is found only in Philippians among the Pauline writings and so is a unique contribution to theology and to the preservation of an early expression of faith.

The letter ends with the final exhortation to *rejoice in the Lord.*

This letter/fragment of a letter is noteworthy in that it is a deep expression of a warm and genuine relationship between Paul and the Philippian community; there are no immediate problems to be addressed and Paul can write in exhortation to a community that he founded and who in turn was supporting him in his ministry. The letter serves to tell the Philippians about his situation – imprisonment – and his plans, and also to commend Timothy as a co-worker. The news of Ephaphroditus' illness, his usefulness to Paul, and yet his being sent back also contributes a personal touch and adds to the warmth of the relationship.

3:1b-4:9: polemic against Jewish and pagan antagonists which was new information received by Paul.

In this letter/fragment there is a complete change in topic, context, language, vocabulary, and tone. There is no mention of an imprisonment; this might suggest that this letter was written after Paul's release from prison and new information regarding the situation in Philippi had reached him. The concern in this letter is that Paul fears Judaizing and pagan infiltration in Philippi which seems to have happened in the communities at Corinth and in Galatia: *look out for the dogs, look out for the evil-workers, look out for those who mutilate the flesh...I have often told you about them, and tell you again with tears, they live as enemies of the cross of Christ. Their end is destruction....*The letter also provides more autobiographical details than other letters.

The letter starts with the warning that Paul will be repeating himself, but that such repetition is good for the community: *to write the same things* (τα αὐτα γραφεἰν) *to you is not irksome to me and is safe for you.* There seem to be two categories of opponents: the first are external elements infiltrating the community, and secondly internal squabbles affecting the unity of the community.

The presence of external elements who are encouraging teachings contrary to Paul is acknowledged, *look out for the dogs, look out for the evil-workers, look out for those who mutilate the flesh* – either they have already entered into the community, or they are posing a threat from outside. Their teachings include mutilation of the flesh (perhaps subjecting the body to lashings or other forms of torture as a 'spiritual' discipline, or mutilation of the flesh through circumcision etc...). The threat is a combination of Judaizing teachings and pagan practices. The warning is, *put no confidence in the flesh.*

As an example of the contrariness of their teachings, Paul gives the illustration of his own life: his impeccable Jewish credentials – *circumcised on the eighth day, of the people of Israel, of the tribe of Benjamin, a Hebrew born of Hebrews, as to the law a Pharisee, as to zeal a persecutor of the Church, as to righteousness under the law blameless.* These autobiographical details show that Paul would have had no trouble in attaining salvation, instead he says, *whatever gain I had, I counted as loss for the sake of Christ* (ἀλλα ἅτινα ἠν μοι κερδη, ταυτα ἥγημαι διατομ Χριστον ζημιαν). *Indeed, I count everything as loss because of the surpassing worth of knowing Christ Jesus my Lord. For His sake I have suffered the loss of all things and count them as refuse in order that I may gain Christ....* In many ways these autobiographical remarks are an account of Paul's conversion experience: he realized that the effort to observe all the requirements of the law did not lead to salvation; salvation was received through faith: ...*and be found in Him, not having a righteousness of my own, based on law, but that which is through faith in Christ, the righteousness from God* (την ἐκ Θεου δικαιοσυνην) *that depends on faith...* When he realized this, then all his impeccable Jewish credentials and efforts were of no use, he had only to accept the salvation offered by God through Jesus by faith. His past had to be left behind, he could only look forward, so he could say, *forgetting what lies behind and straining forward to what lies ahead, I press on towards the goal for the prize of the upward call of God in Christ Jesus.* The illustration of his life leads Paul to the call to *join in imitating me, and mark those who so live as you have an example in us.* The external threat also includes those whose *god is the belly and they glory in their shame, with minds set on earthly things.* This opposition seems to be a combination of Jewish elements insisting on the Mosaic dietary laws and pagan practices which emphasized the exhibition of the body. Paul's answer is, *our commonwealth is in heaven, and from it we await a Saviour, the Lord Jesus Christ, who will change our lowly body to be like His glorious body...* Therefore, the exhortation, reflecting the warmth of the relationship with the Philippians, *whom I love and long for, my joy and crown, stand firm thus in the Lord, my beloved.*

The second, or internal dissentions in Phillipi, are illustrated by Euodia and Syntyche, who had worked along with Paul and another worker, Clement, and who now disagree among themselves but their disagreements affect the unity of the whole community, so everyone is asked to help them to overcome their differences,*I entreat Euodia and I entreat Syntyche to agree in the Lord. And I ask you also...help these women, for they have labored side by side with me in the gospel together with Clement...* What exactly was the cause of the differences is not mentioned, but it does seem to be serious as it is mentioned along with the external threats to the community.

Having dealt with the issues that threaten the unity of the community, the letter closes with the epistolary ending of *rejoice in the Lord always; again I will say, Rejoice....The Lord is at hand...have no concern about anything, but in everything by prayer and supplication with thanksgiving let your requests be made known to God...And the peace of God...whatever is true, whatever is honourable, whatever is just, whatever is pure, whatever is lovely, whatever is gracious...think about these things* (ὅσα ἐστιν ἀληθη, ὅσα σεμνα, ὅσα δικσια, ὅσα ἅγνα, ὅσα προσφιλη).....*and the God of peace will be with you.*

In many ways this letter/compilation of letters is the most attractive of the Pauline letters, reflecting the warm affection of the apostle for his brothers and sisters in Christ. It contains one of the best-known passages on the graciousness of Christ who emptied himself and took the form of a servant even unto death on a cross. However, the writing poses many difficulties since its unity and integrity have long been questioned – where was Paul when he wrote the letters? What is the date of composition? When and where was it compiled? etc... Nevertheless, these questions do not take away from the beauty of each of its component parts, their lofty ideals and expressions, and their challenges to preserve a united community following the example of Christ's humility and Paul's witness of having given up everything for the sake of Christ.

Select Bibliography for Philippians

Beare, F. W., Philippians, Black's New Testament Commentaries, London: Black, 1973.

Brown, R. E., An *Introduction to the New Testament,* Bangalore: Theological Publications in India, 2000.

Bruce, F. F., *Philippians*, New International Biblical Commentary, Peabody, MA: Hendrickson, 1989.

Kummel, W. G. *Introduction to the New Testament,* London: SCM Press, 1975.

Murphy-O'Connor, Jerome Paul, *A Critical Life, Oxford:* Oxford University Press, 1996.

Wintle, Brian C. "Philippians" in Brian C. Wintle (General Editor), *South Asia Biblical Commentary,* Udaipur, Rajasthan: Open Door Publication, 2015, pages 1648 – 1659.

Deutero-Pauline:
C. Colossians

The founding of the community. Occasion and purpose of the letter. Authorship/authenticity and integrity. Place of writing and Date. Brief analysis and commentary on the text. Select bibliography for Colossians.

The founding of the community

The city of Colossae was situated on the upper Lycus River valley on the highway that led eastward from Ephesus. In the mid-first century Colossae was an insignificant market town in contrast to the larger and more flourishing neighbouring towns of Hierapolis and Laodicea; these three cities formed a rough triangle and were often associated with each other. The area was well-known for its crops of figs and olives and the good quality of sheep's wool. There was a considerable population in these three cities especially because of their association with the linen trade and purple dye. Many Jews settled in the Lycus valley after the Babylonian exile; ancient records show that there were at least 10,000 adult Jewish men in the valley and that they were granted permission to freely practice their religion. During his two years and three months' stay at Ephesus (Acts 19:8-10), Paul had two strategies: while he stayed in Ephesus dedicating himself to the foundation of that community, he sent others out from Ephesus, the capital of the province of Asia, to spread the gospel to neighbouring cities. One of the missionaries so commissioned went far eastward to his homeland, *Epaphras, who is one of yourselves* (4:12). How and where Epaphras met Paul is not known, but the best possibility is that they met in Ephesus where Epaphras had come for business purposes and was converted. Since he was a local Colossian, Epaphras would have had access to people, homes and community and was therefore an ideal person to entrust with the message of the gospel. **Paul did not found the church in Colossae,** and had not even visited it prior to the letter to Colossians (2:1); **the community was founded by Epaphras, a beloved fellow servant** (1:3-8); similarly the other cities in the triangle, Hierapolis and

Laodicea, were also founded through the work of Epaphras (4:13); house churches are mentioned in Laodicea and the home of Nympha; a house church is mentioned in Philemon 2 (see section in Philemon, above). The community consisted mostly of Gentile Christians (1:21, 27; 2:13), but there must also have been Jewish Christians since there was a considerable Jewish population in the city. Thus Epaphras, a Greek, belonging to the Pauline mission with its centre at Ephesus was found to be a beloved fellow servant *and that he has worked hard for you and for those in Laodicea and in Hierapolis.*

Occasion and purpose of the letter

The community at Colossae were threatened by the danger of false teachers who had made a strong impression on Christians there (2:4, 8, 20): *let no one delude you with beguiling speech...See to it that no one makes a prey of you by philosophy and empty deceit...If with Christ you died to the elemental spirits of the universe, why do you live as if you still belonged to the world? Why do you submit to regulations "do not handle; do not taste; do not touch..."?* Some of the teachings include: observance of feasts, new moon, and Sabbath (2:16), dietary prescriptions (2:16, 21), the intention of which is strongly ascetic (2:20ff) and serve to mortify the body (2:23). There is also an insistence on *veneration of angels* (2:18) and the *elemental spirits of the universe* (2:20) which were believed to have power over human beings. The practice of these teachings was to prepare the person for direct contact with the angelic powers/elemental spirits through visions (2:18). The Gnostic secret wisdom, *philosophy and empty deceit* are to be avoided. The nature of the false teachings seem to have both Hellenistic and Jewish elements giving rise to the opinion that it was some type of syncretistic teaching being proposed – a combination of Hellenistic ascetic-ritualistic veneration of elements along with the Jewish speculation of angels and dietary prescriptions, and Gnostic ideas of secret wisdom that would lead to salvation; it is usually referred to as *the Colossian Heresy* since there is this mixture. The Colossian Heresy is understandable from the point of view that the region was known for its fascination with magic and mystery cults that promised access to the gods to those who were initiated into their secret rituals.

In response to this infiltration, the writer emphasizes Christ as the true teacher, the origin and head of the universe, of all creatures, also of angelic beings, the reconciler, the one who triumphed over spiritual powers in the cross, and in whom the fullness of the Godhead dwells (1:16; 2:10; 1:20-22; 2:14ff; 2:9, 3). The Colossian heresy raised doubts about Christ's having overcome the spirit world and so they proposed to please the spirit world by cultic and ascetic measures, therefore the author stresses the cosmic role of Christ and the overcoming of spiritual powers by Him (1:15-17, 19; 2:9ff, 15).

Hence the **occasion and purpose of the letter was to combat false teachings in Colossae and to stress again the true teachings**. In this process, Colossians makes a unique contribution to Christology through its insistence on the role of the cosmic Christ.

Authorship and integrity

Paul as the author of Colossians was first disputed in the early nineteenth century and since then there has been much study as to the authorship of this letter. Its affinity with Ephesians, ideas from Hellenistic mystery religions, and the Gnostic ideas against which the author is writing led scholars to doubt that Paul could have been the author in addition to the fact that he was not the founder of the community. The criteria for careful testing of the authenticity are:

1. Language and style: Colossians have distinctive features in vocabulary and sentence structure. There are several *hapax legomena* (rare words, see also Ephesians), and several words found elsewhere in the New Testament, but not in the Pauline writings. The style of synonyms is also to be noted: *praying and asking; in all wisdom and spiritual understanding* (1:9); *holy and blameless and unimpeachable* (1:22); and other grammatical peculiarities. In his *Introduction to the New Testament*, Kummel writes, *the style is cumbersome, wordy, overloaded almost to opaqueness with dependent clauses, participial and infinitive constructions, or substantives with* ἐν. *For example, 1:9-20 is one sentence!* Many known Pauline concepts are missing such as justification, righteousness, law, salvation

etc....

2. Since it has been agreed that the Colossian Heresy is a form of Gnosticism and especially of Christian Gnosticism prevalent in the second century, Paul's authorship has been doubted. The manner in which the false teachings have been combated is un-Pauline: the Gnostic terminology is not repudiated, but simply given a Christian understanding: Christology, ecclesiology, soteriology, eschatology, baptism are all given a Christian interpretation without repudiating the Gnostic understanding. The presentation of the "cosmic Christ" as the "head of the body, the Church" (1:16-19; 2:9ff., 19) does not first negate the Gnostic understanding, but only builds on it and Christianizes it! This is also seen in the quotation of the pre-Christian (with editorial additions) or Hellenistic Christian hymn of 1:15-20, where Christology has been expanded to include an understanding of the "cosmic Christ" which is a major contribution of Colossians although there are antecedents in the genuine Pauline letters, (e.g. I Cor. 2:8; 8:6; II Cor. 4:4; Gal. 4:3,9); the earlier letters which use this imagery do so while describing the functions of a body, but here, the "head" (= source rather than supremacy) is used as the highest authority in the Church; in other words, the Christology of Colossians has developed much further than what is found in the earlier writings.

3. None of the Pauline eschatological ideas such as *parousia*, resurrection of the dead, judgment etc... are found in Colossians.

4. The close relationship of Colossians with Ephesians in vocabulary, style and concepts (almost 70% similarity) raises the issue of similar contexts in which the writings arose and the question of dependency of one writing on the other.

In the light of the above, it can only be concluded that **Colossians does not come from Paul himself** but perhaps from someone in the

Pauline school of thought and therefore is to be placed among the **pseudonymous deutero-Pauline writings;** this is the position taken in this study (however, there are many who would attribute Colossians to Paul).

One of those who has much in his favour as the author of this letter is Epaphras, the founder of the community and someone trained and commissioned by Paul and who would therefore reflect Pauline ideas. When Epaphras was unable to go to Colossae to deal with the problem of false teachings the only solution was to write to the community. The fact that in the letter the close association of Paul and Epaphras is emphasized, and the commendation of Epaphras as a co-worker, and the assumption that Epaphras is a fellow-prisoner with Paul (4:7ff; 4:12ff), strengthens the claim of Pauline authorship (i.e. not from Paul himself but someone in the Pauline circle), and is perhaps a pointer that Epaphras, a close associate of Paul, has written with authority in the name of the apostle.

Further, Colossians and Philemon have much in common where names of individuals are concerned: Paul as a prisoner (where and under what circumstances is not known)(Col. 4:10,18; Philem. 1, 9, 23); Timothy is present in both (Col.1:1; Philem. 1); Epaphras is present in both (Col. 4:12; Philem. 24); Aristachus, Demas, Luke, Mark, Onesimus, Archippus are all common names (Col. 4:9; 4:10; 4:14; 4:17; Philem. 2; 10-12; 24). The individuals would have been associated with the Asia Minor area except for Mark which is a give away: Mark was not with Paul on the second missionary journey as Paul had refused to take him (Acts 15:36-40). Hence Mark's inclusion in the list of names is probably an attempt to cover the later and pseudonymous nature of the writing in order to make it acceptable and authoritative.

Place of writing and Date

The writing claims that Paul is a prisoner (4:3, 10, 18) but no place of imprisonment is mentioned. The most logical place would be Ephesus since it was the capital of the province of Asia to which the cities (Colossae, Laodicea and Hierapolis) in the Lycus Valley belonged. Also, the association of several names found in Ephesians and Philemon serves to give credibility to Epaphras who is a native of the area (Philem 23, Col. 1:8; 4:12). It is to be assumed that Epaphras, for whatever reason, had been imprisoned and that news of the situation in Colossae was greatly distressing him. Since he could not travel himself, he did the next best thing: a letter sent with a trusted co-worker, Tychicus (4:7ff) to counter the immediate situation, a letter written in the name of Paul who was still regarded as the apostolic authority in the area.

As is the case with Ephesians, the occasion and purpose for the writing of Colossians is to address a post-Pauline situation which could have been prevalent anywhere in the Hellenistic outreach of the church in Asia. Since Colossians is a post-Pauline writing its earliest possible date has to be after A.D.70, and since it was included in the Pauline corpus the latest possible date would be towards the end of the first century, therefore the best dating would be between **A.D 80 – 100**. In the light of accepting Colossians as a post-Pauline writing, the references to Paul as a prisoner (4:3, 10, 18) can only serve to substantiate the pseudonymous nature of the writing since it was well known that Paul had been a prisoner on several occasions; such references are meant to strengthen the link and add to the authority of the writing. **The affinity with Ephesians might suggest Asia Minor as a place of writing, but that can be no more than a possibility.**

Brief analysis and commentary

1:1-8: Opening Formula and Greetings

Timothy is listed as a co-sender as is also the case in Philippians and Philemon. It is known that Timothy was often Paul's emissary in the Lycus Valley region, so mention of his presence strengthens the alleged link with Paul, especially in a pseudonymous writing. The author is well aware that the Colossians have received the gospel well and makes a commendation of Epaphras (Epaphras introducing himself as the founder of the church so proposing an authenticity to the writing): ... *we have heard of your faith in Christ Jesus and of the love which you have for all the saints...the gospel which has come to you...as you learned it from Epaphras, our beloved fellow servant* (Ἐπαφρι του ἀγαπητου συνδουλου ἥμων)...

1:9-2:23: Indicative section of the letter

The indicative section of the letter is to express statements and facts; it is not argumentative, nor does it imply that any action must be taken. The section starts with the statement that the author's prayer is that the Colossians *may be filled with the knowledge of His will in all spiritual wisdom and understanding, to lead a life worthy of the Lord.... May you be strengthened with all power...for all endurance and patience with joy....* The reason for this emphasis on the understanding of Christ is to combat the false teaching that was infiltrating the churches in the region. So great emphasis is given to the person and work of Christ: *God has delivered us from the dominion of darkness and transferred us to the kingdom of God's beloved Son, in whom we have redemption, the forgiveness of sins.*

The understanding for a comprehensive knowledge of Christ is made through a famous Christological hymn (1:15-20) in which the work of Christ is described first as a mediator in creation and then as mediator in reconciliation. Most scholars agree that the hymn was already existing and familiar to the Colossians; the ideas expressed in the hymn were further sharpened/edited by additions of Christology which allowed the hymn to be used in combat against the false teachings.

The Son as mediator in creation: *He is the image of the invisible God* (ὅς ἐστιν εἰκων του Θεου του ἀορατου), *the first born of all creation* (πρωτοτοκος)... Since God cannot be seen, the Son – Jesus – becomes the image of what God is imagined to be like. The pre-existence of the Son is brought out – *in Him all things* (ἐκτισθη τα παντα) *were created, in heaven and on earth, visible and invisible...all things* (τα παντα) *were created through Him and for Him. He is before all things* (τα παντα), *and in Him all things* (τα παντα) *hold together.* The hymn's emphasis on *all things* (τα παντα) brings out the superiority of Christ over *thrones or dominions or principalities or authorities;* it also emphasizes that *in Him all the fullness of God* (πληρωμα του Θεου) *was pleased to dwell.* This would combat the Gnostic idea that fullness referred to the rays that emanated from God but were not God; God was above the emanations. But here the fullness (πληρωμα) is a reality that dwells completely in Christ and therefore Christ is not only the first born of creation, but also the creator of all things. This first section establishes the supremacy of Christ over all things.

The Son as mediator in reconciliation: *(Christ) is the head of the body, the Church* (αὐτος ἐστιν ἥ κεφαλη του σωματος, της ἐκκλησιας); *He is the beginning, the first born from the dead...in Him all the fullness* (πληρωμα) *of God was pleased to dwell, and through Him to reconcile* (ἀποκαταλλαξαι) *to Himself all things* (τα παντα), *whether on earth or in heaven, making peace by the blood of His cross.* This would combat the Gnostic 'redeemer myth" – someone who would come as the special messenger from God as the redeemer, i.e. to restore the relationship with God. Here it is very emphatic that Christ is the mediator of reconciliation through his work on the cross – a reconciliation not only with God but also with *all things* (τα παντα). In many ways this is a very comprehensive picture of reconciliation, the hope of a renewed, reconciled creation which includes the present-day environmental concerns.

Christ's reconciling work is summed up thus: *you, who once were enemies of God, separated from God, estranged and hostile in mind, doing evil deeds, He has now reconciled in His body of flesh by His death, in order to present you holy and blameless...* with the proviso that they *continue in the faith, stable and steadfast, not shifting from the hope of the gospel which you heard...*

The author sees his sufferings as a continuation and completion of the *sufferings of Christ for the sake of Christ's body, the Church.* The author's task is to make the word of God fully known, *the mystery* (τα μυστηριον) *hidden for ages and generations but now made manifest to his saints,* especially among the Gentiles. The use of *mystery* vocabulary evokes images of Gnosticism and the Hellenistic mystery religions; *mystery* is a theme that appears several times in Colossians (1:26,27; 2:2; 4:3) as the point being made is that the *mystery* is no longer a mystery! The revelation which Jews and Gentiles struggled to find is no longer a secret; it has been revealed in Jesus Christ; this is what is proclaimed so that everyone *may be presented mature in Christ.* The mention of *I want you to know how greatly I strive for you, and for those at Laodicea...* immediately associates the writing with Epaphras, the founder of the churches at

Colossae and Laodicea, emphasizing that *though I am absent in the body, yet I am with you in spirit*. They are encouraged to remain *knit together in love, to have all the riches of assured understanding and the knowledge of God's mystery of Christ in whom are hid all the treasures of wisdom and knowledge.... rooted and built up in him and established in the faith, just as you were taught...* Although the exact problem is not stated, nevertheless, reading from a mirror image, this is a clear reminder that the Colossians are to stand firm against any false teaching so that *no one may delude you with beguiling speech*.

This warning leads to the author's response to the Colossian heresy. There are allusions to *philosophy and empty deceit, according to human traditions, according to the elemental spirits of the universe, and not according to Christ;* there are repeated references to *mystery:* all indicative that the Colossians are dealing with a complex set of teachings (see Occasion and Purpose, above) and confusion about the need to observe Jewish regulations on matters of circumcision, dietary laws, festivals and Sabbath – probably a syncretistic expression of Jewish and Hellenistic-Roman philosophies, practices, and mysticism: *in Him you were circumcised with a circumcision made without hands...buried with Him in baptism..raised with Him through faith...Therefore, let no one pass judgment on you in questions of food and drink or with regard to a festival or a new moon or a Sabbath. These are only a shadow of what is to come but the substance belongs to Christ. Let no one disqualify you, insisting on self-abasement and worship of angels....Why do you live as if you still belonged to the world?....according to human precepts and doctrines. These have indeed an appearance of wisdom in promoting rigour of doctrines and self-abasement and severity to the body, but they are of no value.....*

The points being made in the section are that Christ is the supreme head, the creator and reconciler, and that false/faulty theological presuppositions/teachings that miss the centrality of Christ result in an equally faulty course of action. The Colossians are warned about this false/faulty teaching and encouraged to hold fast to what has been taught/preached to them.

3:1-4:6: The Imperative section of the letter:

The imperative section of the letter is to suggest a life-style that must be implemented as an ethical expression of the new life in Christ – actions that will totally negate the old life-style and emphasize the centrality of Christ: *if then you have been raised with Christ, seek the things that are above, where Christ is, seated at the right hand of God. Set your minds on things that are above...* for when Christ appears *you also* will *appear with Him in glory.*

A list of vices to be avoided is given: *immorality, impurity, passion, evil desire, and covetousness, which is idolatry....in these you once walked; now put them away.* Further to be avoided are: *anger, wrath, malice, slander, and foul talk from your mouth. Do not lie to one another.... Put off the old nature with its practices and out on the new nature...after the image of its creator.* Any new lifestyle that does not involve a complete break with the past continues to pose the danger of falling back into the old ways; syncreticism (taking something from the old background and incorporating it into the new) is also to be avoided. In the new lifestyle, *there cannot be Greek and Jew, circumcised and uncircumcised, barbarian, Scythian, slave, free, but Christ is all and in all* (ἀλλα παντα και ἐν πασιν Χριστος). In an earlier passage – Gal. 3:28 – *all are one in Christ,* but here the emphasis has changed to Christology and it is Christ who is all in all.

The virtues to be practiced in the new lifestyle are: *compassion* (σπλαγχνα οἰκτιρμον– literally 'bowels of mercies'), *kindness, lowliness, meekness and patience, forbearing one another...forgiving one another... And above all, put on love, which binds everything together in perfect harmony... And be thankful.*

Finally, in the list of imperatives, the *haustafel* or instructions concerning household relationships, are given: *wives, be subject to your husbands.... husbands, love your wives...children, obey your parents...fathers, do not provoke your children... slaves, obey in everything...*The *haustafel* or household codes were certainly influenced by contemporary ethical lists, but a new Christological dimension was added: *in the Lord...serving the Lord Christ...Master in heaven....* The rules for the household are now under the Lordship of Christ (see also the section Eph. 5:21-6:9, above). In any present-day interpretation, these culturally conditioned texts must be looked at from the Christological perspective with which they are presented. In other words, a whole new dimension of relationships is being presented – a Christological re-interpretation, and a specific Christian contribution to the understanding of household relationships, and by extension, of relationships in society. It is also to be noted that the household relationships are listed after the imperative on love and that *whatever you do, in word or deed, do everything in the name of the Lord Jesus*... This would indicate that cultural patterns are subject to renewal/re-interpretation in the light of Christ's ethical demands. Thus, it can be said that *there cannot be Jew or Greek... all are one*. This is one more 'mystery' of God revealed in Christ that affects every aspect of day-to-day life and calls for change.

4:7-18: Greetings and Concluding Formula:

Many of the names given in the greetings are parallel with names listed in Ephesians and Philemon (see above, and comments in Ephesians and Philemon) which are important in discussing the introductory issues of authorship, place of writing etc... Tychicus and Onesimus (in Philemon, he is the runaway slave being sent back, but here he is a mission worker) were entrusted with taking the letter to Colossae and in giving the Colossians information concerning the author: *Tychicus will tell you all about my affairs; he is a beloved brother and faithful minister and fellow servant in the Lord. I have sent him to you for this very purpose...Onesimus, the faithful and beloved brother...who is one of yourselves...they will tell you everything that has taken place here.*

The mention of Mark among those present raises the issue of Paul's authorship as Mark was not with Paul on this journey or during Paul's stay in Ephesus/Colossae/Asia (Acts 15:36-40). The reference to Archippus is interesting: he is mentioned in Philemon 2 (see comments on Philemon, above), and perhaps was the son of Philemon. It closely associates/connects the letters to Philemon and Colossians. The instructions to be passed on to Archippus: *see that you fulfill the ministry which you have received in the Lord*, may perhaps reflect that Archippus was somewhat taken in with the false teachers and was leaning towards them; here he is singled out for correction.

There are instructions to share the letter with the community at Laodicea and also to read the letter to the Laodiceans. The letter to the Laodiceans seems to be lost, but many hold that the letter to the Ephesians was actually the letter to the Laodiceans (see introductory issues in Ephesians, above) even if it bears the nature of a covering letter for the collection of Pauline letters. The common bonds with Laodicea would be: Epaphras, who was also responsible for founding the community in Laodicea; the geographical proximity of the two cities; the probability that both cities faced the same situation of false teachers; the list of common names found in Ephesians, Philemon and Colossians; the possibility that both letters were written by Epaphras in the name of Paul.

The letter ends with copying the usual style of Paul – writing the final greetings and blessings – once again trying to be convincing regarding the authorship and authority issue.

Select Bibliography for Colossians
(see also bibliography for Ephesians and Philemon, above)

Bruce, F. F. *The Epistles to the Colossians, to Philemon, and to the Ephesians*, New International Commentary on the New Testament. Grand Rapids: Eerdmans. 1984.

Dunn, James D. G.*The Epistles to the Colossians and Philemon*, New International Greek Testament Commentary. Grand Rapids: Eerdmans, 1996.

Nicholls, Bruce and Brian C. Wintle.*Colossians and Philemon*, Asia Bible Commentary. Manila: Asia Theological Association, 2006.

Sanyu Iralu. "Colossians" in Brian C. Wintle (General Editor), *South Asia Biblical Commentary*. Udaipur, Rajasthan: Open Door Publication, 2015, pages 1660 – 1668.

Deutero-Pauline:
D. The Thessalonian Correspondence – I & II Thessalonians

The founding of the community. Authorship/authenticity and unity. Occasion and purpose of the letters. Place and Date of writing. Brief analysis and commentary on the text. Select bibliography for the Thessalonian Correspondence.

The founding of the community

Thessalonica was the capital of the Roman province of Macedonia and lay on the west-east highway which linked Rome with the East. It was a populous city which had a synagogue (Acts 17:1) and many non-Jewish *devout Greeks and not a few of the leading women* (Acts 17:4). On the so-called Second Missionary Journey, towards the end of A.D. 49, Paul came from Philippi to Thessalonica along with Silvanus (Silas) and Timothy (Acts 17:1-10; 18:5); their work n Thessalonica resulted in the founding of the community there. The community was almost entirely from a Hellenistic background (I 1:9; 2:14, Acts 17:4). According to Phil. 4:16, the Philippians sent aid to Paul in Thessalonica more than once. The community must have developed quickly as they are held up as examples (I 1:7ff) for Macedonia and Achaia. However, according to Acts, Paul's stay there was short – three weeks only Acts 17:2–as Jews in the city created trouble for him, so along with Silas he had to flee by night to Beroea (Acts 17:5ff), but there too, Jews from Thessalonica followed him and created trouble, so Paul moved on to Athens and thence to Corinth (Acts 17:13ff), leaving Silas and Timothy in Beroea with orders to join him as soon as possible in Athens, but they met up with Paul in Corinth (Acts 18:5). However, the story in Acts does not agree with what is said in I Thess. 3:1-6, presumably by Paul, where the persecution seems to have set in even before he left.Also, Philip.4:16 states that the Philippians sent money to Paul n Thessalonica several times, a description that suggests more than a few weeks' stay. Nevertheless, regardless of the journeys of Paul and his companions, and the length of his stay, **Paul is regarded as the founder of the community in Thessalonica.**

Authenticity and Unity

There are two letters to the Thessalonians in the New Testament. Some claim that they were originally one, whereas others detect four letters. This has to be examined in some detail before proceeding with other introductory matters and commentary.

A characteristic feature of all Pauline letters is the thanksgiving which immediately follows the address and introduces the main themes of the letter (see Analysis of other letters, above and below). A quick reading shows the similarities between I Thess. 1:2-10 and 2:13-14 – two thanksgivings. Many feels that instead of two thanksgivings, there is only one thanksgiving from 1:2 to 3:10; this constitutes too long a thanksgiving passage which is the main section of the letter and therefore implausible.

Also recognized are two conclusions: I Thess. 3:11 to 4:2 and 5:23-28. These sections contain a number of elements normally found in the conclusion of a Pauline letter: the blessing and the desire to see the recipients (3:11ff.; 5:23ff); and the phrase *finally, brethren…* (4:1); and the instructions for the letter to be read to all (5:27).

In the light of the above, the position accepted here is that **I Thessalonians is a compilation of two originally independent letters: 2:13 – 4:2 (Letter 1) with its own thanksgiving and conclusion inserted into another letter which consists of 1:1 - 2:12 + 4:3 - 5:28 (Letter 2).** This sort of compilation is not unusual among the letters of Paul; it was observed in the Corinthian correspondence (7 letters, see above) and in Philippians (3 letters, see above). When there is a compilation, the letters are usually truncated because the beginning and the ending of each becomes superfluous if it is to be presented as a single letter. Thus, it is not surprising that 2:13 - 4:2 lacks the address and the normal ending of a letter with the peace and grace benediction. The question raised by the acceptance of this hypothesis is: why was 2:13 - 4:2 inserted into the middle of 1:1-2:12 + 4:3- 5:28?

The answer is that there is similarity between 2:11-12 and 4:1-2 which fits in well with the instructions of 4:3-12 which originally must have followed 2:11-12. The *call of God* in 2:12 matches the *word of God* in 2:13, so they fit well together. Therefore, there is a continuity of thought between these two letters and they naturally fit together giving the impression of a single letter.

The letter consisting of 2:13 - 4:2 (referred to as Letter 1) can be seen to be prior as it expresses a deep sense of relief (2:17-18) that persecution (2:14)had not forced the Thessalonians to give up Christianity (3:2-3,5,6,7); the joy experienced at coming to know the steadfast faith of the Thessalonians seems to be the occasion for this letter; it was the writer's sense of relief that prompted the letter and not a response to any query or problem.

The letter consisting of 1:1-2:12 + 4:3-5:28 (referred to as Letter 2) makes no reference to persecution and is a calm didactic (teaching) letter without the endearments expressed in 2:13 - 4:2. Most of the letter consists of explaining Paul's image among the members of the community (2:1-12) and when he returns to the needs of the Thessalonians, it is to instruct them in the demands of Christian living and to deal with issues concerning the *Day of the Lord* (4:3-12, 13; 5:11, 12-22). Also, there is no expression of a desire to see the Thessalonians indicating that the writer is quite satisfied with the situation in which the Thessalonians find themselves – a situation where they are an example to others (1:7-8, 4:9).

II Thessalonians repeats most of Letter 2 (above) for the address, thanksgiving and conclusion. The only section that remains is the corrective regarding the *Day of the Lord* (2:1 - 3:15). Therefore, there is not much debate on the unity of the writing although there is much debate on the authenticity of the letter which many ascribe to a disciple of Paul written towards the end of the century. This is especially based on the thinking of the nearness of the end time and related fantasies of apocalypticism which are regarded as un-Pauline. Nevertheless, II Thessalonians is usually accepted as a unified writing (Letter 3) although with a question mark over its authenticity as it brings out a corrective to the eschatological perspective from the one in Letter 2.

In the light of the above, the Thessalonian correspondence consists of three letters:

1. **Letter 1 – I Thess. 2:13 - 4:2;**

2. **Letter 2 – I Thess. 1:1 - 2:12 + 4:3 - 5:28;**

3. **Letter 3 – II Thessalonians.**

The authenticity of the Thessalonian correspondence has always been attributed to Paul and perhaps even as his earliest writings, but the compilation of the correspondence would have been after Paul, hence **the compiled letters, as found in the New Testament, are placed among the pseudonymous deutero-Pauline writings.**

Occasion and purpose of the letters

Letter 1: The letter consisting of 2:13 - 4:2 (referred to as Letter 1) can be seen to be prior as it expresses a deep sense of relief (2:17-18) that persecution (2:14) had not forced the Thessalonians to give up Christianity (3:2-3,5,6,7); the joy experienced at coming to know the steadfast faith of the Thessalonians seems to be the occasion for this letter. Paul had wanted to visit the Thessalonians but had been prevented (2:17), so he sent Timothy (3:2) to them and Timothy had returned with the good news of the steadfastness of the Thessalonians (3:6). This was the cause of Paul's joy and the occasion of the letter. **It was the writer's sense of relief that occasioned the letter and not a response to any questions or problems. The purpose was simply to express this joy.** It was a warm letter, emotionally charged, and expressing a close relationship with deep concern.

Letter 2: This letter consisting of 1:1 - 2:12 + 4:3 - 5:28 has more to do with ethical imperatives (4:3-8) – what the Thessalonians are expected to do rather than with the situation of persecution, the immediate threat of which is evident in Letter 1, seems to have passed. There are also hints that perhaps all is not well in the community (5:12ff.) and they are exhorted to live in peace and harmony. The *Day of the Lord*

(5:2ff.) also seems to be a concern that needed to be addressed. Thus, **this letter is occasioned by the concerns for the community and its purpose was to address certain issues which the community was facing.**

Letter 3: This consists of the New Testament letter of II Thessalonians. There is much similarity between Letter 2 and II Thessalonians (Letter 3) because much of the subject matter is the same. **The occasion and purpose of the letter was to correct any misunderstandings/ misinterpretations that might have arisen from Letter 2 concerning the Day of the Lord.** II Thessalonians reflects an exaggerated expectation of the *Day of the Lord* – whether it has already come or is so near that antinomianism (no need for obeying laws/rules and regulations) resulted and relationships ignored (chapter 2); this apocalyptic fascination and fanaticism led even to giving up of work (3:9ff.) – a situation which had to be firmly dealt with and a community discipline imposed.

Place and Date of writing

Since three letters have been identified, the place and date of the writing of each has to be examined.

Letter 1 (2:13 - 4:2): The occasion and purpose, as outlined above, was to express relief that the Thessalonians had stood firm in their faith in the light of persecution. Timothy had been sent from Athens to Thessalonica to encourage the community there to stand firm in their faith (3:2); Timothy had now returned to Paul (3:6) with the good news of the Thessalonians' faith and love. Where was Paul when Timothy returned to him? It would seem logical for Paul to remain in Athens so that he could be found easily even though he does not seem to have had much success in his missionary work in Athens (Acts 17:16ff. records Paul's speech at the Areopagus in Athens, but the response was to put him off till another time; whether he ever preached there again is not recorded either in Acts or anywhere in Paul's letters). **The letter of relief after Timothy's return would have been written from Athens about early A.D. 50.**

Letter 2 (1:1 - 2:12 + 4:3 - 5:28): From Athens, Paul moved to Corinth (Acts 18:1). Acts 18:5 records that Silas and Timothy joined him there, but I Cor. 1:19 indicates that Paul, Silvanus and Timothy are together in Corinth during the founding visit there; hence, from primary sources, the move to Corinth from Athens was only after the return of Timothy from Thessalonica. While at Corinth, Paul seems to have received fresh information regarding issues at Thessalonica and in response, he wrote Letter 2 with its ethical imperatives, exhortations to live in peace and harmony, and concerns regarding the *Day of the Lord*. Hence **1:1 - 2:12 + 4:3 - 5:28 would have been written from Corinth towards the end of A.D. 50/early 51.**

Letter 3 (II Thessalonians 1:1 - 3:18): Many hold that II Thessalonians does not originate from Paul but from a disciple writing in his name at a later date, based on the fact that much of I Thessalonians (Letter 2) is repeated in II Thessalonians (Letter 3) but with a difference – the eschatological images are incompatible with each other and are closer to later apocalyptic writings like Revelation. However, if as stated above, II Thessalonians was written to correct the misunderstanding/misinterpretation of the *Day of the Lord,* then the similarities are understandable and so also the change in the eschatological imagery used in the process of correction. Whoever brought the news to Paul of the situation in Thessalonica (3:11) stirred up in Paul the concern which he had expressed in Letter 2 regarding the unrest/unease there and prompted him to write an even sterner warning (II Thess. 3:6, 11). Hence **II Thessalonians would have been written from Corinth in the spring/summer of A.D. 51.**

The Thessalonian correspondence would be much like the Philippian correspondence – three original letters by Paul but with editorial activity and compilation at a later stage (see introductory issues for Philippians, above). Hence the three original letters by Paul to the Thessalonians could be dated between A.D. 50 to 51. However, **the compilation and editorial activity after the time of Paul would have to be dated between A.D 80 – 100 placing the Thessalonian correspondence among** the pseudonymous deutero-Pauline letters. It would be logical to accept that any editorial activity during the compilation of the letters would have been carried out at the place where the letters were preserved as honoured writings and instructions from the founder of the community, i.e. in Thessalonica, but it could be at any other place where a collection of Pauline writings was preserved.

Brief analysis and commentary

Since three letters/fragments have been identified (see discussion above), the brief analysis and commentary will follow the sequence of the letters/ fragments as identified above; otherwise the frequent shifts in thought present difficulties in the integrity, understanding and interpretation. The texts will be analyzed in the following chronological order:

1. **Letter 1: I Thess. 2:13 - 4:2**

2. **Letter 2: I Thess. 1:1-2:12 +4:3-5:28**

3. **Letter 3: II Thessalonians**

Letter 1: I Thess. 2:13 - 4:2 – Letter of relief and thanksgiving after Timothy's return:

Paul, Silvanus and Timothy had to flee from Thessalonica due to opposition from some Jewish elements there; they went to Beroea, but when the Jewish elements followed them there, they had to leave there as well and came to Athens (see Acts 17 and the introductory issues, above). Paul's success among the Gentiles in Thessalonica angered the Jews who aroused the crowds against Paul and party; in I Thess. 2:2 Paul speaks of *great opposition* (πολλῷ ἀγωνι) in Thessalonica. Having had to leave in a hurry, Paul was naturally anxious about the community he had left behind and to know how they were dealing with the situation of persecution, especially since he had not been with them for too long a period to be convinced of the firmness of their faith. There was an intense desire to visit the Thessalonians again even though it was such a short time since he had left them, but this was not to be: *since we were bereft of you, beloved, for a short time, in person not in heart, we endeavoured the more eagerly and with great desire to see you face to face; we wanted to come to you, but Satan hindered us.*

So, Timothy was sent from Athens, *willing to be left behind in Athens... we sent Timothy...to establish you in your faith and to exhort you, that no one be moved by these afflictions.* Paul's concern was that the Thessalonians would give in under pressure/threat of persecution, *I feared that somehow the tempter had tempted you and that our labour would be in vain.* The exact nature and form of persecution is not mentioned; the only thing to be assumed is that it is a continuation of the persecution that Paul suffered and which caused him to flee the city – a persecution from Jews: *you became imitators of the churches of God in Christ Jesus which are in Judea;* – and persecution from the Gentiles: *you suffered the same things from your own countrymen.*

Timothy's return to Paul with the good news that the Thessalonians had stood firm, *Timothy has come to us from you, and has brought us the good news of your faith and love...so even in all our distress and affliction we have been comforted about you.* Paul's relief and joy at the news results in a thanksgiving: *for what thanksgiving can we render to God for you, for all the joy which we feel for your sake before our God....?*

The letter ends with the hope that Paul could still visit them: *may our God...direct our way to you.* He again exhorts them to remain firm in their faith: *finally, beloved, we beseech and exhort you in the Lord Jesus... how you ought to live and to please God.*

It is a warm letter occasioned by relief and expressing confidence in the community.

Letter 2: I Thess. 1:1-2:12 + 4:3-5:28 – Ethical imperatives and concerns regarding the *Day of the Lord.*

This letter does not refer to a situation of persecution as in Letter 1 nor does it refer to Paul's ardent desire to visit the Thessalonians or to the relief at Timothy's return with good news. Hence it seems to be a completely separate writing in which Letter 1 has been inserted since there is similarity between 2:11-12 and 4:1-2 which fits in well with the instructions of 4:3-12 which originally must have followed 2:11-12. The *call of God* in 2:12 matches the *word of God* in 2:13, so they fit well together. Therefore, there is a continuity of thought between these two letters and they naturally fit together giving the impression of a single letter.

The letter opens with the customary greetings, *Paul, Silvanus and Timothy* are mentioned as the co-authors. This is followed by a long thanksgiving (1:2-10): *we give thanks to God always for you all, constantly mentioning you in our prayers, remembering...your work of faith* (μνημονευοντες ὑμων του ἐργου της πιστεως) *and labour of love* (του κοπου της ἀγαπης) *and steadfastness of hope* (ὑπομονης της ἐλπιδος) *in our Lord Jesus Christ....you are an example to all the believers in Macedonia and in Achaia....*

Paul's attention then shifts to himself and his image among the members of the community, thereby indicating that there are no immediately pressing problems at Thessalonica and also instructing them through personal example. He rates his work at Thessalonica as successful though he faced problems: *you yourselves know, beloved, that our visit to you was not in vain, even though we had already suffered and been shamefully treated at Philippi...and declared to you the gospel of God in the face of great opposition...we have been approved by God to be entrusted with the gospel...we never used words of flattery as a cloak for greed ...or demands as apostles of Christ. But we were gentle among you...we were ready to share with you not only the gospel of God but also our own selves, because you had become very dear to us.* He then enumerates the work that he did among the community: *you remember our labour and toil* (μνημονευετε τον κοπον ἡμων και τὸ μοχθον)*...we worked day and night, that we might not burden any of you, while we preached to you the gospel.* Presumably this is the time when the Philippians sent financial aid to Paul so that he would not be a burden to the Thessalonians (Phillip. 4:15-16).

Paul's attention shifts back to the Thessalonians from 4:3ff when the spells out the demands of Christian living – the ethical imperatives 4:3-12; 5:12-22) – and issues concerning the *Day of the Lord* (4:13 to 5:11). In the ethical imperatives, he exhorts them to *abstain from immorality* (ἀπεχεσθαι ὑμας ἀπο της πορνειας)*...to take a wife in holiness and honour, not in the passion of lust like heathen...no one should transgress and wrong another in this matter...God has not called us for uncleanness, but* *in holiness* (οὐ γαρ ἐκαλεσέ ἤμας ὅ Θεος ἐπι ἀκαθαρσια ἀλλ᾽ ἐν ἅγιασμῳ). They are already examples of love and loyalty within the community and do not need further instructions, nevertheless, he exhorts them, *concerning love...you have no need to have any one write to you...love one another* (το ἀγαπαν ἀλληλους)...*and we exhort you to do more and more, to aspire to live quietly, to mind your own affairs, and to work with your hands...so that you may command the respect of outsiders, and be dependent on nobody.*

Questions regarding the *Day of the Lord* seemed to have arisen among the community. The early Christian communities were highly eschatological – i.e. they believed that they were living in the end times and that the Lord would return soon. But the delay in the Lord's return began to raise doubts and questions. Apocalyptic imagery and vocabulary were used as an apologetic to explain the situation, especially the issue of those who had died before the return of the Lord, as is the case here: *we would not have you ignorant concerning those who are asleep that you may not grieve as others do who have no hope.* The message of hope was that because of the death and resurrection of Christ, all would share in the same experience: *through Jesus, God will bring with Him those who have fallen asleep.* The apocalyptic imagery helps in explaining Paul's position: *we who are alive, who are left until the coming of the Lord, shall not precede those who have fallen asleep...the Lord will descend from heaven with a cry of command...with the sound of the trumpet of God. And the dead in Christ will rise first, then we who are alive...shall be caught up together with them in the clouds to meet the Lord in the air; and so, we shall always be with the Lord.* No time or date can be attached to all this: *as to the times and seasons...you yourselves know well that the day of the Lord* (ἤμερα κυριου) *will come like a thief in the night....* Overall, the encouragement is: *let us be sober, and put on the breastplate of faith and love, and for a helmet the hope of salvation... whether we wake or sleep we might live with Him* (ἵνα εἰτε γρηγορωμεν εἰτε καθευδωμεν ἅμα συν αὐτῳ ζησωμεν). *Therefore encourage one another and build one another up...* The concern here is not to suggest a timetable of the last events, nor even to suggest that the day of the Lord will defy the law of gravity, but the concern is pastoral – to calm any disturbance in the community with the pastoral instructions to love, encourage and build one another up. In this sense, the eschatological thinking is much like the Gospels (Mark 13 and parallels) and Acts (Acts 1:6-8) – there is a surety in its coming, but when and how is left to God. Nevertheless, the passage reflects the Christian eschatological images which had come down from early times, and which are still prevalent today – images of clouds, trumpets, angels, dead rising from their graves, Christ descending and believers ascending. It must always be understood that apocalyptic imagery is a symbolic and colourful way of expressing that the end time will take place with events which involve human beings, but over which human beings have no control, hence the use of supernatural beings and other natural phenomena.

The concluding section of the letter is a series of directions/ exhortations/imperatives:

1. *Respect those who labour among you…who are over you in the Lord… who admonish you…esteem them highly in love;*
2. Be at peace among yourselves;
3. Admonish the idle;
4. Encourage the fainthearted;
5. Help the weak;
6. Be patient with all;
7. See that none repays evil for evil, but always seek to do good;
8. Rejoice always;
9. Pray constantly;
10. Give thanks in all circumstances;
11. Do not quench the Spirit;
12. Do not despise prophesying but test everything;
13. Hold fast to what is good;
14. Abstain from every form of evil.

All of the above instructions are for the building up of the community. The letter ends with the blessing and prayer that *your spirit and soul and body be kept sound and blameless at the coming of our Lord Jesus Christ.* The request for prayer and the instruction to *greet one another with a holy kiss* breaks down barriers of Jew and Gentile and builds up community. There are instructions *that this letter be read to all the community.* The final greetings follow: *the grace of our Lord Jesus Christ....*Thus, the letter begins with 'grace' and ends with 'grace'.

Letter 3: II Thessalonians - 1:1 - 3:18 – Correcting misunderstandings and emphasizing concerns and instructions from Letter 2.

It would seem that circumstances forced Paul to return to the same subjects as covered in Letters 1 & 2, and especially Letter 2, so there is much similarity in language. There are two passages from Letter 2 which easily lend themselves to misinterpretation providing the occasion for the letter: *you yourselves know that the day of the Lord comes as a thief in the night* (I Thess. 5:2), and *God has not destined us to wrath but to obtain salvation...whether we wake or sleep we might live with Him* (I Thess. 5:9). These will be examined in more detail below in the attempt to correct the misunderstanding in Letter 3 which is II Thessalonians.

The letter opens with the greetings – the same three from Letter 2 – *Paul, Silvanus and Timothy,* perhaps indicative that the letters were not very far apart. The thanksgiving section (1:3-10) praises the faith and love of the Thessalonians even in the midst of their persecution and suffering: *we are bound to give thanks to God always for you, beloved, as is fitting, because your faith is growing abundantly, and the love of every one of you for one another is increasing....in all your persecutions and in the afflictions which you are enduring.* The Lord Jesus will inflict vengeance and eternal punishment on their persecutors, while they will be given rest and glorified: *they (the persecutors) shall suffer the punishment of eternal destruction and exclusion from the presence of the Lord...when He comes on that day to be glorified in His saints...*So, Paul prays that God will make them worthy of their call.

Paul then immediately takes up the issue that has caused misunderstanding in the indicative section of the letter– *the coming of our Lord Jesus Christ and our assembling to meet Him.* He cautions them *not to be quickly shaken in mind or excited either by spirit, or by word, or by letter purporting to be from us, to the effect that the day of the Lord has come. Let no one deceive you in any way; for that day will not come....* He goes on to use accepted apocalyptic signs that must precede the coming of that day – apostasy, lawlessness, appearance of anti-God and the activity of Satan (2:3-12). The reference to *by letter* probably refers to Letter 2 (I Thess. 4:13ff) where he initially dealt with the same subject and which seems to have been misinterpreted. Perhaps the Thessalonians were in an intense expectation of the soon coming of the *Day of the Lord after* receiving Letter 2 and even thought that the *Day* had arrived secretly. This interpretation was probably facilitated by reduced suffering and persecution as signs of Christ's presence among them since persecution is not mentioned in Letter 2 as much as it is the cause of concern in Letter 1. The Thessalonians are encouraged *to stand firm and hold to the traditions which you were taught by us, either by word of mouth or by letter* (ἀρα οὐν, ἀδελφοι, στηκετε, και κρατειτε τας παραδοσεις ἅς ἐδιδαχθητε εἰτε δια λογου εἰτε δι᾽ ἐπιστολης ἥμων). The reference to *letter* twice in this section indicates that Letter 2 had been misunderstood and so a corrective was supplied.

In the imperative section of the letter, Paul requests, *pray for us, that the word of the Lord may speed on and triumph, as it did among you, and that we may be delivered from wicked and evil persons.* Paul affirms that *the Lord is faithful; the Lord will strengthen you and guard you from evil.* He then gives a specific command, *that you keep away from anyone who is living in idleness and not in accord with the traditions that you received from us.* Possibly the Thessalonians had legitimately concluded that their salvation was guaranteed *(whether we wake or sleep we might live with Him, I Thess. 5:9)* and thus some had given up jobs, and perhaps even practiced immorality, as an ethical lifestyle seemed useless since they expected an imminent *Day of the Lord.* This was not imitating Paul who had worked hard to support himself during his stay at Thessalonica. Consequently, *if anyone will not work, let them not eat!* (εἰ τις οὐ θελει ἐργαζεσθαι μηδε ἐσθιετω). To mark the seriousness of the command, a further order is given, *if anyone refuses to obey what we say in this letter, note those persons, and have nothing to do with them, that they may become ashamed.* In spite of the stern warning, the pastoral side still comes through: *do not look on them as enemies but warn them as beloved members.* The ultimate purpose of church/community discipline is not excommunication or any form of punishment, but a correction leading to the building up of the person and the community.

The letter closes with a prayerful wish for peace – a prayer that would have been appropriate for a community confused with regard to the *Day of the Lord,* and the problems caused by those who refused to work. Paul gives the final greetings in his own hand.

Thus the Thessalonian correspondence is a cameo of an early community: a community facing persecution, yet remaining firm in their faith giving cause for thanksgiving; a community with a close relationship with their founder to whom they look for continued guidance; a community that was faced with logical theological questions about the end times and what they could/should expect; a community that needed correction when they misunderstood/misinterpreted the apostle's message; and a community that was willing to be corrected. It is no wonder then, that the letters to the Thessalonians were carefully preserved and compiled at a later date to form part of the Pauline corpus.

Select Bibliography for the Thessalonian Correspondence

Best, E. *Harper's New Testament Commentary Series.*New York: Harper and Row, 1972.

Bruce, F. F., Word *Bible Commentary.*Dallas: Word, 1982.

Cherian, Jacob. "I Thessalonians" in Brian C. Wintle (General Editor), *South Asia BiblicalCommentary.*Udaipur, Rajasthan: Open Door Publication, 2015, pages 1669 – 1676.

_____, "II Thessalonians" in Brian C. Wintle (General Editor), *South Asia Biblical Commentary.*Udaipur, Rajasthan: Open Door Publication, 2015, pages 1677 – 1681.

Fee, Gordon D.*The First and Second Letters to the Thessalonians,* New International Commentary on the New Testament. Grand Rapids: Eerdmans, 2009.

Marshall, I. Howard. *New Century Bible Commentary Series.* Grand Rapids: Eerdmans, 1983.

CHAPTER - 5

An Introduction to the Trito-Pauline Letters:
The Pastorals –
A. I Timothy B. II Timothy C.Titus

The Recipients / Addressees. Historical and Theological Issues. Purpose. Place of writing. Date. Brief Analysis and Commentary on the text. Select bibliography for the Pastorals.

The name 'Pastoral' or Shepherd Letters for I & II Timothy and Titus originated in the 18th Century when it was recognized that their main aim was instructions and admonitions for the fulfillment of the pastoral office in the early Christian communities. These instructions were addressed to Paul's close co-workers and companions, but they are not 'private' letters, rather they are, as the Muratorian canon records, official communications for "for ordering Church discipline". These three writings form a group among themselves within the traditional writings ascribed to Paul. I Timothy and Titus are closely related, but all three presuppose false teachers, the same church organization, and similar conditions in the communities which received them; they have similar theological concepts and use similar language and style of writing.

The Recipients/Addressees

I & II Timothy: Both letters are addressed to Timothy in Ephesus (I Tim. 1:3; II Tim. 1:15). Timothy was from Lystra in Lyconia, the son of a pagan (Greek) father and a Jewish-Christian mother (Acts 16:1); his grandmother's name was Lois and his mother's name was Eunice (II Tim. 1:5). Paul recruited Timothy at Lystra and had him circumcised to prevent any problems with the Jews, especially entering of synagogues since they knew that his father was a non-Jew (Acts 16:3).Since that time Timothy was a close colleague of Paul for many years (Acts 17:14ff; 18:5 19:22; 20:4;Rom. 16:21; I Cor. 16:10; II Cor. 1:1, 19; Philp. 1:1, 2:19; I Thess. 1:1; II Thess. 1:1); he accompanied Paul while delivering the collection to Jerusalem (Acts 20:4); and was with Paul in the places of his imprisonment (Col. 1:1; Philm. 1). Paul treated Timothy as *his child in the faith* (I Tim. 1:2, 18; II Tim. 1:2) and regarded him highly commending his work (I Cor. 16:10-11; Philp. 2:19ff.; I Thess. 3:1ff.). The circumstances surrounding the reference to Timothy in Heb. 13:23 remains unexplained from the known information regarding Timothy in the New Testament. The later tradition of the Church holds that Timothy was made the first Bishop of Ephesus and died as a martyr towards the end of the first century (The feast of St. Timothy is celebrated on 26 January in the Roman Church, and on 22 January in the Eastern churches. In the early history of the Church, both the Feasts of St. Timothy and St. Titus were observed on 26 January, a day after the Conversion of St. Paul which is observed on 25 January, in order to show the close relationship between St. Paul and his two disciples).

Titus: The letter addresses Titus as being in Crete (Tit. 1:5). He was a Gentile Christian and was a companion of Paul to the Apostolic Council in Jerusalem (Gal. 2:1, 3). Paul resisted the demand for Titus to be circumcised probably as a demonstration/example of what he was preaching – that one did not have to become a Jew first in order to be a Christian. Titus carried the "Letter of Tears" to the Corinthian community, resolved the tensions between the Corinthians and Paul, and was the main fund raiser among the Corinthians in the collection for Jerusalem (II Cor. 2:13; 7:6ff., 13ff.; 8:6ff); Titus also bore the "Letter of Thanksgiving" to the Corinthians(see the Corinthian Correspondence, above). Titus is mentioned in II Tim. 4:10 as having left Paul and gone to Dalmatia.

(Did Titus leave Paul in Rome or from some other place of imprisonment? Some early church traditions hold that Paul, after release from his first imprisonment in Rome, stopped at the island of Crete to preach. Due to the needs of other churches, requiring his presence elsewhere, he ordained his disciple, Titus, as Bishop of that island, and left him to finish the work he had started. Later Paul summoned Titus from Crete to join him at Nicopolis in Epirus. The New Testament does not record his death, but tradition holds that Titus died an old man towards the end of the century in Crete where his relics are interred. The Roman church celebrates the Feast of St. Titus on 4 January; the Eastern Orthodox churches observe the Feast on 25 August.)

Historical and Theological Issues

The historical and theological problems of the Pastorals are integrally linked with the question of whether the Pastorals originated with Paul. The attestation for them in the early church is not very satisfactory and they are missing from Marcion's canon (about mid-2nd century); only from the end of the 2nd century, is there evidence that the Pastorals were used/quoted and considered to be among the letters of Paul. The Pauline origin of the Pastorals was questioned in the 19th century on the basis of language and biographical information; other scholars showed that the theology of the Pastorals reflects a period much later than that of Paul. A sort of in-between position emerged where many held that at least some fragments could be traced back to Paul, especially some of the autobiographical notes like where he planned to spend the winter (Titus 3:12), the first judicial hearing of his case (II Tim. 4:16-17), and the names of many friends and opponents not mentioned elsewhere (II Tim. 1:15-18; 2:17; 4:9-21; Titus 3:12-13); but the problem was how to identify the fragments and what criteria to use. So, the present position that is accepted by most scholars is that the Pastorals reflect a later period much after the time of Paul. This is based on the following reasons:

1.   Language and style

There are a great difference between the language and style of the Pastorals and that of the epistles of Paul and the deutero-Pauline epistles. Statistical observations on the use of words and grammatical constructions show that the Pastorals are quite different from other writings. To assume Pauline authorship would mean that there would have to be an assumption that during Paul's Roman imprisonment he was greatly influenced by Latin and that his language and style changed drastically towards the end of his career – an assumption that is difficult to defend. **Language and style are held to be decisively against the origin of the Pastorals from Paul himself;** they could originate from those within the Pauline circle working in various mission fields, hence showing the characteristics of pseudonymous writings.

2.   The historical situation

A. I Timothy presupposes that until a short time previously, Paul and Timothy had worked together in Ephesus then Paul journeyed to Macedonia and left Timothy in Ephesus to carry on the struggle against false teachers (I Tim. 1:3). The letter is an instruction as to how Timothy is to carry on during Paul's temporary absence (I Tim.3:14, 4:13). But Timothy did not need written instructions since he had been commissioned orally as a trusted helper of Paul (I Tim. 1:3ff); further, Paul is to return soon so long term arrangements were not necessary. The instructions in the letter are intended more for the congregation in which Timothy is to carry out his official commission.

B. II Timothy reflects the personal and the official more closely intertwined than in the other two Pastorals. The letter purports to show Paul in prison – Rome? – (II Tim. 1:8, 16ff.; 2:9); he has already had one hearing of his case; a list of those who had visited him, stayed/are staying with him, and those who have left him is given in 4:9ff. Paul thinks that he is near death and that Timothy should try to come to him before winter and bring Mark with him, they are to bring Paul's cloak and books which he had left at Troas (II Tim. 4:6ff, 18; 1:4; 4:9; 4:11; 4:21; 4:13). Where Timothy is located is not stated; the greeting to Prisca and Aquila (II Tim. 4:19) may suggest that Timothy is in Ephesus. None of the historical situations presupposed in II Timothy can be corroborated from the other letters of Paul or Acts.

C. Titus presents Paul as having been in Crete and having left Titus behind to carry out the organization of the communities on the island (Titus 1:5ff.). The aim of the letter was to instruct Titus and to designate him as having been commissioned by Paul. Titus would soon be replaced by Artemas or Tychicus and Titus is to join Paul as soon as possible in Nicopolis where they will spend the winter (Titus 3:12). As far as is known, Paul had never been in Crete or in Nicopolis; he had passed along the shores of Crete on his voyage to Rome (Acts 27:7ff.), but there was no missionary activity and Paul had spent the following winter in Malta (Acts 28:1ff.). Therefore, none of the historical situations mentioned in the letter fit into the life of Paul as known from his other letters and Acts.

Therefore, the presupposed historical situations reflected in the Pastorals must belong to a time after Paul's imprisonment in Rome as is known from Acts 28.

3.   False teaching

The Pastorals are written against two main areas of false teaching: Jewish Christianity and Gnosticism and the syncreticism of the two. The Jewish roots can be seen in the references to the *circumcision group* (Titus 1:10); arguments concerning *the Law* (Titus 3:9); *Jewish myths and human commandments* (Titus 1:14). In I & II Timothy, false teachers pride themselves on their *superior knowledge* (I Tim. 1:4; 4:7); they practice asceticism through the prohibition of marriage and prohibitions concerning food (I Tim. 4:3; Titus 1:14ff.). Their teaching represents a Gnostic background: redemption by means of access into the mysteries of the upper world and through ascetic achievement; teaching that the resurrection of the dead has already occurred (II Tim. 2:14);they make a favourable impression on highly excitable women (II Tim. 3:4; Titus 1:11); teaching on eschatological perversion on all areas of life (I Tim. 4:1ff.; II Tim. 3:1ff.; 4:3ff.). The Jewish-Christian-Gnostic false teaching which is being combated in the Pastorals refer to false teachers *in the last days*(I Tim. 4:1ff.; II Tim. 3:1ff.; 113; 4:3ff.);there are also references to combating the false teachers in the present (I Tim. 1:3ff., 19ff.; 6:20ff.; II Tim. 2:16ff., 3:8; Titus 1:10ff., 3:9ff.), but there is no reference to "living in the last days" when predicting the end times; also the false teachers are not contradicted by being confronted with their teaching, but are countered simply by reference to the traditional teaching which is to be held fast and from which they have erred (I Tim. 4:1; 6:20; II Tim. 1:14; 2:2; Titus 3:10ff.). **The lack of any substantive debate, and a reference to teaching which has already become "traditional" is again a pointer that Paul is not writing these letters.**

4.   The community situation

In the instructions that Timothy and Titus receive, foremost are the officials as leaders of the community: presbyters and bishops (I Tim. 3:1ff.; 5:17ff.; Titus 1:5ff.). They are ordained by the laying on of hands (I Tim. 5:22) and supported by the community (I Tim. 5:17ff.). In addition, there are deacons (I Tim. 3:8ff.) and widows (I Tim. 5:9ff.). The chosen officials are guardians of order in their individual communities and accordingly there are strict requirements which they must meet; they have to assume the lead in the struggle against the false teachers (I Tim. 3:2; II Tim. 2:2; Titus 1:9). It cannot be determined exactly whether the Pastorals presuppose a single bishop over several presbyters (monarchical episcopacy), or whether they are all equals with the person having superintendence over a particular area being referred to as a bishop. Further presbyter is not used as an indication of age as is usual in the rest of the New Testament, so it is clearly an office assumed after the laying on of hands (I Tim. 4:14; Titus 1:1). In I Tim. 3:4ff. and 5:17 as well as Titus 1:1, 7, the offices of presbyter and bishop are interchangeable, so the office of bishop had not as yet developed into the structure of the monarchical episcopacy as found in the later church. However, what is clearly stressed is that these offices represent a chain of tradition whose beginning lies with the apostle (II Tim. 2:2ff., 8). This is already making provision for the on-going work of the church after the death of the apostle and is in contrast to Paul's expectation of a near end of the age; also, the task of preserving the tradition through the offices of presbyters and bishops is not known to Paul. Further, the office of widow whose task it is to be in continual prayer and sexual abstinence is totally foreign to Paul's thinking. In short, as one scholar puts it, **the Pastorals are documents of an already far developed church law in a community which is establishing itself in the world as Paul never knew it.**

5.   The Theology of the Pastorals

The Pastorals do contain ideas central to Paul: e.g. salvation of sinners through Christ (I Tim. 1:15), revelation of the grace of God through Christ (II Tim. 1:9ff.), justification not by works (Titus 3:5), but along with these ideas appear Hellenistic terminology which is totally foreign to Paul for describing the redemptive event: e.g. *the King of kings and Lord of lords, who alone has immortality and dwells in unapproachable light...* (I Tim. 6:15-16); *Christ...manifested....and Saviour* (II Tim. 1:9-10) for the earthly appearance of Christ; *the appearing of the glory of our great God and Saviour Jesus Christ....*(Titus 2:13) – a clear equation of Jesus with God; this is evidence of a Christological stance quite different from the other Pauline writings. There is also the use of the word 'faith' (I Tim. 1:5; 3:9; 6:10; II Tim. 4:7) to refer to a body of traditional material or 'sound doctrine' which has been handed down; this is also found in expressions such as *words of the faith and* the *good doctrine...* (I Tim. 4:6), *sound words and teaching which accords with godliness* (I Tim. 6:3), *...give instructions in sound doctrine* (Titus 1:9; 2:1). There are also rationalistic ethical demands for Christian living, e.g. I Tim. 2:2, II Tim. 1:14, Titus 2:2, which can be summed up as *guard the faith which has been entrusted to you.* **These theological differences show that the Pastorals come from a writer other than Paul and are greatly influenced by the language of Hellenistic Christianity of a later date.**

Many have noted that there are close similarities between the Pastorals and Luke-Acts and have used this to propound a hypothesis that the same person wrote them, or at least the writers were in co-operation with each other. Some examples of these similarities are: the reference to Paul's sufferings in II Tim. 3:11 at *Antioch, at Iconium, and at Lystra what persecutions I endured* echoes the journey of Paul found only in Acts 13:14-14:20; presbyters in every town (Titus 1:5) is found in Acts 14:23; presbyters who were bishops/overseers are attested in Acts 20:17-28 along with the warning of false teachers, *after my departure, fierce wolves will come among you;* aged widows who refuse remarriage and spend their time in prayer (I Tim. 5:5-9) is also reflected in Luke 2:36-37 (the prophetess Anna in the Temple); Luke-Acts is dated towards the end of the first century, close to the date of the Pastorals. One tradition of the church is that Luke and Titus were constant companions of Paul because they were brothers. However, none of the above, while interesting, can really be sustained as proving any relationship of the Pastorals with Luke-Acts.

On the basis of the above historical and theological issues, it can be concluded that the **Pastorals** exhibit all the characteristics of **a pseudonymous writing** that comes from a date later than even the deutero-Pauline writings as the Pastorals are quite different in their outlook. Hence, they are put down as a third generation after Paul or **Trito-Pauline writings.** The late date of the Pastorals and their acceptance into the canon of the New Testament would affirm that there still continued to be a firm link with Paul and that Paul's influence was still accepted as authoritative in the churches.

Purpose. Place of writing. Date.

The Pastorals are not all of similar contents. I Timothy and Titus contain instructions for the organization of the community, membership, and the combating of false teachers thus constituting writings for church order. II Timothy consists of a warning from the apostle, who purportedly is near death, to his pupils to stand firm in their faith and to fight against false teaching. As per the points mentioned above, the Pastorals are pseudonymous writings using the name of Paul and to make it sound more authentic, many personal references are included, and names of co-workers and acquaintances are also used. As seen above, it was difficult to fit the historical/personal references into the life of Paul as it is known from his other letters and Acts, however, the nature of the pseudonymity as such shows that the authority of Paul is still very much accepted in the churches and that writings in his name, though with some attempts at authenticity, are still accepted as authoritative. The purpose therefore is that the authority of Paul has been appealed to in order to instruct churches, threatened by false teachings, to stand firm in their faith and to hold fast to the traditions that were passed on to them; **this is part of the Pauline legacy**

employed by the pseudonymous writer to meet a later situation in the churches where the delay in the coming of the Lord has led to false teachings.

The place of writing cannot be determined with any accuracy except that the references to the Pauline heritage would obviously appeal to the communities founded by the apostle or which were closely associated with the apostle through his representatives. Titus does not specify the place from where it was written; I Timothy indicates Macedonia; and II Timothy, with its references to prison and death, seems to indicate Rome; but none of these presuppositions can be proved. Hence 'Timothy' and 'Titus' would be names that would immediately make the writings sound authentic and authoritative. **Since these two persons were associated with communities in the East, and since many of the Hellenistic/Gnostic ideas were from the East, any place in Asia/Asia Minor would be the possible place of origin.**

The letters were not widely known till about the middle of the 2nd century, and since the description of the false teachings shows a type of Jewish-Hellenistic-Gnostic syncreticism that was prevalent towards the end of the 1st century/beginning of the 2nd century, probably **the date of the Pastorals could be placed around A.D. 120-140.**

Brief analysis and commentary

The contents of I Timothy, and to a large extent Titus which is closely related to I Timothy in terms of content, show a very complicated sequence: at times instructions to the individual (I Tim. 1:3-20; 4:116ff.) and at other times directions to the community (I Tim. 2); some topics at the beginning (false teaching, church structure) are broken off and picked up later. Therefore, for the study of I Timothy and Titus, it would be better to take both together and to study the texts under three headings: church structure, false teaching, community relations. Since the two letters are similar in many respects, they will be studied one after the other; later II Timothy which seems to be the last of the three Pastorals. In this way, scattered/disconnected material can be brought together.

I Timothy and Titus

I Tim. I:1-2 and Titus 1:1-4: Opening Formula

The author, using the name of Paul, identifies himself as an *apostle of Jesus Christ by command of God our Saviour* (Θεου σωτηρος ἡμων) *and Christ Jesus our hope*. The title *our Saviour* for God is unusual as it is normally used only for Jesus. Timothy is addressed as *my true child in the faith* obviously in an attempt to closely associate the writer with the addressee, thus building a basis on which instructions can be issued.

The opening formula in Titus is long and some suggest that the opening of Titus might have originally functioned as the introduction to all three Pastorals. Some propose that the opening formula in Titus was meant to get him public support for the difficult task that he was set of organizing the church in Crete. Titus is also addressed as *my true child in a common faith.*

I Tim. 3:1-13; 5:3-22a and Titus 1:5-9: Church Structure

In I Timothy there are two unconnected segments in which this topic is treated:

1. *I Tim. 3:1-13:* concerning bishops and deacons: The qualifications for aspiring to the office of bishop are given: *a bishop* (ἐπισκοπος) *must be above reproach, the husband of one wife, temperate, sensible, dignified, hospitable, an apt teacher, no drunkard, not violent but gentle, not quarrelsome, and no lover of money. He must manage his own household well.... must not be a recent convert...must be well thought of by outsiders....*Some scholars have felt that these are qualifications for those ministering to Gentile house congregations, but there is nothing in the text that would specifically point only to Gentile groups. The qualifications certainly indicate that the person has to be settled in the community and well known. The claim that *anyone who aspires to the office of bishop desires a noble task*, shows how highly the position was esteemed.

The qualifications for those to be deacons (διακονος) are: *must be serious, not double-tongued, not addicted to much wine, not greedy for gain, they must hold the mystery of faith* (ἐχοντας το μυστηριον της πιστεως) *with a clear conscience. They are to be tested first...must be the husband of one wife...manage their children and households well...* The order of deacons includes also women who meet the qualifications; they must be *serious, no slanderers, but temperate, faithful in all things.* The noun deacon (διακονος) and the related verbs (διακονεω, διακονειν) suggest 'service', one who serves – so deacons are to provide service to the communities (in Acts 6, they are appointed to oversee the daily distribution of food). The condition that the deacons who *serve well will gain a good standing for themselves* may indicate the possibility of them moving on to become presbyters/bishops which would explain why most of the qualifications for deacon and bishop are the same. If that is the case, then women can also rise to assume the highest offices in the Church. Here too the qualifications suggest that the persons for the office of deacon should be settled persons in the community, not nomadic or itinerant evangelists. These qualifications would probably exclude Paul and most of his co-workers as they seemed to have been unmarried and were not settled in any one place/community.

Titus 1:5-9: Church structure was one of the main issues in the Pastorals. The Muratorian Fragment (an early canon of the New Testament dated around the end if the 2nd century) says that although they were written from personal feeling and affection, they are held in honour in the church catholic in the matter of ecclesiastical order. Titus mentions only the order of presbyter-bishops. The designations seem to be interchangeable (see discussion below). The qualifications for presbyters given are: *blameless* (ἀνεγκλητος), *husband of one wife, children are believers, not open to the charge of being profligate or insubordinate.* The qualifications for bishops are: *blameless* (ἀνεγκλητος), *not arrogant or quick-tempered or a drunkard or violent or greedy for gain, but hospitable, a lover of goodness, master of himself, upright, holy, and self-controlled; he must hold firm to the sure word as taught, so that he may be able to give instruction in sound doctrine and also to confute those who contradict it.* The qualifications show that they are to be blameless in their family and personal lives, and in their doctrinal standards.

2. *I Tim. 5:3-22a:* Widows (χηρας) constituted another group (5:3-16) but it is not clear as to whether they constitute holding an office or are a part of an order. The instruction to *honour widows who are real widows* may suggest that the criteria was not just that their husbands were dead but that there was a special role in the Church for them for which qualifications were listed: *she has been left all alone, has set her hope on God and continues in supplications and prayers night and day...not less than sixty years, having been the wife of one husband, well attested for her good deeds, brought up children(i.e. not having dependent children), shown hospitality, washed the feet of the saints, relieved the afflicted, and devoted herself to doing good in every way.* It is also envisaged that these women have no personal wealth (5:5, 16) so that the church becomes their family and they supported by church funds which are to be used to help *real widows.*

There is a sharp tone for younger widows who are not to be enrolled among the group of real widows – the ineligible widows who *grow wanton against Christ in their desire to marry...they learn to be idlers, gadding about from house to house...gossips and busybodies* (ἀργαι ἀλλα και φλυαροι και περιεργοι). These younger widows ought *to marry, bear children, rule their households,* indicating that they should not be a burden on the church structures and funds.

Elders (πρεσβυτεροι) constituted another group of church official(I Tim. 5:17-22a). Their duties are preaching and teaching. People should be careful about bringing charges against them and witnesses are needed (it would seem that the system was well in place in Ephesus where Timothy was located). In Titus 1:5-9 there are qualifications for the combined offices of presbyters/bishops. Since I Tim. 5:17 indicates that only certain presbyters were involved in preaching and teaching, probably not all presbyters were bishops. There does not seem to be a clear demarcation of the two offices; the titles are used interchangeably.

Thus, the church structure in I Timothy consists of bishops, presbyters, deacons, and widows with only the roles of deacons and widows clearly defined; in Titus the office(s) are presbyter-bishops. The duties of the bishops and presbyters seem to overlap with both having responsibility for preaching and teaching. The basic idea seems to be that the presbyter-bishops would provide a leadership faithful to the received teaching and thus protect the faithful from innovations/ false teaching.

Presbyter-bishops in the Pastorals: A brief summary of the general consensus on what is envisaged in the Pastorals is as follows:

1. Normally the designation of presbyter (πρεσβυτερος) would refer to an older person, usually sixty years or more as applicable to widows (I Tim. 5:9), but a younger person noted for good judgement might be considered 'old' in wisdom and so be called an elder. The Jewish synagogues had elders who gave guidance in policy matter and community finances; probably the duties of elders in Christian communities included this function, and as the name suggests, with the added responsibility of providing pastoral/ shepherding care for the community and individuals.

2. In I Timothy and Titus 'presbyter' is used in the plural – presbyters (πρεσβυτεροι), and 'bishop' is used in the singular (ἐπισκοπος). This gave rise to the thinking that there may have been one bishop over many presbyters, a sort of monarchial episcopacy that developed in the later church. But in the Pastorals the designations are used interchangeably, so both were probably had overseeing responsibilities with the addition of preaching and teaching. There is no comparison to Christ and the apostles or to the Jewish order of priests and Levites, so there does not seem to be an hierarchy as such.

3. Before appointment the qualifications were to be carefully examined. It was not to be a charismatic sort of leadership that simply claimed the guidance of the Spirit so that anyone could claim the leadership roles; but there was the process of a very strict screening. The screening process involved meeting the following qualifications – I Tim. 3:1-7 and Titus 1:6-9:

   a. Disqualifying factors: *not arrogant, not quick-tempered, not violent, not quarrelsome, not a drunkard, not greedy for gain, not loving money;*

   b. Qualifying factors: *faultless, above reproach, hospitable, gentle, loving good, devout, just, showing good sense, self-controlled, sober, dignified;*

c. Social standing, or qualities that set an example for others in the community: *married only once, children are believers, not loose-living or insubordinate, not a recent convert;*

d. Skills related to their work: *good reputation with outsiders, manages their own household well, a good teacher, holds fast to the teaching of sound doctrine.*

The qualifications given in (a) and (b) are sometimes called 'institutional requirements' – qualifications that a community could like, admire, and emulate. The qualifications in (c) and (d) indicate that the person being considered should be residential and not a wandering charismatic. The qualification of not being a recent convert would indicate that the church/community was already at least a generation old. The purpose was that the leader of the community had to set an ideal example for the community in their own family life.

4. In Titus 1:5 there are the instructions to Titus to appoint elders in Crete, but there is no indication of how the continuity of presbyters would be preserved after the departure of Titus. There are already elders in Ephesus where Timothy is alleged to be, as appointed in Acts 14:23 and 20:28, but the selection seems to have been made more on the basis of 'charisms' which is frowned upon in the Pastorals and there is no mention of how it was to be continued. There are references to the 'laying on of hands' in I Tim. 4:14; II Tim. 1:6-7; I Tim. 5:22 (ἐπιθεσεως των χειρων), but whether this refers to some type of 'ordination' is not clear. Perhaps the 'laying on of hands' was a ritual which was used to designate a presbyter-bishop, but there does not seem to be a uniform practice for this ritual in the late 1st century/early 2nd century.

So, at the time of the Pastorals, the appointment of presbyter-bishops, deacons, widows, was seen as an answer to the threats to the communities' survival which was to be found in terms of structure. Many of the communities founded by Paul during his missionary activity did not have a structure of authority to ensure the nurture of the community and to direct its on-going life and witness. That deficiency

was now being set right in the Pastorals and presbyter-bishops were
to be appointed. The authority vested in these leaders would ensure
the nurture of the local communities thereby protecting them from
false teachings and disintegration.[2]

I Tim. 1:3-20; 3:14 – 4:10; 6:3-5; and Titus 1:10-16: False Teaching:

False teaching was an issue in Paul's own life time (e.g. the Corinthian
and Galatian correspondence, see above), and certainly was a major
issue towards the end of the 1st century as especially seen in the
Pastorals. However, from the description of the false teaching it is
not clear whether it is all the same false teaching or whether there
are varieties of false teaching – all are placed/referred to under the
category of false teaching. The first description of those who teach a
different doctrine is, *to occupy themselves with myths and endless genealogies*
(μυθους και γενεαλογιαις βάπεραντους) *which promote speculations
rather than the divine training that is in faith…. desiring to be teachers of the
law, without understanding either what they are saying or the things about which
they make assertions* (I Tim. 1:3-7).There is reference to the Jewish law:
the law is good (I Tim. 1:8) but only if it is used lawfully; *the law is not
laid down for the just, but for the lawless and disobedient…and whatever else is
contrary to sound doctrine* (I Tim. 1:8-11). So, while there is reference to a
Jewish background the reference to myths and genealogies is unclear.
Timothy is urged to keep the faith *in accordance with the prophetic utterances
which pointed to you…that you may wage the good warfare, holding faith and a
good conscience. By rejecting conscience, some have made a shipwreck of their faith*
(I Tim. 1:18-20). Further descriptions of the issues being faced are: *giving
heed to deceitful spirits and doctrines of demons…(persons) who forbid marriage
and enjoin abstinence from foods which God created…for everything created by
God is good and nothing is to be rejected…* (I Tim. 4:1-10). Further issues
are listed in I Tim. 6:3-5 including making of money. mSome of the
issues can be identified with matters from the Jewish apocrypha and
Jewish Gnosticism, but that again is only a part of the false teaching
being encountered.

---

[2] For a detailed discussion on Church Structure in the Pastorals and other New
Testament writings, see the relevant chapter in Vol. IV of this series.

In Titus 1:10-16, the same problem arises – there is no precise description of the false teaching only generalizations, thus it is hard to distinguish between the false teaching and *many insubordinate men, empty talkers and deceivers, especially the circumcision party* (οἵ ἐκ τῆς περιτομῆς); *they must be silenced since they are upsetting whole families by teaching for base gain where they have no right to teach…Jewish myths or to commands of men who reject the truth…their minds and consciences are corrupted. They profess to know God, but they deny Him by their deeds, they are detestable, disobedient, unfit for any good deed.* There is reference to a Jewish element – *the circumcision party* and *Jewish myths* – but the rest of the polemic, from verse 12 is against the Cretans. Again, the false teachings are not precisely defined, only that they are causing problems in the community. What the problems are and how they are being caused will be discussed in the next section on community relations.

I Tim. 2:1-15; 4:11 – 5:2; 5:22a – 6:2; 6:6-19 and Titus 2:1 – 3:11: Community relations

In I Timothy, the section starts with the instructions to pray *for all, for kings and all who are in high positions that we may lead a quiet and peaceable life.* This is followed by a Christological affirmation with the claim that the author was appointed *a preacher and apostle…. a teacher of the Gentiles in faith and truth.* There are instructions for men and women in worship (I Tim. 2:8-15) where *the men should pray lifting holy hands without anger or quarreling….*This leads on to household relationships: the instructions to women are that they should *adorn themselves modestly and sensibly in seemly apparel…* and no ostentatious jewelry, further *they should learn in silence with all submissiveness, no woman is permitted to teach or to have authority over men; she is to keep silent.* The patriarchal argument of Adam having been created first and then from Adam the woman was created is tempered with the observation that the woman finds redemption in child-bearing, but only if she *continues in faith and love and holiness, with modesty.* These stern strictures against women would not have gone down well in the first century and certainly would evoke very negative reactions today. However, as scholars point out, the strictures are probably not against women in general but probably against only the rich and wealthy women (reference to gold, pearls, and costly attire, 2:9) who had the leisure to go from house to house causing trouble (5:6,13). These women would have been vulnerable targets of the false teachers and were probably already causing trouble in the community and are compared to Eve who deceived Adam. The salvation of women through child-bearing and the urging of young widows to remarry and bear children (5:14) may have been to contradict those who forbade marriage (4:3). There is much evidence that this was the case in the late 1st and early 2nd centuries along with teaching rejecting the eating of meat, drinking wine, and participating in sexual intercourse. The household instructions also extend to the slaves who *must regard their masters as worthy of all honour...those who have believing masters must not be disrespectful on the ground that they are fellow members of the community; rather they must serve all the better since those who benefit from their service are believers and beloved (6:1-2)*. Anyone who does not teach or agree with the *sound words of our Lord Jesus Christ...knows nothing; they have a morbid craving for controversy and for disputes about words.... they are depraved in mind...and imagine that godliness is a means of gain. But there is great gain in godliness with contentment (6:3-8)*. Following the household codes there is a distrust of wealth in 6:5-10, 17-19 including the well-known saying that *the love of money is the root of all evils* (ῥιζα γαρ πἀτὠ τὠ κακων ἐστιν ἡ φιλαργυρια).

So the instructions to the community in I Timothy give some idea of the community and social relationships.

There are several hymnic passages in this section the most well-known being 3:16: where the *mystery of our religion* – the incarnation, life, death and resurrection of Christ are praised. Other hymnic passages are 6:7-8 and the benediction of 6:15-16 which comes from a liturgical ritual: *the blessed and only Sovereign, the King of kings, and Lord of lords; the one who alone is immortal, dwelling in unapproachable light, whom no one has ever seen or can see* (ὁ μακαριος και μονος δυναστης, ὁ βασιλευς των βασιλευοντων και κυπιος των κυπιευοντων, ὁ μονος εχων ἀθανασιαν, φως οἰκων ἀπροσιτον, ἀν εἰδεν οὐδεις ἐδἐιν δυναται) (a well-known hymn by Walter Chalmers Smith in 1867 is based on this text: *Immortal, Invisible, God only wise, in light inaccessible, hid from our eyes....*).

In Titus 2:1 – 3:11, community relations take up the major portion of the letter. The first section is a household code: instructions to *older men to be temperate, serious, sensible, sound in faith, in love, and in steadfastness. Older women must be reverent in behavior, not to be slanderers or slaves to drink…they are to train the young women… Young men must control themselves….Slaves must be submissive to masters and give satisfaction in every respect.* Titus is urged to be *a model of good deeds, and in your teaching show integrity, gravity, and sound speech that cannot be censured… Let no one disregard you* (mhdeij sou perifroneitw). The same situation as in I Timothy (above) seems also to prevail in the letter to Titus. The community is reminded to be *submissive to rulers and authorities, to be obedient, to be ready for honest work, to speak evil of no one, to avoid quarreling, to be gentle, and to show perfect courtesy toward all…* Before conversion, Christians were *foolish, disobedient, led astray, slaves to various passions and pleasures, passing days in malice and envy… but when the goodness and loving kindness of God our Saviour appeared, He saved us….* There is again the unusual reference to God as *our Saviour.* Salvation is the greatest motivation for a Christian lifestyle of obedience in response to God's mercy and grace.

The point being made is that in community relations Christian belief and manner of life should go together as two sides of the same coin. Pastoral instructions are based on what Christ has done and therefore what is expected of Christians.

I Timothy 6:20-21 and Titus 3:12-15: Concluding Formula

I Timothy ends with a passionate plea: *O Timothy, guard what has been entrusted to you, avoid godless chatter……*

The concluding formula in Titus gives rise to the hypothesis that Paul had a second career beyond what is narrated in Acts, after he was released from prison in Rome. However, the historicity of this hypothesis has been found to be untenable (see introductory issues above). The final greetings indicate a wider readership than just the individual Titus.

Concluding/Summary remarks from analysis and study of I Timothy and Titus

1. Paul is referred to as the apparent writer even to the extent of supplying details about his personal travel. Yet for reasons listed above, this has been challenged and present scholarship accepts that the writer was a disciple of Paul so having continuity with Paul's thought, but writing after the time of Paul;also, not so close a continuity as seen in the deutero-Pauline writings, so perhaps a second-generation disciple-writer, hence the writings can be listed as Trito-Pauline.

2. The purpose was to strengthen local church organization which would act as a bulwark against false teachings and false teachers. The appeal to Paul is indicative that the Pauline heritage was still a strong factor and that Paul's name could still be used as authoritative.

3. The church structure envisioned in the Pastorals goes beyond Paul's life time. The concern for church structure to preserve true teaching is not found in other letters of Paul. This is a concern that would have become more pressing as it became clear that the apostolic and sub-apostolic (the time just after the apostles) period was coming to an end or had perhaps had already ended.

4. The main structure was the presbyter-bishop system with deacons and widows forming supplementary offices.

5. The false teaching is not clearly defined but from descriptions of some of the issues it would seem that the teachings were influenced by Jewish Gnosticism and Hellenistic Gnosticism mixed with the influences of the mystery religions and other philosophical teachings. Thus, it was a syncretism that would have been hard to define and the only defense against it would have been to emphasize the true teaching and to have structures that would preserve true teaching.

II Timothy

The letter to II Timothy is usually treated separately from the other two Pastorals (for introductory issues, see the general introduction to the Pastorals, above). I Timothy and Titus seem to be related, but II Timothy is quite different. It does not show any awareness of a previous letter having been written to Timothy, and it has no reference to Church structure which is a central issue for I Timothy and Titus. As seen from the introductory issues, above, Paul's career as known from Acts and the undisputed letters of Paul could not be fitted into the situation as known from II Timothy. There are three ways of understanding the background of II Timothy:

1. Many scholars posit a 'second career' for Paul after having been released from prison in Rome: a career that would have included a ministry with Titus in Crete, a return to Ephesus where he left Timothy in-charge, and then a departure to Macedonia; at the end of this 'second career' Paul was once again imprisoned in Rome and wrote II Timothy just before he died. This would make II Timothy the last known writing of Paul.

2. Some scholars feel that there is no need to posit an alleged 'second career' but that after the first two years of relatively easy imprisonment in Rome (Acts 28:30-31), Paul was subjected to a more rigorous imprisonment and wrote II Timothy before he died. The location of Timothy is nowhere mentioned; the greeting to Prisca and Aquila (4:19) may suggest that Timothy is in Ephesus; however the reference to Troas (4:11,13) may mean that Timothy is in Troas which may not be impossible since Acts 20:5-13 mentions that on his way to Jerusalem, Paul met Timothy and others at Troas and stayed there seven days, so he could have left his books and cloak behind which he now wants Timothy to bring to him.

3. II Timothy is a pseudonymous writing from the end of the 1st or early 2nd century by someone who knew about Paul's last days, so that biographical material could be included; this gave rise to creating a 'second career' and a second Roman imprisonment for Paul so that he might speak final words about issues troubling

the areas that he once evangelized. It is this third alternative that is followed in this study (for other introductory issues, see the general introduction to the Pastorals, above).

Brief analysis and commentary

1:1-2: Opening Formula

It resembles the opening formula of I Timothy except that the author refers to himself/herself as having been designated as an apostle by the *will of God* and not by the command of God. Timothy is called *my beloved child* (Τιμοθεῳ ἀγαπητῳ τεκνῳ) indicating that it is probably an older person writing to a person young enough to be his/her child, and also indicating that this young person is a trusted colleague.

1:3-18: Personal details, thanksgiving and exhortation

The writer recalls the close relationship with Timothy: *I God...when I remember you constantly in my prayers...I remember your tears...I long night and day to see you*. Timothy's grandmother and mother, both of Jewish descent, are also recalled strengthening the bond between the writer and Timothy. There is reference to *the gift of God that is within you through the laying on of my hands* (δια της ἐπιθεσεως των χειρων μου). This recalling of personal details between the writer and the person being addressed is typical of pseudonymous literature in an attempt to show a close relationship and thus presenting a convincing picture in order to have the writing accepted and received with the authority of the apostle.

The writer exhorts Timothy to follow his example in proclaiming the gospel especially the example of *do not be ashamed of testifying to our Lord, nor of me his prisoner.... For this gospel I was appointed a preacher, and apostle, and teacher... I am not ashamed* (οὐκ ἐπαισχυνομαι), *for I know whom I have believed* (οἰδα γαρ ᾧ πεπιστευκα), *and I am sure that He is able to guard* (πεπεισμαι ὅτι δυνατος ἐστιν τηνπαραθηκην μου φυλαξαι) *until that Day what has been entrusted to me... Follow the pattern of the sound words* (ὑγιαινοντωνλογων) *which you have heard from me.... Guard the truth* (την καλην παραθηκην φυλαξον). *That has been entrusted to you...* There is also the warning, almost a certain prediction, that suffering would ensue, *take your share of suffering for the Gospel in the power of God.*

The last few verses of the chapter go back to personal relations: *all in Asia turned away from me, and among them Phygelus and Hermogenes...* Probably many had become ashamed of being associated with a person who had ended up in prison, and also given that any association may have brought trouble on themselves. And greetings and good wishes: *.... the Lord grant mercy to the household of Onesiphorus* who had rendered service in Ephesus and Rome.

2:1-26: Exhortations continue and call to faithful ministry:

There is the exhortation to *be strong in the grace that is in Christ Jesus... take your share of suffering as a good soldier.* Examples of hard work are drawn from military imagery – *the work of a soldier* – from the world of athletes – *compete according to rules* – and from the agricultural images – *the hard-working farmer.* There is again a personal reference to the writer's own situation: *remember Jesus Christ, risen from the dead, descended from David...the gospel for which I am suffering and wearing fetters like a criminal.* Nevertheless, the writer's conviction is strongly presented: *but the word of God is not fettered* (ἀλλα ὁ λογος του Θεου οὐ δεδεται). There is also the exhortation and concern for the continuity of the Gospel message and the transmission of tradition: *what you have heard from me... entrust to faithful persons who will be able to teach others also.*

The words of an early hymn are quoted in verses 11-13 affirming that salvation and suffering leads to eternal glory. Therefore, *do your best to present yourself to God as one approved, a workman who has no need to be ashamed, rightly handling the word of truth.* Ethical behavior must be observed, especially *avoid godless chatter...* Two men from the community seem to have fallen prey to false teaching/misinterpretation: *Hymenaeus and Philetus who have swerved from the truth by holding that the resurrection is past already.* Ethical behavior is to *aim at righteousness, faith, love, and peace... have nothing to do with stupid, senseless controversies...the Lord's servant must not be quarrelsome, but kindly...an apt teacher, forbearing, correcting opponents with gentleness.*

3:1-17: Warning about stressful times/last days

This is a section on apocalyptic imagery: *understand this, that in the last days there will come times of stress...* A list of behavior patterns is given leading to the final comment that people who follow such patterns *hold the form of religion but deny the power of it. Avoid such people.* Such people influence weak and idle persons in households especially of the wealthy and so cause trouble. The example of *Jannes and Jambres* who opposed Moses and did not get very far. The writer cites personal details from Paul's own example of suffering, saying *all who desire to live a godly life in Christ Jesus will be persecuted.* There is an emphasis on the utility of *scripture inspired by God* for continuing what Timothy had learned from childhood in order to teach and correct and thus counter evil imposters.

4:1-18: A farewell charge

In the final chapter, Timothy is again charged, *I charge you in the presence of God...preach the word, be urgent in season and out of season, convince, rebuke, and exhort...* There is also a foreseeing that false teaching would have its effect on the community: *people will turn away from listening to the truth and wander into myths.* So, the exhortation to *always be steady, endure suffering, do the work of an evangelist, fulfill your ministry.* The writer sees himself/herself near death: *the time of my departure has come,* but in a reflection on life, he/she faces the future confidently: *I have fought the good fight, I have finished the race, I have kept the faith* (τον καλον ἀγωνα ἠγωνισμαι,τον δρομον τετελεκα, την πιστιν τετηρηκα.....). *Henceforth there is laid up for me the crown of righteousness which the Lord, the righteous judge, will award to me on that Day...*

In closing, various names are mentioned of those who have visited the writer, those who have left and those who are still with him/her; perhaps the representation of the pseudoepigrapher putting together information found in other Pauline letters and Acts. Finally, the writer again exclaims that he/she has been faithful in carrying out his/her task of preaching in the face of difficulties, *the Lord stood by me and gave me strength to proclaim the word fully...*

4:19-22: Conclusion

There are greetings to close friends and concern expressed over a sick friend at Miletus. There is an urgency for Timothy to *do your best to come before winter.* Greetings are sent from those at the writer's place, and the concluding benediction of *the Lord be with your spirit. Grace be with you.*

In many respects, II Timothy is similar to farewell discourses found in the Hebrew scriptures and other parts of the New Testament (e.g. Deuteronomy as Moses' farewell to Israel; the farewell discourse in John 13-17). Some of the characteristic features of a farewell discourse found in II Timothy are:

1. The writer announcing his/her departure (4:6-8);

2. Words of reassurance to those left behind (2:1-2, 14-15; 4:1-2);

3. Writer's situation and past life (1:11-13, 15-18; 3:10-17);

4. Urges unity among those left behind (2:14, 23-25);

5. Foresees dangers from enemies (2:16-17; 3:1-9.12-13; 4:3-4);

6. Encourages faithfulness, promising reward (2:11-13; 3:14, 4:8);

7. Expresses love for those being left behind (1:4-5; 2:1 – "my son");

Thus, there is a farewell atmosphere in II Timothy as though it is the writer's last letter to Timothy and to all his disciples. The letter is a powerful writing expressing concern that the work started by Paul be continued beyond his death through his disciples; the writer may be in fetters, but exclaims with assurance that God's word is not fettered. Thus, II Timothy, though a pseudonymous writing, contributes to an understanding of Paul's life and times, to a loving relationship with one whom he considered as his son, and to his concern for the on-going life of the church, and so the writing finds a place in the canon.

Select Bibliography for the Pastorals

Brown, R. E. *An Introduction to the New Testament.* Bangalore: Theological Publications in India, 2000.

Cornelius, Paul "I Timothy" in Brian C. Wintle (General Editor), *South Asia Biblical Commentary.* Udaipur, Rajasthan: Open Door Publication, 2015, pages 1682 – 1692.

_____, "II Timothy" in Brian C. Wintle (General Editor), *South Asia Biblical Commentary.* Udaipur, Rajasthan: Open Door Publication, 2015, pages 1693 – 1700.

_____, "Titus" in Brian C. Wintle (General Editor), *South Asia Biblical Commentary.* Udaipur, Rajasthan: Open Door Publication, 2015, pages 1701 – 1704.

Dibelius, M. and H. Conzelmann, I *& II Timothy and Titus,* Hermenia Series, 1972.

Kelly, J. N. D. *I & II Timothy and Titus,* Harper New Testament Commentaries Series, New York: Harper & Row, 1960.

Kummel, W. G. *Introduction to the New Testament,* London: SCM Press, 1975.

Prior, M. P. Paul the Letter-Writer and the Second Letter to Timothy, *Journal for the Study of the New Testament,* No. 23.

Murphy-O'Connor, J. *Paul: A Critical Life,* Oxford: Oxford University Press, 1996.

_____, *St. Paul the Letter-Writer: His World, His Options, His Skills.*

Good News Studies, Collegeville: Liturgical Press, 1995.

Stott, John. *The Message of I Timothy and Titus,* The Bible Speaks Today. DownersGrove: Inter Varsity Press, 2001.

_____, *The Message of II Timothy,* The Bible Speaks Today. Downers Grove: Inter Varsity Press, 2001.

CHAPTER - 6

Some Issues in Pauline Thought

A. Sin. Law. Righteousness. Salvation. Justification by faith.

B. Ἐν Χριστῳ (en Christo): Life in Christ. Individual and corporative perspectives.

C. The Church: Jews and Gentiles in the Church. The Body of Christ. Sacraments. Spiritual gifts. Γλωσσαλαλια (glossalalia) – speaking in tongues.

D. Eschatology and the summing up of all things in Christ.

E. The place and contribution of women in the Church. Women as partners in ministry.

F. Creation and ecological concerns (Rom. 8:18-23, Col. 1:15-20).

Select Bibliography.

General Introduction

Paul did not theoretically and systematically develop his thoughts concerning God, Christ, creation, sin, salvation etc..... which are normally the topics in a systematic theology: scholars are agreed that the organizational principles of later theology should not be imposed on Paul. Paul developed his thoughts fragmentarily in his letters, and always in relation to a specific and actual occasion to which he was writing. Paul was able to take concrete life-situations/issues and lift them to the level of theological considerations and in this sense, he became the founder of Christian theology. His theological thinking was not an abstract, speculative system, but his theology was always related to the significance of God for the human being and the human situation. Similarly, he did not think of the human being and the world as they are in themselves, but only in relation to God. So, the three foci of the classical theological triangle were very evident in Paul and held together in close interdependence: God, human beings, world (rest of creation). For this reason, Bultmann holds that Paul's theology is at the same time, anthropology – every assertion about God speaks of what God is doing in history and therefore the basis of God's relationship with, and God's demands of, human beings. Similarly, every assertion about Christ is associated with salvation and therefore Paul's Christology is at the same time, soteriology (R. Bultmann, *Theology of the New Testament, Vol. I,* London: SCM Press, 1971).

The study of Paul and his letters, as above, very clearly bring out that Paul originated in Hellenistic Judaism (i.e. Judaism outside of Palestine): his home was Tarsus in Cilicia (Acts 9:11; 21:39; 22:3); here he would have come into contact with Hellenistic culture, philosophy, and religious syncreticism; some of the ideas of Hellenistic philosophical systems, the mystery religions and Gnosticism find expression in his theology. He is also said to have received his strict rabbinic training as a Pharisee under Gamaliel (Acts 22:3) in Jerusalem; his rabbinic interpretations of Hebrew scripture bear out his strict conservative and traditional Jewish background. Since he was not a personal disciple of Jesus, his understanding of the Christian faith came through the preaching (*kerygma*) of the Hellenistic Church – raising the issue of whether he was willing to accept Jesus as the expected Messiah not just for the Jews, but for the whole world. This brought Paul's whole Jewish theology into question as the Hellenistic mission was open to non-Jews receiving the benefit of God's salvific activity in Christ. Recognizing how basically Judaism was being confronted by this *kerygma,* Paul a Pharisaic champion of Judaism, turned persecutor of the Hellenistic mission. Paul was able to see that Jewish theology of *striving after righteousness by doing the works of the Law* was being called into question by the *kerygma* that proclaimed God's salvific activity in Jesus as freely available. Paul viewed this *kerygma* as being God's judgment on the whole Jewish system. In his conversion experience, Paul submitted to this judgement of God as he puts it:

> *a Hebrew, born of Hebrews, circumcised on the eighth day, of the people of Israel, of the tribe of Benjamin, as to the law a Pharisee, as to zeal a persecutor of the Church, as to righteousness under the law blameless. But whatever gain I had, I counted as loss for the sake of Christ. Indeed, I count everything as loss because of the surpassing worth of knowing Christ Jesus my Lord. For His sake I have suffered the loss of all things, and count them as refuse, in order that I might gain Christ and be found in Him, not having a righteousness of my own, based on law, but that which is through faith in Christ, the righteousness from God....*(Philip. 3:4-10).

As Bultmann puts it, *Paul's conversion was not rescue from despair; his was not a conversion of repentance; nor one of emancipating enlightenment. Rather it was obedient submission to the judgement of God, made known in the cross of Christ, upon all human accomplishment and boasting* (R. Bultmann, *Theology of the New Testament, Vol. I*). Thus, the very system that Paul was persecuting, now became the system that he proclaimed and vigorously defended as *my gospel*. This conversion experience and the openness to the inclusion of the Gentiles into God's salvific activity is reflected in his theology, soteriology, ecclesiology etc… hence Paul's theology is always contextual – i.e. arising out of a specific context– and not abstract philosophy.

Keeping the above in mind, some areas of Paul's theology will be discussed here. In many ways, this chapter will be more of a summary, since the issues evolve out of the texts which have already been analyzed in the preceding chapters, above; this is more of a 'bringing together' for convenience.

A. *Sin. Law. Righteousness. Salvation. Justification by faith.*

This section deals with the human condition before and after being confronted by God's act of salvation in Christ.

A.   Sin

As mentioned above, Paul's theology is contextual and so it is necessary that sin must have a sphere in which to operate i.e. there must be a structure in which sin exists. There are two terms which Paul uses to describe this structure, terms that must be understood before dealing with the concept of sin.

The most comprehensive term that Paul uses to describe this structure is *soma* (σῶμα) or 'body'. All existence – whether physical or spiritual – is somatic existence; there cannot be an existence without a *soma*. So, when Paul talks about *let not sin dwell in your mortal soma* (Rom. 6:12), or when he says *present your somata* (bodies) *as a living sacrifice....* (Rom 12:1) it means not just an outward shape or form but the whole human person, body, mind and spirit. The body has its members which comprise a unity (Rom.12:4ff; I Cor. 12:12-26); personal physical presence is the *presence of the body* (II Cor. 10:10); Paul bears on his body the *marks of Jesus (Gal. 6:17)* – perhaps scars from beatings; there are people who *deliver their bodies to be burned* (I Cor. 13:3); he *pommels and subdues his body* (I Cor. 9:27);the body is the seat of sexual life – *Abraham saw that his body was dead* (Rom. 4:19)– i.e. no longer able to procreate; the wife and husband rule over each other's' bodies (I Cor. 7:4); unnatural lust is a *dishonouring of the body* (Rom. 1:24). These are examples to show that *soma* describes existence in general and that all life is somatic – i.e. the *soma* belongs to the very essence of human existence and without it there is no existence. This means that *soma* enables the human being to be able to relate to one's self and to others; so, the human being is called *soma* in respect to being able to be the object of his/her own actions, or to experience himself/herself as the subject to whom something happens. The *soma* simply means human existence; it is neither good nor bad, but because of *soma* there is the possibility to be good or evil – to have a relationship for or against God.

When the *soma* opts for corruption – evil – then the *soma* is said to be under the control of *sarx* (σάρξ) or 'flesh': the 'flesh' suffers (Gal. 4:13), there is *a thorn in the flesh* (II Cor. 12:7), the *two shall become one flesh* (I Cor. 6:16) when talking of marriage and using that metaphor to illustrate joining with a prostitute. *Sarx* can therefore be understood as the passions/lustful desires/evil power that is at enmity with God and the power that has the *soma* under complete control: *I do not understand my own actions for I do not do what I want, but I do the very thing*

I hate...nothing good dwells in me, that is in my flesh....I do not do the good I want, but the evil I do not want is what I do. This complete overpowering of the *soma* by *sarx* leads to the understanding that *if I do what I do not want, it is no longer I that do it, but sin which dwells in me* (Rom. 7:15-20). So very clearly *sarx* is descriptive of the *soma* which is completely under the control of sin. The *soma* is the human being while *sarx* is a power that lays claim to the human being and determines the relationship that the human being has within himself/herself and with God and with others. That is why Paul talks of life as *according to the flesh* (κατα σαρκα) but never of a life according to the body (κατα σωμα) so he yearns *to be delivered from this body of death* (Rom. 7:24).

So, for Paul, human existence is an embodied existence – *soma* – which is under the complete control of *sarx*. Therefore, Paul can say that all are sinners (Rom. 1:18-3:20); that through Adam sin and death came into the world and all humanity shares in the sin of Adam (Rom. 5:12ff.). *Sarx*, being in complete domination of *soma* is seen as a power over which the human has no control (see the Rom. 7 passage); this power is obviously something more than personal sinful acts; it functions as a myth (a deep life changing experience but having to use human language for expression/description) expressive of a world in which individuals are forced to be other than what they desire to be(cf. Rom. 7); this power can be represented by the idea of sin – at enmity with God and others – spelt with a capital 'S' – Sin, and *all persons, Jews and Greeks are under the power of Sin*(Rom. 3:9). This power of Sin is manifested in the *passions and desires* of the flesh (Rom. 7:5; 8:13; Gal. 5:24) which are to be crucified. Sin (ἁμαρτια) is the power to which the *soma* falls prey and is then described as *sarx*. The nature of Sin is such that it forces all human beings into slavery (Rom. 3:23; Gal. 3:22); its origins can be traced back to the sin of one person (Rom. 5:12, 16, 19), Adam. Sin came into the world and achieved dominion enslaving all human beings (Rom. 5:12, 21; 6:6, 17ff., 6:13; 7:14); Sin pays its wages (Rom. 6:23); Sin is universal (Rom. 1:18-3:20). Sin, for Paul, was not an external, other worldly force, but a reality within humanity. Thus Sin (ἁμαρτια) and flesh (σαρξ) can be used as synonymous terms.

This power of Sin which holds the *soma* captive has to be destroyed/broken. Otherwise, the *sting of death is Sin* (Rom. 15:56); *if you live according to the flesh (sarx) you will die* (Rom. 8:13). However, for Paul, the human being is powerless to break the power of Sin since *all have sinned* (Rom. 1:18-3:20). An external force has to be brought into play to deal with the power of Sin. There are two external forces that are brought into play – the Law and Grace. The Law (the Mosaic Law) fails to be the antidote to Sin as it brings the knowledge of sin (Rom. 7:7-12. See further discussion on Law, below). It is only Grace (χαρις), the free and undeserved gift of God that can be the antidote to Sin (Rom. 3:23-25; 6:23). Once grace has broken the power of Sin, the human being lives no longer under Sin's power (Rom. 6); the person is now *dead to Sin and alive to God in Christ Jesus* (Rom. 6:11).

Law

Related to the concept of Sin, is the understanding of the role and function of the Law. In Paul, Law refers to the Mosaic Law found in the Hebrew scriptures – *Torah*– and indeed the whole Hebrew scriptures, which is the basis of Judaism and definitive of all relationships – with self, with God, and with fellow human beings. In Greek, the word used is *nomos* (νομος). In the *nomos* God's demand (how humans are to respond and behave) encounters the human being with the purpose of leading the person to life (Rom. 7:10; 10:5; Gal. 3:12b). The *nomos* is the totality of legal, cultic, ritual, ethical demands and the human response that is expected is total obedience. In most cases, when Paul speaks of the Law he talks of its ethical demands (Rom. 2:1-3:20) and of the Law as a means to salvation. Both Jews and Gentiles stand under this demand of God in the Law – the Jews because they have the *precepts of the Law* (Rom. 1:32; 2:26; 8:4), and the Gentiles when they keep the Law in their conscience (Rom. 2:14ff.).

The Law as God's demand naturally means that it has to be obeyed/fulfilled. However, Paul's position is that the Law is unable to lead to salvation, only to death (Rom. 1:18-7:6; Gal. 3:1-5:12). But this does not imply that the Law does not contain God's obligatory demand; Paul clarifies this in the question, *what then shall we say, that the Law is sin?*

(Τι οὖν ἐρουμεν; ὅ νομος ἁμαρτια;) and answers his question with a strong, emphatic *certainly not* (μη γενοιτο); he goes on to say that *the law is holy, and the commandment is holy and just and good* (Rom. 7:12), the Law *is spiritual* (Rom. 7:14). Thus, the keeping of the Law would bestow life (Rom. 10:5; Gal. 3:12).

However, for Paul, there is no question of being able to fulfill the Law because, *if it had not been for the Law, I should not have known sin. I should not have known what it is to covet if the Law had not said "You shall not covet" ...the very commandment which promised life proved to be death to me....*(Rom. 7:7-10), that is why the written code – the Law – kills (II Cor. 3:6). Paul goes even further still by saying that a person not only cannot achieve salvation by the Law, but that the Law was not even intended to do so: *no human being will be justified in God's sight by works of the Law since through the Law comes the knowledge of sin* (Rom. 3:20; Gal. 2:16). This was a very radical statement coming from a Jew and certainly an understanding/interpretation of the Law that Judaism would not have accepted. But for Paul, *Christ is the end of the Law, that everyone who has faith may be justified* (Rom. 10:4). Here the context of Paul has to be taken into account: he is trying to universalize salvation and take its message beyond Judaism to include the Gentiles, but at the same time, he cannot totally negate the understanding that God has acted for human salvation in and through the Law. So, the only way out is to re-interpret the Jewish understanding of the Law and Paul does it convincingly from his rabbinic-Pharisaic background. The human effort to achieve salvation by keeping the Law only leads to sin as it gives credit to human self-righteousness/boasting and takes away from the gracious gift of God in Jesus Christ – righteousness as a free gift of God – grace. The logical question now arises: *did that which is good, then, bring death to me* (Rom. 7:13)? And again, *Why then the Law?. Is the Law against the promises of God* (Gal. 3:19ff.)? The answer is the same emphatic *certainly not*. Paul's understanding is linked to the interpretation of the story of Abraham (Rom. 4 and Gal. 3:6-9): the promise of inheritance given to Abraham and his descendants was given before the Law came into existence, thus the promise was founded on faith, not on the works of the Law and it was this faith that was reckoned as Abraham's righteousness (Rom. 4:3; Gal. 3:6).

It therefore becomes clear that the demand of God in the Law leads only to the acknowledgement that the Law cannot be kept by human effort and that God's grace is needed. Therefore, for Paul, the ethical demands of the Law (behavior and relationships) must continue to be observed, but the Law is no longer the means to attain salvation; salvation is the free gift of God in Jesus Christ, undeserved and unmerited – the gift of God's grace. In this way, Paul was able to maintain the sanctity of the Law as well as go beyond it to see its fulfillment in Christ for all people.

Righteousness

If the human being is under the power of Sin before salvation, then after salvation the person receives life. If being under Sin is the striving to live out of the person's own ability to keep the Law which leads to death, then life is the complete surrender of the self to God's grace. This is how Paul understands "righteousness" or "being right-wised" i.e. being put into a right relationship and the pre-condition required for that relationship. In other words, "righteousness" is the pre-condition required for receiving salvation/life. Abraham's righteousness was the pre-condition for receiving the promise of inheritance (Rom. 4:13), so now the one who is righteous will receive life (Rom. 1:17; Gal. 3:11). Since the connection between "righteousness" and "salvation" is so close, righteousness itself becomes the essence of salvation and the two can be used as synonymous terms: *striving after righteousness* (Rom. 9:30ff.; Gal.2:16), the concern of the Jews, could also be expressed as "striving after salvation". The connection between the two terms becomes even closer still when it is understood that it is not just salvation/life that is the gift of God, but even the (pre)condition for salvation/life is the gift of God. Therefore the question is: what is meant by "righteousness" (δικαιοσυνη) and especially the phrase "righteousness of God" (ἡ δικαιοσυνη του Θεου).

The Greek noun for 'righteousness' is *dikaiosyne* (δικαιοσυνη); the adjective, 'righteous person' (δικαιος) is also used. The words are used in an ethical sense (doing what is right; having right relationships), and in a forensic sense (legal). When the word is used as the pre-condition for salvation, or as the essence of salvation itself, then its usage must be seen from a forensic (legal) background. In this sense, righteousness is not merely a quality but descriptive of a relationship – i.e. it is not merely something that a person possess of himself/herself, rather it is something that is pronounced about the person by the forum to which the person is accountable. As a forensic term, therefore, righteousness is pronounced by a judge to indicate that the accused person is not guilty – pronounced 'righteous' or pronounced as being 'right-wised' (in a proper relationship). The person is pronounced 'righteous' not to the extent that the person is innocent, but to the extent that the person is acknowledged to be innocent and that the person is in favourable standing in the eyes of others. Thus, it is said of God that God is righteous – i.e. God is acknowledged to be righteous (Rom. 3:4 quoting Ps. 51:4 where God is right in God's judgements).

However, in Judaism, as the thinking moved towards the future restoration of the Davidic kingdom, "righteousness" came to be something that was seen as a future condition – God right-wising at the last judgment – i.e. there was a shift in the understanding of "righteousness" from a specifically forensic term to one that had eschatological implications, e.g. *those who hunger and thirst after righteousness* (Matt. 5:6) is not to be understood as those who continually work towards attaining righteousness on their own, but those who long for God to pronounce the verdict of being "righteous" as God's decision at the final judgment. Hence **"righteousness" came to be a forensic-eschatological term**. What the pious Jew endeavours to do is to fulfill the pre-conditions for this favourable verdict –i.e. keeping the Law. So, Paul can refer to this endeavour as *righteousness based on the Law* (Philip. 3:9), whereas his thesis is that *the righteousness of God* (ἡ δικαιοσυνη του Θεου) *has been manifested apart from the Law* (Rom. 3:21).

In Paul, the forensic-eschatological aspect of "righteousness" are two sides of the same coin and must be taken seriously – i.e. "righteousness" is already a present reality. Rom. 3:21-4:25 deals with faith as the pre-condition for being right-wised following which, Rom 5:1 begins with, *therefore since we are justified by faith, we have peace with God....* Similarly, *since now we are justified (right-wised) by His blood...* (Rom. 5:9) and *if Christ is in you, although your bodies are dead because of sin, your spirits are alive because of righteousness* (Rom. 8:10). In the key verses of Rom. 1:16-17, Paul says that the Gospel *is the power of God for salvation.... for in it the righteousness of God is revealed...*

As a present reality – a paradox in which God's eschatological judgment/verdict is already pronounced in the present. Therefore the "righteousness" that God adjudicates to the person in the present is not a state of "sinlessness" in the sense of ethical perfection, but "sinlessness" in the sense that *God was in Christ reconciling the world to God self, not counting their trespasses against them....* (II Cor. 5:19). This emphasizes the understanding of the concept of Sin as a power that is broken in the salvation process, rather than sin as individual acts of omission/commission. "Righteousness" should be understood in this forensic-eschatological sense rather than in the sense of ethical perfection. This also becomes clear in *for as by one man's disobedience many were made sinners, so by one man's obedience many will be made righteous* (Rom. 5:19). This is the peculiar double character of "righteousness" in Paul: future and yet already present.

This double character of "righteousness" is further described as God's righteousness/the righteousness of God (ἡ δικαιοσυνη του Θεου): salvation is not *righteousness based on Law,* but *the righteousness of God based on faith* (Rom. 1:16-17; ch.4; 5:1; Gal. 2:16; 3:6, 8, 11,24; 5:5; Philip. 3:9). It is a quality of relationship that belongs to God and which God imparts to the human being through Christ and appropriated by the human being through faith (Rom. 3:21-27). The "righteousness of God" therefore cannot be won by human effort, it is a sheer gift, expressed by the word "grace" (χαρις) (Rom. 3:22-24; 5:15, 17; Gal. 3:22). "Righteousness" then belongs to God and has its origins in God's grace; it is God-given and God-adjudicated righteousness (Rom. 1:17; 3:21ff.; 10:3; Philip. 3:9) [God's grace prepares the person to receive the gift of God's righteousness – John Wesley's concept of 'prevenient grace']. However, it must be noted that God's grace is not "cheap grace" (the words of

Dietrich Bonheoffer, a noted 20th century theologian); having had the verdict of "righteousness" in God's judgment makes it obligatory to keep the ethical demands of the Law which ensure proper on-going relationships (see section on "life in Christ").

Salvation: The act of Divine Grace consists in the fact that God gave God's Son to die on the cross – *Christ died for our sins* (Rom. 5:6, 8, 14-15; I Cor. 15:3; II Cor. 5:14); Christ *gave himself up* for us (Rom. 4:25; 8:32; Gal. 1:4; 2:20); Christ is preached as *the crucified* (I Cor. 1:23; 2:2; Gal. 3:1); therefore the gospel can be called *the word of the cross* (I Cor. 1:18), a *stumbling block*(I Cor. 1:23; Gal. 5:11); the enemies of the gospel are *enemies of the cross of Christ* (Philip. 3:18). The cross (death) and resurrection of Christ are bound together in one salvation-occurrence (Bultmann, *Theology of the New Testament, Vol. I*): *he who died* is also *he who was raised up* (Rom. 8:34; II Cor. 5:15; 13:4). The salvation-occurrence then includes the death and resurrection of Jesus. Such was the tradition that Paul had received and passed on (I Cor. 15:1-4): for Paul, the sole decisive event for the salvation-occurrence is the death and resurrection of Jesus (thought of as one event).

How is this act of Divine Grace appropriated and experienced by humans? Paul's answer would be that the salvation-occurrence is a compelling and transforming power and he uses a number of images to bring home the point:

1. Jesus' death is understood in terms of the Jewish sacrificial system – a **propitiatory sacrifice** by which forgiveness of sins is brought about, *Jesus, whom God put forward as an expiation by His blood, to be received by faith* (Rom. 3:25 ff.); *we are now justified by His blood* (Rom. 5:9); the Lord's Supper is also thought of as a propitiatory sacrifice (I Cor. 11:24ff.). It is referred to as a Passover sacrifice (I Cor. 5:7) though the Passover sacrifice was not originally for the forgiveness of sins, but it came to acquire this meaning later. This is probably a tradition that was taken over by the earliest Church (see analysis and commentary on I Cor. 11:23ff.) and Paul crystallized the tradition by formulating it into words.

2. Jesus' death is also understood as a **vicarious sacrifice** – a sacrifice on behalf of another – *instead of us, in place of us, for us* (Gal. 3:13; II Cor. 5:21; Rom. 8:3).

3. Jesus' death is also the means by which people are *redeemed from the curse of the Law* (Gal. 3:13) – using an image from the legal system.

These images explain that Christ's death is thought of as a release from Law, Sin and Death. The power of these forces has already been destroyed (καταργουμενοι, I Cor. 2:6); *the old has passed away, behold the new has come* (II Cor. 5:17). This salvation-occurrence meets the human being in the proclamation (κηρυγμα) where the *word of the cross* meets the believer and demands a response.

> (κηρυγμα, *kerygma*, is the proclamation of an edict from the sovereign by an authorized person such as a "herald" or an "apostle" and thus it demands a response from the hearers)

Justification by faith

This topic in Pauline theology is related to "righteousness" (discussed above) and in Reformation theology/emphasis, it is held to be the central theme in Pauline theology. "Justification by faith" (δικαιοσις ἐκ πιστης) was a theme that had to be developed by Paul in order to express his theological understanding that the salvation offered as a gift by God through the life, death, and resurrection of Christ was open to all – Jew and Gentile. Yet the whole understanding of salvation originated in the Jewish understanding of God's redemptive acts in Israel's history. For Paul, and the New Testament writers, these acts of redemption are continued in Christ – the *heilsgeschichte* – but now go beyond the borders of Judaism to include the world. It was therefore important to develop a concept that would take into consideration the continuity of God's acts of salvation originating in Judaism, and the new understanding of salvation that must also include the Gentiles. In the development of that concept, two backgrounds must be kept in mind:

1. The Jewish background of the Law which held that a person's salvation depended on a person's ability to adhere to all the precepts/demands of the Law. Salvation was something that a person had to work towards and in order to fulfill the demands of the Law, the person had primarily to be a Jew and therefore an inheritor of the promises of God.

2. The background of the Greco-Roman law court vocabulary/concepts (as seen above), where the term righteousness/justification (δικαιοσις, δικαιοσυνή) was a legal/forensic term whereby the judge declared the person "righteous" or not guilty; it was the verdict pronounced by a competent authority and not a quality by which one could describe oneself or quality that one could assume for oneself.

Paul clearly saw that the Jewish background would be too limiting – God's act of salvation was not limited to Judaism but was for the whole world. In developing this understanding of God's universal act of salvation, Paul used the vocabulary of the Greco-Roman courts whereby a person was pronounced "righteous" by the judge. So, for Paul, God pronounced as "righteous" – not guilty – all who by faith would receive God's gift. As a gift, it was free, and no work was required to appropriate its benefits, thus abrogating the Law. The person accepting this gift, by faith, was pronounced "righteous" by God irrespective of whether the person was a Jew or Gentile. In Rom. 4 and Gal. 3, Paul brings out the understanding that *Abraham believed the promises of God and it was reckoned to him as righteousness.* This was before the Law was given through Moses, thus everyone who believes like Abraham did receives righteousness or salvation; it is the *righteousness through faith and not righteousness based on the works of the Law* (Rom. 9:30, 31; Philip. 3:9). Paul had to develop this understanding to ensure that the gracious gift of God in Jesus Christ would be of primary importance for Jews and Gentiles and that doing the works of the Law had become irrelevant: *Christ is the end of the Law, that everyone who has faith may be justified* (Rom. 10:4). In this sense, 'justification by faith' became a major Pauline concept though it may not be viewed by all as *the* central theme in

Pauline theology. The concept of justification by faith was re-iterated by Luther in the Reformation when he too had to propose a means of understanding that salvation was not by doing works but was a free gift of God appropriated by faith (*sola fide*). Wesley took the Reformation theme a step further and added, justification by faith *through grace* (and developed his concept of 'prevenient grace'), thus further emphasizing the nature of the free gift of God in Jesus Christ.

B.   Ἐν Χριστῷ (*en Christo*): Life *in Christ*. Individual and corporative perspectives.

The first section of Pauline Issues dealt with Sin, Salvation, Justification etc…or the process of salvation. This section will deal with the Pauline understanding of how the believer is to continue after salvation. The phrase *en Christo* (ἐν Χριστῷ) – in Christ – is used variously in Pauline theology.

> It can have an *instrumental* usage where Christ is the instrument of salvation: *God was in Christ reconciling the world to Godself* (II Cor. 5:19);

> 'In Christ' can simply mean to be a Christian (Rom.3:24; 8:39; 16:12; Gal. 3:14, 28; Phile. 16).

> 'In Christ' is the medium in which the Christian lives (Rom. 12:5; Gal. 3:28); it expresses a relationship with Christ;

> 'In Christ' describes the on-going participation in the Christ-event: *if anyone is in Christ, there is a new creation* (II Cor. 5:17; Gal. 2:20);

> In Christ' expresses the basis and goal of final salvation: *there is no condemnation for those who are in Christ Jesus* (Rom. 8:1); *I press on toward the goal for the prize of the upward call of God in Christ Jesus* (Philip. 3:14). In this sense, 'in Christ' is an eschatological term.

'In Christ" was earlier thought to refer to a mystical experience/ relationship with Christ; it expresses the believer incorporated into the person of Christ and who lives out the Christ-like life: *it is no longer I who live, but Christ who lives in me; and the life I now live in the flesh, I live by faith in the Son of God...* (Gal. 2:20). This Christ-like life is lived out in the community, therefore ἐν Χριστῳ has an ecclesiological dimension; the individual is taken into *the body of Christ* (I Cor. 12:13) or simply *into Christ* (II Cor. 1:21; Gal. 3:27). To belong to the *ecclesia* (ἐκκλησια), the 'called-out-community', the Church is to be 'in Christ' (Rom. 16:7,11; I Cor. 1:30). So ἐν Χριστῳ, 'in Christ' is primarily an ecclesiological expression where the new sphere of existence is to bring the person into right relationship with God and which would make the person a part of the "new creation" (II Cor. 5:17). The fact that a person is 'in Christ' does not free them from responsibility for their actions; they are to *have the mind of Christ* (Philip. 2:1-5) in their relationships in the community.

This ecclesial-eschatological term determines the life and goal of the individual as lived out and expressed in the life and goal of the community. Therefore, 'in Christ', ἐν Χριστῳ, has both individual and corporate perspectives.

C.   The Church: Jews and Gentiles in the Church. The Body of Christ

Sacraments. Spiritual gifts. Γλωσσαλαλια (glossalalia) – speaking in tongues.

The *kerygma* – proclaimed word – calls and gathers people into the *ecclesia* (ἐκκλησια), the 'called-out' community. Since the *ecclesia* comes into existence through the word which proclaims the eschatological salvation-occurrence, the *ecclesia* is itself an eschatological community, i.e. it is a community that has its existence in the end time when it is called out to be different from the world around. Just as the *ecclesia* is called into existence by the proclaimed word, so in turn it is the forum in which preaching takes place; only in the *ecclesia* is there authorized preaching, *the ministry of reconciliation* (II Cor. 3:6ff.) – i.e. apostolic preaching stands within the framework of salvation history of the People of God (I Cor. 12:28).

The *ecclesia* sometimes means the total (universal) Church and sometimes the local congregation reflecting the peculiar character of the eschatological community; the individual believer stands within the congregation, and the individual congregations are joined together into one Congregation – the Church. At first the *ecclesia* does not denote individual congregations, but the total 'people of God' – the fellowship of the chosen, elect at the end of days – the eschatological congregation. This means that the individual congregations are the present visible manifestations of the eschatological Universal Congregation (I Cor. 10:32, 11:22, 12:28, 15:9; Gal. 1:13). The local church as a manifestation of the total, universal Church is probably meant in the expression occurring in the prefatory greetings of letters: *to the Church (of God) in* (τῃ ἐκκλησιᾳ του Θεου τῃ οὐσῃ ἐν) (I Cor. 1:2; II Cor. 1:1), or in the references to "house churches" (Rom. 16:5; I Cor. 16:9; Col. 4:15; Philem. 2). 'The Church' is therefore simultaneously thought of as a visible local congregation in the world and having to deal with the issues of the world – *the church in Corinth, the church in Ephesus etc... -* and as the invisible, Universal, eschatological Congregation (expressed in the Nicean-Constantinopolitan Creed as the *"One, Holy, Catholic Church"*). The eschatological Congregation is present in the cultic gathering (I Cor. 11:18) in which Christ is confessed as Lord (I Cor. 12:3; Philip. 2:11), and where the Lord, through the presence of the Spirit, bestows *spiritual gifts* (I Cor. 14) so that *if an unbeliever or outsider enters.... they will worship God and declare that God is really among you* (I Cor. 14:24-25).

It must also be noted that in the undisputed letters of Paul, the Church is a "charismatic" community, i.e. having no definite structure or liturgical pattern though Paul insists that worship should be orderly (I Cor.14:26-33). The letters that reflect a more structured liturgy and church order (Ephesians, Colossians, the Pastorals) are held to belong to a period later than Paul.

Jews and Gentiles in the Church

Jewish Christianity was represented by the earliest Church in Palestine as it had not separated itself from Judaism and the concept of the eschatological Congregation of the Jewish people (see Acts where the disciples are closely associated with the worship of the Temple; later followed by

Paul who always first goes to the synagogue in the City where he is visiting). This Congregation took for granted that a non-Jew, desirous of joining the Congregation had first to submit to the laws of Judaism, i.e. had to become a Jew. In contrast to this, and in the presence of Hellenistic Judaism (i.e. Judaism outside of Palestine which had also incorporated influences of other religions), there arose Hellenistic Christianity which did not require the person to first become a Jew. This Hellenistic Christianity or Gentile Christianity represented by Paul achieved recognition at the Jerusalem Council (see Acts 15), but the so-called Judaisers still persisted in insisting on the precepts of Judaism being followed before admission to Christianity. Their mission personnel had penetrated Pauline areas of ministry and caused trouble (see the Corinthian Correspondence and Galatians). In the undisputed letters of Paul, he struggled with this problem of Hellenistic Christianity acknowledging the ethical demands of the Law yet rejecting the validity of the Law as a means of salvation; Paul came up with the concept of justification by faith (see above). Further, in the eschatological Congregation, this world's distinctions have lost their meaning, therefore *there is neither Jew nor Greek, there is neither slave nor free, there is neither male nor female, for you are all one in Christ Jesus* (Gal. 3:28). This indifference to worldly distinctions also extends to *let each one remain in the state in which the call of God encountered them* (I Cor. 7:17-24), a differentiation that does not mean a sociological programme for change, but one which has validity and takes place only within the eschatological Congregation. Thus, for Paul, and his interpretation which he refers to as *my gospel,* Jews and Gentiles have an equal place in the Church.

The Body of Christ

Paul uses many images to describe the eschatological character of the Church: *new covenant* (I Cor. 11:25; II Cor. 3:6ff.), *the Israel of God* (Gal. 6:16), Abraham as the father of those who have faith (Rom. 4; Gal. 3), in the Church all promises find their fulfillment (Rom. 15:4; I Cor. 10:11). The most characteristic image is that of "the Body of Christ" used to express the unity of the Church and the foundation of this unity (Rom. 12:4-8; I Cor. 12:12-31). The expression of the Church as a "body" was developed from the classic Greek tradition which used this image to describe an organically developed and compact community where all the parts have equal importance and work together to present a unity – the organic role of the image of the body. The individual is taken into the "body of Christ" by baptism (see below) (Rom. 12:4-5;I Cor. 12:12-13; II Cor. 1:21; Gal. 3:27), so that further existence is "in Christ". The *en Christo* (ἐν Χριστῳ) phrase is here used primarily as an ecclesiological formula though it also retains its eschatological implications: *if anyone is "in Christ", they are a new creation* (II Cor. 5:17) – both a present reality in the Church and a hope for the future when all of creation is renewed.

The use of the phrase "body of Christ" in Ephesians and Colossians is somewhat different. Here the Church is imaged as an actual body with Christ as the head (Eph. 1:23, 5:30; Col. 1:18, 24), i.e. as the superior organ – the functional role of each part of the body taken separately. This change in the meaning of the imagery also contributes to the letters being placed in the deutero-Pauline writings.

The Church differs from all other human groupings in so far as its unity is not only functional but also organic. An autonomous Christian is an impossibility! Like all the parts of the body, the believers are held together functionally and organically by love – *without love I am nothing* (I Cor. 13:2), which necessarily means a relationship to another person; the independent self is absorbed into the functional and organic unity of the "body of Christ".

Sacraments

There has always been a debate on how to define sacraments. The classic Aquinas definition of 'an outward sign/symbol of an inward grace' is still quoted but added to – 'an act which by natural means puts supernatural powers into effect' (Bultmann) usually through prescribed wordings, formula, in and through a rite. A further definition could be added: a sacrament is a symbol/act which signifies participation in the means of God's grace.

In Paul, the two sacraments of Protestant Christianity – baptism and eucharist – are closely linked with the salvation-occurrence and "the body of Christ".

1.   Baptism

The individual is taken into the "body of Christ" by the sacrament of baptism – *for by one Spirit we were all baptized into one body* (I Cor. 12:13) or simply as *in Christ* (II Cor. 1:21; Gal. 3:27); it is a rite of initiation into the ecclesial-eschatological Congregation, *dying with Christ .... And rising with Christ* (Rom. 6:3-6, 8).

Baptism was a Jewish practice (ref. John the Baptist/Baptizer, Mk. 1:4ff. and parallels) related to a public confession of sins in the presence of witnesses, and a symbol of the sins having been removed. Paul uses this dimension of baptism as purification in *you were washed, you were made holy, you were made righteous...* (I Cor.6:11). As it developed in the Christian tradition, it not only expressed a forgiveness of sins but also came to be an initiation rite where the person baptizing does so in the name of the Trinitarian formula (Matt. 28:19). Therefore, the name of the person being baptized was pronounced so that the named person became a member of the eschatological Congregation. Baptism was therefore considered not just as purification from sins, but a conquest over death and the acquisition of life. In one of the main passages on his understanding of baptism – Rom. 6 – Paul brings together the freedom from Sin and the rite of baptism in which the future resurrection guaranteed by baptism is a present reality which is realized in ethical conduct:

> *...how can we who died to sin still live in it? Do you not know that all of us who have been baptized into Christ Jesus were baptized into His death? We were buried with Him in baptism...so that as Christ was raised from the dead...we too might walk in newness of life...if we have been united with Him in a death like His, we shall certainly be united with Him in a resurrection like His....Do not yield your members to Sin as instruments of wickedness, but yield yourselves to God...and your members to God as instruments of righteousness.....* (quotations from Rom. 6)

The same thought is expressed in Ephesians 2:5ff. and Colossians 2 & 3. It is in this sense, baptism was often referred to as *rebirth* – dying with Christ in the water of baptism and rising to newness of life.

This idea of 'dying-rising' may have come from the Hellenistic mystery religions where it was used to express the idea of oneness with the divine. However, in Paul it is not a mystical act but the expression of the experience of sharing in the benefits of Christ's death and resurrection which leads to a renewal of life.

Baptism therefore, as a cultic rite, finds its meaning when it takes place within the "body of Christ" as a response to the experience of the salvation-occurrence.

2.   Eucharist

In the Pauline understanding of the Lord's Supper – Eucharist – there are some influences from the Hellenistic mystery religions: participation in the eucharist effects communion with the crucified and risen Jesus by means of the bread and wine, eaten and drunk. However, he disregards the mystical effect because the eucharist is a real meal in which all participate (I Cor. 11) and which leads to community (κοινωνια); further, it is a proclamation taking place within the "body of Christ" which is the only forum in which it will have meaning.

The liturgical words that Paul uses, I *received from the Lord what I delivered to you* (I Cor. 11:23ff.), indicates a very early date for the origin of the practice. The liturgy includes 1. an interpretation of the elements: *this is my body... this is my blood;* 2. Jesus' death thought of as a sacrifice to establish a new covenant: *this is my blood of the new covenant;* 3. Jesus' death thought of as an expiatory sacrifice for the *forgiveness of sins;* and 4. Participation in the eucharist is a means to *proclaim the Lord's death till He comes.* Further, *the cup of blessing...is it not a participation in the blood of Christ....the bread which we break, is it not a participation in the body of Christ? ...for we who are many are one body...* (I Cor. 10:16-18) is indicative of the fellowship/unity/oneness (κοινωνια) that is effected by the eucharist, especially in the Corinthian context where differences in social and economic status were to be completely set aside when participating in the eucharist, because the purpose of the meal was to overcome divisions in the community.

Thus, like baptism, eucharist is also regarded as a sacrament and finds its meaning when it takes place within "the body of Christ" and as a response to the salvation-occurrence.

Spiritual gifts

In "the body of Christ" the members are differentiated by their various capacities for service; each has a different "spiritual" gift (because it is bestowed by the Spirit, πνευματικοι χαρισματα, is the divine power/gift that stands in contrast to all that is human, or an empowerment to minister to the community in ways that went beyond natural talents) which is for the common good of the community (I Cor. 12:4-11). All these gifts are for service in the community and each gift finds its place for expression: *for just as the body is one and has many members, and all the members of the body, though many, are one body, so it is with Christ....*(I Cor. 12:12ff.). These gifts are manifested in the Church through the services rendered: *God has appointed in the Church first apostles, second prophets, third teachers, then workers of miracles, then healers, helpers, administrators, speakers in various kinds of tongues....*(I Cor. 12:27ff.). The coming of the Spirit, in Jewish Christianity and Hellenistic Christianity was seen as an eschatological event – something that will take place in the last days (Joel 2:28-32; Acts 2:14ff.) so in the manifestation of 'spiritual gifts', the eschatological event is already present in the community. The Spirit is given to the Church into which the individual is received by baptism and endowed with a gift. The gift may not be expressed at all times, but it is there in times of need to upbuild the community; above all, the working of the Spirit and the exercise of gifts of the Spirit are experienced in the service of worship in which the eschatological Congregation is present and takes its form.

It can be seen that there are two types of "spiritual gifts" : 1. those that are given and exercised for the benefit of the community as a whole – *for the common good* (I Cor. 12:7); and 2. The gifts of special ability (apostles, prophets, teachers, administrators etc...) to help others carry out an effective ministry (I Cor. 12:27-31). All of these gifts are exercised 'in house' or within the community.

Therefore, spiritual gifts are present in the cultic gathering of the congregation (I Cor. 11:18) where Christ is present and demonstrates His presence by the working of the Spirit in the various "spiritual gifts" (I Cor. 14) so that an outsider/stranger can say, *truly God is among you* (I Cor. 14:25)

Γλωσσαλαλια (glossalalia) – speaking in tongues

The ecstasy of being filled with the Spirit was manifested in the phenomena of γλωσσαλαλια– speaking in tongues; it was a manifestation that was causing a problem in Hellenistic churches (I Cor. 14), but a manifestation that was part of the early history of the community, and it is a manifestation that causes problems and misunderstandings in the Church today.

Acts 2:1-13 tells the story of the descent of the Spirit on the day of Pentecost when the manifestation of speaking in tongues first appeared (see section on Acts 2, above). Pentecost was the Jewish festival occurring 50 days after Passover and celebrating the giving of the Law on Mount Sinai. Pentecost was a pilgrim festival so Jews from all over the world were expected to travel to Jerusalem to celebrate the festival. Rabbinic interpretations were that the Law was given in all the languages of the earth (depicting the spread of Judaism beyond the borders of Palestine), therefore in Acts 2 people from all over the world were present, making the important point that the languages could be understood, and communication was possible (Acts 2:11). In depicting God's appearance at Sinai, the scene was described as one including thunder, lightning, smoke etc…. (Exodus 19:16). Rabbinic interpretations hold that angels took the Law on tongues of flame to the people at the bottom of the mountain and to all the people on earth. Acts evokes the same imagery and presents Pentecost in Jerusalem as the renewal of God's covenant – a covenant that will ultimately include the Gentiles as well. It should also be noted that Peter's speech (Acts 2:14ff.) following the Pentecost event closely links the event with the history of Israel thereby indicating that the mission that will follow is a continuation of God's mission with Israel – the *heilsgeschichte* – the history of salvation continued in the Church. This is the impact of

Pentecost: the disciples had become a broken group, leaderless and directionless; it was the end of their world. With the coming of the Spirit at Pentecost, the end becomes a new beginning, a new life; the lack of leadership and direction is transformed into an experience of the empowerment of believers who will become the Church.

However, in the Hellenistic Church, influenced by the experiences of ecstasy in the mystery religions, the speaking in tongues – that is speaking in a language in which one was not normally competent –was a much sought after manifestation (I Cor. 14), especially since it was the most visible of the Spirit's gifts, and included by Paul in the 'spiritual gifts' listed in I Cor. 12:10, 28, 30; 14:18, 26.It can be inferred from chapter 12 that *charismas* (gifts) and offices in the community had become a troublesome feature as one gift was thought to be more superior than the other; Paul clearly saw that the 'charismatic', 'led-by-the-spirit' sort of behavior and worship which had infiltrated the Corinthian community would only result in chaos, indiscipline and finally disintegration; this danger had to be avoided. The *charismas* were not being belittled or discriminated against, but were being seen from the perspective of the whole community with emphasis on interdependence and recognition of the fact that not all members possess gifts and offices:the basic message is that all the *charismas* and offices are needed for the common good and to build up the community(I Cor. 12:27-30) [see section on I Cor. 12 & 14, above].

Paul critiques this so-called charismatic manifestation in several ways:

1. *One who speaks in a tongue speaks not to people but to God…* (I Cor. 14:2)

2. *Those who speak in tongues edify themselves…* (I Cor. 14:4)

3. *The one who prophesies is greater than the one who speaks in tongues…* (I Cor. 14:5)

4. *Speaking in tongues requires an interpreter otherwise it is not beneficial…* (I Cor. 14:14:13)

Better to speak five words in a tongue that everyone understands than ten thousand words in a language that no one understands (I Cor. 14:19).

Paul's critique was a direct answer to the spirit-people who had infiltrated the Corinthian community and who insisted that speaking in tongues was the ultimate demonstration of a person having received salvation.

Paul asks the rhetorical question: *if I come to you speaking in tongues, how shall I benefit you....unless I bring you some prophecy?* His answer is: *if you in a tongue utter speech that is not intelligible, how will anyone know what is said? For you will be speaking into the air....if I do not know the meaning of the language, I shall be a foreigner to the speaker and the speaker a foreigner to me...* He advises that *since you are eager for manifestations of the Spirit, strive to excel in building up the church.* The criterion for the exercise of a gift is always for the good, the building up, of the community: and the answer to his rhetorical question is: *in church I would rather speak five words with my mind, in order to instruct others, than ten thousand words in a tongue* (I Cor. 14:6-19).

The sort of disorder that speaking in tongues caused when they came together for worship had also to be corrected: *when you come together, each one has a hymn, a lesson, a revelation, a tongue, or an interpretation. Let all things be done in order for edification.* There follow instructions for proper order to be maintained in worship so that all are edified rather than allow confusion to prevail *for God is not a God of confusion but of peace* (I Cor. 14:26-33).

Modern charismatic movements from the 19th century onwards exhibit a variety of *charisms*, but the greatest attention is paid to speaking in tongues, probably because it is the most visible of the *charisms*, and which holds that the only criteria for being recognized as a Christian is to speak in tongues. Indeed, the phenomena is still as divisive today as it was in Paul's time and Paul's corrective to the Corinthian situation is therefore as valid today as well and should be paid careful attention.

Therefore, the gift of γλωσσαλαλια– speaking in tongues – should not be seen as an ecstatic manifestation of doing something beyond one's normal abilities, but the **empowerment to communicate in understandable languages** to enable the vast reach of evangelism that will ultimately bring all into the fold of the people of God.

D.   Eschatology and the summing up of all things in Christ

In theological usage, eschatology (ἐσχατος– last time, last things, end + λογος– study) can be used in two ways: 1. studying about the last things, end time, end of the world and the various things associated with the end such as return of Christ (παρουσια, *parousia*), judgment, heaven, hell, and images such as clouds, trumpets, angels, graves opening up, and the state of the person after death etc... 2. Understanding what God has done in Christ – salvation – which is something that is thought of as coming about in the future, but which is already present, thus the Christ-event is an eschatological event, salvation is an eschatological moment, the Church is the eschatological Congregation etc....(Bultmann, *Theology of the New Testament, Vol. I*) [for discussion on topics, see above].This is Bultmann's category of 'existential eschatology' following the German philosopher Martin Heidegger, where the future is already present within one's existence. In this sense, eschatology is not the chronological end of things, but the quality of what has taken place is the more important issue. Therefore, eschatology is the centre or starting point of Pauline theology and not its end; as one Pauline scholar, Gunther Bornkamm, puts it: *eschatology in Paul is the study of the first things and not the study of the last things* (G. Bornkamm, *Paul*). For Paul, the new age which is supposed to come at the end, is already present through the work of Christ and the benefits of the new age are already present (see above discussion on various issues in Pauline theology): *if anyone is in Christ, they are a new creation, the old has passed away, behold the new has come* (II Cor. 5:17) [note that the verbs, even in the English translation, are in the present tense, emphasizing that it is a present reality].

Paul was certainly influenced by apocalyptic ideas of his time (ἀποκαλυπτω– reveal, usually with reference to revealing something pertaining to the end period) – the end of the world in dramatic images such as *the Lord Himself will descend from heaven with a cry of command, with the archangel's call and with the sound of the trumpet of God*. The imagery is given a Christological interpretation: *the dead in Christ will rise first; then we who are alive, who are left, shall be caught up together with them in the clouds to meet the Lord in the air; and so, we shall always be with the Lord* (I Thess. 4:15-17).

Some apocalyptic ideas such as the passage quoted, are often referred to as "vertical eschatology" or the abrupt breaking in of supernatural powers to bring history to an end. A further example is the παρουσια or what is commonly referred to as the 'Second Coming' of Christ (I Cor. 15:23-24) which was expected very soon (I Cor. 7:28-29; 15:51).

In Pauline thought there is also a 'personal eschatology' and a 'cosmic eschatology'. The 'personal eschatology' deals with the state of the individual after death (I Cor. 15; II Cor. 5; Philip. 1:21-26; I Thess. 4 & 5). 'Cosmic eschatology' deals with the end of space and time (Rom. 8:18-25; I Cor. 15:28; Philip. 2:10-11; II Thess. 2) [there are many other passages in the New Testament that also deal with cosmic eschatology, e.g. Matt. 24; Mk. 13; Lk. 21; II Pet. 3:10-13; Rev. 21]. A few passages will be dealt with below to bring out Pauline eschatology.

The passage in **I Cor. 15** has to be understood in the context of the discussion on the resurrection which was a topic that was questioned by some in Corinth especially in the light of the delay in the *parousia*. Paul argues that the resurrection is a certainty based on the resurrection of Christ and that there is no meaning of the Gospel if this certainity is removed. The distinction between the living and the dead is broken down because all enter the process of new life in Christ through a process of change, *a mystery*, where the living and the dead *must put on immortality...the perishable will put on the imperishable...and then shall come to pass the saying, Death is swallowed up in victory...*(I Cor. 15:51-55). There is both a continuity and a discontinuity in this personal eschatology – the physical puts on the spiritual. This personal eschatology leads into the cosmic eschatology: *each in its own order: Christ the first fruits, then at His coming those who belong to Christ. Then comes the end, when He delivers the kingdom to God the Father after destroying every rule and every authority and power...the last enemy to be destroyed is death* (I Cor. 15:20-28).

In the **II Cor. 5:1-10** passage, the same idea of the relationship between personal eschatology and cosmic eschatology is seen, along with the concepts from Hellenistic thinking and Judaism. Hellenistic thinking, especially Gnosticism, saw the body as being 'evil' and the person having to be delivered from it. The Jewish idea was that all life was embodied and that the body was good since it was created by God. Paul brings these two ideas together in the images of a tent (a temporary dwelling place), and the image of a *house not made with hands, eternal in the heavens* (II Cor. 5:1), so life moves from the temporary shelter to the permanent house, thereby preserving both Hellenistic and Jewish thought.

The **Thessalonian church** was expecting the *parousia* in their own life time, and so became concerned about those who had died before the *parousia*. So the idea of a general resurrection is mooted – *we would not have you ignorant concerning those who are asleep ...through Jesus, God will bring those who have fallen asleep...the dead in Christ will rise first; then we who are alive, who are left, shall be caught up together with them in the clouds to meet the Lord in the air; and so we shall always be with the Lord* (I Thess. 4:1ff.).The event cannot be given any time frame *for the day of the Lord will come as a thief in the night* (I Thess. 5:1ff.). Here too, personal eschatology is closely intertwined with cosmic eschatology.

The **Rom. 8:18-25** passage is a classic expression of cosmic eschatology: human redemption is closely linked with the salvation of the whole of creation: *the whole creation has been groaning in travail together until now, and not only the creation, but we ourselves...as we wait with hope* (see section on Ecology, below).

All of Paul's eschatological thinking takes place within the eschatological Congregation as the place where all things are summed up in Christ: *...for God has made known to us in all wisdom and insight the mystery of God's will, according to God's purpose which God set forth in Christ as a plan for the fullness of time, to unite all things in Christ, things in heaven and things on earth* (Eph. 1:9-10) – the vertical view of eschatology, breaking into history, gives way to the horizontal view of eschatology, i.e. God working in and through the processes of history in the eschatological Congregation to finally sum up all things in Christ. This horizontal view of the summing up of all things in Christ is also the thought of Col. 1:15-20: *....in Christ all things were created, in heaven and on earth, visible and invisible.... through Christ, God reconciles to Godself all things, whether on earth or in heaven, making peace by the blood of Christ's cross.*

There is an underlying unity in Pauline eschatology – the personal and the cosmic, the vertical and the horizontal, must be taken together as a whole to give a full understanding of the present life of the believer and the future hope: 1. there is the certainity of the final victory of God who will complete the work of redemption begun in Christ. 2. The apocalyptic imagery is always related to the human being and the world and the imagery is used to emphasize and reinforce the idea of the future being already present in the life of the believer. Thus, Pauline eschatology is the motivational force for the present – it is the first things rather than simply/just the last things.

E.   The place and contribution of women in the Church. Women as partners in ministry

There is much said today about the role of women in the church and in ministry. It has given rise to a contextual concern of feminist theology. This section, however, will not go into the concerns of feminist theology and methodology etc… it will deal only with the texts that mention the role of women. There seem to be contradictory texts in Pauline thought with regard to women, so the texts must always be understood in their own context before making a generalization or a norm for all time. The above commentaries deal with the texts in greater detail; here they are only extracted to highlight the issue of the place and contribution of women, and women as partners in ministry.

Acts 16:13-15 and Philip. 4:2-3

This is not an attempt to combine various writings to form a so-called 'biblical theology' but simply to illustrate the role of women in a Greek city – Philippi. The context of the Acts story is during the so-called Second Missionary Journey when Paul and his group entered Macedonia and the city of Philippi. Among a gathering of ladies at the riverside, they met up with Lydia, a businesswoman in the trade of selling purple goods (cloth, woollen) for which the city of Thyatira was famous. She was a Gentile devotee of Jewish worship and was attracted to the message of the Gospel. She and her whole household were baptized and then invited Paul and his group into their home. In the Philippian passage, two women, Euodia and Syntyche, seemed to have had some differences among themselves which may have been affecting the life of the community; other members of the community are asked to help the women to resolve the differences. These two women are referred to as having ....*labored side by side with me in the gospel*... In the point under discussion, the place and role of women in a city like Philippi is quite clear. Lydia seems to have a leading role in her own household and can make decisions without reference to men in the household; Euodia and Syntyche have worked alongside Paul in the ministry and he seems to have great respect for them. So, in Philippi, women are an accepted part of ministry and leaders in the Philippian community.

Romans 16:1,3,6,7,12,13,15

The closing chapter of Romans has been textually suspect (see discussion on commentary on Romans, above), but the point being looked at here is the presence of many women in the greetings. The first is *Phoebe, a deaconess of the Church at Cenchreae.* There is no description of the work of a deaconess, but it is probably the same as that of a deacon – an office of service. Phoebe seems to have been associated with Paul in his work in Asia and possibly the carrier of the letter to the Romans from Ephesus. Her service – she *has been a helper of many and of myself as well* – is commended to the Roman community. *Prisca* is known from Acts probably as the more prominent of the husband-wife team in Corinth and Ephesus and Rome. Since *Mary* is mentioned without any reference, she must have been a well-known person that needed no introduction. A pair is mentioned – *Andronicus and Junias* – where most feel that "Junias" is a woman's name and that this may be a husband-wife team. If that is the case, then this is the only time a woman is referred to as an *apostle.Tryphaena and Tryphosa* are referred to as *workers in the Lord; the beloved Percis who has worked hard in the Lord.* Greetings are sent to *Rufus, eminent in the Lord, also his mother and mine.* Among the saints at Rome is one *Julia and the sister of Nereus.* Paul had never visited Rome, but most of chapter 16 consists of greetings; it is noteworthy that Paul recognized the contribution of women in the Church and mentioned them by name and achievements/relationships. The conclusion is that these women had rendered praiseworthy service so that they were commended even by those who had never visited Rome.

I Cor. 11:1-16 and 14:34-35

The first letter to the Corinthians deals with various divisions in the community of which Paul had heard, and some of the issues that the Corinthians were facing and for which they had written to Paul. The passages under review in this section deal with various issues related to community worship or "liturgical behaviour" – the men must participate in worship with their heads uncovered and the women with their heads covered, finding support for this in the creation story of Genesis 2:21-22 where God is shown as creating male and female in different ways. It is significant that Paul accepts the gender difference between men and women as being part of God's creation so that a man must look like a man (short hair!) and a woman must look like a woman (long hair!). This emphasis on the physical appearance of men and women probably relates to the issue of blatantly homosexual men and lesbian women participating in worship rituals at Corinth, all as part of the understanding of "charismatic" worship prevalent in Corinth (see commentary, above). This confusion of the sexes led to confusion in worship which had to be corrected (I Cor. 14:26-33 – ...*let all things be done for edification....* for *God is not a God of confusion but of peace*). Paul suggests two ways for this correction: 1. The important point that the Genesis 2 story should not be used for the inferiority and subordination of women – 11:11-12 – *in the Lord, woman is not independent of man nor man of woman* – the text expounds the complete equality of women, backed up further by Paul's interpretation of the Genesis 2 story, that *just as woman was made from man, so man is now born of a woman. And all things are from God.* By this Paul overturned the traditional argument of the priority of the male in the creation story by highlighting the priority of the woman in the birth of a male, both aspects being part of God's plan for creation; equality is emphasized not complementarity. 2. 14:34-35 – perhaps in the charismatic type of worship service some confusion had been caused and in the light of the instructions that worship should be for the edification of all, women should ask their husbands questions at home rather than disturb the worship setting; it is not an injunction not to speak, but an injunction not to cause confusion, *for God is not a God of confusion, but of peace.*

II Tim. 1:5; I Tim. 2:8-15;3:11; 5:9-16 and Titus 2:3-5

It must first be noted that the Pastorals are trito-Pauline writings, i.e. not from Paul himself, but by a later disciple many years after the time of Paul (see commentary on the Pastorals, above), and so while there may be some similarities to the undisputed letters of Paul, there will also be several differences.

The passage in II Tim. 1:5 refers to the faith of Timothy's grandmother, *Lois*, and his mother, *Eunice*, and the influence that they had on Timothy's life. It would seem that these two women played a very significant role in imparting the faith to Timothy for the author emphasizes that Timothy's faith was nurtured by his mother and grandmother, and Timothy is urged to continue in what he has learned from his childhood (II Tim. 3:14-15). The role of women in nurturing the faith is emphasized.

The other two passages, i.e. I Tim. 2:8-15 and 5:9-16 are usually interpreted to present Paul as a misogynist and patriarchal in his thinking. Apart from the caution that the Pastorals are probably not from Paul himself, the context must also be taken into account. The first passage is an instruction to men and women regarding how to behave in worship and disproportionately corrective of women. The stress on modesty and decency in dress leads into a demand that women be quiet and submissive. However, the corrective should be seen in the context of the presence of wealthy women – *braided hair, gold, pearls, costly attire* – who spent their time in *gadding about from house to house, and not only idlers but gossips and busybodies, saying what they should not.* The corrective also applies to younger widows who may be thinking of remarriage and because of their wealth, they need not be a burden on the Church funds which should be used for really needy widows. The false teachers and false teaching seem to have made a great impression on these widows who had leisure and wealth and were the cause of much upset in the community, so the very strong corrective. So, it was not a misogynist writing, but one who was concerned for church organization and order.

The community to which I Timothy is addressed also had women as deacons (I Tim. 3:11) and like the male deacons, their qualifications are listed: *serious, no slanderers, but temperate, faithful in all things.* Presumably the women deacons rendered the same service as the male deacons – a recognized ecclesiastical office of service.

The concern for Church order and sound doctrine forms the context of the Titus 2:3-5 passage (the chapter opens with *teach what befits sound doctrine*) where sound doctrine is also part of the community structure and lifestyle instructions for older men and older women, younger women and younger men and slaves (part of the household codes or *haustafeln*). The older women *are to be reverent in behavior, not to be slanderers or slaves to drink; they are to teach what is good, and to train the young women to love their husbands and children.* The young women are *to be sensible, chaste, domestic, kind, and submissive to their husbands...*By relating their lifestyle to belief and sound doctrine, Christians were to be differentiated from others in their behavior and relationships so *that the word of God may not be discredited.*

In summary, these few passages from Paul and the Pauline writings sufficiently indicate that women were very much a part of the community structure, contributed to worship and the care of the home; the women were partners in ministry and are commended for their service which was on par with that of men; women were ministers of the church (deacons) in precisely the same sense as men. Their gifts were recognized and commended. In all the letters, Christian communities were always commended to work out a life style, individually and for the community, that would make them stand out in their environment showing the difference between the Church and the world, and excellently summed up in Paul's words to the Galatians: *there is neither Jew nor Greek, there is neither slave nor free, there is neither male nor female; for you are all one in Christ Jesus* (Gal. 3:28).

F.   Creation and ecological concerns (Rom. 8:18-23; Col. 1:15-20)

There are two texts from Pauline thought that will be lifted for discussion on the concerns of creation and ecology. A basic consideration to be noted is that Paul and Pauline thought does not deal with the subject of ecology in the sense that the 20th and 21st centuries have come to understand and relate to the term, and in the development of 'eco-theology' and/or 'green theology'. The concern for life-threatening issues related to ecology and environment – pollution, depletion of natural resources by human exploitation etc... – which have been identified in the 20th and 21st centuries were not issues in the 1st century. The Pauline texts are much more in terms of God's act of creation and therefore God's salvific act for the whole of God's creation. The fact that these texts can now be used as a biblical and theological basis for modern concerns is indicative that theology, and the relationship with God and creation, must be viewed and understood wholistically; in this sense, Paul and the development of Pauline thought in the New Testament are well ahead of their times, not because they foresaw an ecological/environmental crisis, but because they were able to see that God's act of salvation in Jesus was an interrelated event and meant for the whole creation, not just one part of it.

In the earlier section, it was seen that Paul envisaged the human being as embodied (σῶμα); this embodied existence has to take place in an environment – the created world. It is only in the world that the possibility for the σῶμα (body) to be good or evil can take place. So, Paul has to go back to Jewish tradition/theology to understand God as Creator: creation was the first act of God's revelation – the first act of creation, light (Gen. 1:3), was not just a physical brightness to enable sight, but more of a metaphysical and mythological expression to realize that it is only in and through creation that the relationship with God is understood. God commanded light to shine out of darkness (II Cor. 4:6 reflecting Gen 1:3), and created human beings, male and female (Gen. 1:27), each for the other (I Cor. 11:5-12); the earth with its contents is God's (I Cor. 10:26 alluding to Ps. 24:1). This understanding of God concerns the human being in the fact that the earth as God's creation is at human disposal for human needs (Gen. 1:26) hence there is nothing unclean (I Cor. 10:25ff.). Yet the creation is characterized by creaturely responses (Rom.1:23, 3:20ff.) and so was subjected to "futility", "the bondage of decay" and awaits the time when it will be set free (Rom. 8:20ff.). Thus, the earth has a peculiar character: on the one hand, it is the creation of God and placed at the disposal of human beings for their use and benefit; yet on the other hand, it is the sphere in which evil takes place subjecting it to demonic powers.

In the Genesis story of creation, the earth was cursed because of Adam's sin (Gen. 3:17-19; 5:29 expresses the hope that Noah would bring people relief) and so in Jewish apocalyptic thought there are hopes of a "new heaven and a new earth" (Is. 65:17; 66:22). Logically therefore, as part of the contrast between Adam and Christ (see commentary on Rom. 5, above), Paul speaks also of Christ's healing effect on all creation – Rom. 8:18-23 – *creation itself will be set free from its bondage to decay and obtain the glorious liberty of the children of God…the whole creation has been groaning in travail together until now…waiting for redemption.* The Greek words used are συνστεναζει και συνωδίνει from the images and vocabulary of labour pains at the time of childbirth: intense pain followed by joyous reward. For Paul then, the whole of creation is alive and human salvation cannot be thought of apart from the salvation of the whole of creation, and if human beings are responsible for creation's subjection to futility, the human beings have to take the responsibility for seeing that creation is freed from decay and bondage in order to achieve the glorious liberty of the children of God. Paul sees this as having not yet taken place, but *in this hope, we were saved…we wait for it with patience* (Rom. 8:24-25); this hope of human salvation is inextricably linked with the salvation of the whole of creation.

The deutero-Pauline writer of Col. 1:15-20 uses a Christological hymn to bring out the idea of a cosmic salvation (see commentary on Colossians, above). The basic point in the Colossian passage is the mediation of Christ, first in creation and then in reconciliation. The Hebrew creation story is re-interpreted in Christological terms; thus, the creative power of God is revealed in the action of God's chosen – Christ – whose participation in creation extended to "all things" (τα παντα). Since Christ is the one through whom "all things" were created, Christ is the one through whom "all things" are reconciled. This brings out the idea that there is a tension in creation which needs to be reconciled which Christ does *by the blood of His cross*. Christ is ascribed this cosmic role as mediator and reconciler of creation after the cosmic disorder into which creation had fallen after the human fall. In this passage, as in the Romans passage, there is an inextricable link between human salvation and the salvation of creation: human salvation cannot be thought of apart from the salvation of creation; both have one Creator/mediator in creation, and both have one reconciler.

In conclusion it can be stated that though the origins of Pauline thought had no context of an ecological crisis, nevertheless, the inclusiveness of the Pauline concept of salvation necessarily involved the understanding of God as Creator, the relationship of creation to human beings, and the act of God for the salvation of all creation. In this sense, Pauline thought lends itself to an ecotheology and provides the biblical basis for the theological development for addressing environmental concerns.

Select Bibliography

Barrett, C. K. *Essays on Paul.* London: SPCK, 1982.

_____. Paul: *An Introduction to his Thought.* London: Chapman, 1994.

Bornkamm, G. *Paul.* London: Hodder & Stoughton, 1971.

Bultmann, R. *Theology of the New Testament, Vol. I.*London: SCM Press, 1971.

Dunn, J. D. G. *The Theology of Paul the Apostle.* Michigan: Eerdmans, 1997.

Kasemann, E. *Perspectives on Paul.* London: SCM, 1971.

Kittel, G. (Ed.) *Theological Dictionary of the New Testament.* London: Eerdmans, 1974.

Murphy-O'Connor, J. *Paul: A Critical Life.* Oxford: Oxford University Press, 1997.

The Relevance of Paul for Today

There is much literature available on Paul and his letters, and much discussion on his theology. A study of Paul is heavy going, especially when it comes to unraveling his complicated arguments and sometimes seeming contradictions. Usually there is one of two reactions to Paul: being put off or a fascination with the man and his message. After having been introduced to his writings in the New Testament, this chapter will be a sort of summary and will try to appreciate Paul's contribution to the Church of his time and to the on-going life of the Church today under two categories: his life and letters, his disciples and their writings.

His life and letters

Paul supplies the reader with the most autobiographical information of all the writers in the New Testament; indeed there is more biographical information about Paul than even Jesus. Artistic representations of Paul draw freely on this information to paint/sketch Paul especially highlighting the information in Acts – lying prostrate on the road at the time of his conversion, arguing with scholars – and from the image of a letter writer: a short, bald headed man with a sharp pointed face and beard bent over a desk furiously writing on a script. Paul's description of himself is somewhat different:

> ....Great labours, several imprisonments, countless beatings, and often near death. Five times have I received at the hands of the Jews the forty lashes less one. Three times I have been beaten with rods; once I was stoned. Three times I have been shipwrecked; a night and a day I have been adrift

at sea; on frequent journeys, in danger from rivers, danger from robbers, danger from my own people, danger from Gentiles, danger in the city, danger in the wilderness, danger at sea, danger from false brethren; in toil and hardship, through many a sleepless night, in hunger and thirst, often without food, in cold and exposure. (II Cor. 11:23-27)

In addition, the "we" passages in Acts, if written by Luke the physician, show that Paul might have been prone to illness and some kind of recurring problem (many have suggested epilepsy and malaria). In II Cor. 12:7, Paul talks of a "thorn in the flesh" – possibly a physical problem that recurred often (a different position is taken in the commentary above). In II Cor. 10:10 he quotes his opponents as saying: *his letters are weighty and strong, but his bodily presence is weak, and his speech of no account.* Amid the splendor and grandeur of the Greco-Roman culture, philosophy and architecture (the ruins today are still a testimony to this), Acts 17:16ffpaints the picture of a man trying to present a criminal as messiah and having been raised from the dead; it is no wonder that he was called a "babbler" and they "mocked" him. Probably the most painful of all reactions was the total rejection by his own people – the Jews (lashes and being thrown out of synagogues) – which made it more difficult to bear all the other rejections. Combining all these descriptions paints an awesome picture which is difficult to comprehend – the picture/image of a man who went through much torture, suffering, and personal attacks for the sake of his convictions and his commitment to the Gospel. In addition to all this, other Christians created trouble in the congregations that he had founded whom he refers to as *false brethren attempting to preach a different Gospel* (Gal. 1:6ff); the Corinthian correspondence also shows this anxiety for the congregations.

What was Paul's motivation for enduring all this suffering? There was no need for suffering in Paul's background – he came from a well-to-do family (they were Roman citizens), his Jewish credentials were impeccable (Philip. 3:4-6), his letters show that he was well educated, and in terms of Jewish tradition he was *advanced beyond many of his contemporaries* (Gal. 1:14); he was well connected with the Jewish authorities and hierarchy (Acts 9:1-2; Philip. 3:6; Gal. 1:13), and in terms of religious observances, he was blameless (Philip. 3:5-6). The sudden change is explained in three narrations in Acts of his conversion experience, and by Paul in Gal. 1:12,16; but these "revelations" do not fully explain his change. Philip. 3:9ff gives a further glimpse of the change – his whole background of which he is so confident is given up as *loss because of the surpassing worth of knowing Jesus Christ my Lord.* But the question still remains as to whether all of this was enough to justify his proclamation that the Gentiles could attain salvation without the works of the Law. It is suggested that something of far greater significance had happened on a personal level which motivated Paul.

Paul had known the love of God through the Jewish tradition, but now he discovered a love that went beyond his previous experience - .... *Christ Jesus has made me his own* (Philip. 3:12); *I have been crucified with Christ.... I live by faith in the Son of God, who loved me and gave himself for me* (Gal. 2:20). He must have had the personal experience of what he wrote in Rom. 8:35-37: *Who shall separate us from the love of Christ? Shall tribulation or distress, or persecution, or famine, or nakedness, or peril, or sword?...... No, in all these things we are more than conquerors through him who loved us.* The experience of God's love through Christ was the motivation for Paul: *the love of Christ controls us....if any person is in Christ, they are a new creation....*(II Cor. 5:14,17). This *love of Christ that surpasses knowledge* (Eph. 3:19) *that* had captured Paul had to be shared through his preaching: *how are they to hear without a preacher and how can there be preachers unless they are sent (Rom. 10:14-15).*

Thus, for Paul, his life and letters show that the mission to the Gentiles was not simply a mental, theoretical conviction, but an absolute necessity/compulsion as a response to God's love in Christ; the message that *while we were yet sinners, Christ died for us* (Rom. 5:8) and *for me to live is Christ and to die is gain* (Philip. 1:21) was the translation of his own experience of being caught up by God's love in Christ that was his motivation: the love that caused him to affirm, *the greatest of all gifts is love* (I Cor.13:13) and the love that constrained him to say that he was the least of the apostles (I Cor. 15:9); the love that had so encaptured and motivated him that he was able to say, *we have this treasure in earthen vessels......we are afflicted in every way but not crushed; perplexed, but not driven to despair; persecuted, but not forsaken; struck down but not destroyed* (II Cor. 4:7-9) and in a moment of eloquence, to declare,

> *In all these things we are more than conquerors through him who loved us. For I am sure that neither death, nor life, nor angels, nor principalities, nor things present, nor things to come, nor powers, nor height, nor depth, nor anything else in all creation, will be able to separate us from the love of God in Christ Jesus our Lord* (Rom. 8:37-39).

His disciples and their writings

Paul had a small group of friends who are mentioned often in his letters – Timothy, Titus, Silas, Silvanus – who are seen as carrying Paul's letters and messages and acting on his behalf in very difficult circumstances and whose loyalty to Paul was never questioned. Aquila and Priscilla were willing to move with Paul from Corinth to Ephesus and to precede Paul to Rome; Apollos joined them in Ephesus as a successful preacher and even made a name for himself in Corinth (Acts 18:24, 19:1; I Cor. 1:12, 3:4). The slave Onesimus who attached himself to Paul (Philemon) and the deaconess, Phoebe (Rom. 16:1-2) are warmly recommended.

Apart from those mentioned there are friends/disciples who remained anonymous but wrote about Paul or in his name. Most prominent among them was the author of Luke-Acts, Luke the beloved physician. Luke devotes more than half of the book of Acts to Paul and gives Paul the credit for the spread of the movement outside Palestine. Luke's work places Paul on par with the original disciples of Jesus. Paul claimed that God's revelation to him was that *he should preach him among the Gentiles* (Gal. 1:16), but the credit for making known the full implications of that revelation to the history of the Church goes to Luke who dramatized Paul's introduction to the Church first as a persecutor and then as its most zealous missionary, tracking Paul's story from Jerusalem (the death of Stephen, Acts 7 & 8),the Jewish capital, to Rome, the Gentile capital, showing in a symbolic way the spread of Christianity from essentially a movement within Judaism, to a world religion. Indeed, Luke has contributed enormously to the image of Paul through the biographical details concerning Paul in Acts.

Great tributes to Paul also came from his disciples who in his name wrote the pseudonymous deutero-Pauline epistles (see introduction and commentary on each letter, above) that come from the last quarter of the first century. Each of these writers found in Paul an authority so forceful that even after his death letters could still speak in his name and with the authority of the Apostle. The letter to the **Philippians** tells of a loving relationship with the Apostle and his anxiety for problems that had arisen in the congregation. The **Thessalonian correspondence** lays to rest the concerns for an immanent *parousia* (return of Christ) with practical advice for getting on with daily living. The letter to the **Colossians** includes a liturgical style developed with a new depth of Christology, ecclesiology and eschatology. In the four major writings, Paul himself concentrated on local problems and issues faced by the churches; in Colossians these ideas are expanded to apply to the universal church: the image of the necessity for all parts of the body to co-ordinate their functions (I Cor. 12:22ff) is developed into the image of the Church as the body of Christ with Christ as the Head (Col. 1:15ff); the concern for the salvation of the groaning creation (Rom. 8:22-25), is brought together in the all-pervading concern of God *to reconcile to Godself all things, whether on earth or in heaven....(*Col. 1:20ff); and Paul's influence is again demonstrated in the insistence that *above all things put on love which binds everything together in perfect harmony* (Col. 3:14). **Ephesians** is the contribution of yet another disciple of Paul bringing out the impassioned eloquence about Christ, ...*the grace to preach to the Gentiles the unsearchable riches of Christ and to make all see what the plan of the mystery is hidden for ages in God who created all things, that through the Church the manifold wisdom of God might now be made known....* (Eph. 3:8-10), and again the insistence on love, ...*that you, being rooted and grounded in love may have power to comprehend...(*Eph. 3:17-18). The development of the exaltation of the name of Christ, *(God) raised him from the dead and made him sit at his right hand in the heavenly places, far above all rule and authority and power and dominion, and above every name that is named, not only in this age but also in that which is to come....(*Eph. 1:20-21). Paul's insistence on "one" – body, bread, spirit, mind (Rom. 12:5; I Cor. 10:17) – is combined in an even higher degree, *there is one body and one spirit, just as you were called into one hope that belongs to your call, one Lord, one faith, one baptism, one God and Father of us all, who is above all and through all and in all* (Eph. 4:4-6). The disciples of Paul were not only inspired by him but took this inspiration to even greater heights thus adding to the Pauline heritage.

By comparison with the deutero-Pauline writings, the **Pastoral letters** (I & II Timothy and Titus) – trito-Pauline writings – are more mundane in their concern for church structure, heretical dangers and concern for women. However, the very reason why these letters are called "Pastoral" is well within the scope of Paul's concern – it ensures that the dangers of church disintegration are avoided by developing a criterion for choosing leaders and of passing on authority to them. Similarly, the "sound doctrine" that was instilled in the congregation had to be carefully protected. Finally, in II Timothy, probably the last of the writings associated with Paul, the author captures the Apostle's spirit at the end of his life in the saying, *I have fought the good fight, I have finished the race, I have kept the faith....*(II Tim. 4:7). Beyond this epitaph, the author of II Timothy has the Apostle declare, *...the gospel for which I am suffering and wearing fetters like a criminal. But the word of God is not fettered* (II Tim. 2:8-9). The trito-Pauline letters affirm that the Gospel cannot be fettered even if its proponents are, and that ensures that the message of Paul and the Gospel will move into the indefinite future, still powerful, still filled with praise and with God's love.

Thus in summary, the relevance of Paul for today is to understand what he himself had left behind (his Jewish background), his heritage (letters), his life and the eloquent expression of his own submission/surrender to the grace of God and the experience of God's all-encompassing love, his disciples who continued his mission and their writings – these are Paul's lasting legacy to the Church, of the first century and of today. It is no wonder then that at every time of theological debate, at every time of church reformation, at every liturgical moment of the Church, and even in every Christian's death, it is to Paul that people turn to rediscover how Jesus is to be interpreted and expressed, and to rediscover God's love in Christ for the salvation of all humanity, and to express the hope that in the final analysis, after all the suffering has passed, the believer can affirm, *I have fought the good fight, I have finished the race, I have kept the faith. Henceforth there is laid up for me the crown of righteousness, which the Lord, the righteous judge, will award me on that Day, and not only to me but also to all who have loved his appearing* (II Tim. 4:8).